For my husband,

YOU HAVE ALWAYS *loved* ME,

supported ME, AND *believed* IN ME.

THIS *dream* WOULD NOT HAVE

COME TRUE WITHOUT *you.*

Rain

WET PUDDLES
FALLING PLOPPING FLOODING
RAIN IS OFTEN INSPIRING
RAIN

DAVY Z

Prologue

TWO WORDS.

That's all I was given. That's all that was said.

I knew this moment was coming, and I didn't really expect much to happen. Well, maybe I did a little, but it was the silence of the moment that I can't seem to forget. The silence is so loud that I can actually hear the air ringing off of my eardrums. I want to throw my hands over my ears to make it stop.

Two words . . . eight letters that have forever changed my life.

I thought that I would feel different. I don't know why. I'm sure it's coming—the difference—but at this moment, I don't really feel like anything has changed. This moment looks just like the moment an hour ago, and I suspect that in one hour from now, the moment will look the same. Or maybe it won't.

I think maybe I'm frozen in this moment. My father sits next to me in the other high-back chair. I can see him out of the corner of my eye, and he leans over with his elbows on his knees and his head is dropped down. Soft piano music plays. It comes from somewhere in the background. They play for her. My mother always loved the piano. The sunlight streaks rays through the window into the room. Dust particles swirl around in the air.

My hands are down next to me and my fingers keep rubbing the fabric of the chair, back and forth, back and forth. The fabric feels almost like velvet, so soft. I officially hate velvet.

I continue to watch the dust swirl, and somewhere in the background voices murmur, but I don't know what they're saying. The ringing in my ears has turned to more of a thumping. My pulse, my heartbeat, I focus on the thumping and the dust.

Someone touches my shoulder and breaks me from my frozen moment. I turn to look up and see my father. I can't help but notice the dark rings under his eyes. He looks like he has aged so much recently. How did I not notice this before? He shouldn't look like this. He's only thirty-nine.

It's then that I realize the moment has changed. Everything has changed. My heartbeat drops from my ears to my chest, and as I look around, it begins to pound faster and harder. The imprint of the dragonfly on my skin burns. A hole is being burned straight into my heart. The room has gone dark. The dust has disappeared and my eyes begin to blur with tears. The music isn't playing, and she isn't here anymore.

Two little words.

"She's gone."

Chapter One

ALI

TWENTY-SEVEN DAYS.

That's how long it has been since I've talked to her, hugged her, smiled at her—seen her. She consumes almost all of my thoughts as if she is still here—but she isn't.

Standing on the beach, I look out to the horizon and the beacon lights from a few ships shine back at me. I breathe in the cool freshness of the morning air and remind myself once again, I am not on vacation and she is gone.

Dad decided after her funeral that instead of trying to move forward with our lives, that it would be best for him and me if we just move on. "Let's start over," he said. Within three weeks, he sold our home in Denver, found a new one on the beach in Florida, and had movers come in and pack up all of our belongings. He transferred offices for work and registered me in a new high school for my senior year. I really didn't get a say in any of this.

Just like that, my entire life changed. I'm not quite sure why I never saw this coming. I should have. Once someone you love dies, nothing really is the same ever again.

I have officially been living in my new house, in a new town, in a new state, for three days.

I look up and down the beach of Anna Maria Island. There are only a few people out, a couple of other runners and a few elderly women looking for shells while drinking their coffee. I can tell that the mornings here are going to be my favorite time of the day.

Mom always loved the beach. I remember her saying over the years that when my father retired, she wanted to live on the beach. The question is: why didn't we? If it's possible for us to do it now, why didn't we then? It also makes me wonder why we didn't go to the beach more often. We took vacations at least twice a year, but they were always to places like New York City, Seattle, or New Orleans. Dad liked cities, and he thought it was important that I was exposed to culture, but what about what my mom wanted? Maybe by him moving us here this is his way of giving her something that she always wanted.

I reach up and rub the dragonfly charm that hangs from a silver necklace.

Over the last week of my mother's life she began to drift in and out of consciousness. She gradually became less responsive to our touches and to our voices. Three days before she died, she quietly told me she loved me and asked that my father go ahead and give me my gift. By the time he returned, she had fallen back asleep, only this time was the last time. She never woke again.

The charm and necklace had been placed in a black velvet box, and it was wrapped with silver wrapping paper and tied up with blue ribbon. The charm of the dragonfly isn't very large, maybe about an inch in size, but what's striking about it are the royal blue Swarovski crystals that make up its body and tail. It is delicate, elegant, and I love it.

Attached to the gift was a letter . . .

My darling daughter Ali,

I love you. I want you to know that you have been the light of my life and you have given me more precious memories than one person should be allowed. This is my wish for you. I hope you will experience a life filled with dancing, kindness, adventure, and love.

Dragonflies are known to live their lives to the fullest. Whenever you see one, I want you to hear me saying, "It's time to let go." You are always so serious and focused. Sometimes you need to look for a little joy. Lighten up your life and make it brighter. Seek out some happiness because you, my darling girl, deserve to live each day smiling with not only your eyes, but your heart too.

Think of me like you think of the wind . . . you can't see it, but you can feel it. I will always be with you.

I love you.

Mom

In the weeks following her death, I did a lot of research on dragonflies. It wasn't like I was asking the big questions and looking for the meaning of life, but I was looking for symbolism. It's the last thing that she gave me, and for that reason, I needed to know all I could and why.

I read that because the dragonfly evolves from growing in the water to moving through the air, it's supposed to show wisdom when it comes to transformation and adaptability in life. I can only hope that I'll be granted this wisdom too. I feel as if I'm evolving in reverse, from the air in Denver to the water of Florida.

The beach feels different this morning than it did yesterday. I try to pin point the changes, but all I can really come up with is that today it is more . . . more accepting, more inviting, and more captivating.

I drop my iPod on my towel, fold over the edge to hide it, and take off running toward the tip of the island. As much as I love music, this morning I just need the peace of the water as it washes up on the shore and the soft sounds of the seagulls as they fly overhead.

My heart pounds in my chest, and I can't tell the difference between the ache for my mother and the ache from the exertion. I push myself harder to go faster, keeping my feet in line with the packed sand that's left behind by the receding tide. I don't even mind the slight downward slope of the beach; it just makes me push harder.

By the time I'm finished with the run, I need to head inside to get ready for school, but the water looks so inviting. Kicking off my shoes and socks, I strip down to my sports bra and underwear, and walk into the water. It's cool, refreshing, and calms my overheated skin. Turning around, I face toward the beach and fall straight backward. My ears slip under the water, muting everything, leaving only the peace and quiet that I need this morning.

Floating on my back, staring up at the sky, I want to laugh at how surreal all this seems. Five days ago, I was sitting on our back deck staring at the Rocky Mountains. Four days ago, I was somewhere in the middle of the southern states. And today, I'm here, living in Florida, swimming in the Gulf of Mexico. Strangely enough, I feel at home here. Maybe it's just acceptance, or maybe I've begun to realize how adaptable my life really is.

Suddenly, something crashes into me, pulling me down. Water rushes over my head.

I'm further out than I thought, and my toes don't reach the bottom. Frantically, I kick my feet to free myself and push on whatever has hit my stomach. It's an arm and that fear turns to panic. Thoughts of drowning flash in my mind.

The arm moves and I scramble to break the surface of the water, gasping for air.

I'm not a very good swimmer. Flailing my arms, trying to stay afloat, my hand shoots out and hits the person in the face causing them to groan. It's a guy and I turn toward the sound. He jerks down on his goggles, and I see his pissed off glare just before he pushes me away.

"Watch where you're going! Didn't you see me swimming here?" he snaps. I've swallowed some water and I start coughing. My hair is covering my face and it floats around me, making it hard to catch my breath.

"I'm sorry," I choke as I keep slipping under. His hands find my waist. I grab onto his upper arms and he pulls me above the surface. My hair is now smoothed back. "I didn't mean to get in your way. I'm not sure how I got this far out. I'm sorry."

His eyes lock on to mine and I'm frozen. He's beautiful.

His hands are warm wrapped around my bare waist, and it shocks me to realize how close I am to him. I haven't been this close to anyone in weeks, and even then they were pity hugs from people who had no business coming near me in the first place. To say that this guy and I are in each other's personal space would be an understatement, but for some reason, I can't bring myself to move. It seems he can't either.

I should say something, or do something, but I can't. He has rendered me speechless.

Water drips off of my lashes, down my face, and over my lips. His eyes scan every inch and detail. He watches the drops of water as they fall across my mouth.

A mixture of emotions cross over his face. The wrinkles smooth out of his forehead as his immediate anger turns to confusion. Slowly, his brows unfurrow and his eyes snap back up to mine. Whatever he's thinking, amusement has now lit up his face.

"No worries. Although I have to admit, I'm a little surprised to see you out here." Half of his mouth smirks up into a smile and his eyes are now sparkling.

"Why?"

"Because of all of the shark sightings lately." He says this as if it's just another everyday thing and there's nothing to be concerned about.

"Sharks!" My eyes widen, hands tighten on his arms, and my nails dig into him slightly. His eyes crinkle in the corners, and he starts chuckling, while biting down on his bottom lip.

"Sorry, I just couldn't resist." He's full-blown smiling at me now. The effect causes my heart to slam so hard into my chest that it hurts.

Wherever this guy came from, he's unlike anyone I've ever seen. I'm spellbound and internally rocked. His skin is smooth, and tanned from the sun. His shoulders and across his nose are sprinkled with freckles. I want to run my fingertips over them and play connect the dots. His jaw is square and covered with day-old stubble. There's a ring left around his eyes from his goggles that make them even more stunning than they already are. Like me, he too has brown eyes—only his are highlighted with flecks of gold.

"So, no shark sightings?"

He shakes his head.

"You think that was funny?"

He nods.

A moment of silence lingers between us, as he gauges my reaction. He's gone back to biting on his bottom lip, trying not to smile at me, but it isn't working. His smile is infectious and slowly the corners of my mouth begin to twitch.

"All right, funny guy. You got me."

The look on his face switches from amusement to thoughtfulness.

"Yes, I do." His voice is deep, rich, and slightly southern. I like the way he sounds and butterflies take off. The good ones that come from being excited, as well as the bad ones that come with nerves. He's making me nervous, and my heartbeat pulses throughout my entire body.

"You know on average there are only sixteen shark attacks per year in the United States, resulting in only one death every two years." *Why did I just say that? Ugh . . .*

"Is that so?" The smirk is back. I know I should stop talking now, but my nerves feel like they've been electrocuted, and all rationality has left me.

"Yes. In fact, if you wanted to be worried about something, it should be lightning strikes. More than thirty-eight people a year die in the coastal states."

He chuckles at me. "Why do you know this?"

It's a very good question. Why *do* I know this?

"Not sure . . . must have read it somewhere. Why are you looking at me like that?"

His expression is one of tenderness and almost familiarity. "No reason, you just remind me of someone. You're not from around here, are you?"

"No, whereas I take it you are."

The freckles across his cheeks move when he smiles. "Yes, I am. So what are you doing out here?"

"I went for a run and the water looked so nice, so I decided to float."

"Hmmm." His brows furrow, and his gaze once again drops from my eyes to my mouth. Mine do the same. His lips, although pursed together, are perfect. They're evenly matched, full, and just the right shade of pink. I can't help but wonder what he's thinking.

"Do you swim here a lot?" *Please keep talking to me. I don't want this moment to end.*

"Every day." He answers.

I will definitely be adding running each morning to my schedule. I can't think of a better way to start the day than to see this guy.

"Wow . . . dedicated, aren't we?"

"You could say that." A shadow flashes across his face and then it's gone. I'm momentarily lost in his eyes, and can't think of anything to say.

We just stare at each other for an indefinite amount of time.

His hands lightly squeeze my waist and there's a slight pull toward him. I gasp and he stills. His lashes are so long, thick, and dark, that they give off the illusion he's wearing eyeliner. My eyes have grown large and I feel a blush spread through my cheeks. I shouldn't be here with him. I don't know him, yet I desperately want him to pull me closer.

Neither one of us moves.

A small wave comes by, and the current from it is just enough that without realizing what is happening, it has pushed me in to him. My fingers slide up his muscular arms and around his shoulders. His hands leave my waist, and his arms wrap tightly around me. He drops down in the water a little. I no longer have to look up at him. We're now face to face and only inches apart.

The water that rolls between us is warm. I can't remember if it was warm already or if it is now because it's pressed between us.

The water continues to sway us and each time my body pushes into his. It's setting off sparks across my nerve endings, causing my mind to scream *what are you doing*, but my body is whispering *live in the moment*.

One of his hands leaves my waist and travels up my back, across my neck, and into my hair. A small sound escapes me and his eyebrows shoot up. He's watching my reaction to this situation very closely.

Unconsciously, my legs lift and wrap around him. His mouth twitches like he's going to smile, but he doesn't.

"Sorry," I say while trying to let go of him. The skin-on-skin contact shocks me. I've never been this intimately close to a guy before, and vulnerability spreads through me.

"Don't go." His voice is hoarse and he blushes, while gripping me, holding me still.

This guy is making me so nervous, in a good way, and he hasn't even done anything. I'm the one that's wrapped around him.

"Hi," I whisper, and he smiles, making me feel like the luckiest person in the world to be on the receiving end of it.

"Hey." His eyes sparkle and his hand tightens on the back of my head. The other leaves my waist, travels up my thigh and underneath my bottom. No one has ever touched me like this. He's still holding me and pulling me closer. Even in the water, his fingers are branding me.

The warmth from his breath brushes up against my cheek and I become acutely aware of how his mouth is just inches away from mine. I could sit here and breathe in this handsome guy all day long.

His eyes focus on my mouth and my tongue licks across my bottom lip, wetting it. He moans just a little and his chest vibrates against me. His eyes slide back up to mine. The color has now deepened to a dark chocolate, and the way he looks at me makes desire shoot through me. This is a foreign feeling, but it's welcomed.

"Is it crazy how badly I want to kiss you right now?" His voice is barely a whisper.

"But you don't know me." A moment of silence passes between us. Reaching up, he tucks my hair behind my ear. His hand drops to my shoulder, runs down my arm, and finds its way to the spot on my back between my shoulder blades. My skin tingles.

"You're beautiful."

I don't know what to say, so I just soak up the compliment and lose myself in this moment.

There is something so incredibly sexy about kissing someone who's so good-looking and a complete stranger. It's a kiss that should be forbidden and saved for someone who has true affection for me, but I just can't help myself. My emotions mirror his. I want him to kiss me like I have never wanted anyone ever before.

He sees the want in my eyes. He's found his answer.

His face comes closer, and his cheek brushes up against mine. The stubble on his jaw is slightly scratchy, but the friction of it feels so good. Even though the water is warm, he shivers. His lips linger below my ear, and feather light kisses sweep across my jaw. My legs have tightened around him, and my fingers tangle in his hair on the back of his head.

So quickly I went from feeling like I was drowning in the water to drowning in him. No guy has ever stirred these types of emotions in me or caused the sensations rippling through me. I never want to come up for air.

His mouth lingers over mine, and electricity shoots between us. My stomach, and every muscle beneath it, has tightened in anticipation of this kiss.

This first kiss.

My toes have curled, my chest is pressed up against his, and I'm not breathing.

Time has stopped.

I no longer feel the sun beating down and warming my skin. I no longer hear the waves crashing against the shore. I no longer see anything—nothing at all—only him. A storm could be blowing in all around us. We could be the last two people on the island and I wouldn't even know it.

His lips lower on to mine, and he doesn't move. My eyes drift shut, and I let out a small sigh at the sensation of him on me. His lips move and gently brush across my bottom one, pulling it between his. His lips are exactly what I thought they would be, full and perfect.

A seagull flies directly over us and lets out a cry. It's so loud and piercing that it startles both of us and he pulls back. His eyes lock back on to mine, and the intimacy walls he had let down, seem to slam back up.

The moment is over, and an ache stabs at my heart. His face has completely turned to stone, and he looks at me as if he's downright confused and slightly furious. I must be looking at him as if my heart was just broken.

He lets out a deep sigh, pushes me off of him while still holding on to my waist, and glances toward the shore. A moment of silence passes between us. His mood has completely changed and done a one-eighty.

He lets me go, grabs my arm, and starts walking us to the shore. He pulls me behind him. No words are said, yet I feel as if an entire conversation is taking place.

"Wait!"

He lets go of my arm. I can touch the bottom now, and the cool sand squishes between my toes.

"Who are you?"

He barely turns back around to me. My heart sinks. The expression on his face is one of sadness, and I don't understand this.

"No one. I'm no one," he says to me as he stomps out of the water and up onto the beach. I can't seem to look away as he crosses over the dock footpath that leads to my street. Not once does he look back at me.

What. Just. Happened?

If someone had told me that this morning, my life would be forever changed by one small encounter with a stranger, I would have thought that they were insane. But that's exactly what happened. I still feel his eyes smiling at me, I still feel his lips on mine, and I still feel branded by his fingers. How could I have felt such a strong connection to him? He's a stranger, and that entire interaction probably lasted no longer than five minutes. But it wasn't just a physical attraction, either. With his arms around me, I genuinely felt safer and calmer than I have in the last six months.

I can't help but think about him leaving the way he did. Was it something I did? Then again, how would I know? I never act this way. I've only kissed one other boy before, and that was a long time ago.

I guess in the end, where we were and who he was with

crashed down, and he didn't like what he saw. Considering I'm hardly wearing any clothes, I'm humiliated. Uncomfortable nerves take over my body causing my hands to shake.

I don't want him to think I'm following him, so instead of heading back to my house, I sit on my towel and look out across the water.

All I know is that this guy is the most beautiful person I have ever seen. Despite all of the complete insecurities I feel right now, given another chance, I'd do it all over again. It's welcoming to feel something other than loneliness and grief.

Who is he? What will happen the next time I see him?

Reality engulfs me, and I pull my knees up to my chest. What am I thinking? This guy doesn't want to see me again. His actions just proved that, and he's way out of my league. Tears fill my eyes. I must look like a little girl to him, but I'm not a little girl anymore. I stopped being a little girl a long time ago.

My heart pauses as I think of her, and I think of the one thing I know for certain.

I know I will never see her again, and this makes my heart ache even more.

I reach up and rub the dragonfly charm. Just one hour ago, I thought I was evolving and adapting. Now . . . I'm not so sure. I miss my home. I miss my life.

I miss my mom.

DREW

OVER THE WEEKEND, Beau was first to notice our new neighbors across the street. The moving truck must have been there on Friday while we were on our way back from Beau's tennis match, because we never actually saw anyone unload anything. Only now, there's a white Range Rover and a black BMW sitting in the driveway, both with Colorado license plates. The BMW has a decal on the back window of a dancer. It must be a girl's car. This end of the island really is hit or miss on neighbors, especially with the waterfront properties. Would they become residents, or would they use the house as a rental property?

Before it went on the market, the owners had used it as a vacation home and they would occasionally loan it out to some of their friends. For at least two years, Beau and I had a great time making memories with the owner's daughter and her friends. Those were some good times.

Fifty years ago, my grandfather, on my mother's side, started a land developing company. After my mother married my father, he eventually took over the business. When my grandfather passed away, my father changed the name to reflect his and he added a real estate portion on as well. One of dad's agents on the residential real estate side sold the house, and I was surprised at first that dad didn't mention who the new neighbors are, especially since I suspect there's a girl there about our age, but then I realized he never would have mentioned her, because in his mind she would just be a distraction.

Beau, Matt, and I know firsthand how he feels about distractions. He's drilled it into us enough over the years, especially to Beau and Matt. Perfection is what he expects. Perfect grades, perfect athletes, perfect family, perfect community name . . . but inside these walls we all know the truth.

"What's wrong with you?" Beau asks me after we drop Matt off and pull out of his elementary school.

"What do you mean?" I glance over at him.

"I don't know. You just seem like you have a lot on your mind, and whatever it is, it isn't making you happy. You're stewing over something." Beau has always had this ability to read me so well. But what could I say to him? Oh, I just met the most gorgeous girl in the world, got spooked because I was afraid someone was watching us, treated her like she was nothing more than a mistake, and I never even asked for her name. No, some things are better left unsaid.

It doesn't matter anyway. It's not like I'm ever going to see her again. On any given day there are more tourists here than there are locals.

My lips still burn from touching hers. I can still feel her hands in my hair and the feeling of being wanted, knowing that she knew nothing about me. My cheeks flush and my heart aches. I'll relive that moment with that beautiful mystery girl over and over in my mind.

"Maybe . . . nothing worth talking about, though, so don't give me any grief about it. I see you analyzing me." He cocks his head to the side. He's watching me, and I let out a sigh.

We pull into the high school parking lot and Beau curses under his breath.

"Shit. Are you kidding me? Who the hell has the audacity?" He's angry someone has parked in my spot, but I couldn't care less.

"Relax, Beau. It's not a big deal."

"It's the point, Drew. It's such a slap in the face and a complete disregard to hierarchy. This freshman needs to get with the program." Beau has always worn his emotions on his sleeve. In many ways, I think that's good for him because he needs to be able to let it out, but other times, I think he really needs to rein it in. It leaves him vulnerable and exposed. If I could teach him anything, it would be how to show indifference.

I pull up and back into the spot next to mine. I see the BMW and Colorado plate before I see the girl. Then Beau yells at her.

"Hey! You're parked in our spot!" He stands out the top of the Jeep, and looks at her as if she's an idiot. She turns around to face us and adrenaline punches me in the chest. I reach up to rub the spot. It's her.

I had just assumed she was vacationing, not living here permanently. We know everyone who lives here. At least I thought we did.

Embarrassment takes over. I wanted this girl, gave in to the moment, and then I just dismissed her, not even caring how that might make her feel. Now, I have to see her every day. I'm an asshole.

This girl is tiny and beautiful, but in an understated way. Her dark brown hair is pulled up messily on top of her head. She wears tiny, little white shorts, a light yellow button down with the sleeves rolled up, and gray Chuck Taylors. *Chuck Taylors!*

Most guys would probably say that she was "cute" dressed like this, but to me she is totally hot. Don't get me wrong, a girl's legs in a nice pair of high heels is one thing, but from eight to three during the day at school, those little lace-up shoes do way more for me.

The thought causes me to look at her legs. My gaze lingers and I groan at the memory of having them wrapped around me. My chest aches again.

She looks around on the ground, and then up at Beau. For a split second she appears stunned, and then she glares at him.

"Is there assigned parking?" It's so interesting to see this side of her. She exudes confidence, strength, attitude, and has an edge to her. She's completely different from the girl in the water. The girl in the water was sweet, open, giving, and trusting.

"No, but everyone knows *we* park here!" They continue with their stare-down and then Beau smirks at her. Beau is a good-looking kid. He always has been. Any time we go anywhere, girls seem to flock to him. I mostly find it annoying, but he loves the attention.

He chuckles next to me thinking he's already won this girl over too. Usually that's all it takes, one smile and they're like putty in his hands. Not with this girl though. Her look hardens as if she has decided he isn't worth her time. Then again, after my abrupt and rude departure this morning, she just might be turned off to the male population in general.

Pushing her backpack up higher, she shrugs her shoulders, and walks off putting in a pair of earbuds. She has some fire in her, and I smile at her back as she slips between Cassidy and the girls. I realize I'm not surprised. Thinking back to an hour ago, she might have been nervous, but she was with me every step of the way.

"Did that just happen?" Beau says. We both continue to stare at her as she walks away.

"Yep, I think it did." A small part of me is rejoicing in the fact that she didn't even blink twice at him. But then again, she never even glanced my way. He looks over and catches me smiling at her. I don't even care.

"Beau, who was that?" Cassidy shouts, making sure everyone hears her. Ugh, she's such a snob.

Cassidy, Lisa, and their friends approach the Jeep. Cassidy's voice is like nails on a chalkboard to me. I used to think she was a sweet girl. Boy, was I wrong about that. I'm certain now that it had all been just an act, and I made the terrible mistake of hooking up with her once, early in the summer, at a party. I'd had too much alcohol, and too much anger floating in me that needed to be forgotten. Ever since then, I haven't been able to shake her. For the most part, she steers clear of me. She knows that absolutely nothing will ever happen between us, but at the same time, she uses this so-called attention that I showed her to launch herself, for lack of a better word, to Queen Bee status. The guys really seem to enjoy her friends around and in a way, by Cassidy always being there, other girls have seemed to shy away. I'm thankful for this. I have no time to deal with a girl, even if I want to. It's my last year, and I'm counting down until I am outta here.

"I don't know. Some new girl, I guess. She doesn't look familiar to me," Beau answers her. Cassidy looks back over her shoulder one more time, and narrows her eyes at the new girl.

Beau slips out of the Jeep, and walks toward Lisa, slinging his arm around her. She looks up at him and giggles. She's been his flavor of the month, so to speak. Grant and Ryan, our oldest friends, pull up right after us. The other two girls skip off to be with them.

"Well, didn't you tell her to move?" I look over at Cassidy and I can't help but compare her to the new girl. Cassidy is the quintessential Barbie doll; she's tall, has blonde hair, and a body that most high school girls would kill for. She is always wearing fancy clothes and shoes, and isn't the kind of girl that could ever just be laid back. She really is a pretty girl—that is, until she opens her mouth. Seriously, every day this girl gets on my last nerve more and more.

"Let it go, Cassidy. I mean, who cares. It's just a parking lot." All seven of them freeze and turn to stare at me as I climb out of the Jeep. Really, this is just stupid. I leave them standing there and walk off toward the school.

Beau's feet thump against the pavement as he jogs to catch up. He falls in beside me. "What was that all about?" People look at us as we enter through the front door. Some things never change. As we walk down the hallway toward the lockers, not one person gets in our way. Girls all down the hall giggle, a few say hello, and guys nod "what's up" in our direction.

"That girl drives me nuts with her attitude all the time." I look over at Beau; he's smiling and checking out some girl that's standing across the hall from us. She looks kind of familiar, but I stopped paying attention years ago.

"You know that she thinks it's gonna be you and her against the world this year." He never directs his attention to me but tucks his hands into his front pockets and leans back against the lockers next to mine. Beau has mastered the "boy next door" look that makes him approachable for every girl he has ever met.

"Why would she ever think that?" I briefly think back to the last couple of parties that we've been to, including last night at my house, and not once did I even look at her.

Dad thought that it would be a good idea to show a little hospitality to all of his business contacts by inviting their kids over to our house for a last night of the summer get-together. The guy is really a tool. He'll do whatever he needs to do to try and make himself look good. Sucking up to my friends and other kids so they run home and tell their parents how wonderful mine are is low. Just thinking about him makes me angry.

"You haven't told her differently." I freeze, and then grab on to his arm. He looks at me questioningly.

"You're kidding, right? I haven't told her anything because I don't talk to her . . . ever. As in months!" He shakes his arm out from under my hand. I was squeezing a little too intensely.

"Well, then heads up, because she's spreading rumors." My blood pumps faster through my body as anger washes over me.

"Of course she is. Who told you this? Lisa? You need to stay away from that girl. She's nothing but trouble. When's the next party? I'll squash this then." Part of me doesn't want to wait. I want to drag her into the nearest closet and rip into her. No one makes a claim over me, no one talks about me, and no one will dictate what my life is going to be. I have to deal with enough of that crap at home.

"Yeah. Lisa might have mentioned something to me, and you're right, I'm about done with her too. It was fun while it lasted, but seeing what's walking the halls here, I need to spread the love! Next Saturday, Grant's house."

"You're an idiot." I shake my head at him. "Done. Next Saturday at Grant's. I don't have time for this." I slam my locker door and lean my head against it. The combination of my father and Cassidy is a little too much for me. I wouldn't put it past the both of them to be working together against me. I push off and stalk down the hallway.

"Dude?" I stop and turn to look at Beau. He can see there's more going on with me than just this mess with Cassidy. None of this is his fault, and I let out a deep breath. Our eyes lock on each other as I reach for the door to my homeroom class. People shuffle around us, trying to not get in my way.

"You know how I feel about clingy chicks. Why do you think I always pick a mainlander? They aren't here to bother me day in and day out. I have enough going on without all of that too. I knew better and I don't know what I was thinking. Huge, huge mistake . . ." Silence stretches between us because he knows what I'm talking about. But the question is: am I talking about just Cassidy?

"Whatever, man. I need to stop by my locker. I'll catch you at lunch." We bump forearms, something we've done since we were little kids pretending to be ninjas, and Beau walks off.

I know Beau really wants to have the best time ever this year, and in a way, I'm sad this will be our last year together, but I have to remain focused. Nothing, and I do mean nothing, can get in the way.

Since June fifteenth, I have been counting down my "last first-days" here. Today is my last first day of school. There are only 298 more days until I am out of here. If it wasn't for Matt, I doubt I'd ever return . . . who knows, maybe I won't.

I take a seat by the window, hoping people won't attempt to talk to me. They should know better by now. The bell rings.

Looking out the window, I close my eyes. I see dark hair smoothed back, big beautiful brown eyes, and flawless ivory skin. She's gorgeous. My stomach tightens at the memory, and then sadness. I'm overcome with the emotion, because that's all she'll ever be, a memory.

The morning announcements come and go, typical morning, and then she walks in. Of course she does. Aren't I being punished enough?

The teacher points in my direction, and with her head down, she sits in the last desk in the class, right in front of me, and she doesn't even know it.

Little brown hairs have fallen out of the messy bun and are floating around her neck. I can't help but to remember how her neck and skin felt under my fingers.

She lets out a sigh and I wonder why.

The second I walked away from her this morning, I missed her. I don't even know her, yet there's something about her that makes me want to. The storm that was brewing in her eyes calmed the longer she looked at me. I had this over-whelming sense to want to make her happy, and I don't want to make anyone happy. I want to be forgotten.

She reaches down with one hand to grab a notebook and pen. Vanilla and citrus drift my way, and I inwardly groan. How am I going to make it every day knowing not only where she lives and what classes she has, but how she felt wrapped around me? If only that seagull had waited just a few more seconds, then I would know what she tastes like too.

ALI

I CAN SEE out of my peripheral vision that people are looking at me as I walk up the front steps to my new school. I park my car on the far end of the lot away from the cliquey groups, hoping to not be noticed. I have zero interest in being Ren McCormack, from *Footloose*, who drives in and parks front and center, drawing the attention of everyone around him. So much for that plan. In a matter of five minutes, I've pissed off the popular crowd.

The school is prettier than what I had originally thought. The building is large, made of white stucco, instead of traditional brick, and the roof is made with rust-colored clay pot tiles instead of shingles. It gives off a Mediterranean or beach feel. The landscaping is tropical, and although the building looks newer and clean, it's small and I realize immediately there's no way I can blend into the crowds here. I step under a Bougainvillea that's in full bloom with dark pink flowers arched over the entrance. I love it.

Walking through the front doors, my earbuds blare "Closer" by Tegan and Sara, and in a way, it calms me. It has such a happy beat, and right now, I need something that makes me feel happy. I hate every second of this.

The office is through the main doors and directly on the right. A bell chimes as I open the door and I'm met with a whiff of tropical flavors, very fitting given the location. The smell definitely makes the room more inviting. At the front desk sits Leila. I had met her over the weekend at the Beachside Café. Her aunt owns the place and she works there part time.

"It's about time you got here! I was so excited to see you this morning." She smiles at me, and it reaches all the way to her bright blue eyes. "Everyone is talking about how you parked in Drew's spot." She bounces in her chair and her strawberry blonde hair sways with the movement.

"I thought the spots weren't assigned. I didn't see any numbers, and just wanted to park in the back." Why do I have to keep defending where I parked my car? If I had known all this was going to take place, I would've walked to school or parked on the street.

"Oh, they aren't assigned. Drew and Beau sort of claimed the back corner and have parked there since Drew started driving three years ago. You threw everyone off this morning. You parked in Drew's spot, Drew parked in Grant's spot, Grant parked in Ryan's spot, and so on." Her excitement about this is over the top, and I can't help but raise my eyebrows at her.

"You do realize how stupid that sounds . . . it's just a parking lot."

She giggles and hops down out of her chair.

"Yes, but that's *major* first day of school gossip. I already

24

pulled your class schedule, and I'm going to give you a quick tour and show you to your locker before I head off to class. I guess you could say I'm your official welcome wagon." She skips out from behind the counter just as the second bell sounds. The classroom doors from the hallway begin to close and I let out a momentary sigh of relief. Leila will be able to show me around without curious eyes.

The layout to the school is fairly easy, and my locker is right in the middle of the senior hallway. After showing me where the library, gym, and cafeteria are located, Leila eventually makes her way around to my first class, but instead of saying goodbye she stops and looks at me.

"So, what did Drew say to you?" Her smile is gone and she looks at me questioningly.

"Who's Drew?" Did I miss part of a conversation somewhere?

"Drew, you know, you parked in his spot this morning." Her look changes and now it basically says, "Come on, you know who I'm talking about." She seems pretty obsessed with this Drew guy. It's the second time she's brought him up in the last ten minutes.

"Oh, I don't think he said anything to me. The guy in the passenger seat was the one who stood up and yelled at me." She nods at me like she is agreeing with me.

"That was Beau, and that would make sense. Drew never says anything to anybody. He's definitely more of the "sit back and observe" of the two, whereas Beau has the classic middle child syndrome. He's always demanding attention and likes to be heard. But you know, it works for them, and people are always trying to get their attention." This Drew person sounds like a guy from my own heart . . . sit back and observe. Aside from dancing, I've always been the type that wanted to blend into the crowd versus stand out.

"Seems a little excessive for just two guys. There have to be more around here that are just as good or popular, or whatever you want to call it." I think back to my last school and there were a ton of popular guys, at least enough to go around.

"You don't understand. These guys aren't just popular— they are everything. Every guy wants to be them and every girl wants to be with them, if you know what I mean." Her eyes attempt to take on a dreamy look, but what I see underneath is sadness and this confuses me. She must have some history with one of these guys.

"But why?" It just doesn't make any sense to me how two guys can have this much power or effect over the general student body here.

Leila's look was one of confusion, as if there was something incredibly obvious that I just wasn't grasping. "For starters, they're both beautiful. Even though their looks are completely opposite, they always look like they could step out of an Abercrombie poster. Ah, and let's see . . . they're rich, smart, and famous." Famous? She has my attention now. I've never met anyone famous.

"Why are they famous?"

"Have you seriously never heard the names Drew Hale or Beau Hale before?" Something about the name does kind of ring a bell, but I can't remember.

"I don't think so." Her face registers shock and I almost feel a little stupid like I should know them.

"Well, Drew swims and Beau plays tennis. They win everything and have begun competing on a large scale. Rumor has it that Olympic coaches are looking at Drew. Both brothers were featured earlier in the year in *Teen People* and the 'Kids in Sports' issue for *ESPN*." By the look on her face, I can tell that she loves being the one to tell me this.

"Wow, I guess that's impressive." I wasn't expecting that answer. These two guys are basically local celebrities. No wonder she's asking about them. They probably live front and center in the gossip news feed around here.

"You guess? You crack me up. Like I said, every guy wants to be them and every girl wants to say they've been with them." Hearing her talk like this, I almost feel sorry for them. It seems that people care more about what they are versus who they are. Then again, they probably love all the attention— name one high school guy who wouldn't.

"Well, I can tell you that I don't want to be with them. That's not really my thing." She just smiles at me as I reach for the door handle of my first class. The smug look on her face says that she doesn't believe me. Oh well . . . time will tell.

"Seniors here have open lunch, so you have the choice of eating here or leaving campus for an hour. I hope I'll see you later." She's smiling from ear to ear.

"Okay, that sounds great." With that she spins on her toes and skips off.

The morning announcements have just ended as I walk into my homeroom class. I hand the teacher my office slip and she points to an empty desk at the end of the front row next to the window. I try not to look at the other students, and the room has taken on a blurred quality as I walk to my seat. Of course it's in the front of the class. All eighteen sets of eyes are burning into the back of me. Blood floods into my cheeks— whatever, never let 'em see you sweat, right?

With one hand, I reach down to grab a notebook and a pen. With the other, I gently rub the dragonfly charm between my thumb and forefinger. The teacher starts her introduction and I find myself staring at the clock, willing the minutes to tick by.

DREW

I END UP having two classes with the new girl, not that she would know. She hasn't looked at me one time. I'm also shocked to see that her locker is three over from mine. Why I'm paying any attention to this girl, I have no idea.

Thankfully, this year, Cassidy isn't in any of my classes. Honestly, she isn't that smart, and there's no way she'd be able to keep up; but mostly, I'm thrilled that I don't have to worry about her over-the-top, constant, flirtatious behavior.

I'm not as fortunate at lunch. Beau and I grab a table outside in the courtyard, and she and her friends come waltzing over to plop down in our space. Cassidy sits down right next to me and tries to turn on the charm. She wraps one arm around my shoulders, and gives me a squeeze like she's hugging me. I'm certain that people see her. It's all for show and not for sincerity. Everything that this girl does is calculated.

"Hey, how's your day going so far?" she asks.

I abruptly stand up, knocking her off of me while shooting her a glare that leaves no room for discussion and says *back off*. She lets out a slight gasp and she jerks backward.

Looking over at Beau, he's seen the entire scene play out and he shakes his head at me. I turn around and walk off without saying anything to anyone. No one says anything to me either. That girl has a lot of nerve.

I decide to run over to Beachside to grab a sandwich. It'll get me off campus and away from roaming eyes. I pull the top up, crank on the AC, and open up Spotify to the latest album for Artic Monkeys. Even though I'm parked in the shade, August in Florida is freaking hot, and sweat begins to drip down my back.

The more I think about Cassidy, the more I think there must be something else motivating her crazy behavior. She never tried to pull this stuff with me last year. Even over the summer, after that party, she kept her distance. Whatever. She just needs to stay away from me.

Walking into Beachside, I let out a sigh seeing there isn't a line to order food. During August the tourists max out on the island, and it's always a little crowded in here for lunch.

"Well hey, darling. How are ya?" Aunt Ella's behind the counter. That's what we all call her, Aunt Ella. Technically she's Leila and Chase's aunt, but she wouldn't have it any other way.

Aunt Ella and her husband own The Beachside Café. Both of them have lived on the island their entire life, so most of us grew up with them. Aunt Ella is tall, thin, and graceful. She smiles at everyone, loves to give hugs, and I don't think I've ever heard her say one bad thing about anyone. If I had an aunt, I'd want her to be just like Aunt Ella.

"I'm good and starving." She knows I'm on a lunch break, so she'll get my order up as soon as possible.

"You want your usual?" Just thinking about her Cuban sandwiches, my mouth starts to water.

"Do I ever order anything else?" I say, smiling at her, while pulling out my wallet.

"Nope. Take a seat over there and I'll have it up in five." She smiles at me and a pang of jealousy rips through me. Aunt Ella and her husband are so genuinely kind. Her son, Ben, who is in college now, he has no idea how lucky he is.

Turning for the lounge couches, I stop dead in my tracks.

She's sitting there and I just stare.

What do I do? Do I go over and talk to her, or do I pretend I don't even see her? I should just stay away from her.

Letting out a sigh, I know I need to man up and face her. It's bound to happen at some point.

"Hey," I say to her. She looks up at me and her eyes widen. She's so tiny and curled up in this big leather chair with her legs underneath her. She leans against the armrest, using it as a prop for her book, and she's eating a sandwich, a Cuban sandwich. My chest starts to ache.

"Hi," she says quietly, her eyes never leaving mine. A moment of silence passes between us, and I reach up to rub the back of my neck. She's so beautiful. It hurts me to look at her.

"So, I'm glad I ran into you because I want to apologize to you for this morning."

Her cheeks and ears turn beat red, and she drops her gaze looking down at her lap.

"No, no, no, not for what you're thinking. I'm not sorry about that."

She looks back up and I give her a small smile.

"I'm sorry for the way I left you. I was rude, and for reasons I can't go into, but it had nothing to do with you. I'm sorry, please accept my apology." Her face is blank, but she's studying me now. I think about how this might have sounded to her. I basically gave her the *it's not you but me* line. I feel like an idiot.

"Okay." She smiles and my heart melts. Just like that, she accepts and forgives. I don't deserve her smiles. She should be giving them to someone worthy of them, and I'm definitely not. "Do you want to sit down?" she asks me quietly.

"Um, sure." I know that I shouldn't be sitting here with her. Nothing can ever happen between us, not that she'd even want it to, but if all I can have are a few stolen moments with her here and there, I'll take them.

"So, do you live around here?" She looks around the café. She must wonder if I am here with anyone else.

"Yes, just a couple of blocks that way." I point toward the north end of the island. It's such a basic question, and although I already know where she lives, I can't help but smile at her.

"Me too." She grins back. My eyes are drawn to her lips. They're bee-stung and perfect. "Well, that explains why I ran into you. Sorry about that by the way. I hope I didn't hurt you anywhere." One of her hands has moved from her lap and now fidgets with a charm that hangs off of a silver chain. Am I making her nervous?

"No need to apologize. I wasn't paying attention either, and it was equally my fault. Nope, no injuries." Her eyes are so large and pretty. They're a shade of brown that's a little on the lighter side, almost like a milk chocolate. She's drawing me in and she doesn't even know it. Ugh, I need to stay away from her.

"Well, since I know that you swim every morning, next time I'll make sure I stay out of your way."

What I want to say is, "please don't," but I know I never can. Just the thought of seeing her first thing every morning . . . my stomach tightens, and not in a good way.

Swimming in the mornings is the only time of the day where I feel I truly get to be myself. For ninety-five percent of the day, I have to wear a mask to cover up the truth. No one really wants to know the truth. The truth is ugly, and every day, I feel ugly. But buried under the water, I don't have to pretend. I can bear my soul, and pour out my broken heart without fear of discovery.

I feel guilty for not wanting her there. She's done nothing

wrong.

"No worries." I give her a small smile and she blushes again. The color on her face makes her even more breathtaking than I already think she is.

"Darlin', food's ready," Aunt Ella calls out to me. Standing up, I rub my hands across my thighs, not even realizing they're sweating.

Without thinking, I start to lean over, and almost put my hand on her arm. She sees the movement and I jerk back.

What am I doing? What is it about this girl that pulls me to her? I'm acting like a completely different person. I don't talk to girls, touch girls, or really even acknowledge them for that fact. So why can't I help myself around her?

A piece of her hair has fallen across her cheek and my attention zeroes in on it. Should I? Or shouldn't I? What the hell . . . I reach over and tuck it behind her ear. She blinks at the contact, but doesn't flinch.

Every part of me feels like it's vibrating. It's been only five hours and I feel like I need her, want her. I don't even know her.

I take a step back, stand up to my full height, and watch as her eyes run over the length of me. She may as well be touching me, because that's what it feels like.

"See you around?" she asks. There's hope in her voice and it makes my heart flutter.

"Maybe," I shrug my shoulders and give her one last look. Aunt Ella smiles at me as I grab the sandwich and head out the door. I can feel the new girl's eyes following me and in so many ways, they're undoing me.

Eating in the Jeep, in the parking lot at school, is my choice every time, instead of going home. My thoughts are on her and I need to clear my mind. I need to stay focused.

Popping open the glove box, I grab the envelope I received at home in the mail last week. Taking out the letter, I read it again and my blood boils with sheer anger.

Mr. Drew Hale,

On behalf of the Athletic Department here at the Western Florida University, we would like to say thank you for your family's sizable donation to the Aquatics Facility. We look forward to having you join our swim team next year and look forward to talking to you sometime soon.

I want to crumble up this letter and burn it. Instead, I use it as motivation to keep me moving forward with my plans to get out of here. There is no chance in hell I'm ever going to that school. It's just like my father to try and bully his way in also. Paying off the school so he can choose where I go to college. I don't think so. He's such an arrogant asshole.

Coach Black told me he had received some inquiries from a few other coaches across the nation, and I encouraged him to keep that bit of information to himself. I have a feeling he knows what my father is like behind closed doors. He gave me some great advice when he mentioned I go down to the post office and open a P.O. box to keep my college interest separate from my daily mail. Once I have an address, he'll provide it to people he thinks are worthy of it and to the schools I've already applied for. I need to go and take care of that today after school.

If things go my way, I'll end up at USC. I want to be as far away from here as possible. I know I should be thinking about Matt and my mother, but Beau only has one year left, and I need to start thinking about me. The older I get, the more I can see clearly what my father is trying to do to us, and the only person who can change the cycle is me. I need to be free.

I lean over and drop the envelope back in the glove box next to my last stack of college applications. I want to include the new P.O. box address on these and then get them in the mail soon. I slam the glove box closed and lock it just as she pulls back into the spot next to me. She cracks open her door and puts one foot out before she turns off the car. "Paradise" by Coldplay is blasting through the speakers. She likes Coldplay. I smile to myself.

I watch as she yanks off a pair of aviator sunglasses and tosses them onto the passenger seat. She climbs out of the car, pulls her shorts down since they've ridden up, throws on her backpack, and walks off. This girl seems real, and I think that might be something that draws me to her. She also seems to have a bit of sadness that follows her around, and it makes me feel like I know her.

Ugh! Why am I even thinking like this?

Climbing out of the jeep, I shake my head to clear away the thoughts, and slam the door.

Chapter Three

ALI

THIRTY-FOUR DAYS.

It's been over a month now, and today feels harder than all of the others.

I start my day, just like every other day, by looking at her picture on my book shelf. This picture is one of my favorites of her. Shannon, my best friend back in Colorado, had come over for dinner with this crazy new fancy camera she had finally bought, and she must have taken at least a thousand pictures of us. She said she wanted to work on her candid shots.

Mom was standing in the kitchen stirring a pot of spaghetti sauce when all of a sudden some splattered out on her shirt and we all busted out laughing. You can see in this picture she's happy and healthy. A little contentment fills my heart that I can still remember what her laugh sounded like. When I close my eyes, I remember this night with complete clarity. Today, I remember more of the good moments than those from over the last couple years. I think that's why it's so hard. I miss those moments the most.

Georges Duhamel said, "Sometimes you will never know the value of a moment until it becomes a memory." He was so right.

Dad is always gone. I've been here a little over a week and I've seen him twice: the night I arrived, and for a few hours on Saturday. His company's offices are located down in Sarasota, which is about forty-five minutes south, so that's where he's spending his time. He says he's working on a large project which requires him to be there more often, longer hours and weekends, so he's staying in one of the company-appointed condos. I don't know if this is the truth or if it's an excuse. Then again, I don't know why I thought that it would be any different here in Florida. He was never there for me at home either. The depth of my loneliness is slowly getting deeper.

Ever since Mom was diagnosed with breast cancer, Dad has needed his space. He began working longer hours and was definitely not with me anymore. He closed himself off. But when he was at home, he followed my mother around, helpless because he didn't know what to do for her. I felt bad for him, but I felt bad for me too. Did it never occur to him that I might have needed him too?

He and my mom married so young. They were high school sweethearts and so excited to start their life. I came a year later, and afterward my mother couldn't have any more children. I know they always wanted more and I think they even considered adopting, but by the time she was thirty, she was diagnosed with breast cancer for the first time.

She went through months and months of treatments, and even surgery. I didn't know much about this stuff at the time, but boy I sure learned pretty quickly. Eighteen months later, we were told that she was in remission and all three of us sighed in relief. Little did we know that it was going to come back, raging like a herd of bulls, seven years later.

The part of me I'm continually battle with is the anger. For months, I was so mad at her. She should have gone in for more checkups. She should have been able to recognize the signs; after all, she went through this once already. She should have been stronger to fight it better. I know it isn't her fault she left me, but sometimes that's just how I feel.

I pull into school today, wanting to be left alone. I already know that today is going to be hard for me emotionally. I just need it to be over.

Without even thinking, I park in the same spot as the first day of school. I pop my earbuds in, crank a little "XO" by Beyoncé, and climb out of the car.

Out of nowhere a hand reaches up and grabs my arm, jerking me backward.

What the . . .

"Hey, New Girl! Didn't you hear me when I said this is where we park?" Whoa. Seeing this guy up close now, I feel a little awestruck. Leila was right, he is good-looking. I can see why girls would throw themselves at him. However, his attitude seriously needs to be worked on. He genuinely seems angry about where I parked, and that he has to move one spot over. As his glare continues to get sharper, I can't help my own reaction to him, and my blood starts to fire through me.

The four girls from the other morning step up behind me and I feel trapped. My hands tighten on the straps of my backpack.

"Hey, douche bag! Didn't you see that I just don't care?" I don't know how long we continue to stare at each other. It could have been seconds or minutes, but there's no way I'm going to back down to this guy.

"New Girl . . . have you ever heard of the phrase "rule of thumb?" Did you know it's derived from an old English law, which states that you can beat your wife with anything less than the width of your thumb?"

What? Is he joking? Who comes up with this kind of stuff and actually says it out loud? "Are you threatening me?" I snap back at him.

"Nope, just stating . . ." One of his friends approaches. He too, is smirking at me, but he looks over at someone in the Jeep and shakes his head like this guy in front of me is an idiot, which he is. There's a glare on the windshield and I can't see who he's looking at. Whatever, I too can play this game.

My voice drops so it's low and monotone. "Well, then you should remember this . . . nutmeg is extremely poisonous if injected intravenously."

His friend breaks out in laughter behind him. After a moment of silence passes between us, he finally looks me over from head to toe, and then cracks. He starts laughing. I roll my eyes and turn around to leave.

If this guy thinks he's going to intimidate me, he has another thing coming. I can dish it out just like everyone else, maybe even better. And I certainly don't back down.

The girls are still standing there and their expressions are a cross between shock and anger. Looking at the two in front of me, neither one of them says anything. They're all wearing dresses again today, and it occurs to me that they don't look much different than the other day. They each have on fancy shoes and jewelry, full makeup, large designer sunglasses, and their hair is done. Looking at them, I almost feel insignificant. Almost. I'm 5'2" to begin with, but next to them in their heels,

I feel like a child. They look like they should be stepping out on a runway, not going to school.

The initial wow I had over their appearance is drifting away. If they continue to look like this every day, I can see how it would lose its effect. If I was a guy here, I wouldn't see beautiful as much as I would see high maintenance.

"Move," I say to no one in particular, but all of them at the same time.

"You move your car." One steps toward me. Aside from the clothes, this girl is seriously stunning. She has long legs, a great figure, and perfect blonde hair. She must be every guy's fantasy come true. No wonder she's friends with these guys. Beautiful people tend to stick together.

"Really?" But at the same time how stupid is this girl? Her eyes widen a little, and then something sparks in them. It's as if I just issued a challenge and she is accepting.

She makes no effort to move, crosses her arms over her chest, and smirks at me. Nothing about her screams *I'm gonna kick your ass*, so why she's acting all big and mean is beside me. These girls look more like the *I'm gonna be your worst nightmare* kind of girls.

"This is pathetic." Walking forward, I bump my shoulder into her as I slip between Blondie and her friend. She stumbles on her high heels, and one of her friends reaches out to steady her. Beau laughs again, I'm so glad I'm able to amuse him.

Where there is anger, there are tears. Walking away from them, I reach up to rub the dragonfly and try to regain control over my emotions. What did I ever do to these people that's so bad?

All of my classes seem to fly by and before I know it, today has passed by in a blur. I am completely enveloped in my own grief. I didn't go out of my way to talk to anyone. I don't even think I looked at anyone if it wasn't necessary.

I don't want to live this life without her. I need her to hug me, love me, and talk to me. I don't have anyone who does that now and I feel so alone.

I walk into The Cave at 5:15, completely skip my warm up, and go straight to dancing.

A few days ago, I had found this multipurpose room next to the locker-rooms. I was so excited, I immediately knocked on the coach's office door.

"Come in."

I pushed the door open and slipped inside. The office looked like a typical coach's office, there was athletic gear lying everywhere and the walls were lined with trophies and plaques. I couldn't help but smile at the man looking at me.

"Well, well, I can't say that I get many girls wandering in this way. What can I do for you?" I sat down in the chair that is across from his desk.

"I was wondering if it would be possible for me to use the multipurpose room next door after school." He raised one eyebrow at me and leaned back in his chair. It squeaked under the weight of him.

"What for?"

"Ah, to dance in, sir."

"Oh, you're a dancer. Are you new here?" He propped his elbows onto the armrests and steepled his fingers together.

"Yes, sir." There was a brief pause in the conversation. I could feel him trying to assess me with his eyes.

"What's your name?" Suddenly, I was really nervous. That excitement that I had felt coming in here drained away. What if he decided to not let me use the room? I would have to find a studio to rent time at, or possibly build one down in the garage. The thought of being in a non-air conditioned garage in Florida was not appealing to me at all.

"Allyson Rain, but everyone calls me Ali." My hands started sweating and unconsciously I reached up and began to rub the dragonfly.

"It's nice to meet you, Ali. I'm Coach Black. You know we have a dance team here at the school, and I can talk to the coach for you if you're interested in joining."

"Thank you, but no. Not that kind of dance." Both of his eyebrows shot up at this and I could feel the blush rise across my cheeks. I was completely aware of how that came out.

"What kind of dance are you talking about?" Half of his mouth smirked up. I could see that he was finding my reaction funny.

"I have a Juilliard audition in the spring, and I need a place to work on choreography."

He smiled from ear to ear. "Julliard, you say. Well, that's fantastic. I don't think that we have ever had anyone graduate from here and attend Juilliard. The guys have wrestling practice in there until 4:30, but they are always cleared out by 5:00. I don't mind giving you a key for evening use, but understand only you and I will have the key, so if something happens it's on you."

Relief flooded through me and I let out a deep breath. "I really appreciate that, Sir. You have no idea how much. I'll take care of the room and please, I'm a bit of a private person, so please don't tell people I'll be in there."

"No worries, kid." He opened the top drawer to his desk and pulled out a key that had *The Cave* engraved on it.

I cracked a smile at this because the name fits that room perfectly. There are no windows to let in any natural light, only one in the door that opens to the hallway.

"This key is for the back door in the room, which leads to

the outside. That way you won't have to walk through the school after hours and set off the security sensors. Since you're going to be here after school hours, don't forget to lock it after you when you come inside. Better to be safe than sorry, if you know what I mean. Let me know if you need anything else." He smiled at me warmly. It had been a whole lot easier than I had expected.

My mother loved ballet the most, so today I dressed the part: tight bun, black leotard, pink tights, short black sheer wrap skirt, and pink toe shoes.

I turn the music up a little louder than usual because I need to feel the vibrations echo through the room and through me. I need to feel something other than this all-consuming loss. It's when I'm dancing that I feel the closest to her. Maybe that's another reason I have been putting in so many hours lately.

I've finally accepted that this is now my home and this is my school, but these things are all just the physical aspects that are a *part* of my life. What about my actual life? What about me?

Living here, in this strange place, going to a strange school, none of it feels like who I am. Who am I now? I'm struggling with what I'm supposed to be doing all the time and who I'm supposed to be. I feel so out of place, and really just out of myself. She's supposed to be here to help me.

If I was still in Denver, I would feel like I had direction, a sense of belonging. My mother helped me lay out a plan. We knew what I had to do next and who I needed to do it with. Here, there is no one. I'm unguided in my training, I have one friend who is barely even that. The other girls and guys at this school don't like me at all, and not once has my dad asked me how I am doing.

The backs of my eyes prick, and I close them as the tears begin to fall out.

Tears.

At some point you would think that they would stop coming, right? But nope, every day they still show up like clockwork. I should be thankful for the tears because if I didn't have them I'm not sure what kind of person I would be.

My heart fills with them as the ache in my chest grows deeper and deeper until there's no more room and as they leak out. My heart drains of that all-consuming sadness only to repeat over and over again.

I constantly find the weight of this grief so heavy that unconsciously I pull my arms in and hug myself. It's compressing so tightly that I can't breathe. It's during these times, I wish the most that she was here to hug me. I miss her arms, I miss her warmth, I miss her compassion, I miss her love.

Closing my eyes, the music takes over.

Behind my eyelids visions of my mother flash like a home movie. I can see the two of us at the mall getting a pedicure. Helping her in the kitchen, to cook anything and everything—I loved her cooking. Laughing as the three of us—my family that is, mom, dad, and me—open up presents around the Christmas tree. And seeing her stand in the audience at one of my performances, clapping like crazy because she was proud of me.

I'm so grateful for all of the beautiful memories of her, and so sad over the ones I'll never get to have. She'll never see me perform in New York, won't get to help me pick out a wedding dress, and she'll never get to hold my children. She would have been the best grandmother.

Without opening my eyes, I move flawlessly across the floor: stretching, reaching, lengthening, and twirling. I know this break down is probably of epic proportions, but I just don't care and I'm so thankful that no one is around to witness it. But then again, if someone was here, I wouldn't be so alone.

Alone. That's what I am now.

DREW

I DON'T KNOW why I walk toward The Cave again. I need to stay away from her, but I know she'll be in there. She's been there almost every night this week, and I suspect that she was last week as well. I round the corner, and am surprised to hear "TKO" beating through the walls. I peek in through the window and can't help but stare. She has on a sports bra, the tiniest black shorts that I have ever seen, and her hair is down. When we were in the water, her hair was wet and smoothed straight back. This is the first time that I have seen it dry when it's down, and she looks like a different girl. She looks completely exotic with it falling around her face, down her back, and it's kind of wild from the dancing. Completely sexy. She's been working hard tonight, and every inch of her is sweat-covered. She looks so good.

Yesterday, "Say Something" by a Great Big World was playing, and I was so mesmerized by her dancing, technique, and gracefulness that I couldn't tear my eyes off of watching her move. In about ten seconds, I realized this girl isn't in here every night dancing just to dance. She's trained, and she's practicing or rehearsing or whatever it is that dancers say they do.

She was wearing typical ballerina clothing of tights and pointe shoes. Her legs looked amazing and so long for such a tiny girl. When I finally glanced up at her face, I was shocked to see the pain and sadness written across it. She was completely absorbed into the music, her eyes were squeezed closed, and tears were streaking down her cheeks. She had no idea that she was being watched, and I felt horrible for invading her private moment. My chest twinged again and I rubbed the spot over my heart. What was happening to me? I should have walked away, but I just couldn't. The music finally came to a stop. She ended up in some pose on the floor, and silence took over.

I watched as she curled up into a ball on the floor and cried. Anxiety ripped through me. Every part of me screamed to go in there and comfort her, but instead, I turned and walked away. I hated walking away when I wanted nothing more than to throw the door open and go completely caveman on her. I wanted to demand she tell me what was wrong. I wanted to take away or fix whatever it was that was making her feel this way. I wanted to protect her.

What strikes me odd about these feelings is that I've never ever felt protective over a girl before. Other than trying to protect my brothers and my mother, I've never wanted to be there for anyone else. I'm just not wired this way. All of these feelings confuse me and because of this, I can just add it to the list of reasons why I should be staying away from her. I also know that if she had seen me watching her, she would have been embarrassed and I don't want her to feel that way.

I tried to remember when the last time I cried was, and then it came to me. I was fifteen and Beau was fourteen. For whatever reason, Beau was in a bad mood that day. It was definitely Beau against the world, and no one was getting in his way, except for my father that is. Beau was in his room storming around and throwing things, really minding his own business, when my father walked in and started hitting him. Beau was so angry that he actually fought back. I wish I had asked him why he was so mad. I think it was the last time he ever fought back.

At some point, my father had picked up Beau's tennis racket and decided to hit him in the arm with it. Even from the doorway I could hear the crack. Beau started screaming and fell to the floor. Matt and I were both standing there crying, and that's when my father saw me.

"What the hell are you crying for? I swear all of you are worthless and no better than a trio of girls. Boo hoo hoo! You think this is worthy of crying over? Huh?! Next time you'll think twice about crying . . ." And he turned around and hit Beau in the arm again. Beau passed out from the pain, and I ran from the house and down to the water.

Kicking off my shoes I dove straight in, clothes and all. Under the water, no one could see my devastation or my tears. I needed to swim out the heartbreak and get control of the guilt. I caused this to happen to my brother. Matt was only seven. Seven-year-olds cry, not boys who are fifteen.

My mother ended up taking him to the emergency room. His humerus, the upper arm bone, was cracked in half. I'm certain that after the first hit it was just fractured, and I know that it was because of my tears that he had his arm broken in half. I have to live with this knowledge. I did this to him, and that day I vowed to never cry again.

Refocusing back to Ali and thinking over the last couple of days, it kind of makes sense. Although she doesn't necessarily do anything that screams, *hey, there's something bothering me*, I've seen it. I saw it in her eyes in the water, and I see it in her body language when she thinks no one is watching. The logical explanation is that it has something to do with why she moved here. I wonder if she has told Leila, since she seems to be the only person here Ali talks to.

I've watched a few guys approach her in the hallway, but her attitude and complete lack of interest screams *closed off.* Last week, there was a lot of buzz about her in the locker room; not so much this week. I think most guys thought she was like a shiny new toy, only she didn't want to be played with and she made it known immediately.

After that last encounter with Beau, she continues to park in my spot every day. I don't mind. Turns out I like knowing where she is and in a way, it makes me feel like she's mine. I know I shouldn't think this way, but I do.

Beau still continues to harass her on a daily basis, but she completely ignores him or fires back one of his useless facts at him. I'm not gonna lie, I like that she ignores him. Girls seem to trip over themselves to get to him, but not this one. He thinks she's playing hard to get, but she's not. She wants people to leave her alone, just like I do.

"Holy shit, dude! She's a B-girl!" Beau had walked up behind me. I didn't even realize he was standing there watching her too. In fact, how long has he been standing there? A flush of anger sweeps over me. I don't want him watching her.

"Nah, man. She's more than that." She is so much more than just this.

"What do you mean?" His gaze moves from her to me. Why did I have to open my big mouth and say anything about her? Beau has always had this uncanny ability to understand what I'm thinking and how I'm feeling without even saying anything, and most of the time, I wish he didn't.

I turn to face him and run my hand from the back of my head to my forehead, smoothing down the hoodie I had pulled up. Not that it really makes much of a difference, but if she saw me looking through the door, I wouldn't want her to know who I am.

"I've seen her a couple of times this week. She dances all different stuff."

"When did you see her?" His eyebrows furrow and he shifts his weight. He is full on watching me now.

"Around." He lifts his brows as he continues to study me.

"I've never seen her." He's trying to challenge me, but I've got news for him, I'm not going to engage.

"Let it go." His eyes soften and he looks at me like he's been let in on the biggest secret.

"She's not a freshman, is she?"

"Nope." Beau slaps me on the shoulder and now he's smiling from ear to ear. Ugh.

I step away at the exact moment that she must've looked over because Beau had glanced back to her and he immediately throws his hands up in the air like he's been caught stealing something. I can't stand here any longer and watch him watch her. It doesn't sit right with me. It's time to go. I shouldn't even be thinking about this. I shouldn't be thinking about her . . . I just don't have the time.

"I've got to go and pick Matt up. I'll see you at home."

Chapter Four

DREW

IT'S BEEN A week since I've talked to her, but I see her every day. Even when we aren't at school, the window to her room is directly across from mine, and I feel like I've watched her for hours. I've completely become a peeping Tom, or maybe even a stalker, whatever you want to call me, but I don't care. They always say you want what you can't have . . . and I want her.

"So, how was your swim this morning?"

I hear her voice as I walk out of the water and my soul embraces it. How did I not see her standing there? She watches as I run my hand through my hair and across my face to shake off some of the water.

"It was good. How was the run?" Today, she's only wearing a tiny sports bra with a pair of running shorts. She puts her hands on her hips and looks at the ground. She's still breathing a little hard. Her face, neck, and chest are flushed red from her workout, and she looks so good.

"It was okay. I just don't understand where all of this

smoke is coming from. There must have been a huge fire somewhere." The morning sky is cloudless, but the island is covered with a low hanging haze of smoke that doesn't appear to be lifting. She rubs her eyes. The smoke must be burning them.

"Yeah, my guess is that a house on the north end caught on fire. I don't know what it is about this place, but it seems every couple of months something catches on fire. You'll see. It's like clockwork. The next one will probably be sometime after the first of the year." I run my hand through my hair again and she watches the movement.

"Wow. Why are there so many?" She bends down and removes her shoes and socks. Her toenails are painted pink and she buries them in the sand.

"No idea. Some say arson. Some say the island is haunted. Most likely it's just irresponsible tourists."

"That's kind of sad." She pulls the rubber band from her hair and runs her hand through it, untangling some of the knots. My stomach tightens. I wish that she was using my fingers to do this.

"Yeah. Are you headed in to float?" I point toward the water. I know from watching her that after each run she floats on her back.

She grins at me. "I do like to float. Wanna join me?"

What? I didn't expect the invitation to spend more time with her. Does she feel the pull like I do? "Actually, I need to get home. I've got somewhere I need to be."

Her shoulders drop a little . . . so does my stomach.

"Oh, okay." She looks toward the water. Disappointment flits across her beautiful face. "How about another time then?"

I now feel like I'm being stabbed in the heart. I turn away from her to look at my house and close my eyes. The mask is down, and I feel like if she looks at me, she'll see right through me. I have to remind myself why it is that I can't be with her, and why I'm choosing to walk away.

"Ali, remember at the café when I said that I was rude to you for reasons I couldn't get into, but it had nothing to do with you? This is another one of those situations. I'm sorry." I know her eyes are on me, but I still can't turn and look at her.

"That day in the water, why did you even bother talking to me?"

What? I never in a million years thought she would ask me this. How should I answer this question? Do I give her the truth or make something up? There's insecurity in her voice and right now I hate myself.

"Honestly… because I thought you were a tourist. I didn't expect to see you again." The truth hurts. It hurts me, and I know I just hurt her.

"Oh." A breeze blows over us and out of the corner of my eye, I see her brush her hair off of her face and tuck it behind her ears. "Well, at least I asked and now I know." Her voice is quiet and there's disappointment laced between the words.

She deserves my attention and not a cold shoulder. I look back at her and our eyes lock. She's so beautiful. The haunted sadness she carries around is glaring back at me and I feel like the worst person in the world.

I'm not sure what she sees in me, but after a moment her eyes narrow and she shrugs her shoulders.

She pulls off her shorts, I squeeze my eyes shut, and groan inwardly. "I'll see you around." She walks away from me and out into the water completely dismissing me. I've hurt her feelings and I feel like an asshole.

The outdoor shower's water is warm as I stand underneath it and rinse off. This is a part of my everyday routine, just like swimming, that I usually enjoy—but not today. Realistically, I know it isn't her fault. It's actually my dad's, but I can't do anything about him, and I can when it comes to this girl. She deserves better. I'll never be what she wants me to be—maybe that's what hurts the most.

Walking up the steps to the back deck, I stop to check her out. Even from way back here, her skin looks ivory smooth. She's toned from head to toe, and there isn't one ounce of fat. After seeing her dance, and the way she runs down the beach, it's easy to understand why she's in such great shape. I can't imagine a girl looking more perfect than her. Her being athletic has done nothing but fuel my unwanted interest in her. Wait, did I just think that? Ugh. I should not be thinking about this girl in any capacity.

"Who's that?" Matt asks as walks up next to me, his binoculars hanging around his neck.

"The new girl that moved in across the street." He holds them up and looks out at her as she wades out of the water.

"She's pretty."

"She is."

"You should make her your girlfriend." If only.

I smile at him. He's still so young and innocent. "Seriously? Can you imagine the shit that would go down if dad found out I had a girlfriend?"

He frowns at me. Now he understands.

"Come on, little man, we have to get you ready for school."

I wrap my arm around his shoulders and give him a hug.

Walking into the kitchen through the sliding glass doors, we see my mom standing there making a pot of coffee. Internally I sigh. I love my mother, but where she is, my father is. Most mornings I'm lucky and can get in and out of the house without either of them noticing me. That's not going to be the case today.

"Good morning, darlings." She looks over at us and smiles. My mother really is a beautiful woman. It's too bad she's married to my father.

"Hey, Mom." I lean over and give her a kiss on the cheek. It's the small things like this that I know make her so happy. For the most part, this home is completely devoid of any type of affection. It's not that we all don't want it or want to express it, we just have learned over the years to interact as little as possible with each other.

"Want some coffee?" I can't tell if she is being serious or not. Usually she tries to get me out of any type of direct line of fire, so I decide to say yes, hoping I'll get to spend a few more minutes with her. She points to a bowl of cereal on the table for Matt. He sits down quietly and begins to eat.

"Sure." When I see her eyes skip toward the door, I realize she hadn't been serious. She asked more out of courtesy than a desire to spend a few minutes with me. That look means he's on his way down. I should have said no.

"How's school going? Are you excited it's your senior year?" I take a seat at the breakfast bar and she slides the mug across the counter.

"It's fine. Same as any other year, really. Yes, I'm excited about it being my last year." I flip my eyes up to meet hers. Sadness washes over her face, but she knows I need to get out of here.

"Oh, I smell coffee . . ." Beau wanders into the kitchen. He ruffles Matt's hair and I start to worry about what type of scene is going to occur this morning. All four of us are in the same place at the same time. Right on cue, Dad follows him in.

"Well, well, if it isn't the three most pathetic excuses for sons out there." I hate that he talks like this in front of Matt. He deserves a better life.

I look over at my mother and feign indifference. Giving him a reaction is what he wants. I've learned not to do that over the years. Beau on the other hand chokes on his coffee, fueling the beast.

"What? Can't hold your coffee down? Just like you can't hold a tennis racket?" Beau lost his match last Friday in the finals, and I'm almost certain he did it on purpose. I've watched him so closely over the years that I can feel which moves he's going to make before he makes them, and I am certain that the lack of moves was calculated.

"It doesn't surprise me you lost that tournament. You don't have what it takes to be a winner. I've wasted years of money and time on you, and you're pathetic. Keep it up, son. Keep up the losing and see what happens to you." My father is snarling at Beau with his distaste for him, and my heart breaks for him. Out of the three of us, Beau was always the one seeking approval and love. I gave up on it a long time ago, and poor Matt never even tried at all.

"And you . . ." His eyes swing over to me. "You aren't any better. You may win your swim meets, but we all know the truth—you really aren't that good. Everyone else is just worse. There's no way that you'll ever amount to anything on a collegiate level or higher. Again, waste of my money and time."

On that note, I set down the coffee cup and go to walk out of the room. I've heard all this before.

"Where do you think you are going? I'm talking to you!" he yells behind me.

"Yeah, well I'm done listening."

From behind me, the sound of an impact vibrates across

the room, and an excruciating groan comes from Beau. I turn around and see him doubled over with saliva dripping from his mouth. His eyes are watering and he's trying not to throw up. The asshole punched him in the stomach. Matt has dropped his head too. He's cowering into the table, and I can see the fear written all over him. He thinks he's next.

"You think you can treat me with such disrespect in my house? Just because you take your shirt off to swim doesn't mean I won't put you in your place, too. Or better yet, maybe I need to show you what I am going to do to you on him!" He points to Matt and out of the corner of my eye I see my mother's face cringe. The two of us continue to stare at each other in a standoff. It's so quiet, I can hear the clock ticking from the living room. Eventually, he grabs my mother by the arm and leads her out of the house. No more words are said.

Matt sprints out of the kitchen and I walk over to Beau. I place my hand on his shoulder, but he just shrugs me off and heads back up to his room. He's angry and hurt. My stomach squeezes. Usually after one of these encounters I find myself in my bathroom throwing up. This is my fault. It always is.

For years, it was me who took the hits, slaps, and shoves. But once I started swimming and the clothes came off, he worried more about his reputation than he did about the well-being of me. He redirected the physical abuse to Beau. He almost never takes his shirt off, but when he does, he blames the bruises on being hit with tennis balls. A fist or a ball—they're about the same size.

Twenty minutes later, we leave the house, drop Matt off, and drive to school. None of us say anything to each other. Nothing needs to be said. It's my fault that he hits Beau. It has been for years. I have to live with the guilt that I've failed him as a big brother. He deserves someone better than me.

This day sucks.

ALI

SEEING BEAU STANDING at The Cave door watching me the other night, I felt a mixture of weirdness and indifference. He was talking to someone. I'm not sure who and I don't really care. What I did find interesting though is that this guy just doesn't do it for me.

The first time I saw him, I thought he was beautiful, and he is, but over the last two weeks or so I've seen him at least a dozen times and not once have I experienced nervousness or butterflies. Leila had mentioned that every girl wants him and his brother, and although I haven't met the brother, I can without a doubt say that I don't want him.

I push through the door to the café and am immediately met with a smiling Leila.

"Ali! Yay! My night just got so much better!" I can't help but laugh at her.

The café is so warm and inviting, I feel like I've been coming here for years. The aroma of coffee permeates the air and it smells oh so delicious. I decide that studying here may just be my new favorite place.

"Are you this happy when all of your friends come in?" I say while still smiling at her.

"Nope, just you, girl! It's been kind of slow, as you can see, maybe we can study together?" We don't have any of the same classes, but I can use the company.

"Really? Okay." I look around to see if there are any hid-

den places where we can sit together—nope, just all open tables, and then I see him. He's sitting in my chair, the one that I
always use when I drop by; a big, leather lounge chair. I'm not
sure how I feel about this.

"Yep, best job ever. Remember my Aunt Ella owns this
place, besides we close in an hour and a half anyway. Want a
latte?" I don't respond to her and she follows my gaze to him.
He's looking at me and I'm looking at him. He gives me an
apologetic smile, stands up, and gathers his things.

Walking toward the front door he has to pass us and with
each step my heart pounds harder. He brushes up against me
and goose bumps race down my arm. My body hums from being so near to him. He pauses briefly and looks down at me
through his thick, dark eyelashes. His eyes lock onto mine and
that connection, that pull for him, burns through me. The
warmth radiating from him heats my skin, he's so close to me.
In a perfect world, I would be able to lean into him, but instead
I watch as he walks away. Did he leave because of me? I look
back to Leila. She's watching me.

"Sure. A latte sounds great. Thanks."

She smiles slowly and sympathetically, and then skips off
to the back. Why would she look at me like that?

I head toward the lounge area and drop my bag as I sit
down in the chair he just left. It's still warm and there's a
slight lingering scent of a clean body wash. I know it's stupid,
but I want to melt into this chair knowing that this is where he
sits when he comes in too. Letting out a sigh, I pull out *Mac-
beth*, our English literature assignment, and fold my legs up
underneath me.

I should be opening my book, but instead I glance out the
front windows where the sun is about to set. Beau is standing
outside talking to him and someone else.

My heart aches as I look at him. His hair looks wet and it's perfectly sticking up everywhere like he's run his hands through it. He's wearing a black, long-sleeved T-shirt and gray athletic shorts. The three of them start laughing and I wish I could hear him. He looks happy, and that isn't how he looked when he saw me.

This morning, when he said he thought I was a tourist and that he wouldn't have to see me again, stung. There's a tiny part of me that knows he felt the connection like I did. That entire moment never would have happened otherwise. But that's what makes this so disappointing. I was hoping we could be friends. I know it's stupid to even think about him, but I can't help the way I feel around him, and I don't even know his name.

Wait a minute! Earlier this morning on the beach he said my name. He called me Ali. How does he know my name? I never told him.

The café door opens and their laughter sweeps in. He glances at me through the window one more time before he walks away. That one glance is like an arrow shot straight into my heart. Why does he even look at me if he doesn't even want to be friends?

Beau and the other guy walk through the door. Leila had brought over our lattes and is sitting next to me with her calculus book open. She stands to greet them, and quickly recovers from the frown that had slipped onto her face at the sight of them.

"Look who we have here! It's the new girl!" Beau saunters over, plops down on the couch, throws his arm across the back, and brings one foot up to prop on this other knee. He looks completely relaxed, like he's at home. With a blank expression, he asks me, "Come here often?"

"Did you seriously just ask me that?"

He smirks at me and I watch his gaze travel over me as I'm still curled up in the chair. His forehead wrinkles a little, and not that I care, but I can't get a read on whether he likes what he sees or if I am completely unappealing to him.

After my rehearsal today, I threw my hair into a messy bun on top of my head, pulled on a wide-neck T-shirt that falls off one shoulder, a pair of sweatpants, and flip-flops. I'm definitely not dressed to impress anyone, but I don't look that bad. Whatever, this guy doesn't do it for me anyway. I look away from him, and over to Leila who's talking to his friend at the back counter.

"So, have you talked to Drew lately?" His voice brings my attention back to him and as I look over, I notice he's started bouncing his propped up foot like he's nervous.

"Your brother?" I'm not following his train of thought, or understanding why he's asking me.

"Do you know a lot of Drews?" Boy, he sure has a smart mouth when he wants one.

"No, and I don't know your brother, either. Never met him. Never even seen him. I couldn't even pick him out of a lineup . . . why?" I'm surprised at the confused look that crosses his face. His foot stops bouncing.

Beau is a really hard person for me to read. One minute I feel like he's checking me out, and then the next, he looks at me like he's trying to figure me out. It makes no sense.

For the most part, I'm really good at reading people. I don't need or want to be the center of attention and because of that, I spend more time watching people than trying to entertain them. From what I've seen of Beau so far, he loves to be loved by whoever he's around, but at the same time he's always studying people's interactions. It's like he is trying to measure himself against everyone else to see if he's doing and saying the right thing.

He has this slight bit of insecurity about him, that he tries to rub off as cockiness. I can't imagine why he would be this way. It seems to me he has a lot going for him.

"No reason, I guess."

Leila and the guy start walking toward us. He puts his hand on her lower back and out of the corner of my eye I see Beau's gaze drop to the hand and he flinches. Interesting.

"Hey, Ali, have you met Grant?" Leila introduces us, and I'm glad because I have no idea who he is. I've seen him a lot over the last two weeks, but none of the guys that are in Beau's group have gone out of their way to introduce themselves to me.

"Grant, it's nice to meet you."

He smiles at me and it's friendly. I grin back. He may not be as beautiful looking as Beau, but he definitely has the rugged, handsome beach look going on. His blond hair is a little too long and bleached out by the sun, his body is more muscular than Beau's, and in general he reminds me of a hockey player, although I doubt they have that sport here.

"You too, Ali."

"Your name is Ali?" All three of us turn to look at Beau. No one says anything. "Sorry, I guess I never really thought about it, just been calling you New Girl."

"You're an idiot, and yes my friends call me Ali." I hold out my hand for him to shake and in a very professional tone I say, "Hello. My name is Allyson Rain. It's a pleasure to make your acquaintance." Grant busts out laughing behind me and I turn toward him. "So Grant, come here often?" I try to say it with a straight face, but eventually I end up laughing with him.

"Really, New Girl! Are you trying to poke the bear?"

I turn back to Beau. Although his face is blank, his eyes are smiling at me and this makes me laugh louder. It feels so good to laugh this hard—it's been so long. Grant's eyes flicker back and forth between us. He and Leila are both trying to figure the two of us out. My eyes lock in on Beau's, and he smiles at me. It's genuine and in this moment, I know one day, somehow, we'll be friends.

"Reindeer like to eat bananas," he says.

I bust out laughing again. "A giraffe can go without water longer than a camel."

His smile gets bigger. "So, Ali, Grant's having a party Saturday night. You and Leila should come." Beau glances up at Leila and then over to Grant who are both still staring at us.

Leila squeals, "Oh, that would be awesome. I love parties. Ali, you could just meet me here and we'll go together."

All three of them turn to look at me. They're waiting for my answer.

"All right, I don't see why not."

Leila squeals again from behind me and a bell goes off near the kitchen. She skips to the back to pick up the guys' food.

After the invite is officially out there and accepted, both guys end up moving over to a table not far from where we're sitting. Leila tells me that they come in at least twice a week for dinner. I'm trying to get some reading done, but I end up listening and peeking at the two of them instead. Grant watches as Beau continually glances at me, I'm watching Leila sneak peeks at Beau, and Beau keeps his thoughts divided between her and I.

"Are you into this girl or something?" I overhear Grant ask Beau.

While keeping my head down, I see Beau drop his gaze to

his plate. I wish that I hadn't heard him, but the place is empty and except for some soft music in the background it's unfortunately very quiet.

"Nah, man, it's not like that." Beau says as he twirls his fork between his fingers and I see his leg start bouncing again.

"What's it like then, because you're different around her." *He is?*

"Yeah well, she's different, and you'll see why." *What's that supposed to mean?*

"What does that mean?" *Thank you, Grant, for verbalizing what I can't.*

"Don't worry about it. Just trust me on this one and know that she's off limits . . . to everyone."

Grant sits back in his chair and then looks over at me. I raise my head to match his stare. His eyebrows are furrowed and both of us have an equal look of confusion. He rubs his hand over his jaw and then looks back to Beau.

"Whatever, man."

"Exactly." Beau's leg stops bouncing.

I'm not sure how I feel about him saying that I'm off limits. Part of me is angry and doesn't understand why a nice guy wouldn't be allowed to date me. What have I done that's so wrong for these people to have me blackballed after two weeks? And then the other part of me is relieved. I don't have time to date anyone, and if this means that guys will leave me alone, I'm all for it.

Chapter Five

ALI

WE PULL UP to the home the party is at and my mouth drops open—it's huge. There are cars and golf carts parked all up and down the block and around the circular driveway. Leila says it belongs to Grant's dad—the parent he visits every other weekend—only his dad is never home.

The house sits on the Intercoastal and has one of the largest back patios I have ever seen. There's a swimming pool in the middle that has a volcano off to the side. Inside the volcano is a hot tub and a waterslide. To the left of the pool is a small golf putting area and off to the right is a tiki bar. This patio is meant to entertain and it runs straight up to the seawall. Past that is one long dock. At least two dozen boats are tied to the dock and to each other. People are jumping from boat to boat and it looks so normal for them, but I've never seen anything like it.

Grant is Beau's best friend. He's a junior like Beau, and

also plays on the tennis team. Leila says they've all been friends for years. I can't help but think that those are the best kind of friends to have. The thought causes me to miss Shannon. I've been avoiding her calls lately. I don't know why. I'm just not ready to talk about my life here.

Music blasts from the speakers which are strategically placed around the patio, and everyone seems to be having a great time. There must be at least a hundred people hanging around laughing, drinking, and dancing.

Leila takes my hand and pulls me over toward the large tiki hut bar. We grab two empty stools that are near the end. The guy behind the bar walks over to us and smiles.

"Hey, Lelia." He's cute in a jock kind of way. I've seen him once in the hallway with Beau, and figure he must be one of their friends. Especially if he's behind the bar serving at Grant's party.

"Hey, Ryan. This is a great turnout tonight." She gives him one of her killer smiles and his grin back to her stretches from ear to ear. I can't help but wonder why Leila doesn't have a boyfriend. All of these guys, Beau's friends particularly, plus others around school, seem to trip over themselves whenever she's around. She's so beautiful, and really one of the nicest people I've ever met.

"Yeah, I think Grant extended to a few mainlanders. What do you two want to drink?" His eyes flash over to me and I can see recognition flare in them. He knows who I am and I don't get the feeling that he's checking me out, more like he's curious instead. He picks up a bottle opener and spins it on his finger.

"Ryan, meet Ali. Ali, meet Ryan."

I give him a small smile and he winks at me. A grin splits across my face. He's cute and very approachable. He's not as tall as Grant or Beau, but my guess is that it doesn't bother him. I'm pretty sure he has no problem getting girls. He's the kind of guy who likes to be the life of the party. No wonder Grant posts him at the bar.

"We'll take whatever the drink of the night is," says Leila.

"Coming right up!" He spins around on his heel and heads toward the other end of the bar where there's a large Gatorade cooler, one like you would find on the sidelines at a football game. He grabs two clear plastic cups and two straws, loads them with ice, and fills them up.

Leila swivels toward me. "Every party has a drink of the night. They're always mighty tasty, but take it from me . . . don't drink more than two." She makes a sick face and I laugh at her expression.

"Gotcha." I'm not a big drinker, never have been, and wasn't planning on starting now.

"Here you go, ladies. This one is called 'The Summer Finale,' and I prefer kisses to tips." Ryan wiggles his eyebrows and leans across the bar.

"In your dreams, Ryan." Leila laughs at him. These two clearly have been friends for a long time. He shifts my way and gives me a panty dropping smile.

"Don't look at me . . . I don't kiss people I don't know." Well, mostly that is. His eyes sparkle like I just issued a challenge.

"Well, maybe it's time we get to know each other." He wiggles his eyebrows again.

"Such the charmer you are!" I like him. I have a feeling that no matter where you are or what you're doing, if Ryan is there, it'll be a fun time. I think about Beau, Grant, and Ryan, and I can see why the three of them are friends. They complement each other nicely.

I take a sip of the drink and immediately see what Leila was talking about. It's good. "What's in this?" I need to know how strong these actually are.

"Ah, now if I tell you, I'll have to kill you . . . just kidding. I think that the correct term for this one is Malibu Baybreeze. It's coconut rum, plain rum for extra kick, pineapple juice, and cranberry juice. Do you like it?"

"Ummm, very much." I smile at him again.

"Who invited her?"

I swing around on the stool to see what the commotion is all about, but the only people there are Cassidy and her friends. That's when I realize they're talking about me. My night just went from very promising and having a good time to terrible. Seriously, what is with these girls that they won't leave me alone? Isn't it bad enough that I have to put up with their crap at school? But outside of school, enough is enough.

"I did, so knock it off, Cassidy." Beau comes up from somewhere and slides in next to me at the bar. He wraps his arm around my shoulder and I stiffen. Lisa instantly looks like she wants to rip my throat out.

"Why would you do that? She doesn't belong here." She says in a slow monotone voice, while never taking her eyes off of Beau. A flush spreads across Cassidy's cheeks. Is she spitting mad at his response, or is she embarrassed because he snapped at her? It's known that she's all about pleasing the Hale brothers and trying to be a part of their crowd. It has to be a popularity thing.

"What are you talking about, Cassidy? It's a party! The more the merrier. Besides, look at her, she has definitely improved the scenery."

I can feel my ears tinge pink at the compliment. I look up

at him and see a piece of his perfect hair fall across his forehead as he looks down at me. I know it'll fuel the fire, but I can't help it. I reach up and brush the strands off of his face. His eyes twinkle back at me with mischief. He knows what I'm doing and he lets out a chuckle while squeezing my arm. Smiling back at him, I lean into his side. If he wants to defend me, then so be it. I'm going to soak this up and rub it in their stuck up faces. Just watching them now, they're squirming, and Beau sits his chin on top of my head.

Leila is still sitting on her stool on the other side of me, and her jaw has fallen open at the conversation and our interaction.

"Scenery, more like entertainment! I mean, look at her. I'm certain something will go down with her tonight." Cassidy's eyes travel down the length of me.

If Cassidy thinks she's intimidating me, then she's mistaken. I really don't care.

"I am looking at her . . . and you need to let it go, Cassidy." Beau's voice has switched from casual to serious. He's no longer playing games or humoring her and her bad attitude toward me.

I see Ryan out of the corner of my eye look at me curiously again. He sees what's going down, and he walks over, and stands behind me from the other side of the bar. These two are making a statement, and I have no idea what it's about.

"Beau! You're choosing her over me!" Cassidy now screeches, causing a scene.

"I'm not choosing anyone, so watch your mouth. You should know better by now. However"—he pauses for dramatic effect—"someone else might have chosen her. Yeah, I'm thinking she might already be spoken for."

What's he talking about? Remembering the conversation I

overheard between him and Grant, he said I was off limits to everyone.

"What does that mean?" Cassidy's irritated and it's not a good look for her.

"Like I said, let it go, Cassidy." Beau looks at each one of the girls. Two of them step back.

"Or what? What are you going to do?" If Cassidy thinks throwing this little tantrum is going to benefit her somehow, she's sadly mistaken. Beau slowly lets go of me, stands up to his full height, crosses his arms over his chest, and glares at Cassidy. His lips are pinched into a straight line and his message is coming across loud and clear. I hear another one of Cassidy's friends gasp, and collectively all four of them seem to take another step back. A silent moment passes between everyone, and just before the girls quickly turn and leave, Cassidy pins me one last glare that says *this isn't over.*

Beau turns and looks across the bar at Ryan, an unspoken message is passed between the two of them. Ryan nods his head and then bends down to grab a Corona for Beau.

"Thanks, man! Just what I needed. Well, that and maybe a little female company." The smirk is back in place. He swings his eyes past me to Leila, and smiles a little bigger.

"Don't even think about it, Hale. Not in your lifetime." Beau throws his head back and laughs, but I see Leila's neck flush a little as she turns away. Beau raises his beer bottle to us in a toast as he steps away from the bar.

"Did you know that almonds are not nuts? They're a part of the peach family." Huh, I didn't know that. His eyes are gleaming; he really loves these one liners.

"Sex burns three hundred and sixty calories an hour." *Ohmygod!* I can't believe I just said this to him, but the expression on his face is classic. I shocked him. He didn't see that one coming.

He chuckles and pins me with one last look. "I'll be watching you, Tiny." Then he's gone.

Tiny? Where did that come from? Oh well, I'm not going to complain. If anything, the nickname Tiny is a step up from New Girl. If he decides I'm on their side, who am I to go against the grain. At this point I'll do anything to get these girls to stay away from me.

Leila turns to face me. The wheels are turning in her head.

"Is there something going on with you and Beau?" Her question catches me off guard. Not necessarily what she asks, but how she asks. Her tone doesn't come across as curious, more hurt if anything.

"No. Every interaction I have ever had with him you've been there, aside from the parking lot at school. You're seeing the same crazy behavior from him that I am. I don't know why, though. What do you think he meant by—I think she's already spoken for?"

"I was kind of wondering that myself. That's what made me think that maybe he had chosen you, but then again it's not like he openly flirts with you." She visibly relaxes. Her reaction makes me believe that there's definitely something between them, whether they want to admit it or not.

Leila eventually leaves me to go off and see some of her friends. I decide to walk down to the end of the dock and take a seat on a wooden bench. It really is a pretty night, and I'm enjoying watching all the fun. I can't get over how different Grant's party is versus ones that I would have gone to back in Denver. Those parties were never outside, and if they were, they were in a field.

A few people stop by and introduce themselves, and in general I think that the students at our school are very nice.

The only hostile ones still just seem to be Cassidy and her friends. I occasionally catch them staring at me and whispering to each other. Maybe the more people I get to know, they'll see that their hostile behavior toward me is ridiculous, and they can move onto the next victim.

"Oh my God! Drew Hale is staring at you!" Leila skips up. I didn't even notice her.

"The brother?" I'm finally going to get to see what the infamous brother looks like! Seriously, this guy is worshipped around the school, and I have no idea who he even is.

"Yeah, Beau's older brother. So, I was in the bathroom minding my own business when Cassidy walks in with Lisa and I hear her complaining about how Drew isn't paying her any attention and that he is too busy staring at the new girl, when it dawns on me that they must be talking about you! They leave the bathroom, I leave the bathroom, and sure enough I spot him right away, and he is definitely watching you." She's beside herself with giddiness. Wow, she didn't react like this when she talked about Beau which further confirms what I think I already know about the two of them.

She points up toward the back of the house and to a group of people sitting around the fire pit. My heart skips a beat when our eyes lock, and my hands start to sweat. So many pieces of different conversations fall into place. He is the older brother—gorgeous with dark brown hair, never really talks to anyone, but was laughing with Beau at the café, swimmer . . . how did I not figure this out sooner?

His expression to me isn't exactly one of indifference. There seems to be a slight edge to it. Leila's right, he is staring at me. I can't believe that he's the same guy I secretly look forward to seeing in the mornings. He's become the best way to start my day. He took away some of my loneliness and he didn't even know it.

I inwardly groan to myself.

I must look like a complete idiot to him. First, I run into him in the water, I park in his spot, and then I actually asked him if he wanted to spend more time with me. No wonder he's scowling at me. His girlfriend hates me, too.

Ugh . . . Any dangling possibility where I thought my mystery guy from the beach and I might one day be friends just drifted away with a passing breeze. From what I've heard about him, he doesn't have or want many friends. My heart cracks into a million pieces. Even now if I tried to be friends with him, most likely he would think I was trying to be like every other shallow girl.

Wait! Why do I even care what he thinks? In the end, he doesn't know me and has made it clear he doesn't want to. I let out a loud sigh, break the eye contact, and look down at my hands, which are sitting in my lap. I feel Leila watching me. She doesn't say anything and I'm glad. My heart feels like it is breaking up with him, even though we were never together. This just sucks.

DREW

SHE FINALLY FIGURED it out.

Everyone knows who Beau and I are, and I was certain that she had been given some type of detail about me, but after watching Leila approach her, say a few words, and then her eyes sought out mine . . . I knew.

I wish I knew what she was thinking; the expression on her face tangles between embarrassment and sadness. Leila leans over, grabs her attention, and says something else to her. I watch as her shoulders slump down and she wraps an arm that was lying on her lap across her stomach. If I wasn't such an asshole, I might have actually tried to talk to her. I don't know why she would ever want to talk to me after I blew her off, but it would have been nice.

I know nothing about her other than she dances and is from Colorado. I want to ask Beau what he knows about her, but that would just be strange. Again, we don't talk about girls.

I walked into the party just as she was making her way down to the dock, and she took my breath away. She's wearing a short, little coral-colored strapless dress that's tight through the top down to her waist, and then it flares out a little. She has on a thick belt around her waist, and gold flip-flops. Her hair is pulled back from her face, but the majority of it was left down. I love her hair. For me, she is the complete package.

I didn't even realize that Cassidy and the girls had wandered over until Cassidy walks between my legs and sits down on my lap. I didn't let on to her, but shocked is how I feel about her behavior. She has definitely been getting bolder when it comes to me and what she wants.

Beau had clued me in on their little interaction earlier in the evening and how she was treating Ali. I am officially done with Cassidy.

I break my gaze from the new girl and look into Cassidy's face. She really is a pretty girl and had we run across each other in a different place and a different time, then just maybe I would have considered her more. Or maybe not, since her behavior lately has been terrible. She smiles at me and wraps one arm around the back of my shoulders.

I glance back over to the new girl and see that she and Leila are headed down to Chris's boat.

I grab Cassidy's thigh and pull her tighter and closer on my lap. Her eyes sparkle with excitement and I need to squash whatever she thinks is going to happen between us immediately. Her flirtatious behavior is bordering on annoying.

"What are you doing?" I ask her. She leans her head closer to whisper in my ear. People are watching us and for her sake, I really don't want to make a scene or embarrass her.

"I was hoping to make it perfectly clear what I want to be doing." Her breath grazes my neck and normally this would give my libido a kick, but not tonight.

My eyes flicker down to the boat before they land back on Cassidy's.

"Cassidy, just so there isn't any confusion here, I'm not interested." Her face remains calm, but her eyes register disbelief at what I said and then she tries to switch to a seductive look. Most guys would never turn down a chance to be with her, and maybe it's because I've been there already, I don't know. What I do know is that the only girl I have any interest in, is talking to a guy right now who is not me and I am not happy.

"You were a few months ago, and I thought we were pretty good together." She runs her hand through my hair and I grit my teeth.

"I never made any promises to you. In fact, I'm pretty sure that you have always been quite aware of that one-night deal."

"What deal?" she asks innocently, when we both know she isn't.

"That we are nothing and never will be. We had a good time, one time, but that's all it was and all it will ever be." Direct, direct, direct. Sooner or later it has to sink into that head of hers.

"I know, but it's our senior year, and I think you and I could be good together. Kind of like a power couple." And there it is. She doesn't really want to be with me; she just wants what I can potentially bring her . . . more status, secure popularity, and the one to claim that they landed me.

"Seriously, what makes you think I would ever want that? I have zero interest in being a power couple with you or anyone else. No offense." Does she not know me at all? I have never been into popularity or trying to pull rank above others at school.

"Is that so?" she smirks at me as if she knows a secret that I've not been let in on.

"Yes, you got a problem with that?"

"Well, I guess it is what it is, but can't we still have some fun together?" Her hand leaves my hair and she runs it down the side of my face. She's still trying to go with the seductive route.

"No."

"Really?" Direct, direct, direct. What part of this conversation is she not getting?

"I mean it, Cassidy. Stay away from me. Don't even look at me. Pretend like you don't even know me. If you continue to harass or bother me, you'll regret it. Stop acting like there's something between us when you know there isn't and there never will be . . . ever."

Her eyes narrow and she lets out a small laugh. "I'll regret it? You can't be serious?" Her tone is laced with disbelief.

She's starting to lose a little of her composure and I need to end this conversation before she causes a scene.

"I am. You and your friends like spending time with Beau and my friends, right?" She gasps and pulls back. "Find someone else to direct your attentions on. You are starting to look desperate, pathetic, and we're done here." With that, I push her off my lap and she stumbles on her high heels as she stands up. She always wears the most inappropriate shoes.

Hurt crosses her face, and then anger. "You know our timing is coming. Accept it and things will be a lot easier."

What the hell is she talking about? I'm done dealing with her. I shoot Beau a look and then head over to the bar to hang out with Ryan for a little bit.

ALI

THE PARTY IS actually turning out to be pretty awesome. I've met some of Leila's friends, who all assured me that any friend of hers was a friend of theirs. We had wandered down to someone's boat and we're sitting around the back just keeping to ourselves.

There's Dawn and her boyfriend, Chris, both of whom couldn't keep their hands off of each other. It really was kind of funny. Karrie and Scott who just recently started dating and didn't really seem to into the PDA thing or they just hadn't reached that point, and Leila's cousin, Chase.

Chase is really something else. He's definitely an interesting character, and I mean that in a good way. He thoroughly kept the group entertained and became the gopher for beverages. I occasionally caught him looking at me. Hopefully, he realizes, I'm about as closed off as it gets.

"So, Ali, we know that you've been hanging out with Leila at the café some, but we don't really know anything about you." I'm not surprised that Dawn is the one to initiate the questions. She seems to be Leila's closest friend, and that makes her the most skeptical of me. With Leila now being my only friend, I appreciate how she's looking out for her.

I lean back and cross one leg over the other. I smile, hoping to encourage her to ask away. "What do you want to know?"

"Where did you move from?"

Well, that's an easy one. "Denver. Well, just outside of it," I say.

"Wow! That's far. Why did you move here?" Karrie chimes in.

"My dad is the COO of Outdoor Explorer, and he decided to come here for a while and work out of the Marine branch office." This technically isn't a lie, and they all seem pleased with the answer. I've never asked Dad this, but I've often wondered if Mom had ever been here. I wonder why he picked this island out of all the islands or beach towns that we could have gone to. What is so special about here to him?

Chase perks up at that. "I love that store! We just bought new paddleboards from there. Have you ever been paddleboarding?"

"No." I can't help but laugh. "Up until two weeks ago, I hadn't been to the beach in years. If there was a board involved for me, it was a snowboard." I'm going to miss the snow this winter.

"You snowboard?"

I nod.

"Sorry, but that's totally hot." Everyone on the boat laughs at him and he grins from ear to ear.

"Dude, leave the girl alone. You just met her." Chris swats him in the back of the head and everyone laughs again.

"Do you play any sports?" The conversation shifts back to

Dawn.

"Not really. I just dance." My dad had me play softball when I was a kid, but the practices started competing with dance rehearsals and well, obviously dance won out.

"What kind of dance?" Karrie asks.

"All kinds. I love to dance." Chase moans off to the side and everyone just laughs again.

"What?! It adds to her hotness. I can't help it," he says.

"How old are you?" This question comes from Chris.

"Nineteen, why?"

"That's perfect!" Karrie squeals. "There's this awesome warehouse dance club on the mainland that splits its floors by age. The downstairs level is for eighteen and up so we can go dancing . . ." Karrie throws her arms up in the air, and starts wiggling her hips like she's dancing.

Chris leans over and turns the music up. Speakers from all around the boat fill the night with the latest pop hits. "Talk Dirty" by Jason Derulo comes on and Karrie jumps off her seat, grabs my hand, pulling me up, and we start dancing. Dawn and Leila join us while the guys sit back and appear to be admiring the view. We laugh at them.

I try not to think about Drew. A few times I catch myself looking around the people at the party to see if I can spot him. Only once did I find him by the bar. After watching Cassidy help herself to him a little earlier, I know I need to forget about him. I don't look anything like her, and if that's what he likes, then I'm not the girl for him. Not that he wanted me anyway. He made it perfectly clear that he didn't. Karrie bumps me on the hip and breaks me out of my train of thought. I'm glad for the distraction and I'm happy to be making new friends.

Other people eventually board the boat and before we know it, we've started a little dance party. It feels so good to let go for the evening and enjoy myself. It's the first time in a long time that I'm having fun, and tonight I actually feel like I might be okay here. I feel like I'm starting to fit in.

DREW

WATCHING HER DANCE on Chris's boat made my night. I know I shouldn't be watching her, but I find myself seeking her out even when I don't realize it. Beau and Ryan both catch me staring her, but neither one of them say anything to me.

Cassidy and the girls finally take the hint after I walk away that none of us are interested in entertaining them tonight, and they wander down to the dock to do a little more socializing elsewhere. I'm so incredibly happy she left and isn't anywhere near me. I just hope she takes my warning seriously, and leaves me alone.

Beau and I spend most of the evening together next to the bonfire. We don't really talk about anything important. It's just nice to be talking to him. Practice schedules have become a little crazy lately for both of us and when we're home, we tend to hide out in our rooms. We both agree that some much-needed Matt time is overdue. We decide that tomorrow we'll take the boat out, do a little fishing, and enjoy the sunshine.

Toward the end of the evening, the girl we saw on the first day of school, standing across the hall from us, comes over and sits on the arm of Beau's chair. She's been watching him most of the night, and I guess her liquid courage has finally kicked in. His attention leaves me immediately and moves on to her.

I decide it's time for me to take off, so I wander down to

the dock to let Grant know. This is by far one of the craziest parties that he's ever had. As I pass Chris's boat, I glance at her. At that moment, she laughs. In the last two weeks, I've seen her mad, sad, and indifferent, but never happy. The smile on her face and her laugh—she might as well have been singing to my soul. I'm pretty sure that mine just smiled back at her.

I keep walking because if I stop, then I'll cause a scene, and really I'm not sure what to do with these emotions swirling around inside of me. I shouldn't feel this way about a girl, but I can't help it. I've never been one to believe in love at first sight, and I'm not saying this is love, but it is something, and it happened at first sight.

I find Grant on the last boat. "Hey man, great party, but I'm gonna head out." We do one of those one handed handshake/hug moves that guys do.

"Alright, glad you came, I didn't think you were." He steps back and smiles at me.

"Beau asked me to drop by and hang out with him for a bit since I haven't seen much of him lately." I run my hand through my hair, scratch the back of my head, and stretch.

"Gotcha. So, you and Cassidy, huh?"

Huh? My jaw tenses and my eyes narrow.

"No way! Never going to happen—ever." My nice little mood that I was in after seeing Ali laugh just vanished. I'm seriously never going to be able to escape that awful girl.

"She sure looked pretty cozy earlier." I can't blame him for asking. He just wants to know the specifics. Beau, Grant, Ryan, and I have all had each other's backs for years, and I know that he'll squash any unwanted rumors should he hear them.

"Exactly, that's what she wants it to look like. She's been

warned, and I'm done with her."

"How about the new girl?"

Of course. I shouldn't be surprised that he's noticed me looking at her, too. All three of these guys have serious detective skills.

"What about her?" Tension leaks into my shoulders.

"Interested?"

I'm not sure how to answer his question. I can't date her, but I don't want anyone else to either. Is he interested in her? He sees me thinking and raises his eyebrows at me.

"Nope. Can't. I have to focus on swimming. Last year here, dude, and I can't have any distractions."

"Right . . . whatever you say." He grins at me and pats me on the back. I shake my head at him before climbing off the boat.

What I didn't expect to see was the Cassidy showdown taking place halfway down the dock.

"What are you still doing here?" Cassidy yells at Ali. Lisa and their friends are standing behind Cassidy and on both sides of Ali are Leila, Dawn, Karrie, Chris, Scott, and Chase.

"Leave her alone, Cassidy," says Karrie.

"Or what?"

I approach Cassidy from behind. She doesn't know I'm there, and I spot Beau coming toward us from the other end of the dock. He must've seen what I'm seeing, and he looks pissed.

"Cassidy! I thought I told you to let it go," Beau yells at her.

"I don't answer to you, Beau, and this nobody here needs to learn her place." Ali rolls her eyes at Cassidy and turns around to leave. The second she does, I know it isn't going to end well for someone.

Cassidy's hand shoots out and grabs onto Ali's arm. "Just where do you think you're going? I'm not done with you."

"Yeah, well, I'm not listening to anything you have to say, and you better take your hand off of me."

Cassidy, standing in her heels, towers over Ali. Most girls in our school cower down to Cassidy and her friends, but not her. Maybe that's part of Cassidy's problem; she isn't used to being dismissed. Ali jerks her arm away as Beau steps up and pulls her back into him. I know that he's trying to make a statement to everyone here, and well, I'm in for that too.

"Leave her alone, Cassidy," I bellow out. I can't stay quiet anymore. A hush falls over the crowd.

"Drew, seriously?" She swings around at the sound of my voice as I walk past her—shock evident on her face.

I step up next to Beau and look directly at Ali. She watches me warily, and her eyes on me do funny things to my stomach and my chest.

Cassidy stands there and looks between the three of us, and then she starts laughing. "Oh, I get it now. One brother isn't good enough, you have to have both."

"It's not like that, Cassidy, and you should know better than anyone here that we don't work that way," says Beau.

This is news to me. I didn't know that she had approached him too. I look over at him and he shakes his head in disgust. It doesn't surprise me, though. A few people snicker through the crowd. Cassidy's cheeks turn bright red with what I'm hoping is embarrassment, but the ice in her eyes makes me feel like it is something more.

She looks over to me. "Are you going to let him talk to me like that?" Again, she's trying to stake some kind of claim over me and make it seem like we're more than what we are. Stupid girl.

"Why wouldn't I? It's not like you're anything to me . . . and I just found his last statement quite interesting, although knowing you and your obsessive tendencies, it doesn't surprise me." She gasps and then regains her composure.

"That's right, Drew. You do know me well . . . very well, as a matter of fact."

"Yeah, well enough to know that you're crazy. You and I have never been and never will be anything. So get that through your thick head and remember you've been warned repeatedly. No one here appreciates you being a bitch to this girl for no reason. Let it go. Show's over, folks." I look around at the group that's formed around us.

Shaking my head in disbelief, I turn to look at Beau. He has that look on his face again where he's reading into more than I'm saying. It occurs to me that I just defended Ali in front of an entire audience of spectators, and I never defend anyone, especially a girl. Beau's the talker between the two of us. I shrug my shoulders and the three of us turn around to walk off. Ali is still watching me and I realize I feel good for standing up for her. I also like Ali being in the middle of Beau and me. It feels kind of perfect her being with us. I like her next to me. I could get used to this.

Beau let's go of Ali's arm and a loud screech comes from behind us. Ali's jerked away. Cassidy has grabbed ahold of her skirt, and is attempting to shove her over the edge of the dock.

My reflexes kick in and one arm shoots out and wraps around Ali's waist, pulling her back into me. Ali pushes off of Cassidy and this causes Cassidy to lose her balance on those high heels. Before anyone can react, Cassidy slips over the edge of the dock and into the water. There is a beat of silence before everyone breaks out into laughter. Cassidy instantly starts slapping at the water as if she's never been swimming before.

"Someone help me! My dress and shoes are getting ruined!"

She pushes her wet hair back and looks at everyone standing on the dock. Makeup runs down her face and no one moves to help her. Even Lisa stands there staring with her jaw dropped open. Cassidy's chin trembles as she treads water. She wants to cry, but won't give Ali the satisfaction.

This has to possibly be the most embarrassing moment ever for Cassidy. She's all about being prim, proper, and poised.

Beau looks over at the two of us and then down over the edge.

"Look who turned out to be the entertainment after all!" Beau throws his head back and howls with laughter, fueling the crowd even more.

"Beau, this is all your fault!" she yells at him. He's done listening to her. He shrugs his shoulders, smirks at her one last time, and then turns away from her, dismissing her.

"Just wait, Beau Hale. You're going to regret the day you ever met me!" she screams as she tries to make her way over to the dock's ladder.

Beau turns and smiles at her. "Sweetheart, I already do."

"Oh my god, Lisa, don't just stand there. Help me!" Cassidy screeches, causing Lisa and probably every dog in a five mile radius to wince before rushing to the top of the ladder to help fish her out.

Beau laughs and shakes his head as he turns back toward us. His eyes land on Ali. "You okay, Tiny?" Tiny? When did he start calling her this, and what does it mean?

"Yeah, I'm good. Thanks, Beau." I look down and realize I still have her up against me. Her back is pressed to my front, one arm is wrapped over her chest, and the other is still around her waist. Her hands are curled down around the back of my legs. She's holding onto me tightly, and I like it just a little too much.

I let go of her and instantly feel the loss as her hand drops. She smiles at Beau and then turns to look up at me.

"Thanks." Her smile to me is sad and then she does the most unexpected thing. She reaches up and slowly runs her hand down my arm, squeezes my hand, turns around, and then walks off.

My arm and hand are burning and numb from her touch.

Maybe it's just because I haven't been touched in so long, or that it was tender and affectionate, I'm not sure, but my chest thumps hard again and the ache returns. I rub the spot over my heart and watch as she walks off. I can feel Beau watching me and I know he sees what's happening to me.

ALI

I HAVE TO admit, as I pull into the school Monday morning, I feel better than I have over the last two weeks. People are starting to become familiar to me, and the anxiety that accompanies having to do something new is wearing off.

Most of the hallway is clear as I run through the front door, trying to not be late to class. My run felt especially good this morning and I ended up going farther than I usually do, causing me to be a little behind.

I walk into my homeroom class and head for my desk. Not paying attention, I drop my bag onto the floor and almost hit a very long pair of jean-covered legs that are stretched out underneath my chair. My gaze travels up a pair of muscular legs, over a broad chest, and I'm met with a pair of beautiful brown eyes that seem to be laughing at me.

I feel like the air has been punched out of my lungs as I stare back at Drew Hale. He raises his eyebrows at me and it snaps me out of my shocked moment. A piece of my hair has fallen onto my face and I tuck it back behind my ear. This couple of seconds allows me enough time to pull myself together to say something to him. He watches me.

"Have you been sitting here all along?" Yes, that's the best that I could come up with. Half of his mouth goes up in a smirk. Yeah he is definitely laughing at me.

"Yep."

Even though he just gave me a one word answer, the sound of his voice frees a dozen butterflies in my stomach. His eyes roam over my face and they quickly come back to mine. The gold flecks make them appear lighter today. I love their unique coloring.

"Huh." That's my only response as the second bell sounds. I sit down in my seat and all of a sudden, that calmness I had as I entered the school leaves me.

Glancing back at him one more time, his eyes find mine. I can't help but to look him over. His dark brown hair is perfectly messy, his face is clean from a fresh shave, he's wearing a red T-shirt, and his tanned arms are stretched across his desk. On the inside of his right forearm I spot a tattoo of a saber or sword, this surprises me because I don't remember seeing it before. His left hand twirls a pencil between his fingers.

"Like what you see?" He just totally called me out and I squeeze my eyes shut. Humiliation engulfs me and a flush runs from my neck, through my cheeks, and up to the tips of my ears. I turn back around quickly only to hear him chuckle behind me.

This guy that I have been thinking about for over two weeks has been right here behind me the entire time. That's what I get for keeping my head down. Oh well, it was probably for the best anyway. As it is now, I'm going to have a hard time focusing on the class and not every little sound and movement that comes from behind me.

I think back to Saturday night and how I finally had a name to put with a face. Disappointment washes over me, because not only is he the most popular guy, like ever, but he's so out of my league. Again, this makes me sad.

I'm lost in thought as the end of the period bell rings and I jump in my seat, causing my pen to hit the floor. Before I can grab it, a hand reaches over and picks it up. He doesn't say anything. He just hands it back to me.

"Thanks," I say.

He nods. Both of us grab our bags and head for the door. He's right behind me and his hand grazes across my lower back, leaving a trail of tingles.

My thoughts turn to Saturday night. During that little confrontation with Cassidy, he was behind me then, too. I was shocked when he grabbed me around the waist to keep me from going over the edge of the dock. I would have assumed that he would have grabbed her. Instead, he pulled me in right next to him, and I couldn't help but to reach around and lock onto his legs. Part of me was trying to gain balance and the other part of me felt as if I was trying to melt into him. Being flush next to his body with his arms around me, for those two minutes, I felt safer and more secure than I have in a long time.

Letting out a sigh, Drew's hand lightly grabs my hip.

I look over my shoulder at him and he glances down at me with no expression at all across his face. From this angle, I can see a small scar under his chin and I swear he has the longest eyelashes I have ever seen. He's gorgeous and so tall. He must be at least a foot taller than me. The other students push through the door and the heat from his hand leaves me as we exit the classroom and enter the hall. That's probably the closest I'll ever get to him. My heart frowns.

Part of me feels really stupid. Leila warned me. She said that every girl wants either Beau or Drew, and now I fall into the same pathetic category as the rest of them. I don't know if I actually want him, or if it's more that I'm intrigued by him. His looks alone are unlike anyone I've ever seen before. Of course I'm curious. But the way my body reacts when it's around him; it's never been like this before. Is this how every girl feels around him or his brother? This is the part that confuses me the most.

"Hey, Ali." Chase is walking in my direction and he's smiling from ear to ear.

He's just like his cousin, happy all the time, and I can't help but smile back when I'm around him. Drew's hand lightly grabs my hip again, and Chase falters in his steps. His smile drops a little and he glances up over my shoulder. I turn too. Drew looks angry and Chase seems to be on the receiving end of his glare. The three of us stop moving, and then Drew is gone. He pushes past us and heads for his locker.

"What was that all about?" Chase looks as confused as I am.

"Beats me. He sits behind me in class." I turn to walk down the hall to my locker and stop when I see Drew standing at his, which is only three over from mine. How did I not notice this before either? Oh, I know . . . it's apparently because I never pay attention to anything that's going on around me.

"So, how was the rest of your weekend?" Chase asks me.

"It was good. I got caught up on some studying, went and bought some groceries, you know . . . typical weekend stuff." I open my locker and pull out the books I'll need up until lunch. Chase leans on the locker that's between Drew and me.

"If you're caught up on studying, then that means you'll

be free to join me one night for dinner this week over at Beachside."

I look at Chase and he is smiling at me again. Behind Chase, I hear a locker slam shut, and it causes me to jump. Chase turns around, looks at Drew, and then steps back away from me and into the middle of the hallway. I glance over and this time, Drew pins me with a look that lets me know he isn't happy.

"What?" I say to him.

He doesn't say anything, but I feel as if all the oxygen is being sucked out between us. Again, how have I not seen this guy once in the last two weeks? He shrinks the size of the room and every time I've been near him over the last couple of days my body hums with awareness. Beau walks up and sees the exchange taking place. Drew and I are locked onto each other and essentially everyone around us has disappeared. Beau's head bounces back and forth between the two of us.

"Hey, Tiny! Whatcha doin'?" Beau asks me.

"Hey, Beau." I still haven't broken eye contact with Drew.

Chase clears his throat next to me and gently grabs onto my elbow to gain my attention. Letting out a deep breath, I turn to face him.

"Look, I'll catch you later. Think about dinner, okay?" He takes another step back, drops my arm, and looks up over my shoulder one more time. His eyebrows furrow and then he turns around to head off in the other direction.

Beau starts chuckling and my eyes snap to him. He looks back to his brother and then over to me. "Did he just ask you out on a date?" Why does this guy care so much who I do and do not date? I'm getting kind of sick of him thinking he has any say over it or me.

"What's it to you if he did?" I'm scowling at him.

Beau looks back over to Drew whose look of annoyance has dropped to one of indifference. For whatever reason, he's thrown up a wall over his emotions, and he isn't letting anybody see in. The two of them share a silent conversation and Drew turns around to walk off.

Beau looks back over to me and I slam my locker shut.

"Nothing, you can date whoever you want to. I just think you should get to know a few more people here and enjoy all the new fish in your sea before you tie yourself down."

I'm not planning on tying myself down, and isn't that what I'm doing? The guy just asked me to dinner, nothing else. Ugh, really, it isn't any of his business anyway!

"Were you dropped at birth?"

He busts out laughing and his eyes sparkle as he looks down at me. "Oh, Tiny, I do like you. You're perfect for him."

"For who?"

"No one. Hey, did you know that a woodpecker's tongue is long enough to wrap around its head two times?" He grins at me.

"Yeah, well money isn't made out of paper. It's made out of cotton."

His grin grows wider. "I'll see you around."

And with that, he too walks off. My head is spinning at the strange conversation and then I hear a female voice come from across the hall.

"Stay away from them." I look over to see Cassidy and her friends lined up against the lockers, shooting daggers at me through their eyes.

"Or what?" I take a step toward them and her friends lean back into the lockers, as if that isn't telling enough. These girls are nothing but all bark and no bite. My eyes lock on to Cassidy's, who's now only a foot away, and she appears completely unintimidated by me. "What do you seriously think you're going to do to me? I'll tell you, nothing. Who I talk to or don't talk to is none of your business. So back off and leave me alone. I am so over you." My voice was even and monotone just enough to let them know that I'm not going to be bullied by them in the slightest.

Silence fills the space between us. She says nothing, but in her eyes I see determination. She's not going to let this go. I roll my eyes at Cassidy, and turn away to walk to my next class. Apparently, she's decided to ignore the guys' warnings from Grant's party.

DREW

HOURS TURNED INTO days, days turned into weeks, and before I know it, it's almost the end of October. Ali and I have yet to have another conversation since that day on the beach, but that doesn't mean I've stopped watching her. I smile at her in our classes and occasionally I nod to her in the hallway outside of our lockers. Beau and a few others have spotted my friendly behavior to her and look at me in astonishment. I do understand why they're reacting this way. Smiling at girls isn't normal behavior for me. I rarely acknowledge anyone, much less smile at them too. But for the most part, she keeps her head down at school and moves from class to class. She pops in those earbuds and no one bothers her.

I still watch her at home too. She spends most of her time in her room or on her balcony and she has no idea that she's become better entertainment to me than TV.

She's started talking to Dawn, Chris, Karrie, Scott, and Chase a little more. I'm not gonna lie, seeing her talking to Chase and laughing really pisses me off. I'm not sure if they ever went out to dinner or not . . . I'm hoping not. He's a good dude and all, but he's not the one for her.

Every morning and night her routine is still the same. I see her running and I see her dancing. I've also noticed that the Ranger Rover is hardly ever there. She continues to park in my spot, but I guess after all this time, it officially isn't mine anymore—it's hers.

I wake up in the morning thinking about her and I go to sleep thinking about her. I must have thought of at least a hundred different scenarios where I "accidentally" run into her, invite her out to dinner, ask if she wants to study together, etc. Sooner or later something is going to have to give, because I'm driving myself crazy.

I relive those few moments in the water and on the dock at Grant's party over and over again. It really was just a reflex to reach out and grab her. There was no decision to make. Ever since that first second when my eyes locked onto hers, it has been her, only her. I think about what it felt like to have her up next to me, and she fit perfectly. Thinking back, I'm angry at myself for letting go of her so soon.

The house is quiet this morning as I leave for my swim. The sun has started rising later and when the time changed on the clock, that didn't help either. It's still pretty dark out, but there's an orange glow coming up from the Eastern horizon. I can see just enough as I head over the dock pathway at the end of the street and down to the beach. I look over at Ali's house to see if there are any lights on, and there aren't. The air is cool this morning, which means that the water is going to be getting cooler soon too.

The beach is empty except for someone sitting on a towel with their legs drawn up, their arms wrapped around them, and head down. I don't think much of the person and assume that it's most likely some drunken person sleeping it off or someone who feels the need to do Tai Chi at sunrise. I've seen a few of both of those over the years.

As I come up behind the person to get a better look, I realize this person isn't either of those, but it's her. Ali is sitting here. The size of the person is so small that I should have realized it was her right away. With her legs pulled up, she looks like a little ball and I can hear her crying. Panic instantly fills me, and I scan her body looking for injuries.

I drop to my knees and reach out to touch her shoulder. She jerks backward and her eyes fly open. I've startled her. I didn't mean to, but she shouldn't be sitting out here crying in the dark. Her beautiful eyes are red, swollen, and laced with sadness. Her hair isn't pulled back and it's fallen all around her face and shoulders. She shivers.

"What's wrong? Are you hurt?" She sits up slowly, straightens out her back, and looks around.

"What time is it?" I notice she doesn't make eye contact with me, nor does she answer my question. Tears still stream down her face.

"It's 6:15." I let a few minutes pass as she stares out at the water. The silence around her is driving me crazy, and the only thing I can focus on is the sound of the waves lapping the shore. I don't think she's hurt, but I'm confused and concerned.

"Ali?"

Her eyes flash to mine and neither one of us says anything. I can see and feel her broken heart and it makes my chest feel weird again. Her chin begins to tremble and slowly more large tears drip from her eyes. I'm not sure if I should touch her or not, but I can't help myself. I let out a sigh and reach over to wipe them away with my thumb. She leans her head against my hand and closes her eyes. I wasn't expecting that from her. At this moment, this girl owns me and I would give anything to make her stop crying.

I move and sit next to her on the towel. She still hasn't opened her eyes, so I pull her onto my lap and wrap my arms around her. Her skin is cold. She shivers again, and lays her head on my chest. Her arms find their way around my body, and she hangs on while silently crying. I've always known that she has a sadness in her that follows her around, but this kind of sadness is more like pain and grief. It reminds me of the time I saw her crying when she was dancing. Maybe I should have gone in then?

She takes a deep breath and then lets it out slowly.

"It's been seventy-eight days, and every day just gets further and further away." The sound of her voice breaks. I have no idea what she's talking about and I try to do the math in my head. Seven days a week, eleven weeks ago, whatever happened was in August right before she moved here.

I look down at her and smooth a few pieces of her hair away from her face. "What happened seventy-eight days ago?" I ask her quietly.

"It was the last time that I saw her."

"Saw who?"

"My mom." Oh no. I know where this conversation is headed.

"Why can't you go see her?" I need her to say it, that way I know.

"She's gone… she died."

I have a feeling she hasn't told anyone about this yet, or

really even talked about it. This poor girl is broken and her teardrops are breaking me. I pull her tighter and she hangs on. I had planned on going for a swim, so all I'm wearing are swim shorts. Her skin warms against mine, and her tears drip down my chest. Each drop that falls is falling straight into my heart.

I'm not sure how long we actually sit on the beach, but I do know that I need to take her inside. The sun has finally risen over the treetops and a few more people have started wandering onto the beach—shell pickers mostly, but they don't need to see her like this.

I lean forward onto my knees and then stand up with her still cradled in my arms. This girl is so small, I feel like I can break her. I pick up her towel and flip flops. I don't want to leave them behind.

I walk back up the dock pathway and over the dunes that lead to our houses. Beau is standing in the driveway, looking around, when he spots me. Concern and panic spread across his face and he jogs over to us.

"Yo! What happened to her? Is she okay?"

She tenses in my arms and moves her face from my chest to my neck. She doesn't want him to see her and she's hiding, so I pull her up tighter into me.

"Nothing. She'll be fine. She just sprained her ankle."

His eyebrows lift as he takes us both in. It isn't lost on him how she's nuzzled into me and she never lifts her head to acknowledge him. Considering how she's probably better friends with him than me, her reaction to him, upsets him. Silent communication passes between him and me. He knows I don't want him asking any more questions and he nods his head.

"Oh, okay. Well, I'm gonna head off to school early. I

need to talk to Coach, so I'll catch you later. Ali, I hope your ankle feels better."

She doesn't make a sound or a move. Her warm breath drifts across my skin and under my ear. It's time for me to move. I give Beau a small smile and turn toward her house.

I walk us in through her front door and up the stairs.

Walking into her room makes me feel funny. This is her private, personal space and I feel a little strange being here. Don't get me wrong. I've imagined myself in this room with her so many times, but at the moment, I also feel very under-dressed.

Her bed is all rumpled, and I pull back the covers a little more so I can lay her down. Her tired eyes watch my every move. She lies on her side and curls up. I pull the blankets and tuck her in. She's breaking my heart with her sad eyes. I push some more of her hair out of her face and tuck it behind her ear. Leaning over, I kiss her on the forehead, leaving my lips on her for just a second longer.

"If I could stay here with you today, I would. I have a meet this weekend and I need to be present in school."

There was a brief moment of hope in her eyes, and then it went out. I hate having to say this to her. I want nothing more than to climb into her bed, wrap my arms around her, and make her feel better.

"It's okay. I didn't expect you to." It's like she's resigned herself to the fact that she's going to be here by herself, no matter what. I get the feeling that she doesn't have anyone to expect much of.

Even though we have barely had ten minutes of conversation together total, I feel a responsibility to her and I know I shouldn't. This pull I have toward her hasn't weakened in the slightest. If anything, over the last couple of weeks, it's gotten stronger.

"Do you need anything?" I tuck her blanket in a little tighter.

"I don't think so. I'm just tired." Her eyes lock onto mine and another tear drops out.

"All right, well get some sleep and I'll check on you later, okay?" It's silent for a minute and I take this as my cue to leave. I run my hand down the side of her body and over her leg. I love touching her and just having that connection to her. I stop at her foot and give it a squeeze before I turn for the door.

"Thanks, Drew." She's almost so quiet that I don't hear her.

I turn back and give her a small smile. "So you do know my name."

"Doesn't everybody?" She smiles back at me.

I'm not sure if this statement coming from her makes me happy or annoyed. Oh well, in the end, it doesn't matter. I'm just happy she knows for sure who I am.

"Yeah, I guess they do." I tap the doorframe to her room twice, give her one last smile, and head for the stairs.

With each step that I take away from her, a part inside of me hurts a little more. I don't want to leave her here by herself. I don't want her crying all alone. From what I can tell, she's alone all the time. I can't even begin to imagine how she's dealing with all of this. Seventy-eight days, is that even long enough to grieve the loss of a parent? If you loved them, I can't imagine it is. The thought of her crying every night in this house alone breaks me. My chest is aching so badly I feel like I can't breathe. What is it about this girl that makes me this way? This can't be normal.

I walk back across the street, throw on some clothes, and

head to school. I park in what I now consider to be her spot since Beau is in mine. I stop in the front office to let them know why I'm late and that she won't be in today. They don't say anything to me. Why would they? I'm a golden child to them and I make straight As. I've never caused them any problems, and if anything, I've brought them in money through donations to the school.

The end of the day can't get here fast enough.

The lunch bell rings and students immediately begin filing out of the classrooms and into the hall. Thankfully, most people this morning have steered clear of me. There must be something about my appearance that says "don't bother me." I head to my locker eagerly, wanting to dump my morning class books in, and head out.

"I see you got your spot back." Cassidy has wandered over and leans against the locker next to mine. Of course she didn't notice my "don't bother me" appearance. She's selfish and only thinks about what she wants and no one else. I don't even acknowledge her.

"What, are we not friends now?" she asks in a terribly sarcastic tone.

"Were we ever? Don't you remember what I told you?" I shoot her an annoyed look, wishing that she would go away. Her perfume has wrapped itself around us and I want to gag at how strong and sweet it is. I'm missing vanilla and citrus.

"Come on, Drew. You know we were," her face has taken on her trademark seductive look, and I cringe. "And I still want to be . . . just think about how great we'll be," she whispers, running a finger down my arm.

I slam the locker door shut and stare at her, saying nothing. *How great we'll be?* What is with this girl? Doesn't she understand, *no*? Beau walks up behind her and I can feel him reading the situation.

"What do you want, Cassidy?" Beau says.

She turns her body and her eyes shift from me to him and I can see her confidence begin to falter. Both of us are now giving off a hostile, unwelcoming vibe. I know she isn't smart, but surely she must sense this.

"What do you mean, Beau?" She looks genuinely hurt that this conversation isn't going the way she wants it too.

"Um, let's see . . ." He throws his head back and grabs his chin as if he's in deep thought. "Oh, I remember now . . . Grant's party a couple of weeks ago. I thought Drew was pretty clear when he told you to back off and stay away from him."

Her mouth drops open a little, but I know her well enough to know that no matter what he says, she isn't finished. She's one of those girls who always try to have the last word.

"Gee, Beau, I always thought you were supposed to be the nice brother." Her tone has switched from sarcastic to condescending.

"Well, Cassidy, that's what you get for thinking about me."

A few people have stopped to linger and eavesdrop on the conversation. Lisa gasps as she walks up and catches the tail end of the conversation. Why this girl remains friends with Cassidy after hearing she tried to pick up a guy that she was dating is beyond me. I would have thought that girls would have a similar code as guys. You don't go where your friend is or has been.

"Why are you guys being so cruel today? All I asked was if Drew got his spot back."

Neither Beau nor I say anything, and his eyes flash to me. He knows that's not all she asked, and he's also aware that something else was wrong with Ali; she didn't sprain her ankle. He's on to me as well. He had his suspicions before, but as the weeks passed and I never pursued her, he never said anything. The truth is though, if she means something to me, then she means something to him, and no one talks about the people we care about.

"Wait! Is this about that new girl?" her nose wrinkles in disgust.

On that note, I bump arms with Beau and walk away. I'm certain by doing this I just caused more harm than good. These girls are brutal when it comes to bullying, and I can only hope that they don't further direct their attentions toward Ali. Cassidy has been warned repeatedly—I can only pray that she'll listen. Poor Ali has enough stuff going on without me interfering by adding in a bunch of catty girls that can't take the hint. I'm not interested.

Thinking about Ali, I decide that instead of waiting until tonight to see her, I'm going to pick up lunch and bring her a sandwich. I really should be staying away from her. I've done pretty well so far, I just don't want her there by herself all day. I want her to know someone is thinking of her, even if it is just me. After today, I'll leave her alone. No need to cause the girl more problems.

ALI

I CANNOT BELIEVE that Drew found me having a complete meltdown on the beach.

I'm not even sure what really happened to set it off in the first place. Maybe it's because it would have been her fortieth birthday today and she died so young, or maybe it was because she was so young and she's not here with me anymore. I feel completely robbed of years of time and shared experiences with her. All I know is that I slept terribly last night and when I woke up this morning, I felt like the house was closing in on me and I had to get out. I had to get away.

It should have occurred to me at some point in the early morning he would be making his way down to swim. He's always in the water before I start my run and he pretty much sticks to his routine, just like I do. I wasn't thinking.

After Grant's back-to-school party, I had hoped that once he realized I knew who he was that maybe he would talk to me more and we could be friends. That didn't happen.

He isn't rude to me in any way, but he doesn't go out of his way to ever give me reason I could be something more to him . . . like a friend. He still smiles at me in class and in the hallways, and occasionally in the mornings, I will wave to him and he will wave back. But these are things that you do with anyone you know. I'm sure he smiles at lots of people throughout the day. I'm not any more unique than the next person. Still, it's comforting to know even though we don't talk, he is still here.

I feel grateful for him today. What he did for me this morning—I don't know if a lot of guys would have. Most probably would have checked to see if I was okay on the beach and then left. Not Drew. He carried me home and took care of me. I can still feel the lingering sensation of his lips on my forehead. I miss someone showing me affection, even if it is just a small amount.

There's a knock on the front door, it opens, and then his voice drifts throughout the house.

"Hey, Ali, can I come in?" This morning was the second

time that I've heard him say my name. It did strange things to my stomach then and it's doing strange things now.

"Upstairs." I glance into the mirror on my dresser and take a quick look at my appearance. I'm so glad I decided to take a shower after I woke up. I was a complete hot mess after sitting on the beach sobbing my eyes out.

I hear him skip up the stairs and with each pound against the floor, my heart pounds with it. He rounds the corner and stops in the doorway that leads into my room. All I can do is stare. His dark hair is back to that perfectly messy and perfectly sexy look. He's wearing a light blue T-shirt, a pair of low-slung designer jeans with a thick brown belt, and a pair of Rainbow flip-flops. This look seems to be *his* look. Only a few times have I ever seen him in anything different.

He probably knows that I just checked him out and I find myself unable to make eye contact with him. My gaze lands back on his belt. I've never given much thought to a belt before, but on him, I'm jealous of the belt. It gets to wrap around him, just like I was earlier.

"How are you feeling?"

My eyes jump to his. His are locked on me. I scoot against the head board and pull my legs up. I want him to have room to sit next to me if he wants to.

"As good as to be expected, I guess. You don't have to stand in the doorway. Do you want to come in?"

He shrugs his shoulders and then saunters into my room. Instead of sitting on my bed, he drops a bag and then sits across the room in my desk chair. Disappointment floods through me. Any thought I had of being close to him again just flew out the window.

I have never thought that this room was particularly small, but with Drew sitting here, I feel the space shrinking.

He looks so out of place here. Maybe it's because I've never had anyone over, but at the same time, it feels so right to have him here. I wish he'd be here more often. I frown on the inside knowing my wishes will probably never come true.

"I wasn't sure what you had to eat here, and I think you should eat something, so I stopped and picked up a Cuban sandwich for you from Beachside. That's what's in the bag. I wasn't sure if you would like it or not, but I did see you eating it once before, and it's my favorite. Hope you like it." He's rambling a little bit. Is he nervous?

I reach down and grab the bag, placing it in my lap.

"Thank you. A Cuban sandwich sounds perfect right now. This is very thoughtful of you." I drop my eyes to his hands. He rubs them back and forth across his thighs slowly, unconsciously. He catches me watching the movement and stops. I look back up to his handsome face and my heart squeezes. "Thank you too for helping me out today. I'm sorry you had to see me like that." He sucks his bottom lip in between his teeth and his eyebrows pull down.

At the same time, though, I wasn't sorry at all. At Grant's party I wasn't sure if the sense of safety I felt was from being wrapped up next to him or if it was the adrenaline from the confrontation with Cassidy. Earlier in the evening when Beau had thrown his arm around me at the tiki bar, I felt nothing. But this morning, sitting in Drew's lap and being wrapped up in his arms, I felt the same wave of comfort wash over me. I feel a sense of security and safeness that I haven't felt with another person, since my mother. I felt that no matter what, if he was there, I would be all right. It really is silly and I don't know why this feeling takes over when I'm around him, but it does. I mean, I don't even know the guy.

It also makes me sad, knowing I feel this way around him.

It kind of hurt this morning when he walked away. He took that feeling of calmness, wholeness, and that sense of belonging to someone with him. I was all alone again.

"No worries. I'm glad I was there to help you." He watches me closely now and I just want him to come and sit next to me. "So what happened this morning that makes it so different from other mornings?" I look down at the bed and grab the edge of the quilt. Running my fingers across it, I know I'm fidgeting, but he sits quietly and watches me.

"Oh . . . today was my mom's birthday."

He nods his head, but doesn't say anything in return. I've noticed that he doesn't really talk that much.

"How did you know where I live?" I ask him.

His eyes grow large and his jaw drops open a little. "You're kidding, right?"

I don't know how I should be feeling right now—shocked at his reaction or stupid because apparently I should know the answer.

"Ah, no."

He gives me a small smile and leans forward, placing his elbows on his knees. He glances at the ground and then back up to me. He almost looks like he's a little disappointed. "I take it you aren't a very observant person. I live across the street, literally directly across the street."

Oh. How in the world did I not know this? This is another one of those moments where I begin connecting the dots, just like I did when I figured out who he was. He enters and leaves the beach in the same place that I do. There's never been a random car parked on the end of our block. I had heard he threw a back to school party. The house across the street always has a black Jeep parked out front; Beau rides to school with someone in a black Jeep.

"Oh. I'm sorry. It's not that I'm not observant, I just kind of keep to myself." Suddenly, I feel stupid. Including my little episode from this morning, we can just add this to my list of embarrassing things that I do or have done around him.

"Yeah, I've noticed. So how come you are always here by yourself?" Wow, this guy is pretty direct.

"Whereas, I take it you must be a very observant person." I smirk at him. "My dad works a lot and has a condo next to his office." *Oh, and because he doesn't know how to deal with a teenage daughter now that his wife isn't around, essentially making me feel like an orphan.*

"Aren't you kind of young to be staying here by your-self?" Is he concerned or just being nosey?

"Young? I'm nineteen."

His eyes flash a little brighter. "You don't look nineteen."

And isn't that the story of my life. I don't know if it's that no one ever believes me or if they just need to second guess me. As if I don't know my own age.

"And now you know why I'm still in high school, too. I was born a preemie my birthday is July twenty-ninth, and when I turned six, they wanted me to be the oldest in the class versus the youngest, but they still thought that I was underde-veloped, so they held me back. I started kindergarten when I was seven. It didn't make much of a difference, though. I've always been smaller than most other girls."

"I'm nineteen, too. I started school when I was six, but I repeated first grade. My dad told me that I needed extra time to learn the fundamentals of reading. What really happened is neither he nor my mother ever read to me or helped me with my homework, therefore I fell behind. I overheard him once on the phone say that he wanted me older than the other boys. My dad is crazy. He said it was more important to be bigger for sports as a senior than to worry about age. My birthday is July twenty-eighth. Whatever, I guess he's right. I am bigger and stronger than I was last year. Beau too, he's eighteen. It definitely helps from the competition standpoint." I can't believe he just told me all this.

"So you're one day older than me." I smile at the thought. "It seems kind of unfair for the others who have to compete against you."

He just shrugs his shoulders.

"Couldn't the same be said about you? Oh well, swimming is going to be my ticket out of here, so it is what it is. Listen, I need to head back to school. I just wanted to check on you. You okay?"

No! I don't want him to go yet. I never have anyone to talk to. I want him to stay, I want to get to know him better, and I want to be friends with him.

"I'm good. Thanks, Drew."

He stands up and taps on the bed with his fingers—those same fingers that ran down the side of my body before and squeezed my toes.

"No worries. I'll see you around."

I hope so.

He gives me a small smile and he walks out the door.

After I hear the front door close, I throw myself sideways on the bed and cover my face with my pillow. I take in a deep breath, not believing that Drew was here in my room twice in one day. I throw the pillow off and sit up. I was so caught up with the sight of him in my room that it wasn't until just now that I even register the smell of him lingering in the air. Closing my eyes I breathe in the fresh cleanness of him. There's a mix of a light shower scent with patchouli and musk. It's distinctly him and it sets my heart off even more.

Chapter Seven

ALI

DREW'S JEEP IS already parked by the time I pull into the school's parking lot this morning. I had been hoping to get here first and then hang out and wait so I could thank him for yesterday, but that idea didn't work out as planned.

My next thought was to catch him in one of the two morning classes we share, but as soon as the bell rang he either walked into the class or walked out of it and I never got a chance. Other than him nodding at me as he passes by, or just making slight eye contact, it's as if yesterday never even happened. Oh well, worst case is that I can always stop by his house later today if our paths don't cross.

I decide to leave campus for lunch today, and I'm stuffing my books into my locker when he strolls up to his. He's only a few down from me and this seems like the perfect time. I'm not quite sure why I'm so nervous, but whatever this guy is about, he definitely gives a closed-off vibe. Over the last couple of weeks, I've only ever seen him speak to like three or four people. Even the teachers don't call on him. Not that it matters, I really don't talk to anyone either.

Taking a deep breath I take a couple of steps toward him. Again, I don't know why I am so nervous.

"Hi." He doesn't even acknowledge me. He just shoves his books into his locker and I feel like he's pretending that I'm not even here. He can't possibly understand how much this hurts me.

"I just wanted to say thanks again." He slams the locker and I jump at the sound. The speed in which he closed the door causes the air around us to fan over me and his scent completely immobilizes me. I know that he affects my senses, but this is crazy. His smell is so delicious, and so him, it makes me wonder how I'm going to go every day without getting to smell this. He turns to face me as I'm lost in this thought, and his eyes bore into mine. His glare is so fierce that I take a small step away from him. His jaw locks tight, and he still doesn't say anything. I don't really know what I expected him to say, but I was attempting to have a conversation with him, so something would be better than nothing.

Nothing. This is how he's making me feel at this moment, like I am nothing.

A few too many silent seconds go by and he raises his eyebrows at me like I'm an annoyance to him. My eyebrows wrinkle in as I flash back to the two interactions we had yesterday. He was perfectly cordial and a gentleman. I can't come up with anything that would make me think he wouldn't acknowledge me today. I know it's stupid, but I kind of thought that we had at least become passing friends.

Under his gaze, I look down at the ground feeling completely defeated, inappropriate, and my heart sinks in my stomach. Of course he doesn't want to talk to me, or have me talk to him. I already live every day by myself and alone, pretty much just feeling like a nobody. He's confirming this all over again. I should have let this go. I mean, seriously what was I thinking? He's made no effort at all in the last two and half months to try to get to know me. Why would he want to now all of a sudden? I hear some girls laughing at me from across the hall, which causes me to stiffen, and my heart aches even more.

"Oh . . . I see how it is," I whisper out, still staring at the ground. I look back up to his handsome face, give him a small smile that I know doesn't reach my eyes and lift my shoulders in a small shrug. I officially feel like I've humiliated myself and I need to get out of here as soon as possible. "Well, like I said, I just wanted to say thanks." I'm trying my hardest to keep a brave face.

From behind me, I hear Cassidy laugh a little louder. "Oh, how sweet . . . she actually thought he would give her the time of day."

The other three girls break out in loud laughter and Drew's eyes skip from them to me. His hands, which are hanging down by his sides, tighten into fists. I wrap my arms around my middle. It's an unconscious protective move, and I can't help it. Drew frowns at me, and I can't take it anymore.

I quickly turn around and my eyes blur with tears. I don't want any of them to know they've finally gotten to me, especially Drew. I'm not paying attention and I run right into Beau who's standing directly behind me. When did he join this little conversation? He grabs me by the elbow as I begin to lose my balance and pulls me in toward him. I feel his eyes scan over my face. I can't look at him. My heart is pounding and filling with tears. They're all going to leak out soon and I just need to get out of here before I make myself look like a bigger fool.

What was I thinking? Drew Hale. I knew better. I've heard the stories and was even issued a warning by Leila. This guy is so out of my league. We don't now and probably never will move in the same circles. The only person to blame here is my stupid self.

"You okay, Tiny?" Beau asks me quietly and under his breath.

His concern for me seems genuine, and this hurts even more than if he was just going to be his usual confrontational self. I don't want his sympathy or pity. All I had wanted was to be their friend. Now, I don't want anything from these people.

"Sorry," I mumble. I jerk my arm away from him, quickly step around him, and walk straight out the front doors. I can't get to my car fast enough.

I don't know why I thought we were going to be friends. All he did was sit with me for a few moments on the beach, carry me into the house, and bring me a sandwich. He probably thinks I'm just the poor, pitiful new girl. But to me, he was someone that I talked about my mom with. I haven't talked about her to anyone since I moved here, and it felt good to.

Loneliness washes over me like a complete blanket, and my heart is cracks into pieces in my chest. I feel so unwanted and unloved. How do people go through life like this? Maybe some don't know any better because that's the way their life has always been, but I know. I know what it's like to walk into a home and feel so secure and safe. I know what it's like to walk into a school and have a dozen people stop to say good morning to you before the first bell even rings. I know what it is like to have a mom sit on your bed at night, tuck you in, and when she leaves that spot is still warm and comforting. I know.

By the time I get to my car, the tears are unstoppable. I

click the key fob and throw open the door. As I am about to sit down inside my car, I see it. It sits on top of my car, waving its translucent wings up and down.

My heart just went from breaking to stopping. I can't tear my eyes away and it seems to be returning my stare. Its elongated body is electric blue, eyes are a shiny gray like mercury, and its six little legs are skinny and black. What's it doing here and where did it come from? I look around to see if there are any others and there aren't. I glance back at the roof of my car, and it lifts up and flies away. I watch it until I can't see it anymore. I want to scream for it to stay, but I know that it won't.

I slip into my car and close the door. I pull on my sunglasses, lean my head against the steering wheel, and grab the charm hanging around my neck. That was the first dragonfly that I've seen since she died. I know it's irrational to feel some type of connection to an insect, but I can't help the hopeful side of me that thinks maybe, just maybe my mom is with me.

I think back to the letter she gave me with this necklace and in this moment, I can hear her voice as clear as a bell. *"Sweetheart, dragonflies are known to live their lives to the fullest. Whenever you see one, I want you to hear me saying 'it's time to let go.' You are always so serious and focused. Sometimes you need to look for a little joy. Lighten up your life and make it brighter. Seek out some happiness because you, my darling girl, deserve to live each day smiling with not only your eyes, but your heart too."*

I look out the window hoping to get another glance at it, but it's not there. Wet tears are still falling down my face and I think she's right. My life is dark right now. Only I don't know how to find the light. Suddenly, I'm exhausted.

I sit silently in the car for a few minutes to compose myself. Wiping my eyes with the heels of my hands, I make a decision—I just need to get home, get in my bed, and forget about the rest of today.

DREW

I WOKE UP today knowing it was going to be an awful day. I heard Dad downstairs yelling at Matt and my mom, and there was no way I was going to try and bypass them to go out and swim. Staying in my room was the best decision, but I'm missing my swim and also missing Ali. I wanted to make sure she was okay before we got to school.

Beau and I walked into school at the last minute possible, so I didn't see her before class, and now I don't want an audience when I do talk to her. People are nosy, and I know they will be eavesdropping on our conversation. Ever since those magazine articles went out earlier in the year I feel like everything I do and say is constantly up for discussion by people who don't know me, and I sure as hell don't care to know them.

When we were kids, Beau and I went camping with the Boy Scouts, and I remember this one activity where we sat in a circle around the campfire and our den leader would whisper a secret into the ear of the kid on his left side. That kid would turn to his left and repeat the whisper, and so on and so on until the whispered secret was returned to the beginning of the circle with den leader. Every single time the secret was changed and elaborated. It never ended the way it began, and most people never heard the true secret. In hindsight, the sad part about this exercise was that all of us loved what the secret had become in the end more than what it was in the beginning.

None of us cared to know the truth. And this is the biggest reason why I choose not to talk. No one cares about me, my life, or the truth. It's all about the gossip and who can spread it the fastest. This is why I'm all about being seen and not heard.

Ali didn't see Cassidy and the girls enter the hallway, but I did. I knew they were watching us and I knew if I responded to Ali, they would give her a harder time than they already have, and honestly the girl has been through enough recently. She doesn't need to add this on top of it.

I didn't mean to come off rude to her. I just didn't know how to diffuse the situation. It isn't like she and I are friends, but at the same time I know she feels something deeper for me like I do for her. Don't ask me how I know this, I just do. It's like I can read her through all of the simple things that she does. Like when she acknowledges me with a smile in class or the hallway, or a wave from down the beach as I finish my morning swim, and after having watched her for months, I know she doesn't do this with anyone else.

The girls laugh at her from across the hall. "Oh . . . I see how it is," she whispers out. She won't make eye contact with me.

I look down into her beautiful face and watch as she finally lifts her head and gives me a small smile that isn't real. Her eyes are filled with hurt and it breaks me to know I'm doing this to her. She shrugs her shoulders at me and I can see that she has given up. "Well, like I said, I just wanted to say thanks."

Across the hall from her, I hear Cassidy laugh again. "Oh, how sweet . . . she actually thought that he would give her the time of day."

Glancing over, I see that Cassidy's face is lit up. She's watching me, not Ali, and she's giving me a smug grin.

The other three girls laugh along with her and I want to retaliate so badly that all four of them will never forget who I am as long as they live. I want to make each of them suffer for being so catty and just downright horrible. My hands ball into fists. What has this sweet girl ever done to any of them?

I've never wanted to hit a girl, but at this moment I really wanted to shut Cassidy up. Ali has never tried to approach me before and I know I don't give off a vibe that makes it easy, so for her to come over here to try and talk to me at school in front of other people—I know it was hard for her. I feel like a complete asshole. I hate what this situation is doing to her. It's written all over her beautiful face.

Beau walks up behind her with an evident scowl. He's there just long enough to witness most of the interaction. He hears the girls laugh and he watches as Ali retreats into herself. He's standing so close to her that she easily could have sunk backward into his arms. The thought of him and her together, I decide right then that they're never going to happen. Not if I have anything to do with it.

Ali looks at me one more time and then she whips around so fast to leave that I don't think she expected anyone to be standing there. She runs right into Beau, but keeps her head down. I already know I've hurt her feelings, but to see her feeling so rejected, I wasn't expecting that. She always stands up to Beau no matter where we are or what we're doing. He riles her up and she fires right back. Beau glares at me with a complete look of disapproval.

"You okay, Tiny?" She doesn't even look up at him.

"Sorry." She jerks her arm away from him, keeps them wrapped around herself, and heads for the front door. Oh man . . . and the asshole of the year award goes to . . . ding, ding, ding, that's right . . . me.

Both of us turn to watch her walk away. When the front doors close, Beau turns back to face me, clearly pissed. We both look over to Cassidy who's still laughing with her friends. They're now in the process of switching out books and moving down the hallway toward the cafeteria. They don't even notice how angry we are. They're too caught up in feeling victorious for thinking they finally got under her skin.

"Dick much?" I turn back to look at Beau. He's pulled himself up to his full height and glares at me. I can't help but wonder again what his deal is about this girl. He never shows any interest in her day in and day out, but he certainly defends her every chance he gets.

"What difference is it of yours?" I'm curious and hoping he'll give me an answer.

"Really, Drew, that's all you have to say?"

I don't have a response for him, and he's right. He defends her because of me. He knows that she means something to me. I push off the lockers, pull my keys out of my pocket, and stalk out to the parking lot. I need to make this right with her. She needs to understand.

Ali doesn't see me approach the Jeep. I probably could have talked to her here, but damn if there aren't eyes everywhere always watching my every move. I climb into the Jeep and look over at her. She put her sunglasses on and her hands are gripping the steering wheel with her forehead lying in between.

A pain shoots through my chest and I automatically reach up to rub it. She takes a deep breath, wipes her cheeks, puts the car in reverse, and leaves the school.

I made her feel this way and in this moment, I feel like the worst person in the world. Maybe I should have talked to her. She just wanted to thank me. It wasn't like she wanted to walk down the hall and hold hands.

I follow her home and pull up behind her as she climbs out of her car. I know she knows I'm here, but she doesn't even look at me.

"Ali." My emotions are running crazy, so calling out her name comes across very quietly. She hesitates mid-step, but then keeps right on walking. I follow her into the house without asking for permission. I don't ask and she doesn't stop me.

Just like yesterday I notice that all the blinds are shut and the lights are off downstairs, making it very dark. If I didn't know that she lived here, I would have thought the house was vacant. She throws her keys and her bag on the island in the middle of the kitchen, opens the refrigerator for a bottle of water, and heads up the stairs. I keep following her and she keeps ignoring me.

Once we get to her room, she grabs some clothes off of her bed and goes into the attached bathroom to change. I didn't really have a chance to look around her room yesterday, but today all I can do is stare.

Most girls would probably say this room looks vintage or what's that other description—shabby chic. In the middle of the far wall is a queen sized bed with a wrought ironed frame. The bedding is all white except for a quilt that's folded up at the end of the bed. There's a large, white fur rug in the middle of the floor, a white desk, a white dresser, and a floor-length mirror leaning against the wall. All of the furniture has a distressed look to it and honestly, it looks pretty cool. The walls are a pale blue and all of the windows, including the French doors, have long, thick, dark gray curtains. She has one book shelf next to the desk and it's covered with keepsakes, books, and a few photos.

What strikes me the most however are the framed, movie-sized posters of her in full dance costume of whatever performance she was in at the time. They're beautiful and she looks breathtaking.

The bathroom door opens and Ali walks out wearing a tiny camisole top, little cotton boy shorts, and her hair is pulled into a ponytail. She closes all of the curtains except for one, cracks open the balcony doors, and climbs into her bed.

I know I'm staring at her. I can't help myself. She has so much skin showing that it's messing with my brain. As she moves around her room I'm awestruck again by how beautiful and perfect I think she is.

"What do you want, Drew?" She lets out a deep sigh, curls up on her side to face the balcony door, and closes her eyes.

"I'm sorry." I know these two words aren't going to mean much to her after today, but it really is the truth.

"For what?"

She doesn't open her eyes, and I don't say anything back to her. I push my hands into my front pockets and wait. I need her to tell me how she's feeling right now so I can fix this.

"Whatever. I wasn't trying to upset you or your girlfriend." Here we go . . .

"Trust me when I say that I don't have a girlfriend." I hate how I've done nothing to encourage this, yet everyone seems to think that she is. I'm starting to wonder if she is telling people that we're together?

"Does she know that?"

"Yes." She damn well should. I feel like I've told her over and over again.

"All right, well thanks for stopping by."

"Ali . . ." I know that she's still hurting. I don't want to be dismissed. I did this to her and it's my responsibility to make her feel better.

"What, Drew?" The tone in her voice says I'm starting to annoy her.

"What are you doing?"

"What does it look like I am doing?" She opens her eyes and I feel the weight of them as they land on me.

"School's not over."

"So? And why do you care?"

I don't want to be there without you. Not that I can say this to her.

"We're friends."

She frowns and looks at me as if I've lost my mind.

"No, we aren't."

Don't say that. Please don't mean it.

"I'd like to be." Truth time.

"Honestly Drew, if this is how you treat your friends . . . no thank you." I deserved that comment.

"I said I was sorry."

"Fine, apology accepted. You can go now."

"What if I don't want to?" *Please don't ask me to leave.*

"Are you planning on taking a nap with me then?"

"I'll take that as an invitation and the answer is, yes."

Before she can say anything I walk to the far side of the bed, put my phone on her nightstand, kick off my flip-flops, undo my belt, drop my jeans, and climb into the bed next to her. I leave on my T-shirt and am wearing a pair of boxer briefs. She rolls over to face me and I match her position by lying on my side with my head propped on my hand. Her eyes are huge as she watches my every move.

"I wasn't offering an invitation, and you can't just climb into my bed." She's flustered and nervous. It's like she knows the appropriate response should be to kick me out, but the curious side of her is winning.

"Well, I did and I'm here now."

She pulls the covers around herself a little tighter and up to her chin, confusion still evident on her beautiful face.

"Why?" she asks.

Because I don't want to stay away from you anymore.

"Why not? I promise I don't bite." A piece of her hair has fallen out of place from the ponytail and I reach over to tuck it behind her ear. I love doing this. Her hair is so soft and I watch as her cheeks blush a little. She's so stiff she barely moves a muscle.

Silence stretches between us. She closes her eyes and I know this is the moment where she decides if she lets me stay or if she wants me to go. I feel her let out a deep breath and I have my answer. My heart sighs in relief.

"You look beautiful in the posters." She watches me look at each one. I want to see her smile again.

"Thanks. My friend Shannon, back in Colorado, was all into photography and graphic design, so she made those for me. I'm a dancer."

"I know."

A look of surprise registers across her face. "How do you know?"

"Because, I check on you every afternoon once I get done with swim practice. You know, just to make sure you're okay."

"I've never seen you, just your brother once."

"Doesn't mean I wasn't there." I'm not sure if I expected her to be angry or not now that she knows I've been watching her, but what I didn't expect was the look of approval on her face. Does it make her happy to know that I stop by and check on her?

"Oh . . . You should come in sometime. It's nice to take a break every now and then."

"Okay." If she wants to see me, then I'm definitely going to start stopping in.

"Drew . . . I'm so tired," she says quietly. Tears fill her eyes and I know she isn't talking about being physically tired. I can't even imagine how emotionally draining it must be to miss someone like your mother.

"I know. Come here." I pull her into me. She seems a little hesitant, but she doesn't resist. We tangle our legs together, while one of my arms slides under her head and I wrap my other arm around her. She snuggles up right next to me, and if you didn't know she was there, most people probably wouldn't have even noticed her. I completely surround her and block her from the outside world. All I can hope for is that I can provide her some kind of comfort. After all, I was the one who set her off into this mood in the first place.

"Ali, I need to tell you again how sorry I am about today. I loved that you wanted to talk to me, but I saw Cassidy and her friends behind you. I've known these girls a long time. If I had talked to you, shown interest in you, whatever . . . their claws would come out more than they already are. I wasn't trying to hurt you. I was trying to prevent you from having further hassle."

She's stiffens and I run my hand up and down her back to ease out some of that tension.

"Then why were you so mad at me? You looked like you wanted to rip my head off." Sadness leaks out of her. It is coming through loud and clear.

"I wasn't mad at you. I was mad at them. I seriously at one point could have put my fist in Cassidy's mouth."

She relaxes and then giggles. It's the best sound in the

world.

"I wish you would have."

"Yeah, something tells me that if I had, we wouldn't be here together right now."

"Thanks for coming after me. That means a lot to me."

I run my hand over her head. Gently, I tangle my hand in her ponytail and pull back so her face angles toward me. I need her to look me in the eyes when I say this to her. I'm nervous. She makes me nervous, and my heart is pounding in my chest.

"Ali, I don't talk to a lot of people. In fact, I don't really talk much at all. It's not my thing. But, you need to hear me when I say this. I know that whatever we are . . . is different. It has been, from that first moment. I don't know why, but I feel like I can just be myself with you, and I like that. I really do care about you. Seeing what happened to you today broke my heart. I don't ever want to make you sad and I'm never going to intentionally hurt you. Okay?"

Her face is expressionless, and then she blinks. Slowly, a small smile forms on her lips. "Okay." She says quietly.

I break eye contact and drop my eyes to her mouth. Her face is only about six inches from mine and it would be so easy to lean forward and take her lips with mine. She watches me and she licks her bottom lip. Remembering the way her mouth felt against mine, heat surges through me. Inwardly, I groan. Against every instinct I have, I let go of her hair and pull her back into me, resting my lips on her head. I don't want her thinking I came over here for any other reason than to apologize.

It doesn't take long for her breathing to even out, but I on other hand am going to need a little more time. Being this close to her is affecting me in more ways than just one.

The obvious distraction is how she curls up and fits perfectly in my arms. Her skin is so soft and she smells so good. There's no way I'm ever going to be able to smell vanilla again and not think about her. The faint citrus smell adds to the overall effect and I want to just lay here and breathe her in.

The other thoughts running through my head are more like, "what am I doing?" I have never cuddled, snuggled, or whatever you want to call it with another girl. Yes, I have been with a couple of them over the years, but once we were done, I was done. I don't do clingy and I don't do relationships. The thought of my dad ever finding out about me being serious about a girl—it makes my skin crawl. I can hear him chanting in the back of my mind, *There is no excuse for distractions! If you want distractions, I'll give you something to think about.*

At some point my phone starts buzzing, waking both of us up. I reach behind me to grab it off the nightstand and I lie on my back, staring at the ceiling. She tucks her body in a little closer to me and one of her arms slides across my chest. I pull her tighter next to me. I really like the way she feels.

"Dude, where are you?" Beau sounds worried.

"At home." There's no need to tell him exactly where I am. I hear him let out a breath.

"You okay?"

"Yep." I'm better than okay. If I had my way, I'd stop time and lie here with her forever.

"Are you headed back up later to swim?" Ugh, swimming is the last thing on my mind at the moment, and unfortunately I know that it should be the first.

"Yeah, I'll be there in about an hour. I need to make up for this morning."

"All right, I'm headed to Grant's after practice. Come get me later?"

"Sure."

"Later."

He hangs up and I put my phone down. The only sound in the room is the waves crashing on the shore. I easily could have gone back to sleep, but reality is calling. I roll over toward her and look down into her face. Her big brown eyes stare back up at me. My heart squeezes again and I want to rub that spot on my chest. Instead, I trace my finger over the dragonfly charm that's slid over her collarbone. She gasps slightly at the unexpectedness of this.

"Why didn't you swim this morning?"

"My dad was home and I was trying to avoid him." I don't make eye contact with her as I say this. I don't want her to be able to read any type of emotion in me.

"Why?"

"It's complicated." My tone lets her know that I'm done with the questioning about my father. The further I keep her from that part of my life, the better off everyone will be. She takes the hint.

"I've never slept next to a guy before." A grin stretches across my face. That's the last thing I ever thought would come out of her mouth. It also couldn't have been more perfect. The thought of her with another guy is enough to make me see red.

"I've never slept next to a girl before."

Surprise registers on her face. "Really?"

"Really." I'm not going to go into detail with what I really did with girls. She doesn't want to hear it, and suddenly I feel bad for it, which is stupid. "I need to take off and go eat something before I head to the pool. Food needs time to settle and all that."

She lets out a little whine, scoots closer to me, and her arm that's wrapped around me clamps down tight. I can't help but chuckle. She's so cute.

"Oh . . . okay." She sighs into my chest. She's disappointed and this makes my heart swell. She wants me here.

"Are you coming up to dance later?"

"Yes, I need to stretch." She pulls back and looks up at me. Her hand moves to my hip and I can feel her fingertips lightly squeezing me. I think about her stretching in front of me, and yeah no, it's not going to be good for me.

"Okay then." My eyes drop to her mouth again. I want to kiss her more than anyone else I've ever kissed before. But I know me and if I start kissing her while lying here, I won't be able to stop. My eyes flash back up to hers and I give her a big smile before sliding out from underneath her. She sighs again. It's nice to know that I affect her like she affects me.

I slip my clothes back on, facing away from her. She doesn't need to see how my body is reacting to being that close to her. Once I slip my flip-flops on, I stop at the foot of the bed. She's curled back up into a ball, and she looks so little. I can't help but to run my eyes all over her. She really does make me feel funny things. I reach over and squeeze her foot just like I did yesterday.

"You okay?" I ask her. She looks a little sad.

"I don't know how to answer that anymore."

I don't have a response to that, but I understand why she feels this way.

"I'll see you later?"

She nods her head. I turn to leave, but stop as she quietly says my name.

"Drew . . . thanks again for coming over." Cracking a smile at her, I wink, and leave.

Chapter Eight

ALI

THE SCHOOL IS pretty much empty when I arrive at 5:15. I park next to Drew and then let myself into The Cave. Throwing on a little country in the background, the air fills with "Everything has Changed" by Taylor Swift. My body is still tingles from being around Drew.

I never expected him to follow me home. I thought he was mad at me. He comes across so standoffish to everyone, but I really do think it is all an act. Aside from today in the hallway, he's never intentionally given me the freeze out. But after hearing him talk about Cassidy, I can understand why he's the way he is at school. In the last two days, I've seen such a different side to him. I really like this side.

I spend most of the first hour stretching and doing yoga. Along with perfecting moves, it's just as important to work on flexibility and strength. This also allows me the time to replay over and over again what happened earlier in the day.

When Drew walked into my bedroom and started taking off his clothes, I think a part of me forgot to breathe. I mean, yes I have seen him in nothing but those tight swim trunks for weeks now, but there's something extremely personal about a guy taking off his clothes in front of you, because of you.

I didn't even hesitate in allowing him to climb into bed with me. I so desperately have been craving physical and emotional closeness with someone, especially him, that I could have cried tears of relief. I still don't know what it is about him, but I do know that it has to be him. I can't imagine anyone else being in room or in my bed. That thought kind of makes me shiver and makes me feel uncomfortable. I just want Drew.

Feeling the warmth coming off of him, his hand running up and down my back, how he smelled, the combination put me to sleep immediately. It was some of the best sleep I've had in a long time. I wish I could ask him to sleep with me every night.

About two hours into my practice, the door to the room quietly swings open and I jump in surprise. I've been dancing in here for two months and no one has ever come in. His eyes find mine and both of us smile. I know that I was hoping that he would stop by sometime, but I didn't actually think it would be today. I'm over the moon with happiness and I don't even care if he sees this. I want him to know he makes me happy.

Drew walks through the door wearing a long-sleeve, dark blue T-shirt with a hood, white athletic shorts, and flip-flops. The hood is pulled up with only a few pieces of his brown hair curling out from underneath it. His shirt fits him almost like second skin and his shorts fall low on his hips. I can't take my eyes off of him. He is so beautiful. It's not fair to the rest of us. It's crazy to think that just a few hours ago, this gorgeous guy was wrapped all around me and snuggled up under my blankets. I feel lucky to know that I was given that at least once.

"So how was swimming?" I walk over and turn down the music.

"About the same as always, perfect the stroke and beat the clock. Condition, condition, condition. How's the dancing?" He walks over to the wall next to the back door and drops his bag.

"Good today. I needed it. So much of dance is expressed through emotion, and well, you and I both know I've had a lot of that lately." I smile shyly at him.

He leans against the wall and slides down it so he sits with his knees pulled up.

"How did you get into dance? From what I've seen, you seem to do all kinds and you're really good at it."

I walk over and sit down in front of him to start stretching again. There's no need for us to yell at each other across the room. He watches me closely and I can't tell if it is unraveling me in a good way or not.

"Oh, I've always danced. I don't remember a time when I wasn't. My mom was a dancer, so I guess you could say her love of it rubbed off on me."

"Why do you dance so much? Every day seems like a lot." I like that he's curious about me.

"I'm auditioning for Juilliard."

Shock registers across his face.

"In New York City?"

"Yeah, that's always been my dream."

"Wow. I didn't see that coming. That's impressive. When's the audition? Are you nervous?"

I can't help but giggle at his reaction. He smiles at my giggle and my heart takes an extra beat—he's so handsome.

"No, I'm pretty much ready for it. I've been ready for this for years." And that's the truth. After attending the Summer Intensive Camp in New York before my junior year, I knew I was ready. The choreographers and teachers from different dance schools were continually watching me, and I took that to be a good sign.

"So, you never intended on sticking around this place?"

"Ah . . . no. If you haven't noticed already, I don't really have much here."

"Hmm." A look of regret slips onto his face and leaves as quickly as it came.

"I passed the pre-screens, and my audition is toward the end of February in Miami."

"Is it strange if I say I'm proud of you?"

Well, that's something I haven't heard in a while. I take the compliment, but I can feel my cheeks heating up.

"No. Thank you. I'm glad someone is." I look down at the floor and bend over to stretch my lower back, breaking the eye contact.

"Your dad isn't?"

"I haven't told him."

"I don't know what to say to that."

"There's nothing to say. Besides, he has his own issues to work out right now." I stand up and walk over to the audio system. I grab my iPod and pick up my bag. As much as I love talking to Drew, the father conversation is a closed topic for me as well. At this moment, my day is winding down perfectly and I don't want to ruin it with emotional whatnots. I approach him and he stands up. "You ready to go?"

"Yep." He looks at me hesitantly, "How do you feel about cheeseburgers?"

I smile at him. "I love cheeseburgers." He smiles back

and his eyes sparkle.

"Okay, I have to run to pick up Beau and Matt. Care if we drop over shortly with some takeout?"

"Who's Matt?"

"Oh, he's my younger brother. He's eleven." I didn't know that there was another brother. With all of the gossiping about him and Beau I'm surprised it never came up. The thought of Drew hanging out with both of his brothers makes my heart smile.

"I'd like that. I'll make brownies. Fries too?"

"Of course!" Drew smiles a little bigger and then takes my bag from me.

We walk out together, and I think to myself that I can definitely get used to this.

DREW

OVER THE NEXT couple of weeks, I unintentionally fall into a routine with Ali. I wave to her in the mornings, I nod at her in the hallways, and after swim each night I wait for her to finish practicing. Occasionally, we grab a bite to eat afterward, but most of the time she goes her way and I go mine. If my dad ever caught wind that I have interest in a girl—I just can't even imagine.

Without even saying anything, if I'm gone too much from home, he would automatically catch on that I'm spending a little too much time being preoccupied or distracted—that's his word—by a girl, and not focusing enough on what's important. And that would be making him look good, as if everyone hasn't already heard enough, but I'm his gifted and talented son. I'm going places and apparently I'm supposed to be taking him with me. No thanks.

Every night, I look forward to walking into The Cave. Honestly, it has become my favorite time of the day, and knowing I have to finish my practice before I can get to her, has actually shortened my times. Coach Black noticed that I've been shaving a few seconds off here and there, and he hasn't asked me about it, but I'm sure he can guess. The quicker I can get finished, the quicker I can get to her.

I've enjoyed talking to her and discovering all of the little ins and outs of her mind. She's smart and interesting. I've never found a girl to be interesting before. I guess I've never really taken the time to get to know one.

It doesn't hurt either that she's so beautiful that sometimes, it hurts just to look at her.

I've already been in the room watching her for forty-five minutes. She thinks I'm studying, but I'm not. I've never been one to think much of dancing, but when she moves, I can't take my eyes off of her. She transforms and molds into the music and flows with the beats as if they were written and composed just for her. I don't know how she does it, but even I, with my naïve eye, can tell she's the real deal. There's no way this school isn't going to offer her a place in their program.

She finally cuts off the iPod and wanders over to stretch in front of me. She never sits in the middle of the room or uses the barre that she brought in and had me help her build. She always sits with me and asks me about my day. The first couple of times she did this surprised me. I mean, no one ever asks me how my day was. It's taken me a bit to open up. I don't talk to anyone ever, but once I did, I found her to be so easy to talk to. I love talking to her.

"So what are your plans for Thanksgiving next week?"

I'm super-excited that she asked and initiated this conversation. I've been wondering what she's going to be doing as well.

"Nothing much. Grant is planning on throwing a TBT party, a Tuesday before Thanksgiving party, that way everyone can come. My mom will probably cook dinner and then I'll be around the rest of the week. How about you?"

"Leila mentioned something about the party, but I haven't decided if I'm going or not yet. I'm not too sure about a dinner yet, either. I'm guessing my dad will come over, but who knows with him. It seems lately he's been coming less and less." She frowns at this last comment and I hate to see her sad.

"I kind of figured as much. I never see his car there. When was the last time you saw him?"

"Last weekend."

I've never met her dad and I already don't like him. Ali is the most awesome person I've ever met. He's so lucky to have her as a daughter, and he doesn't even realize it.

"Are you okay being there by yourself all the time?" At night I worry about her. What if I'm not the only one to notice that she's there by herself all the time? I know girls live by themselves, but those girls aren't my girl. Wait . . . is she my girl?

"I guess. What choice do I have?" She leans to the right and lays over her right leg which is stretched out, I can't help but tip my head with her.

"Have you thought about getting a dog?"

Her eyes sparkle and she giggles. "What would I do with a dog?"

"I don't know. It'll keep you company or something."

"No thanks. Too much work. Plus, what would I do with it when I move to New York?"

At least once a day, I think about her moving to New York, and how I'm going to feel when she leaves. It's not a good feeling.

"Fair enough. It was just a thought."

"I'm all right. Don't worry about me." She sits up and then lays over the left leg, wrapping her fingers over her toes.

"But I do."

Her eyes lift to meet mine, silence grows between us, and then she smiles. I love her smile. When she smiles, it lights up her whole face.

"Thanks." She looks away, but not before I see the smile drop and hurt flash through her eyes. I've always thought that I would love to live on my own, to finally not have to worry about anything or be responsible for anyone else, but then I look at her and I don't know. I guess the difference is that she didn't choose this life, but I would.

"I also think you should go to Grant's party. I hear the cocktail of the evening is supposed to be cranberry flavored."

A small smile forms, lighting up her face. I want her to feel wanted. She has to have an idea after all this time that she's wanted by me.

"All right, I'll go." Ali pulls her legs in and leans all the way over stretching her arms straight out. She sits back up, stretches her arms up toward the ceiling, and stands up. "I'm ready when you are."

I grab her back pack with mine, throwing them both over my shoulder. We walk out the back door and she locks up. The parking lot is completely empty except for our two cars and I realize, I'm surprised that rumors and gossip haven't run because of this. Without meaning to, I reach down and grab her hand. Out of the corner of my eye, I see her head drop and she smiles.

"Hey, Drew?"

"Yeah." I look down at her.

"Why do you sit here with me every night? Don't you have better things to do?"

"No, I don't or I would do them, and I'm here because I want to be."

"I don't understand. Why would you want to?"

"I don't like knowing that you're up here by yourself."

She pulls her hand away from mine and stops walking. I recognize the look she's giving. It's the same one she gives Beau every time he teases her about something.

"I don't need a babysitter." She frowns at me.

"I never said you did." If she wasn't so mad, I would laugh at her. She's super-cute when she's scowling.

"I'm perfectly fine here by myself."

"I never said that you weren't. What I said was I didn't like it."

Her gaze goes from glaring and angry to downright icy.

"Just so we're clear, I don't need you to watch out for me. I didn't ask you to nor do I want you to."

"Ali, what are you doing right now?"

"Drew . . ." I reach down and grab her hand again, lace my fingers through hers, and begin walking toward the cars. She doesn't resist and walks with me.

"Listen, I know you don't need anyone to watch out after you. I come here at night because I like to be around you, all right?" I look down at her and she looks away. "It makes me more comfortable to know that should you sprain your ankle or God forbid something worse, that I can be there for you. Okay?"

"Okay."

We reach her car and I squeeze her hand not letting go of it.

"It's not a bad thing that I come in to see you, is it?"

She turns and looks up at me. "No, I just always thought you did because you're my friend."

"I am your friend."

She doesn't say anything back and I can see straight into those milk chocolate eyes of hers. She's happy in this moment, and I'm so thankful I made her feel this way. Her emotions kind of remind me of a yo-yo. She angers quickly, but then she forgives too. I'm so used to anger all the time, that the quick turnaround to her being happy again makes me feel calmer. She never stays mad for long.

I tug her toward me and her free hand lands on my hip. I bend down and put my lips on her forehead, kissing her lightly before turning my head and resting my cheek on top of her.

"Listen, I have a meet this weekend, so I won't be home. Will you be all right?"

"I should be. I'm having dinner with Leila and Chase to-morrow night, and I plan on studying on Sunday."

I stiffen when she mentions Chase's name, and I'm certain she felt it. I can't exactly ask her not to see him. We're barely friends, much less anything more. Although, I do feel more for her than I should, there's just something about her that pulls me and I can't stay away.

"Will you call me if you need anything?"

She giggles again. "I don't have your phone number."

Stepping away from her, I let go of her hand. I'm furious at myself at the moment. I didn't realize that I've never given her my number, and here I had been thinking this entire time that if she ever needed me she would call. Nope.

"Oh, let me see your phone." I hand her backpack to her and she reaches into the side pocket, pulling it out. She passes it over to me and I call myself.

"I called my phone so I would have yours as well. You need to add me to your contacts."

"Okay." She takes her phone from me and another beat of silence passes between us. "Good luck at your meet this weekend. I'm sure you'll rock it."

I can't help but grin at her. She is so pretty and awesome. I take another step back from her, letting her know that I'm going to leave. If I don't get away from her soon, she's going to have a problem on her hands that starts and ends with me.

"Thanks. I'll see you Monday, okay?"

"Sounds good. Bye, Drew," she drawls out. Taking a backward step toward her car, she then gives me a once over from head to toe while smirking. Her eyes show that she's being a little flirty. I like this side of her and I like having her eyes on me. I groan inwardly.

"Later," I say smiling back at her.

Chapter Nine

ALI

DINNER AT LEILA'S was actually really nice. I've only been over to her house a few times, but each time, it reminds me of what it feels like to belong to a family. They're warm and inviting. They live very simply and don't have much, but they're the perfect example of how you don't need it as long as you have each other.

Again, Leila was dressed in a super cute top and a skirt. I can't help but look at her wardrobe and think maybe I should "southern girl" mine up a bit. Most of my clothes are what you would expect a girl from the mountains to wear—dark and kind of outdoorsy. It's time to buy some beach attire.

What surprised me the most was to learn that Leila doesn't buy a lot of her clothes—she makes them. The girl seriously has a talent for fashion, and she proudly announced that she's applied to fashion schools across the country for college. Who knows, maybe she will get accepted to a school in

New York and we can be there together.

Listening to her talk about something she's so passionate about, causes me to smile. I haven't found a lot of other friends my age that love something as much as I love to dance, and sometimes they find it hard to relate to me, but not Leila. She and I understand each other perfectly.

Chase was his typical funny self, and of course he finally talked me into going paddleboarding with him. He wasted no time in declaring that he would be picking me up at 8:00 on the dot.

I hear his truck pull up outside and I run down the stairs to meet him at the door. It isn't that I don't want him to come inside, I just don't want to have to answer any questions that he may have. Besides, the only people who have been in my house are Drew, Beau, and Matt. I know it's stupid, but I kind of want to keep it that way.

I lock the door and turn around to find Chase standing there smiling at me from ear to ear, holding a cup of coffee.

"Leila told me this is your favorite coffee drink, so I thought I'd surprise you." He looks at me sheepishly and I smile big at him to let him know that I appreciate the thoughtfulness.

"Ohhh, this is an awesome surprise. Thank you." Chase is wearing an old surfing T-shirt and a pair of board shorts. Looking at him, I really don't understand why he doesn't have a girlfriend. He has a sweet baby face, blond hair, and those same blue eyes as Leila. He really is a good-looking guy.

He smiles at me as he hands me the coffee.

"So, where are we going?" I need to change the conversation. He smiles at me again.

"I thought we would head off the island. If we cross the first bridge, like we're heading toward the mainland, there's a pull off for kayaks, flat bottom boats, et cetera. There are a lot of mangrove marshes which makes for pretty sightseeing and not a lot of waves."

"Sounds good to me." No waves means I just might make it up on the board without tipping over. We walk toward the truck and Chase opens the door for me. I glance over at Drew's house and see Beau standing on the front porch, leaning over the banister drinking a cup of coffee, and watching us. I raise my hand and wave to him.

I kind of feel like I'm doing something wrong, although I know I'm not. For whatever reason, I want Beau to see that this is just a friendly outing and nothing more.

"Hey Tiny, whatcha doin?" Beau walks down his front steps, across the driveway, over the street, and stands right in front of us. Chase stiffens behind me.

"Chase's taking me paddleboarding today." I see him take in both of us, what we're wearing, the gear in the back of the truck, and then his eyes settle back to Chase's.

"Hey man, how's it going?" At least Beau is attempting to be nice. Not that he has a reason not to be.

"It's going. I thought we could head out early before it gets too hot." Chase is politely trying to tell him to get lost.

"That's probably a good idea. Not sure why it's been so hot lately. It's November, after all."

"What are you doing today?" I'm trying to keep the conversation light.

"I'm heading over to Grant's later. He agreed to play a few sets with me." Beau laughs at this. "Speaking of Grant, are you going to his party Tuesday?"

Beau talks directly to me and I feel bad for Chase. I look over at Chase and smile at him. He's leaning up against the truck, watching the two of us.

"I'm planning on it. Drew mentioned something about it the other day." Approval lights up in his eyes.

"Good. I like being able to keep my eye on you."

"Whatever, Beau Hale. I've seen what catches your eye and I'm most definitely not it, nor do I want to be."

He laughs openly, wraps an arm around my shoulders, and gives me a squeeze.

"Oh, Tiny, if you only knew." He lets go of me and takes a step back, smiling. "Did you know that if you were to travel to the sun, it would take eight days?"

"Did you know that an ostrich's eye is bigger than its brain?" I wiggle my eyebrows at him and he laughs at me.

"Y'all kids have fun today and don't forget to wear sunblock." With that, he gives a nod to Chase and wanders back to his house.

I climb into the truck. Chase closes the door behind me and walks around the front. His brows are furrowed and I can tell that he's thinking hard.

"What was that all about?" He looks over at me. Of course he's curious. I would be too. After all, the Hale brothers don't really talk to anyone outside of their circle and at school I'm not in their circle.

"Nothing, it's just something that we do." I'm hoping that he means the useless fact part of our conversation and not the whole interaction.

He pauses for a few seconds as if he's deciding on what he's going to say or ask. "Ali, is there something going on between you and Drew?" I know that I should just answer his questions and then tell him to let it go, but he's been so nice to me I feel like I need to tell him more of my story.

"My mom died one hundred and five days ago." I didn't mean to blurt this out, but it just came out. Chase's eyes grow large and his chin drops open a little.

"What? Ali, I'm so sorry. I didn't know." I reach up and start rubbing the dragonfly. More and more it has become an object of comfort and if I am going to talk about my mom, then comfort is needed.

"I know you didn't, which is why I'm telling you. I honestly don't know what's going on between Drew and me, but I do know there's something. Drew is the only other person here who knows about my mom, and I'd like to keep it that way. I'm not ready to talk about her, and for the most part I'm a very private person." Tears fill my eyes as I look at him.

"I won't tell anyone. Thank you for telling me, but if you ever need to talk to anyone, please know that I'm here for you." A tear leaks out and he leans over to wipe it off with his thumb. His eyes are locked on me and I'm trying to read him, but there's a part of him that's closed off.

"I don't want to mislead you, Chase. I really enjoy your company and want to be friends with you. I don't have a lot of friends . . . but that's all I can be."

"Ali . . . I don't have a lot of friends either, and I really want to be friends with you too." He lets out a deep sigh and I reach over and grab his hand.

"I'm sorry."

"What for?" He holds onto my hand and his thumb rubs across the back of it.

"For making you feel like this."

He smirks at me.

"You haven't made me feel any way, and honestly I feel a bit relieved. Leila has been pushing me to ask you out and she's just been through so much over the last couple of years that I wanted to do this to make her happy. Don't get me wrong, I think that you're freaking gorgeous, but I'm trying to get off this island and don't really want any attachments." I'm caught off guard a little with his statement about Leila, but it isn't my place to ask and unless she offers up the information, it isn't my place to know.

"So, are you still going to teach me to paddleboard?"

"Yeah, baby! I've been waiting almost three months for this." He lets go of my hand, starts the truck, and backs out of the driveway.

"Chase, I'm glad that we got this conversation out of the way. I was nervous about what your expectations from me were." It feels good to be able to talk openly to him.

"Darlin', I have zero expectations for you. In fact, I'm glad that we see eye to eye on this subject. Don't get me wrong, if you ever feel the need, and want to make out a little, you can definitely call me. I won't say no."

I bust out laughing.

"So, you and Drew, huh?"

A blush rises into my cheeks. "I don't know. Maybe?" I smile a little bigger and look out the window. I don't want Chase to know how affected I am by Drew.

"Ali, I have known him almost my whole life and I've never seen him react or look at another girl like he does with you. I mean, you've seen the looks he gives me when I'm around. He's very territorial over you, and so is Beau. Cassidy knows it, too. That's why she's the way she is." I thought that Drew was being pretty subtle, but if people are noticing, maybe there's more to us than I thought— or could hope for.

"Nothing has ever happened between us, and it's been months."

"Give him time. It's there. I promise. I can't imagine why it's taking him so long. If I was around you as much as I suspect that he is, fireworks would be going off." He gives me a mischievous grin. "But, there is definitely something going on with him and Beau. They've both become more withdrawn and driven over the years. Neither one of them ever looks happy anymore."

I don't say anything as Chase pulls off the road and into a sand parking lot. I've thought to myself several times that something might be going on with them, and now to hear someone else say it . . . it makes me wonder.

"Come on, short stuff. Out of the truck. If you are going to paddleboard, lesson one is that you carry your own board." He lets out a laugh.

I hop out of the truck and look at the board in the back. "You're kidding, right?"

"Nope." He grins from ear to ear.

"You realize that this board is four times as big as me?"

"Yep."

"Fine, hand it over!" The only way that I can get this board into the water was either to drag it through the sand or hoist it onto my back. I opted for plan B.

Once we make it into the water, it doesn't take me long to get up. I think the board weighs almost as much as I do, so it's pretty evenly balanced. I also learn that unlike a snowboard or surfboard your feet have to be spread wide side to side and not front to back.

Chase hops up onto his and together we paddle through the mangroves. It feels great to get out of the house and out of The Cave. I can't help but to laugh at myself. If Shannon could see me now. I'm sure that right now in Denver the temperature is somewhere between thirty and fifty. Shannon will be putting on a coat and boots, and here I am in a bikini and sunblock.

By the time we're done and back to the truck, it's close to four in the afternoon. We had only intended on going for a few hours, but we were having so much fun that we didn't stop. I'm thankful for our earlier conversation and that over the course of the day we didn't have any awkward moments. As it turns out, I think Chase and I are going to be great friends.

My phone chimes as Chase pulls out of my driveway after dropping me off.

Drew – How was your weekend? A huge smile stretches across my face.

Me – Actually it was really good. How was yours?

Drew – Better now that I'm headed home. What did you do this weekend?

Me – I had dinner at Leila's last night and today I went paddleboarding with Chase.

There's a pause in the texting conversation, so I unlock the door and go into the house. I'm starving. Chase and I didn't stop for lunch, and we didn't really think that we would be gone as long as we were, so we didn't pack any food.

Drew – Did you have fun? Wear sunblock? I laugh at his question.

Me – Yes, I did. Thanks for asking. And what is it with you and Beau and the sunblock?

Drew – What do you mean?

Me – Well, he stopped us while we were on our way out and said the same thing, "wear sunblock."

Drew – You're pale and the sun is strong here. Did you know that two thirds of all cancers are sun related?

Me – Oh my gosh! You just dropped a fact! Beau would be so proud. LOL. Btw - are you trying to make fun of me?

Drew – Nope just stating a fact. :)

Me – You know that you shouldn't be texting and driving.

Drew- I know, just wanted to check on you.

Me – I'm good and thanks.

Drew – No problem. I'll see you later?
Me – Okay :)

I can't help the grin that is sitting on my face. I love knowing that he's thinking about me. At least I'll get to see him tomorrow at school.

DREW

SHE HAS JUST turned off the lights as I skip up the balcony stairs to her room.

"Ali!" I whisper loudly. I knock quietly not wanting to scare her. Instantly, I'm filled with a nervous giddy. I'm swaying back and forth between each foot almost like I'm bouncing and then she opens the door. She looks so good standing in the doorway that for a minute there I forget to breathe. Her dark hair is wet and pulled back into a braid. She must have just climbed out of the shower and she's wearing a gray T-shirt that drops over one shoulder with another pair of tiny little shorts. And she smells so good.

"Hi, what are you doing?" She smiles at me from ear to ear.

"I told you I'd see you later, and I just wanted to come over and check on you."

"I didn't realize you actually meant later as in today. You just talked to me a few hours ago." I'm glad that she's still smiling, or I might have backed out and gone home. I thought that she understood when I said later, I meant a little later, as in a couple of hours—tonight, not waiting until tomorrow, et cetera.

"Well, I didn't really talk to you . . . anyway . . . can I

come in?" Her room is dark, and now I'm not so sure. This seemed like a great idea at the time.

"Sure. I just turned the lights out to go to bed." She opens the door a little wider.

"Oh, well I don't want to keep you up . . ." She giggles, leans forward, and grabs my hand, jerking me into her room. This causes me to chuckle at her. She's so cute.

"So what do you want to do?" she asks. She looks at me and then around her room.

"I don't care. We could watch a movie or go to bed." Fear flashes across her face. I don't think she meant it to, but she couldn't stop the look from happening. I take a step back and start stammering.

"No. Not what I meant. I just meant go to sleep. I want to stay with you tonight if that's okay?" My parents weren't home when I decided to come over here. My Jeep is in the driveway and my door is closed and locked, so they'll never know that I'm actually not there.

"You want to spend the night?" She sounds surprised.

"Yes." The only time that we've slept together was the day after I found her on the beach. I haven't stopped thinking about it since. The thought of her falling asleep in my arms again makes me so happy. Every night while lying in bed I think of having her curled up next to me. I love the feeling of wholeness that I have when I'm with her, and it doesn't hurt that she smells so good too.

"Okay." She closes the balcony door.

"Okay?" My heart pounds in my chest. She wants me here. She really does. I know this shouldn't come as such a surprise to me. I just can't help all of the negative thoughts, which have been shoved down my throat for years that come to the surface. He always said that no one would want me or find me worthy. Maybe he was wrong.

"Yep, come on." She hops up onto her bed and scoots over. I lock her balcony door, kick off my flip flops, and climb in next to her. Just being in her bed feels so good. Mostly, guys don't care much about their bed. We just need a place to lay our heads, but girls are different. Girls are all about textures and fluff. Ali's bed is so soft and I sink into it.

"I'm still a little wound up from the drive home. Do you mind if we put on a movie for a while?"

"Sure. Any requests?"

"Nope."

She flips through the channels and stops when she comes across *Elizabethtown*.

"How's this one?"

"Good, I guess." I don't know much about it except that it's a little older, and the same producer who did *Almost Famous* did this one. It has a great sound track.

"It's kind of a chick flick, but it's about a guy who gets fired from his job, his dad dies, he meets this girl, and his whole life changes."

I like the whole life-changing part. Slowly, I think that she could be changing my life as well.

"All right, I like Orlando Bloom anyway. You've seen the *Pirates of the Caribbean*, right?"

She giggles. "Of course I have."

I prop myself up against the pillows on the head board and wrap one arm around her shoulders. She leans in and lays her back against my side so she can see the movie. I need to touch her, to feel her skin against mine. I run my free hand down her arm closest to me and I pull her arm back a little so her elbow rests on my stomach. I drape my arm across the top of hers and my fingers tangle with hers. This is how we sit throughout most of the movie. I don't want to move, and I gather that she doesn't want to either.

As the movie ends, I lean over and grab the remote to turn off the TV. Darkness immediately engulfs the room. One of her windows must be cracked because I can hear the water from the Gulf crash onto the shore. I forgot that she likes to sleep to the sounds of the beach.

"Drew?" she says quietly.

"Yeah, babe . . ." I feel her turn her face toward me, even though she can't see me.

"Are you really staying tonight?" I'm not following her question. Does she not want me to stay after all?

"Do you want me to?" I've always hated when I ask people a question and then they answer with one in return, but here with her I just really need to know what she's thinking.

"Yes, please." She sounds so sad.

Trying to lighten the mood, I slide both of us down under the covers and pull her into me so her head is lying on my chest. Her arm drapes across my stomach momentarily distracting me.

"Now, I seem to recall being the one who came here to ask if I could sleep over."

"I know. It's just . . ."

"What?"

"I don't want to be alone anymore."

This breaks my heart. I know my sweet girl is lonely and she misses her mom. Yes, I called her mine and somewhere inside of me I feel a cool peace trickle through my veins.

"You aren't. You've got me and I've got you. Okay?" I kiss the top of her head and she lets out a sigh.

"More than okay."

Her chest expands as a deep yawn comes out and she

snuggles in a little closer.

I think about her and me over the last three months. Apart from the day I met her and the day we took a nap, I've never really initiated contact with her. But here we are in her bed wrapped around each other like it's an everyday thing. There isn't any awkwardness or shyness. Feeling her next to me feels completely natural and perfect. I could go to sleep like this every night.

Chapter Ten

ALI

HAVING BEEN TO one of Grant's parties before, I feel more comfortable walking in this time. Chase has one arm slung over my shoulder and one over Leila's. He's completely full of himself tonight as he cracks one joke after another. The three of us are laughing so hard that we've gained the attention of a few, including Grant, who's posted up as bartender. I see him look at me and then nod his head in my direction. I haven't missed either that Drew is sitting in front of him at the tiki bar. Drew spins around on his chair and his eyes lock with mine. For a split second, I see confusion, but just as it came it's gone and that look of indifference that he's perfected down to a science has slipped back on.

I'm coming to understand his looks, even though he tries to give nothing away. It's when his expression changes to the closed-off whatever look, that I know he's having some type of emotion course through him. He thinks that he's being subtle about it. He hates for anyone to know the real him, but I see right through it.

As we approach the bar, I slide out from under Chase's arm and walk over to stand in front of Drew. Other than at school, I haven't seen him in the last two days. I'm not sure what he's been up to, but both last night and tonight he didn't drop into The Cave to see me. Don't get me wrong, he still smiled and nodded at me in class and the hallways. I just missed him in the mornings and in the evening. Hopefully, since school is out for the rest of the week, this will change. My heart races as I walk between his legs and into his personal space.

"Hi." I smile at him. I love knowing that he spends so much time with me and no one else. At least I don't think there's anyone else.

"Hey." He smiles back.

"How was the meet by the way? We never really talked about it. Did you crush some dreams?"

He smirks at me and I feel his walls slip down a little.

"I might have. What did you do this weekend?" He already knows the answer to this, so I'm not following his line of questioning.

"I had dinner with Leila's and Chase's families on Saturday, and then on Sunday Chase took me paddleboarding for the first time."

"Is that so?" His eyes skip from me to Chase and then back. I see Chase take a step toward Leila out of the corner of my eye. He definitely knows something is up and he's smiling at the two of us. "How did you do?" Ah, he's letting Chase know that he knows the two of us went out together. I'll never understand guy macho stuff.

"Pretty well. I got up on the first try and then just took

off."

From behind me I hear Grant ask what everyone wants to drink, but I can't take my eyes off of Drew. Grant tries to redirect everyone's focus so that Drew and I are given the freedom to talk without spectators. He's talking to me in front of everyone and we all know this is out of character for him. I know I shouldn't be making a big deal out of this, but in my mind it feels huge.

"Take a walk with me." It wasn't really a request, more like a command. He swivels in the bar chair and then stands up, grabs his beer with one hand, and throws his other arm over my shoulders. Together we turn and start walking toward the dock.

I can't help but notice all the stares that we're getting. I also notice how gorgeous Drew is tonight and how good he smells.

He's wearing a pair of dark jeans that hang low on his hips and fit perfectly through his thighs, a light blue, long-sleeved, button-down shirt with the sleeves rolled up, a navy T-shirt peeking out from underneath, and his signature flip-flops. His dark hair is parted on one side and styled like he should be at a modeling shoot. I can't help but swoon at him. I wrap my arm around his waist and close the distance between the two of us.

"You're up to no good tonight," I say to him. He throws his head back and laughs. It isn't that often I get to see him be just himself and usually, it's because we're alone after practices, but when he's free to just be, my insides melt even more.

"What do you mean?" His eyes sparkle down at me.

"You know exactly what I mean." His smile is so genuine and meant just for me, that my eyes are drawn to his beautiful mouth. I wonder if and when he might kiss me. The thought of him kissing me sends goose bumps racing down my arms.

"Well, maybe it's just time."

My eyes jump back up to his and I notice they've darkened. I'm busted for looking at his mouth.

"Time for what?"

He doesn't answer my question, but he does smile a little bigger at me as he runs his hand up and down my arm. I love being close to him.

The dock is fairly quiet, only a few boats came in to the party this evening. We walk to the end and he pulls me aboard a twelve person Stingray. The boat is amazing.

In the front of the boat is what looks like two padded built in lounge seats. Drew flops down on one and I sit on the other across from him. He doesn't say anything as he looks up at the sky, and I don't feel the need to question him.

The sky tonight is void of clouds and full of stars. As the moon peaks up over the trees on the Eastern side, it looks huge and orange. I read once that the closer you are to the equator and/or the horizon, the larger the moon can appear. It's the same with the color. If the moon is closer to the horizon, it'll be seen through more layers of the atmosphere, making it appear orange versus when it is directly overhead. Either way, the moon is still beautiful to me.

Drew's head turns to the side and he looks over at me. I'm sitting on the bench with my legs pulled up and my head propped on my knees.

"Ali . . ."

"Yeah . . ." I can tell he's thinking hard about something. He sits up, drops his feet to the ground, puts his elbows on his knees, and angles his body toward mine. I mirror his position and our knees are almost touching. He reaches out, placing his hands on my legs. His fingers slide under my knees. His touch is so warm, it's burning me through the fabric of my jeans, and I can't help but blush imagining how these fingers would feel on other parts of my body.

"Will you spend the day with me tomorrow?" He looks nervous and unsure of himself and this completely catches me off guard. Here's this guy who is so handsome, talented, and popular and yet he's looking at me as if he has never asked a girl out before.

"Yes," I say back to him quietly.

He lets out a deep breath that I don't think he realized he was holding in, squeezes my legs, and he smiles at me—a real smile. I'm still not used to the effect his smiles have on me. My heart races and butterflies take off in my stomach.

He lets go of my legs and reaches out for my hands. I lay mine in his and he brushes his thumbs across the top.

"You've just made me very happy." He looks down at the ground, but continues to rub my hands.

"So what time should I be ready, and what do you want to do?" I don't want him to feel nervous and I want him to know I'm excited to be with him. I would go anywhere and do anything he asked.

He picks his head up. "Can you be ready by nine? And I'm thinking I'd like to spend the day on the water with you tomorrow."

"Nine sounds perfect, and what do you mean 'on the water?'"

"Do you like to ski or go tubing?" I can't help but laugh.

"Yes, I love to ski and go tubing . . . however there isn't any snow here."

His eyes narrow at me and he smirks.

"Ah, I like this funny side of you. You should let her out more often."

"Sometimes I forget she's in there." He doesn't say anything as he continues to look at me. He knows what I'm thinking.

"So, I can't help you with the snow . . . but I love to water ski and go tubing behind a boat. It's so much fun. I also know of a small island where we can go for lunch."

"Okay. What do you want me to bring?"

"Nothing, just your beautiful self." I smile up at him. He glances back toward the house and lets out another sigh. "We should head back up, people might start talking."

"Okay." I don't want to head back. I want to stay right here with him.

We stand at the same time and our bodies couldn't have been more than a few inches apart. His breath on the side of my face is warm and more than anything I want to lean into him. I love being in his arms and wrapped up in the smell of him. He raises his hand and gently tucks some of my hair behind my ear. I close my eyes as he trails a finger down my cheek, across my jaw, and down to my collarbone. He picks up the dragonfly, rubs it between his fingers, and then puts it back. My heart pounds in my chest. His fingertips lightly skim across my skin and my body overheats from a massive blush.

His lips settle against the skin next to my ear and very slowly he drags them across my cheek bone and over the corner of my mouth. He doesn't kiss me, but the contact is so sensual. He rests his forehead on mine. "Ali . . ." he whispers.

"Come on, let's go," I say quietly.

I take him by the hand and turn toward the back of the boat before I do something that he doesn't want me to do and I embarrass myself. He climbs off the boat first and then helps me up onto the dock. Once on the dock, he lets go of my hand. I feel the loss of him and I hate it.

"Are you coming over later tonight?"

He stops walking to think about my question.

"No, probably not. Turns out I now have plans tomorrow and I have a bunch of stuff that I need to do in the morning." I don't know what to say. I'm disappointed, but I don't want to push him.

"Okay. You sure I can't help with anything?"

"Nope, I've got it."

When we reach the patio, he takes a step away from me. I look for Leila and spot her with Dawn over by the fire pit. Beau has arrived and is sitting on the opposite side of the fire pit from Leila with Ryan. He watches us as we rejoin the party. I raise my eyebrows at him, asking him a silent, "What?"

"Tiny! Nice of you to join us." He shoots Drew a look and I see his legs bouncing. I can't get a read on the meaning of it. Is he mad?

"Aww Beau, did you miss me?"

He grins at me, picking up on my sarcasm. I take an empty seat next to Leila and Drew sits down next to Beau. He isn't sitting anywhere near me and this sucks. At least I know when he's looking at me—I can feel his eyes. I like this feeling.

"Of course I did."

Drew smacks him on the back of the head.

"What?" he asks, looking over at his brother.

"Knock it off." Drew scowls at him.

Beau looks back over at me. "So how was paddleboarding?" Oh, Beau is out for blood tonight. He's purposely trying to get Drew all riled up I wonder why.

"It was awesome. We had a great time."

Beau looks over at Drew to see if there's a reaction, but nothing. The indifferent look has returned. Something is going on between the two of them.

"Tiny, did you know that crocodiles can't stick their tongues out?"

"Yeah, so . . . elephants are the only animal that can't jump."

He busts out laughing. "Interesting."

"Beau, I think you've met your match," Ryan says.

"Yeah, I'm all right with that. One of these days I'll get her and she won't have a comeback."

"Whatever you say Beau."

The night turned out to be quite pleasant. A group of about ten of us sat by the bonfire for several hours telling jokes and drinking the infamous Thanksgiving cranberry drink. For a while, I kept watching the gate waiting for Cassidy and her friends to walk in, but they never did. Cassidy hasn't said anything to me lately, but she is still watching me. It makes me uncomfortable, and I get the feeling that she is planning something and just waiting for the next opportune moment to strike. I wonder if they were even invited, hopefully not.

DREW

I WASN'T PREPARED to see Ali walk in under Chase's arm. I had arrived at Grant's a little early to help him set up and had just sat down on the bar stool when I heard her laughing from across the patio. Grant nods at them and I turn around on the stool to watch them walk over. Although Chase has his arms wrapped around Ali and Leila, it still doesn't make me feel any better. I mean, Leila is his cousin after all. Ali and I have spent a lot of time together lately and I don't think she has any romantic interest in him, but then again I've never asked her.

She looks beautiful. She's wearing a pair of dark skinny jeans and a light pink top that hugs all of her perfect small curves. Her hair is down, her lips are glossy as she smiles at me, and I want to drink her in.

When she gets to the bar, she shoots me a know-it-all look and comes over to stand in between my legs. Most people would never be so bold as to approach me this way, but not Ali. She's never played by my social rules.

"Hi," she says. I smile back at her. Being near her makes me so happy. I can feel people watching us. People watch me everywhere I go. I should be used to this, but I'm not.

"Hey." I smile back. A breeze blows over us bringing her scent to me and I have to hold back a moan. She smells so good and so refreshing. I rub my hands across my thighs. They're itching to reach out, grab her, and pull her in closer.

"How was the meet, by the way? We never really talked about it. Did you crush some dreams?"

I smirk at her. I don't even know if she realizes that she just announced to all of those around us that we previously talked, and not about the meet. I love that she thinks about me and the things that I do, enough to ask me about it. No one ever asks me how I do.

"I might have. What did you do this weekend?"

She lifts her eyebrows at my question. I'm confusing her. After all, I already know what she did. But for those who are eavesdropping, I don't want to give them any more ammunition for gossip, so I try to distance us.

I also want Chase to know that I'm on to him. The few times that I've seen him around school I have made it abundantly clear that I don't want him near her. I'm certain by now that he of all people knows I feel something for her. I've known him most of my life and I have nothing against him—

it's just, she can't be with him.

"I had dinner with Leila's and Chase's families on Saturday, and on Sunday Chase took me paddleboarding for the first time." I can see the excitement in her eyes. She must have really liked the paddleboarding. I'll have to take her myself sometime soon.

"Is that so?" I glance over at Chase. He takes a step back toward Leila, but what surprises me is that he doesn't appear intimidated or jealous. He smiles at the two of us. Huh? I wonder if they talked about me. That thought never even crossed my mind, but just maybe. Yeah, he's definitely on to me. "How did you do?"

"Actually, I did pretty well. I got up on the first try and then just took off." Of course she did. She's good at everything. The conversations around us have taken on a bit of a buzz in the background. Being around her, I completely forget everything else. Grant's voice picks up in the buzz and he asks people what they want to drink. He's most likely trying to take the attention off of us and that's when I realize that she and I need to get out of here for a bit.

"Take a walk with me." Leading her away from the party, I decide that the best place will be down on our boat. When Beau and I bought the boat, its purpose was for the three of us to escape. It was a place where Beau, Matt, and I could go and be together and not have to worry about being bothered or found. Other than Grant and Matt, no one is allowed on this boat, until now that is.

She fits perfectly under my arm. This shouldn't surprise me—everything about her is perfect. She starts teasing me as we walk off toward the dock, and all I can do is laugh. This girl gets me, and I don't even have to say anything. Other than Beau, I've never had this and it's a new, but good feeling.

Looking down into her beautiful face, I pull her a little tighter against me. Absentmindedly, I begin to run my hand up and down her arm.

There are only a few boats docked at Grant's and all of them are empty. Everyone must have wandered up to join the party.

The weather tonight is perfect. It's nights like this that make me want to live in Florida forever. It's still warm during the day, but there's coolness in the air at night. Humidity drops off approaching the holidays and the skies are cloud free. Every star is out tonight and I look up to spot Orion's Belt.

Beau is always talking about the stars. I'm not sure why, but he's kind of rubbed off on me. To me Orion's Belt is easily the most recognizable of the constellations and it occurs to me that every time I'm outside at night, I look for it. To the ancient Greeks, Orion was a great hunter and he was considered a hero. In many ways, I want to be like Orion. I want to be strong enough and fearless enough to face all kinds of monsters, like my dad, and then be a hero to my brothers. I want to stand in and fight and kill for them. I love them.

Stepping onto the boat, I instantly feel the need to take it out. The peace and quiet that comes from being on the water is a feeling that I crave constantly. It's a gift that the water always provides for me, whether it's through swimming, being on the boat, or even taking a shower.

I lead us to the front of the boat. There are two seats that are comfortable and private in case anyone should wander down.

Sitting on the chairs, I stare out across the water and then look back up at the sky. I inwardly laugh to myself as I think again about Orion. As a powerful hunter, I can't imagine he would ever be nervous about something like asking a girl out on a date. He seems like he would have been the kind of guy to just take what he wants, and everyone would agree with him.

That's what we're doing here. I've finally decided to ask her out on a date and now I'm trying to work up the nerve. I'm being so stupid. Why wouldn't she want to go out with me? I'm pretty sure that she enjoys my company, so I can't see her saying no. I need to suck it up and ask. Wait! How do I ask her? I've never asked a girl on a date before.

"Ali . . ."

"Yeah."

I decide to change positions. I should be facing her when I ask her. It's important, and I don't want her to think that I'm just casually asking her. She mirrors how I sit and I wrap my hands around her calves before running them up her legs behind her knees. I could sit here touching her all night.

"Will you spend the day with me tomorrow?"

Surprise crosses the features of her face and her big brown eyes light up.

"Yes."

That one little word, coming from her, is the best thing I've heard in a long time. I let out a deep breath because the way she just made me feel is amazing. She wants to spend the day with me! If I wouldn't look like a complete idiot I would fist pump the sky, jump out of this seat, and holler, "Yeah!"

I let go of her legs and reach for her hands. I want contact. I want to feel her skin on mine. She has made me so happy.

We talk for a little longer and eventually decide that we should probably be getting back. We both stand up at the same time and she is so close that I can literally breathe her in. I drop my head down a little and inhale the sweet citrus scent of her hair. I can't help but to rock forward on my toes. I want to close the distance between us and take her mouth with mine. I wonder if she tastes as sweet as she smells.

She breaks the moment by grabbing my hand and leading us off the boat.

As we walk back up the dock to rejoin the party, part of me just wants to take her by the hand and take her home. I really don't want to be here with most of these people. I want to spend time with her.

On the last few steps up to the patio, my hand grazes across her lower back. I know we're about to separate from each other, and I don't know why, but I need contact with her one more time.

I let her step away from me and I follow behind her as she heads over toward Leila at the fire pit. Beau sits next to Ryan and he watches us. He has to know that I walked her down to the boat. I know that it's our thing, but hopefully he's not too angry with me for sharing it with her.

"Tiny! Nice of you to join us." Beau shoots me a pointed look and I get my answer. He isn't happy with me. Oh well. I don't share anything about my life with anyone, so the fact that I've let her in a little is a big deal for me. He should ease up.

"Aww, Beau, did you miss me?" He grins at her. I know that he approves of her or he wouldn't give her the time of day. I sit down next to him and he won't even make eye contact with me.

"Of course I did."

I smack him on the back of the head.

"What?" he asks looking over at me. He's going to acknowledge me whether he likes it or not.

"Knock it off." I can't help but frown at him. He's kind of making me angry.

Beau looks back over at Ali. "So how was paddleboarding?" All right! I get it. I hurt his feelings, but does he really need to push my buttons?

"It was awesome. We had a great time."

Beau looks over at me to see if there's a reaction, but I try to give him nothing. Besides, any reaction that I would have is because of him, not Ali's pseudo playdate.

Beau and Ali continue to banter back and forth. I try to calm down my insides. Maybe I should cancel the date. Beau and Matt are the only two people in this world that I've ever wanted to make happy. He's not happy right now, and it's my fault. If I can't keep him happy, and he's just one person, how am I going to make and keep her happy? I try to push away the things my father has said to me, but one by one they fire through me and my blood thunders in my ears.

You'll never be good enough for anyone. Who would ever want you? You are worthless and good for nothing or no one.

"Stop it," Beau says quietly next to me.

I look over at him and he's leaning toward me, so no one can hear him. He looks mad and concerned at the same time. It's then that I realize I'm white knuckling the arm rests of the chair, and I've got beads of sweat dripping down the sides of my face.

"I'm sorry." I let go of the chair, and run my hand over my face to wipe it off.

"Dude. What are you sorry for? I'm the one who should be apologizing. I'm sorry that I overreacted and made you feel this way. This is all on me."

"I'll cancel." I never should have asked her in the first place. She deserves better.

"Cancel what?"

"I asked her out on a date for tomorrow." A smile splits across Beau's face, and his eyes light up.

"About freaking time, and no, you better not cancel. She's

good for you." He thinks she is good for me? My insides smile. That one line calms me down a little, yet I can't help but ask myself in return—am I good for her?

"I want to take her out on the boat." I don't know if I'm asking him or if this is more of a general statement. I look down at the fire, and I can see Ali out of the corner of my eye watching this conversation with Beau. She can't hear us, but she knows something is going on.

"Then take her. I'm sorry I acted like an ass. It just surprised me, is all. Do you need any help getting ready?"

I look over at him. He's always been so thoughtful and selfless. I'm so proud of him.

"No, I've got it, but are you sure? I can do something else with her."

"Absolutely not! Take her out on the boat. She'll love it. You know she will, which is why you asked her in the first place." He's right.

"Okay."

Beau and I lock our eyes onto each other. He understands I'm telling him thank you, and I see that he truly is okay with me taking her out. A huge part of me feels relief, but the lingering doubt still hangs in the background.

Chapter Eleven

ALI

AT NINE, DREW walks into my house. I love that he doesn't even knock anymore. He's comfortable enough here and with me that he makes himself at home. I head down the stairs and into the kitchen to find him bent over and in my refrigerator. He hears me, stands up, and smiles. I don't think looking at him could ever get old. He's wearing what looks like a comfortably worn Salt Life T-shirt, a pair of navy swim trunks, and a Tampa Bay Rays baseball hat.

"I packed us a lunch, but I don't really know what you like to eat, so I thought if I found something in here of yours, we could pack it."

"Well, aren't you sweet?" His smile grows bigger. "I eat everything, so no worries."

"All right, then." He takes my bag in one hand and with the other he reaches out to hold mine.

As we walk out the front door, I look around for the boat.

"Where's the boat?"

"At Grant's house," he says, throwing me a look like I should have known the answer to this.

"You keep it there?" I ask as I turn around to lock the door.

"Yep, they have plenty of room at the dock, and his dad doesn't care."

"Which one is yours?"

"The one we were on last night." He stops walking and turns to look at me. He sees the confusion on my face and then the clarity.

"That's your boat? It's really big!"

He laughs and throws my bag into the back of the Jeep.

"You know what they say about guys with big boats, right?" He's still laughing and I turn beet red.

"Oh man, you're such a guy." I crack a smile at him and shake my head.

"I know, but you walked right into that one. I couldn't resist."

I huff at him.

"When my grandfather died, he left a trust fund to Beau, Matt, and I. When we turned eighteen we were granted access to it. Beau and I split the cost of the boat."

I can't even imagine how much a boat like that must have cost, nor can I imagine how much money must be in those trust funds for them to feel comfortable enough dropping that much on a boat.

"That's nice. Do you guys get to take it out a lot?" I ask him.

"We did over the summer. Since school's been back in we've only gone out a few times. We like to fish together." He holds the door open for me, I climb in, and he walks around to the driver side.

"I've never been fishing."

He glances over at me with a look of incredulity.

"Really? I thought that Colorado was really big into fishing, especially fly fishing."

"Nope, never. I mean, come on, can you see little ole me standing in a river fly casting?"

He laughs again and it sounds so perfect. I could listen to him laugh all day. "It seems like you and I are going to have a lot of things to do together."

I look over at him and he's watching me. I smile because more than he knows, I want to do everything with him.

We park the Jeep outside of Grant's home and he wanders out the front door to meet us.

"Hey, kids." His eyes skip between Drew and me. "Drew, man, you were here early this morning. I heard you fire up the boat and now I know why."

"Yeah, I needed to get gas and stuff. Here, dude, make yourself useful." Drew opens the back of the Jeep and hands Grant the cooler. Drew grabs my bag and a backpack of his own.

"Gonna be gone all day?" he asks Drew.

I can't tell if us being here together is surprising Grant or if he's just being curious. I watch Drew close up the Jeep, but I can feel Grant assess me from head to toe.

"That's the plan."

"Awesome, sounds like a good time. You pack sunblock?"

I bust out laughing. Drew looks over at me and starts laughing too.

"Did I miss something?" Grant says as he closely watches the two of us.

"No, man, don't worry about it, and yes, I packed sun-block." Drew's eyes are sparkling. He's happy.

The three of us walk around the house and head toward the dock. I trail behind the two of them not listening to what they say. A feeling of contentment washes over me as I take in my surroundings. The sky is crystal blue, the water is sparkling, and the air is cool.

It isn't lost on me that tomorrow's Thanksgiving and it will be the first holiday without her. As much as I feel happy to be here with Drew, I feel guilty at the same time for feeling this way. I look down the dock and on the post closest to me there's an electric blue dragonfly. Its wings are slowly beating up and down. I feel like it's looking at me, and I can't move. Is it the same one? It can't be. I gasp at the significance at seeing this dragonfly at this moment.

Drew must have heard me because he turned around, and now stands in front of me. I didn't even notice.

"Babe?" He reaches out and wraps one hand around my head. The dragonfly seems to startle at his voice and it lifts off, flying toward the house. My heart pounds harder, the farther it flies away from me. Drew wipes a tear with his thumb. I didn't even know I was crying. I look up into his eyes and see he's trying to read what's happening to me.

"I'm sorry," I whisper.

He leans down and rests his forehead on mine. My heart squeezes when he does this because I feel like he's closed us off to the world and it's just him and me.

"Don't apologize. Just tell me what you're thinking." He whispers back. I don't want to tell him about the dragonfly. I feel like that was a gift only for me.

"Tomorrow is Thanksgiving . . . and I feel guilty for being here and being happy right now." I squeeze my eyes shut as another tear leaks out.

"Sweetheart, you shouldn't feel guilty." His thumb lightly brushes back and forth across my cheek and his breath drifts across my face.

"I know, but I do."

"It's okay. Look at me." I slowly open my eyes and pull back a little. So much emotion and concern swim in his eyes— in this moment, I don't feel so alone. He understands me and he's here with me.

"Listen, we don't have to go out today if you don't want to. If you want to go home, lie in the bed and watch movies, that's fine with me. I don't care what we do. I just want to spend the day with you."

He's so sincere and sweet when he says this, that my body leans forward into his and I snuggle my face into his chest. He wraps his arms around me and I soak in the affection that he gives.

Seeing the dragonfly, I hear my mom again. *Find some joy. Go find some light.* I let out a deep breath and feel myself saying—*okay.*

"No, I really want to go. I'm sorry. I just had a moment."

His hand runs down my back and he pulls me in tighter. "Don't apologize for how you feel, ever. Understand?"

"Thanks, Drew." He tucks his face in between my neck and my shoulder. I let out a deep sigh and he chuckles. I pull back and look at him questioningly.

"You're so small." He shakes his head while still smiling. He wipes the rest of the tears off of my face, bends down, and throws me up onto his shoulders into the fireman move. I can't help but laugh. He jogs down the dock and drops me to my feet right in front of the boat.

Grant is already on the boat. I see the cooler and our bags

sitting off to the side. Grant's eyebrows are furrowed, he runs his hand back and forth across his chin, and he stands there watching us. He gives Drew a look and Drew shrugs his shoulders, smiling. Grant shakes his head and grins back. What is it about these guys and their silent conversations?

"Does Beau know about this?" Grant asks, as he motions back and forth between the two of us, and then points his thumb back toward the front of the boat.

"Yep," Drew says. Surprise crosses Grant's face, and then acceptance. He claps his hands together and maneuvers around me.

"Well, all right then, kids, have fun and, Drew, call me if something happens or if you need anything." He pats Drew on the back and then climbs off the boat.

"Thanks, man." Grant gives us each one last smile, and then he walks back toward his house.

"He seems like a nice guy, but why do I get the feeling that me being here with you today is confusing him?" I ask.

"He is, one of the best. Beau and I have known him a long time. And that could be for several reasons. One, I've never spent time with a girl before, so us together is probably throwing him off and two, no one is allowed on the boat. It's always been just for Beau, Matt, and me. Grant knows this." I don't know what to say.

It's so strange to me the reputation that Drew has. Maybe he was different last year, but I don't get the feeling that's the case. In three and a half months, I've never seen him speak to anyone other than Beau, Grant, and Ryan. He doesn't give girls the time of day and is a very quiet and closed off person. Knowing what little I know of him, I can see how Grant would be confused seeing us together.

"Really? Is Beau going to be mad?" I don't want him mad

at me or Drew. If this is their personal sanctuary together, maybe we shouldn't be doing this.

"No, he's good. We talked about it last night."

I think back to the bonfire and to the intense conversation that was privately taking place between them.

"The look on your face right now is concern. I don't want you to be concerned. If Beau wasn't okay with this, we would've done something different today. He's cool, okay?"

"Okay. Well, I guess it's nice to know that I'm the first one to be here with you and this isn't where you take all your dates." I'm teasing him.

He sits down behind the wheel and motions for me to sit next to him.

"Ali . . ." He's thinking hard about what he wants to say. He turns the key and the boat engine fires on. "You're the first and this is the only date I've ever been on." He looks over at me with a little pink on his cheeks. He's nervous to tell me this and yet I can't wrap my head around being his only date, ever.

"Yep, seems you and I are both going to have lots of firsts together." He says, while cracking a big smile, lightening the conversation. "I can't wait to see you on skis, but that'll have to wait. Today, I'm taking it easy on you with just the tube."

I look over at the back of the boat, and there's a large navy blue tube in the shape of a chair with two handles to hang on to and a rope tied to one end.

"Sounds like fun, Skipper. Let's get going."

His eyes sparkle at me again and he laughs. "Skipper? More like Captain to you, Tiny."

"Why does he call me that?" I ask.

"No idea, but it fits you." The boat roars to life and we pull away from the dock.

Most of the morning, we spend trading off and on between driving the boat and tubing. I'm shocked that he lets me drive his boat, but when it's his turn to ride the tube, the playful side of him comes out and he's so cute. It's a lot like snow tubing, but definitely more bouncy as the tube passes over the wakes of the boat. The ride time is also longer.

The weather is perfect. The sun isn't too hot, and the water is still warm enough to get in. Eventually, I sit down next to Drew while he drives and we just enjoy being on the water. "Don't Happen Twice" by Kenny Chesney floats through the air, and as the sun warms my skin, my heart warms too. He points out some of his favorite spots to fish and the name of every bird that we see.

"So last night Beau left with some girl that I haven't seen before. Is he dating her?"

Drew's lips pinch together, he stiffens, and he looks over at me. I can't see his eyes behind his sunglasses, but his eyebrows are drawn together.

"Beau doesn't date." He says this to me very shortly, almost like he is angry with me for asking.

"Oh, so he just hooks up with girls all the time?"

The boat slows and he looks over at me again. I can tell he's studying my face, trying to get a good read on why I'm asking.

"Does it bother you, what Beau does or doesn't do?"

Does he think that I'm interested in his brother? Surely he doesn't. I need to fix this conversation quickly.

"No . . . um . . . I was just kind of wondering if you do the same?"

"You want to know if I hook up with random girls?" His look immediately softens and the corner of his mouth twitches.

"Yes."

He lets out a sigh and I wish I could see his eyes. His

sunglasses make me feel closed off to him. Then again he could say the same about me and there's no way I'm taking mine off. It is way too bright out here.

"I'm not going to lie to you and say I never have . . . but what I can tell you is that I haven't in a long time."

This makes me feel better. I can't be spending time with him if he's interested in other people. I just don't have it in me.

"Okay, I'm sorry for asking you. It really isn't any of my business what you do or who you spend your time with."

"Ali, you can ask me anything." He reaches over and runs his hand across my knee.

"Okay." I look down at his hand. I really like when he touches me.

"Just out of curiosity, would it bother you if I was?"

"Was what, hooking up with other girls?"

He nods his head.

"I'd like to tell you no, but yes, it would bother me." I look away from him and out over the water. I don't want to see his reaction and I don't want him to see on my face, exactly what the thought of him with another girl would do to me.

"So, since we're on the subject, what about you?"

He surprises me with this question and I look back over at him.

"What about me?"

"Do you hook up with guys when you go out?"

I start to laugh. "That's a definite no. I never have."

There's a pause in the conversation as he studies my face. I know he's reading between the lines and I'm okay with that. Should we ever become something more, I was wondering how I was going to break this news to him.

"Never?" His jaw drops a little and I see his eyebrows shoot up. Why does this surprise him so much?

"Nope, not even close."

"How is that possible? You're so beautiful."

I blush at the endearment.

"Dance has always been my focus. Back in Denver, everyone knew that. I wasn't one of those girls who went boy crazy. I've stayed on course with pursuing my dream of dancing in New York."

"I understand dedication, but sometimes it's good to just let off steam."

"That is such a guy thing to say. And believe it or not, I'm proud of who I am and what I have and have not done. Not many girls at nineteen can say this. Trust me I'm not against it, it's just never been in the cards for me. Especially, over the last year with everything that was going on."

He looks over at me and even with the glasses, I can see pity. I don't want to be pitied. I just want him to understand.

"Huh. Well, we might have to change that." He smirks.

"Is that so?" I blush at his bold statement, but I can't help smiling too.

"Maybe," he says.

"Maybe." It's fun flirting back with him.

"Remember, you and me . . . full of firsts." He laughs with a mischievous grin on his face.

Oh, what am I going to do with this boy?

Drew pulls the boat up to a small island in the middle of the Intercoastal. The island is small and filled in the middle with palmettos, pines, sea oats, and other vegetation. There are no houses here. It's just raw with nature. My guess is, if we were to walk around the perimeter of this island, the distance would be about a mile.

He parks the boat out just far enough that it doesn't hit bottom, but close enough where we can jump off and it will be waist deep. Well, waist deep for him that is.

"So, how does this spot look for lunch?" He asks.

"I think it looks perfect."

His faces lights up. He's satisfied with himself for coming up with our little picnic excursion.

"I love coming here. No one ever stops here. They just drive right on by. I like to come here to think."

"Ah, I see. So this is your happy place?"

"I guess you could say that." He smirks at me.

He grabs a bucket, the large thermal cooler bag, his back-pack, and off the back of the boat we go. He holds my hand as we wade to shore. I'll never get tired of him wanting to hold my hand.

Drew packed the perfect beach lunch for us. In the bag, he has a large sheet that he lays down, along with paper plates, paper towels and paper cups. For food he packed two Cuban sandwiches, a bag of potato chips, two oranges, Oreos, and a gallon jug of water. Apparently, Oreos are the perfect dessert because they don't melt in the heat.

"Let's play the 'I didn't know that about you game,'" he suggests, grinning at me.

"That's kind of a long name. What is it?" I ask, while grinning back.

"It's a game where you try to stump me with things you think I don't know about you. Eventually, I'll know just about everything and it'll get hard. But in the meantime, it's a way for me to get to know you more—and I really want to."

Wow. This is really kind of sweet of him. I want to know more about him too. I just haven't been too sure about how to get him to open up.

It isn't lost on me that he said, *eventually*. My insides are giddy because that means he wants to see me more to know more about me. Maybe this isn't going to be a onetime date.

"Okay. I'll play if you do." I push my plate to the side and lie on my stomach with my feet kicked up in the air. He watches me, and his eyes darken.

"Deal! You go first and then it's one for one unless I already know what you told me. Then you'll have to go again. Same for me. So, just try and stump me!" Drew lies on his side facing me, propping his head up on his hand. He flips his hat around backward and I can see every detail of his handsome face.

"Stump me. I think that sounds like a good name. It's short and to the point."

"Okay, perfect." He smiles at me, and butterflies start to move around in my stomach.

"Hmmm, let's see . . . I hate olives. I love food and I'll eat just about anything, but I can't get on board with eating olives. I'm super thankful to not live in Italy. Don't they put olives in everything?!" I shiver at the nasty thought of them and he laughs at me. He's laughed so much today.

"Well, I'm glad I didn't go with an antipasto lunch." He says.

"Yeah, me too. Although, I probably would've eaten it."

His brows furrow a little. "Why?"

"Because you've been so thoughtful to plan all of this. I wouldn't want to hurt your feelings."

"Trust me when I say, there's probably very little you could do that would hurt my feelings. It's just food. But now you have to promise me that if you don't like something I give you, you won't eat it."

"I promise. Okay, now it's your turn." I swing my feet back and forth. His eyes move from my face to my legs and then back to my face.

"When I was eight, I was stung by a sting ray, and almost an entire year went by before I would get back in the water."

"What? No way!" He laughs at my shocked expression.

"Yes way. Even now, I find myself swimming on the top of water whether or not I can stand. It keeps my feet out of the sand."

"That's crazy, Drew."

"Yep. You hear about things like this happening, but I've never met anyone else that it's happened to. I tell myself that it was some freak occurrence or I might not ever get back in the water."

I can't help but laugh.

"I love mystery novels. There's something about the suspense and the "who did it?" that I love. They get my blood pumping and I seem to never be able to put the books down until I figure it out."

He smiles at me, leans over, and brushes a piece of hair off of my face.

"I can totally see you curled up on one of your balcony lounge chairs reading. That suits you. When Beau and I were little we loved the Teenage Mutant Ninja Turtles, and we used to pretend that we were ninjas. Of course we never had swords, so instead we pretended our arms were. That's why we both have a sword tattoo on our forearms. Pretending that we were clashing our swords together became our thing and we've always done it."

"I think that's awesome. It must be so cool to have a brother that you're friends with."

"You have no idea. Beau is more than just a brother to me. He's my best friend and I love him more than anyone could ever imagine." He drops eye contact with me, and looks out across the water—time to change the subject.

"What about the other tattoo?" This one I just recently saw. It was after a morning swim, he waved at me, and that is when I noticed it. I was surprised that I hadn't noticed it before. On the inside of his left bicep there is an inscription. He pauses as he thinks about the answer.

"*Freedom,* it's what it feels like when I'm swimming in the water, being free. Does that make sense?"

"Yep, perfect. I feel free when I'm dancing too. Okay, so I told you the food that I hate the most . . . well, the food that I can't live without, could eat every day of my life, and it's my last supper meal—pizza."

Drew laughs. "Really? Mine would have to be cheeseburgers. So what kind of pizza is your favorite?"

"Any kind really, as long as it doesn't have olives on it—oh yeah, and anchovies. Those little suckers are not meant for pizza. I like all kinds. In fact, I make one mean homemade pizza that only a few of the special privileged have been allowed to taste." I smirk at him.

"What are the chances that I get to taste this super-special pizza?"

"Hmmm." I tap my chin and look up at the clouds like I'm contemplating. "I'd say your chances are looking pretty good, Captain."

"Captain." His smile is so big and infectious. "Sounds like date number two."

"So, you want to spend more time with me?" I ask him teasingly.

"Ali . . . I want to spend a lot of time with you."

I can't help but look in his eyes. Butterflies awake in my stomach again and tingles prickle all over my body.

"My turn," he says, breaking the moment. "I've never been to New York City and I've always wanted to go."

"Oh my gosh, Drew, you'll love it there. Two summers ago I spent three weeks at Juilliard in a dance camp, where we worked on classical ballet and modern dance, and it was amazing. I love the energy, the diversity of the people, and there is so much there to do and eat. You should come and visit me next year." Sadness rips through me and I have to look away from him. I haven't really given much thought to next year and not being with him. I just can't go there yet. I need him so much right now. I don't want to think about losing him.

"You sound pretty certain that New York City is where you're going to be."

"It is, one way or another. I've applied to other programs and schools there. Juilliard is just the one that I want." I wish I could beg and plead for him to come with me. In a perfect world, he would want that too and we would go together. I know I'm getting a little ahead of myself. After all, this is a first date, and I know Drew doesn't really date.

"Well, maybe I'll come and visit you. But when you're making plans for us, just remember that I'm a typical southern beach boy. I swim, wear flip-flops daily, and have never seen snow."

"You've never seen snow?"

He shakes his head at me, and my eyes get huge.

"Oh man, this conversation just took a left turn. The first time you are going to see snow, Drew Hale, is with me in Colorado. Your first time has to be done right."

A slow smile stretches across his face like he was just let in on the biggest secret.

My cheeks flush a little. Of course he's a typical guy and his mind would wander that way. "What? Why are you smiling at me like that?"

"No reason. I just like watching you talk about things that

make you excited. I think my first time . . . in the snow, definitely needs to be done right . . . in Colorado." He starts laughing and rolls to his back. His hand rubs across his chest. He's so handsome.

"As long as you're on the bottom." My face flushes and his head whips over to look at me. "Seriously, two can play this game."

He sits up and his eyes roam all over me. A blush darkens my skin.

"Come on, gorgeous, let's pack this up and go for a walk. See if we can find any good shells." He says, while sitting up.

We find so many perfect shells: starfish of all sizes, sand dollars, perfect conchs, cat eyes, checker boards, olives, scallop shells in all different colors, and more. We even find a piece of coral and two pieces of sea glass. I now see why every morning there are shell pickers on the beach. I love this! I feel like I'm finding little treasures.

"I had a feeling that you would want to keep these shells, so I bought you a large glass jar to put them in. It's in the back of the Jeep, waiting for you."

I'm speechless and stop walking.

He looks over at me out of the corner of his eye, reaches down to grab my hand, and we continue walking.

"You thought of everything today, didn't you?" I say to him.

"I just wanted you to have a really good day. One with good memories." He's so thoughtful.

"Drew, this is the best day I've had in so long. I don't even know how to thank you."

"I can think of one way." He squeezes my hand, and a smirk crosses his features.

"And what's that?"

He stops walking and turns so he's directly in front of me, but never let's go of my hand. He sets the bucket on the ground and steps in closer as he looks down at me. His free hand reaches up and wraps around the side of my face. He runs his thumb and eyes over my bottom lip and then my cheek bone. He tilts my head back so he can look directly into my eyes.

"So . . . there's a question I need to ask you." He takes a deep breath. "I know that you've been spending time with Chase. How do you feel about him?"

Chase who? That's what I want to answer him with.

"Not like this," I breathe out.

"That's good enough for me." He lowers his head and his lips lightly kiss the corner of my mouth.

I tremble in anticipation.

"Ali," he whispers. "I have wanted to kiss you every day, since that very first day. All this time has gone by and now instead of wanting to taste you, I'm at a point where I need to taste you." His mouth hovers directly over mine as he speaks to me. "You have the most beautiful smile. I can't tell you how many times I've forgotten that you aren't mine and I almost lean over to kiss you like it's an everyday normal thing for us."

I'm slipping into one of those moments. A moment where everything around me freezes, and all that matters is him. I'm completely lost in him.

As my eyes close, I lose the sense of sight, but the others pick up with so much more clarity. His breath is warm as it drifts across my lips, and his body heat as he steps closer warms me through the outside in. The pressure from his fingers changes as they tangle into my hair and pull on my hand. The sound of the water as it laps onto the shore and the soft spoken words of the seagulls as they sing to each other.

"I'm not yours?" I ask as I slowly exhale.

"Do you want to be?"

"Yes." My answer comes out in a whisper. I can't open my eyes because I don't want him to see how much I want to be his. I think I'm truly feeling my heart beat for the first time.

In the back of my mind, I smile. See, Mom, I listened. I let go and found some joy and light. Drew's light is so bright, he causes me to see the world differently. Maybe he does want me and maybe I am good enough for him.

DREW

I KNEW AT some point today I was going to kiss her. I didn't know when or how. I just knew that I was.

I've never been one to kiss girls. I can probably count on one hand who and when. It's just never been my thing. Kissing to me, for whatever reason, is so much more intimate than anything else.

Walking down the beach with her, collecting shells, I was so happy in that moment that I needed to wrap her in my arms and hold her to know that the moment was real.

I've never wanted the responsibility of having to deal with another person. I never wanted the strings or drama that comes with having a girlfriend. I've heard all of the guys over the years complain about one thing or another and every time, it just confirmed to me why this was something I never wanted in my life.

And to be honest, I didn't even know if I was capable of emotionally connecting to anyone. I've never been very high on my own self-worth. I mean, if the one person in the world who's supposed to love me more than anything doesn't, why would I think someone else will?

When Ali said that she wanted to be mine, I felt the shell around my heart crack. The walls I've built up around it over the years start to crumble and I can feel each brick fall away. No one has ever wanted to be mine. All these years, girls have chased after me and every time it was the same thing—they wanted me to be theirs. Belonging to someone else was never going to happen. But then Ali crashed into my life, literally, and refused to move out of the way.

Looking down into her beautiful face, she's closed her eyes. This gives me the opportunity to memorize every detail of this moment: her ivory skin that's so soft and perfect, the silkiness of her hair, and her gorgeous bee stung lips. I've never seen anyone as breathtaking as her. Her lips part slightly, and I can't wait any longer.

Closing the distance between the two of us, I finally press my mouth to hers. The moment our lips touch, an electric zap shoots straight down my body and into my toes. Every part of me tingles and hums.

I let go of her hand and move mine around to the small of her back. I pull her into me. I need to feel her body flush with mine. My self-control slowly slips and I am filled with the need to devour her. Her tiny hands gently touch my stomach and she slides them up over my chest, across my shoulders, and to the back of my neck. She flips off my hat and then slides her fingers into my hair, while at the same time, pulling me tighter against her. I can feel her slipping as well.

Everywhere she touches me heats like I've been burned. No one touches me, ever. Having her little fingers feather across my skin is so foreign to me that I shake.

Needing more of her, I tilt her head a little further so I can gain better access to her mouth. I grab on to her bottom lip, suck it into my mouth, and run my tongue across it. I have thought about what her bottom lip would feel like under mine so much that I can't help but lavish in the fullness of it.

A small gasp comes from her and I absorb the sound as she parts her lips. I deepen the kiss and finally get to taste what I've been craving for so long.

Ali tastes like the sun's warm rays on a late lazy afternoon and cotton candy. Comforting, warm, and sweet.

I feel weightless and free.

Her taste, her smell, the way I feel with her wrapped around me, and the little noises she makes—I want to bottle this moment up forever.

I move my lips from her mouth and run them across her cheek, her eyelids, her jaw, and down her neck. I could stand here and taste her forever.

She quietly breathes my name, while letting out a small sigh. She's content with me and happy. I'm making her happy. I never make anyone happy.

The thought of this overwhelms me, and tears burn my eyes and the back of my throat tightens. I don't cry, so why I feel so emotionally vulnerable at the moment is beside me. I bury my head in her neck and let her hair fall around my face. I know I need to pull it together. Focusing on citrus and vanilla, I take deeps breaths and my racing heart begins to slow.

She feels something happening to me because her hands begin to softly run up and down my back. I never want to let go of this perfect girl. I know I should, but I don't think I can.

I've never been one to wish for much, but I find myself cataloging these wishes with all of my other last firsts. I wish for this day to be my last first date and that this kiss is my last first kiss.

Chapter Twelve

ALI

THE HOLIDAYS CAME and went in kind of a blur. My dad didn't spend any more time at the house, even though he knew I was here all break. Drew, Beau, and Matt made it a habit to drop in daily to check on me. Somehow we always found ourselves having dinner together. I often wondered why they didn't eat with their parents. I wanted to ask, but at the same time I don't want them to think I don't want them here. Not one of them ever offers up any information or talks about them. I've let it go for now, but I have an uneasy feeling that if I do ask them, there may be a story to tell. For the moment though, I'm just going to enjoy their company. At the end of the day, it's their business, and I'd much rather they tell me anything they want to in their own time.

Drew and I never really did clarify if and when we're going to have that second date, but I can't help but think that all of this time that we're spending together has to mean something.

I ended up making my famous pizza for all three of them. Both Drew and Beau stopped talking, moaned with delight and satisfaction, and then scarfed it down. I laughed at them as I watched them survey my kitchen for more. Feeding these three boys is tough. They eat like they're bottomless pits. I feel bad for their mother.

At Christmas, Drew and I both surprised each other. We had never talked about exchanging gifts, so when he walked over with one, we ran upstairs to my room where I had his, and just flopped down on my bed grinning at each other.

I bought him a baseball hat with *Captain* embroidered across the front, a huge supply of sunblock, and I made him a coupon book filled with pizza and cheeseburger requests. He laughed when he slipped on the hat, telling me that now he had coupons, I'd never get rid of him.

He had a huge smile on his face as he passed me my gift. I tore the paper off like an overexcited little girl and was left completely speechless. He'd bought me a wind chime for my balcony, decorated with beautiful pieces of sea glass that hung from it, reflecting tiny bursts of colors, where the light hits.

"I know that you like to sleep with your windows open and I thought that you might like this to add to the sounds of the beach," he tells me with a shy smile gracing his handsome face.

"Drew, I don't know what to say. You couldn't have possibly given me anything more perfect. Thank you so much." I'm so moved by his continued thoughtfulness that without thinking I climb onto his lap and kiss him. I'm pretty sure I surprised him, but it most definitely isn't unwelcome.

His strong arms wrap around me as he slowly takes control and I melt into him, not wanting this moment to ever end.

Since our date on the beach, Drew has kissed me a few times, each one has become more gentle and romantic, considerate even, instead of being panty dropping and passionate. Don't get me wrong, I'm not complaining. If the boy wants to kiss me, I'll take whatever I can get, but I can't help but wonder what's lurking underneath all this sweetness.

Drew leans back on my bed and I move to straddle his hips. His eyes darken and his hands rub back and forth across the tops of my thighs. The sight of him lying underneath me has my stomach flipping with excitement and nervousness.

I look at him and then at myself. I just don't understand why he would want to be with me. He is so incredibly handsome, and I can't help but wonder, why me?

I slowly lean forward, placing my hands on either side of his head. His eyes lock onto my mouth, and that's all the encouragement I need to claim his lips with mine. This kiss is slow, sensual, and deep. His hands begin to run up my biceps and over my shoulders. They leave a trail of heat as they descend down my ribcage and settle on my hips. My whole body is on high alert as ever so slowly, his fingers dig into my hips and he pushes me backward and then pulls me forward. He may just be settling my weight better on him, but the feel of him underneath me can't be missed.

Kissing Drew is like a fairy tale each and every time. He makes me feel like there's a once upon a time and a happily ever after all wrapped up waiting for me. I love the feel of him, his warmth, and his taste. Each time we kiss, the hunger radiating off of him intensifies, but he never crosses any lines. He never takes what I'm more than willing to offer him.

FOR NEW YEAR'S Eve, about twenty-five of us end up at a closed party at Grant's. At midnight, we all stand together on the back patio and yell the countdown into the air. As fireworks light up the sky, Drew grabs me away from Leila and the girls, and kisses me. It isn't a little kiss, either. He takes his time and explores every crevice of my mouth. Most people are too caught up doing their own thing to notice, but I do feel the eyes of several land on us, including Leila's.

Drew wraps his arms even tighter around me and instead of letting go, he nuzzles his head into my neck and under my ear. I'm so happy standing here under the stars with him that I could cry.

"So . . . did you come up with a New Year's resolution?" His voice vibrates into my skin.

"No, I haven't thought about it yet. You?" Music plays somewhere in the background and we start swaying together.

"I have, wanna know what it is?" he asks.

I nod my head and his mouth curls into a smile against my skin. Goosebumps race across me.

"My resolution is to spend the night with you every Saturday that I can, starting tonight."

I let out a small gasp and pull back to look in his eyes. He's only spent the night once and every night before I go to sleep, I lay in bed wishing he would come over and knock on my door.

"Are you serious?" I whisper.

His beautiful eyes meet mine and I see him, the real him, not the one that he gives others. His eyes search mine to make sure this is what I want and I see emotions flash through them. The hardness and indifference he puts in place for everyone else is momentarily gone and I fall for him all over again. By letting me in, he shows me that he's mine and I so desperately want to reassure him that I'm his.

Drew bends his head down so his lips brush mine. "Yes."

"Why?"

He pulls back a little and wraps one hand around the side of my head, tangling his fingers in my hair. He runs his thumb across my cheekbone and I lean into it.

"Because I want to spend more time with you. I like being with you, Ali. I like having dinner with you, watching movies with you, playing games with you, curling up next to you . . ." His cheeks blush pink and my heart flutters at seeing him nervous.

"I don't know what to say." Could he be any more perfect?

"Say okay." Drew's hand on my lower back presses into me. I love his hands on me.

"Most definitely okay."

He smiles and then leans down to kiss me again. Everyone and everything around us slip away.

This is the most affectionate he's been in front of other people, and I feel pride swell inside of me. Not because he's the infamous Drew Hale to all of these people, but because he's kind, thoughtful, generous, funny, handsome, and so much more.

His mouth becomes forceful, possessive, and then giving. He's unapologetic and then appreciative at the same time. I can taste the champagne punch that's the drink of the night on his lips, and I want to drown in him. A quiet moan passes his lips and I squeeze closer to him. The length of his body against mine is exhilarating. I can feel every part of him from thigh to chest. Just knowing I'm making him react and feel this way, is almost enough to send me over the edge. I can't get enough of him.

Drew's hand fists into the back of my dress, and the other grabs on to my hip in a possessive move. My back arches, pushing my chest into him, and more than anything I want to strip this dress off of me so I can feel his hands against my skin. We're completely caught up in the moment until somewhere in the background, I register someone chuckling.

"All right, all right! When's it my turn?"

I jerk back from Drew, and look to see Beau standing right next to us. We've gotten completely carried away in front of all of these people and a blush rises up my neck and burns through my cheeks.

"It's okay, Tiny. We all enjoyed the show." Beau says as I drop my head on Drew's chest. He chuckles again.

"Come here, Tiny, and show me some love." Beau snatches me away from Drew, picks me up, and kisses my forehead. "Happy New Year's, Tiny."

"You too, Beau." I smile at him. As he puts me back on my feet, and let's go, a wave of brotherly love for him washes over me.

Beau wraps his arm around Drew and the two of them smile at each other while having a silent conversation. I take a moment just looking at the two of them, and my heart swells at the realization that I finally feel like I have a family again.

Drew grabs my hand and pulls me into the middle of them. The three of us share a hug that I'm certain everyone here at this party is aware of.

"So, Ali . . . let's get out of here," Drew says to me. Beau starts chuckling again.

"Tiny! Did you know, that line is the most used line of all time in cinema?" Beau says, all proud of himself.

"I did!" I can't help but laugh. "Beau, did you know that Bruce was the name of the mechanical shark used in Jaws?"

"I thought that was the name of the shark in Nemo," he says.

"That's where it came from." My eyes are twinkling at him.

"No way!"

"You two kill me." Drew says, while shaking his head.

Drew and Beau lightly tap their tattooed arms together and then Drew pulls on my hand so we can leave the party. I catch Leila's eye as we head for the gate and she gives me a knowing look that says, "Yeah, I'm on to you." I smile real big at her and blow her a kiss.

DREW

SCHOOL STARTED UP again two days after New Year's, and Ali and I fall back into our daily routine. The water in the mornings is now too cold for her, so she no longer floats after her runs. I, however, am used to it and am still working on my open water strokes.

I started riding to school with Ali in the mornings and Beau drives his car instead. It just makes sense since I leave with her after we're finished with swim and dance anyway. Matt doesn't seem to mind. He hops into the first car that leaves and between the three of us, we always make sure that he's at school on time.

I know the gossip mill has been running some since we returned after the holidays, but at school in front of others, I keep my hands to myself. The only exception has been New Year's Eve, but other than that we come across to anyone who sees us as just friends. The thought of some detailed rumor about her and me getting back to my dad has me cringing.

I finally gave in to talking to her in front of others. It hurt my feelings to pretend not to know her, especially when I think she's the best person in the world. Besides, she deserves better than that from me. We now walk to our classes together and spend our lunch hour together, whether it's at school or somewhere else.

I've been hearing little things lately that make me wonder if Cassidy's putting her manipulation skills to the test, and trying to turn the other girls at the school on her. None of them have . . . yet. Ali's really sweet and kind to everyone. She keeps to herself, doesn't pick sides, and is drama free. It's really hard to dislike her, and most girls I think genuinely want to be her friend.

Today is a teacher work day and there's no school. Beau, Matt, and I decided last night that we want take the boat out and do a little fishing. It's been a couple of weeks and I think the three of us need a little time together.

Another fire occurred last night. This one was on the southern tip of the island, Intercoastal side. The house was small and fortunately no one was home. I wonder if Ali remembers me telling her that there would be a fire in January. It's sad that we can now predict when one is going to happen. The thing about the fires is there's no pattern in them. I think that's why the police keep ruling out that it's a string of arson attacks. The houses have ranged from all different sizes and have been in so many different locations.

The breeze travels east so most of the smoke has drifted that way. I take us south to clear out of it, and park the boat near the island where Ali and I went for our date. Beau baits his hook and casts out.

"So, are we ever going to talk about you and Ali?" he

asks, while looking over at me. His face is expressionless.

I see Matt out of the corner of eye. His head has popped up. I know he's curious too.

"What's there to talk about?" I say. I know this will fire him up.

"Dude! I'm your brother and I'm curious. We want to know what's going on between the two of you. You spend a lot of time with her, including every Saturday night. Are you guys dating? Is she like your girlfriend?" I pause to think about how to answer him.

No one really knows about the real Ali and me, and I've kind of liked it that way. I love having her all to myself, and only I know about it. But at the same time, I'm so excited about being with her, I want to tell Beau and Matt just about everything.

I cast my line out, reel in a little, and stare out at the water. "Yeah, I guess you could say that we're dating. We've never really defined anything, but there isn't anyone else for me and I don't think that there is for her either."

He thinks about this for a moment.

"I think that's awesome. She's the perfect girl for you, and you deserve to be happy."

Hearing him say this makes my heart speed up. I know that he means well, but I don't know if I'll ever really deserve to be happy. It's kind of hard when I think about all of the things that have happened to Beau, Matt, and my mom over the years that were a result of something I've done. They're the ones who deserve to be happy.

"She is kind of perfect," I mutter, smiling at that thought. "Saturday nights are the best too. We curl up in her bed and watch a movie while eating pizza. It doesn't get much better than that."

Beau's head jerks over to my direction. "Wait! Her homemade pizza?"

"Yep." I grin back at him.

"I'm officially jealous," he says.

My grin turns into a smile because I know he's really not.

"I honestly can say, I didn't think I would see the day that you would settle down." Beau's eyes lock onto mine and I don't know what to say.

"I told him months ago that he should make her his girlfriend." Matt grins at me knowingly.

"That makes two of us," I say back to Beau. "Most days I just don't feel like I deserve her—she deserves better. But there's something about her that I can't stay away from. She has this pull on me, and she doesn't even realize it."

"I know why you think this, but you're wrong. *He* is wrong. You deserve the best things that life has to offer, so do we for that fact. No matter what he says or does to us, we can't lose sight of that . . . ever."

I look over at Beau and he watches me. I can see that he really means this and it makes me feel things that I shouldn't. Sometimes, I look at him and I can't understand how or why he loves me so much. I'm the reason his life is so terrible.

"Ali's a big girl and she seems pretty smart, too, so keep in mind that she can make her own decisions. If she didn't want to be with you, she wouldn't," he says.

"I suppose," agreeing with him. Ali definitely isn't a pushover. She does exactly what she wants, when she wants.

"As for this pull that she has on you, we can all see it." Beau smirks at me.

"What? What do you mean?"

"You're not as subtle as you think. First off, you've never *ever* looked at any girl, but when it comes to her, you can't keep your eyes off of her. You're constantly watching her and I don't even think you realize it. Second of all, your mood has changed. I know better than anyone what the last couple of years have been like, and with each passing month, you became surlier and well, much more of a pain in the ass. But since October, you've changed. You seem lighter, happier, and we've all caught you smiling when you're with her."

Huh. I don't know how to respond to this. She does make me lighter and happier. For so long, I felt like my life was just getting darker and heavier. It even crossed my mind once that I might be clinically depressed. I mean having to deal with what the three of us do, on pretty much a daily basis, would make anyone feel this way.

"Yeah, I guess you're right." For some reason it no longer bothers me that people can see what I'm feeling. She does make me happy.

Matt gets a tug on his line and he pulls his pole back. He's hooked something and slowly he begins to reel in his line. It's a silver mullet. Matt unhooks the fish and tosses him back.

"Matt, why didn't you keep him? Mom would have made us a great smoked dip," I ask him.

"I didn't feel like it." Matt's been kind of quiet and withdrawn all morning.

"What's wrong with you?" Beau's brows furrow as he asks him this.

"Nothing all right! I'm tired and I just want to hang out with you two and fish, okay?"

"Okay," we say in unison.

Beau and I exchange a concerned look. Matt has been hiding out a lot more lately. After school he says he's going to play with his friends, but we don't really know what he does.

At night he walks through the door right before dad gets home. It's like he can't stay away enough, not that anyone would blame him given the circumstances. Matt rebaits and casts out.

"So, Drew, have you thought about what happens next year? Dad still seems to be pushing Western Florida." I'm not surprised that Beau is asking me this. I feel like I get asked at least once a day by someone what my college plans are. I haven't told anyone anything. Not even Ali.

"I have, a lot. I'm not ready to talk about that yet, but I will when I'm ready. What I can tell you though is I'll never attend Western Florida. It amazes me every day that he thinks he can still control us. You and I are both legal adults. Technically, neither one of us should be there putting up with his shit."

"Tell me about it. I don't know what I'm going to do when you leave. Grant asked me to move in with him and his mom, but I just can't, you know? I think that you and Ali should pick a college together, or at least a city where you both have options."

"We'll see. Her audition is at the end of this month, so that's kind of hanging over us." I feel a tug on my line and I jerk the rod backward. It eases again. Something's circling. It'll hook itself soon enough.

"What audition?" Matt asks.

"She's trying to get into Juilliard. I thought y'all knew this." I glance over at them.

"What?!" Beau's looks completely shocked. "No, I didn't and that's crazy. Now I understand why she's dancing all the time. Does she think she'll get in?"

"I think she does. I can't even imagine the pressure. They only take twenty-four students a year into the dance program, twelve girls and twelve guys."

"Wow. Isn't Juilliard in New York City?" Beau asks.

"Yep." Slowly, I reel my line back in and rebait the hook.

"Well, that's perfect. There are a ton of colleges there for you."

I cast the rod back out and look over at Matt. His eyebrows are pulled down and he's watching me.

"You would move all the way to New York City?" Matt asks, looking angry and slightly panicked.

"I might. We'll see. Don't mention anything to her, though, and I'll let you know once everything gets sorted out. Several things still have to happen before we can 'ride off into the sunset' together."

"Hmm, yeah, but just think about how nice that ride would be," Beau says grinning at me. He's so cheesy sometimes I can't help but laugh at him. I'm going to miss him so much next year.

Matt moves to the other side of the boat facing away from us. I can tell that he's upset and he doesn't want us to see it. Maybe it's better he knows now. It will give him time to prepare for me leaving. I wish I could make his life easier. He deserves better than this.

Chapter Thirteen

ALI

THE DRIVE DOWN to Miami was pretty quiet. I'm thankful Drew let me be, so I could internalize what I need to do over the next twenty-four hours. I've never gone with him to any of his away meets, but maybe he's the same way.

Walking through the doors and into the university's dance department, I really wasn't nervous. I know I probably should be. After all, my future and which path I take in life will be based on this one day, but the things we'll be doing today and the dance that I'll be auditioning with I can do in my sleep. I was born to do this, and I feel completely prepared.

I breeze through registration, walk into a smaller auditorium, and take a seat off to the side. I would say that there are around eighty people here, and I just know I've got this.

"Good morning, ladies and gentlemen. We'd like to thank each and every one of you for taking the time needed to travel here to audition for us. We know how daunting this whole process can be, but we want to assure you that today will be quick and mostly painless.

"As you know, each year the program only accepts twelve girls and twelve boys from across the nation. If you're not chosen to be one of the twenty-four, please do not be too discouraged. There are so many opportunities for dancers, and if you've already made it this far, we're confident in your abilities that you will do amazing things. So please relax, do your best to enjoy today with us, and just be yourself.

"The day is going to be broken down into five different components. Those are: a ballet technique class, a modern technique class, solo performances, a coaching class, and then lastly an interview.

"The ballet technique class is the most difficult of the day, which is why we hold it first. It's here that we will conduct our first round of cuts. You can be cut at any time, during or afterward. Most likely three quarters of you will not continue on past this round. Callbacks will take place, and then we'll move on to modern.

"The next round of callbacks will take place after you perform your solos. Your solo should be kept under two minutes, and we hope you've chosen wisely. It's here that we are expecting to see you at your very best.

"The coaching class is designed for us to see how you work under pressure in an ensemble rehearsal type setting. The conservatory program at Juilliard can be extremely challenging at times, and we have found over the years that some dancers just haven't quite reached a certain maturity level to be able to handle what is expected of them. Should you receive the last callback, you'll meet with all of us for a brief interview.

"Remember to please be yourselves today, and again, congratulations for making it to the audition day for Juilliard."

For the ballet technique class, they broke us up into four groups of twenty, and so began our day. Each class had two instructors, and as we each tried to showcase our technical strengths through barre work and center work. One by one, applicants were dismissed. At the end of this round, there are twenty of us left in total. They were right, three quarters were sent home.

The modern class is my most comfortable. I feel as though I breezed through my routine.

When the call comes for my solo, a wave of love washes over me. Somewhere, somehow I know that my mother is watching me. I can almost feel her with me now.

I decided to perform a ballet piece for my solo and as I stand before the panel, I see all eight of the faculty members look me over from head to toe. For my costume I'm wearing my bright blue pointe shoes, a bright blue tutu, black tights and leotard. I want to stand out and have applied bright blue eye shadow to make my eyes pop. I know my look is severe, and it's exactly as I have envisioned it.

"The title of this piece is the Dance of the Dragonfly. I choreographed it myself, and the composer is Alexander Ray-tchev. Thank you for your time, and I hope you enjoy this."

As I move to the middle of the stage, strike the first pose, and wait for the music, a sense of calm settles over me. I'm not nervous like I thought I would be, but instead I'm so happy.

The music begins and the sounds of the piano notes tinkle through the air. Visions of the eight people watching me disappear, and up on this stage, in this moment, I'm not dancing for them—I'm dancing for my mom. I know that she's so proud of me.

My solo, although it was just a little over a minute in length, was strong, elegant, and graceful. A smile lights up my face as I refocus and the panel comes back into view. I know that this is the best that I have ever felt.

Back in the auditorium, I watch the minutes tick by. Fewer and fewer applicants remain, and by the end of the solo round, there are only three girls and two guys left.

"Miss Rain, please come in and sit down. We want to thank you for the hard work you exemplified today, and congratulations for making it to the interview portion of the audition. Before we called you in, we each reviewed your pre-screen video, your essay, and we watched your solo again from today. We take this process very seriously and when we're talking to you, we want to be completely in the moment with you and only you.

"We have a series of five questions that we'll ask you that are basic and standard. From there, any further questions that might arise, we won't hesitate to ask. The goal here is not only to get to know you better and see if you're a good fit for Juilliard, but to see if Juilliard is a good fit for you. Do you have any questions?"

"No, ma'am."

"All right, let's get started. Most of the time if someone is to ask you to describe yourself you would say that you're a dancer, correct?"

I nod my head.

"Well, we want you to describe who you are, but leave the dancing out."

I look at each of the eight faculty members and feel my heart rate pick up. They don't waste any time trying to get to the core of me and of all the questions they could have asked, I don't know how to best answer this question.

"If I remove the dancing element of my life, I don't know who I am. I think that this is an evolving question because life changes so much, and so often that these changes can have an impact on who you are or who you think you are. If you had asked me this question one year ago, my answer would definitely be different than what it will be one year from now. Who am I today? I'm girl who is trying to follow her dreams." This must not have been the kind of answer they're looking for because each of them just stare at me. I straighten my back, pull down my shoulders, and smile while looking at each of them eye to eye.

"Perhaps you could elaborate on this a little bit more for us. What changes have taken place in your life to make you feel like you don't know who you are?"

"My mother died." All eight of them put their pens down and look up at me.

"When?"

"Two hundred and three days ago. August second."

"We are sorry to hear about the loss of your mother."

"Thank you." I reach up and rub my fingers across the dragonfly charm. Feeling the coolness of the metal reminds me that she's always with me.

"You didn't mention this in your essay. How come?"

Because, I'm not trying to play up the "woe is me" sympathy card.

"The purpose of the essay was for me to describe why I would be a good addition to your program. Bad and unfortunate things happen to people every day, and yes her death has had a profound impact on me, but it really has nothing to do with how I dance, why I dance, or why I will be an asset to your program." A few of them nod their heads.

"We see on your application that you attended our Summer Intensive Camp the summer before last. We were wondering why there was a year gap. Is it safe to assume that she's the reason why?"

"Yes, it is."

"This next question comes in two parts: First, we want to know why you choreographed your solo yourself and second, what does this piece mean to you?"

"After my mother died, my father thought that we needed to start over. He moved us from Denver to an island on the west coast of Florida. Honestly, I was a bit overwhelmed. My new school gave me the use of their multipurpose room, and after installing a barre, it had everything that I needed. The idea of looking for a new instructor for a dance that I needed to have prepared and ready in six months wasn't appealing to me. I'm confident enough in my own abilities, so I worked hard and pieced it together myself.

"The actual title of the music selection is 'May Night, Opus 27, Number 3: Dragonfly.' Did you know that the dragonfly is considered the ballerina of the insect world? The dragonfly, in almost every part of the world symbolizes transformation, change, and light. It's a change that comes in the perspective of self-realization, primarily in mental and emotional maturity, and the understanding of the deeper meaning of life. It's connected to happiness, lightness, and joy.

"My mother gave me this dragonfly charm and necklace right before she died. I hardly ever take it off. But she said to me, "Ali, every time you see a dragonfly remember to let go, and find some light and joy in your life." Dancing brings me joy and although I'm still working on discovering who I am, each day acceptance gets a little stronger and the light around me gets a little brighter."

None of them say anything to me. The pause in conversation lingers until one of them clears their throat, pulling the rest of them out of whatever train of thought each of them was having.

"How do the rest of your family and your friends feel about you applying to Juilliard? Do they support you and understand what type of commitment goes into a program like this?"

"Well, other than my father, I don't have any other family. He's had a rough time over this last year, and for the most part he does his own thing and I do mine. I'm a nineteen-year-old high school senior and I live by myself. I'm self-sufficient and I support myself on what I was given through her inheritance. I do have a couple of friends at this new school, but other than Drew, no one even knows that I'm here. This is my dream, and only I can make it happen."

"Who is Drew?"

"Oh, I guess you could say he's my boyfriend. His name is Drew Hale."

"The swimmer?"

I imagine that a look of shock registers on my face.

"Yes, do you know him?" I look over to the panel member who asked.

She chuckles. "No, I just know of him. My son is a swimmer also. I guess if anyone is going to understand how rigorous your training would become, it's him." I can't help but smile. Drew definitely understands me.

"Why Juilliard?"

"Because it's the best. I'm certain most of us answer this question the same way, but all I know, is that for as long as I can remember, it's where I've wanted to be. When I was eight years old, my mother took me to New York City and we went to see Swan Lake. As most eight-year-olds are, I was mesmerized. There was a brief biography about the principal ballerina in the playbill, and it said she had attended Juilliard. Right then and there I told my mom that was where I was going to go. Juilliard offers dancers what no other place can. The artistic training, the quality, technique, style, reputation and respect that graduates are given, it opens up a much larger world of opportunities for those of us who love to dance."

"And lastly, is there anything that you think we should know about you before we conclude today?"

"Thank you for allowing me the opportunity to be here today. Is it crazy if I say that I wasn't nervous at all? I loved being a part of your classes, going through this process, and just getting to dance. I guess if there's anything that I need to say it's that, as much as I want to be accepted to Juilliard, if I'm not, I'll be okay. It's like we talked about earlier; sometimes in life things go as we have planned and sometimes they don't. It's how we accept what's given to us, how we learn from it, and grow stronger. I hope that what you have seen from me today is enough, but if it wasn't, I'm still going to dance and I'll still find my way because I love it. My life won't be over if this opportunity doesn't work out. I'll just have to chasse off to a different direction." I smile and all eight of the panel members smile back at me.

DREW

HAVING TO SPEND the entire day in Miami, just wondering how it's going for her, is complete torture. I hate that I told her I wouldn't go with her today. I understand her need to want to do this by herself, but sometimes I think she forgets that she's not by herself anymore. She has me.

After lunch I wandered down by the water before returning back to our room. I didn't really want to be out anywhere, and I really didn't want to be in this room, but I have nowhere to go. I feel like a caged animal pacing back and forth.

Sometime close to dinner I finally hear the beep of the keycard and the door pushes open. Although it has only been a couple of hours since I've seen her, I would swear that she somehow became more beautiful.

She's still dressed post-dance, and she looks so good to me. Her hair is pulled into a tight bun on top of her head, and her makeup still looks professionally done. She's wearing a leotard underneath a large, long-sleeve, thin black T-shirt. I know she still has on her tights underneath those gray sweatpants, and a pair of flip-flops. She walks through the door, closes it, and leans back on it.

I'm frozen, trying to get a read on her mood, and the two of us just stare at each other, kind of like a face off. Slowly, but surely, a smile forms on her lips and it stretches from ear to ear. Her eyes crinkle a little in the corners. I can see that she's so happy, and I'm so glad. I had no idea how today was going to go for her, and I have been so nervous.

"Hey," I say to her. My palms are starting to sweat, and I am dying for her to say something.

"Hi." She starts laughing, drops her bag, and runs straight at me. I catch her as she jumps and wraps her arms around my neck, her legs around my waist, and just squeezes.

I'm lost in the feel of her, and the overall joy radiating off of her. I never want to put her down.

"I take it today went well." I chuckle.

She leans back with her hands on my shoulders and locks her eyes on mine. They're sparkling.

"I did the best I could do, and that's all that matters, right? I told them in the interview that no matter what happens

I'm still going to dance, and I am. Hopefully, it will be there, but if not, then it'll be somewhere. Thank you so much for coming with me here. I didn't think that I needed anyone, that I could do it on my own . . . but I can't tell you how much it meant to know that you would be here waiting for me when it was all over." She lets out a big sigh. "I couldn't wait to get back here."

I pull her back into me and hug her tightly. She is so amazing and so giving. I want to give her the world. I desperately want this for her because she deserves it so much.

"Ali, I will always be waiting for you. I'm so proud of you. I wish I could have been there to watch you. I know that you were perfect." Loosening my hold on her, I lean my forehead onto hers. "You have to be hungry. How about we order some room service and you tell me all about it."

"That sounds perfect, but first I need a shower. I am one gross girl." She slowly unwraps her legs from me, and I place her back on the floor.

"Is that an invitation?" I grin at her.

"Yes."

Woah . . . what? A moment of silence passes between us as I look into her face. I know how innocent she is, I know she's ready for more, and I also know that it's been me who's been holding back. Her putting the offer for more out there feels like a lifeline. I want more, crave more, and need more of her, but I in the back of my mind I hear myself saying, *full of firsts*. Her first time needs its own special memory, not one that is wrapped up with another.

In the time it takes me to make a decision, I see the sparkle of happiness in her eyes change to insecurity. She put herself out there and I'm taking too long.

I smile slowly at her and move one of my hands to the

middle of her back. Pulling her closer, her head tilts just enough for my lips to fall onto hers. She hugs me tighter and opens her mouth in response to mine.

I love kissing her and tasting her. Even after all these months, I still think she tastes like the afternoon sun and cotton candy. I run my tongue across her lower lip and she sighs into me.

I slowly begin to walk us towards the bathroom. I flip on the light and push her away from me gently.

"Ali, I'm not saying no. I'm just saying not here. Trust me when I say that you and I in the shower will happen, but when it does, we will not be in a hotel and it will not be after one of the biggest days of your life. This trip needs to be about you and the audition. When you and I finally happen, because we will, I want to be the only thing on your mind and the only thing that is making your blood race. That excitement and adrenaline will come from me and it will be about us and only us."

Her cheeks tinge pink and I love that I have this effect on her.

"Okay, Drew." She looks up at me through her eyelashes. The look is completely sultry and she doesn't even realize it.

I groan and kiss her again before I pull the door shut.

I walk back to the bed, and throw myself down. Staring at the ceiling, I take deep breaths to try and calm my overexcited body. I now know what it feels like to have her legs wrapped around me, and I can't wait until we get home and I can further explore this.

I hear the shower kick on and all I can think of is her in there wet and naked. Why did I say no? I could be joining her right now. Ughh.

I don't know how long I've been lying here, but eventually the shower kicks off and the bathroom door opens. I sit up and see Ali standing in the doorway with steam billowing out, wearing only a towel. Her hair is wet and hanging down her back, and her cute, little blue-painted toes are wiggling up and down.

"I didn't bring in any clothes with me," she says biting her bottom lip.

She's nervous and I can't look away from her.

"I forgot to order the food."

She giggles.

"That's okay. We can do that in a little bit," she says.

I get up off the bed and slowly we walk toward each other.

"I'm not gonna lie. You partially wet and in a towel, is really sexy."

She looks up at me through her eyelashes again and I can't take it anymore. My over stimulated body needs to touch her, taste her, and feel her all over.

Slowly, I grab my shirt from behind my head and pull it off.

Her eyes grow wide and I chuckle at her.

Gently, I slide the shirt over her head and she pulls her arms through. She's so small that my T-shirt falls to mid-thigh on her. I grab the bottom of the towel and yank. It falls to the floor around her feet.

I'm at a loss for words seeing her standing in front of me wearing my shirt, knowing that there is nothing on underneath.

Turning us around, we walk over to the bed and slowly I lie her down on her back. She widens her legs and I step between them while running my eyes all over her. I can see her perfect outline underneath my shirt.

Slowly my hands slide up over her thighs, hip bones,

stomach, ribcage, breasts, and collarbone. I've never openly felt her up before, but tonight there's no way I'm keeping my hands off of her.

Bending over her, I place my forearms next to her head to keep some of my weight off. While resting my forehead on hers, her eyelashes brush against my cheeks. She's breathing a little harder than normal, but then again, so am I.

"Like I said," I whisper across her lips. "This trip is about you. Tonight is going to be about you too. Seeing you here like this, there's no way I can keep my hands off of you. I'm going to take my time with you, explore you, build you up until you are burning, and then watch as that burn turns into a fire. I want to see your beautiful skin blush from head to toe. You, just you . . . sound all right?"

"More than all right. Please, Drew . . ."

With that, no more words are said. I run my tongue across the seam of her lips. She opens up for me and wraps her legs around my waist pulling me more on top of her. My hips are perfectly aligned with her and just the slightest pressure against her feels so good. She moves her hands from my shoulders, wraps them under my arms, and begins running them up and down my back. Her hands and her fingers leave trails of fire over my skin. It feels so good to be touched by her. I pull back slightly and look down into her beautiful face.

Our breaths mix together, and her heart pounds through her chest and into mine. I move my hands and wrap them around both sides of her head, brushing my thumbs across her cheekbones.

This girl owns me and she doesn't even realize it.

Returning my mouth to hers, I take in her bottom lip between my teeth.

Her fingers dip inside the waistband of my jeans. I can't

help but groan, and I push into her a little more. Her hands fall to the front of my waist and she tugs on my belt. It comes undone and then, one by one, she pops open the buttons on my jeans. After the last one, I feel her thumbs hook into the waist and she pushes them down. I kick off the jeans and this leaves me in nothing but a pair of boxer briefs. Not only can she feel the effect that she's having on me, now she can see it.

Her hand gets a little bold and brushes across the front of me. I jerk at the unexpectedness of this.

"Sorry." She looks past my shoulder at the wall. I never want her to feel self-conscious when it comes to us. I lean down and touch my lips to hers.

"Don't be." I take her hand and run it up and down me so she can feel what she's doing to me.

She lets out a small gasp and I groan at the sensation.

"But like I said, tonight is about you." I remove her hand, pull it up over her head, and clamp down on her wrist. My weight is fully on her now and she feels so good underneath me.

My free hand grabs her calf and I wrap her leg back around my waist while running my hand up her bare leg and backside. Her skin is so soft and so all mine.

The T-shirt has shifted up and from the waist down she is naked. It is almost too much for me as I can feel heat pouring off of her while she rocks her hips into me. I want to strip off the rest of our clothes and feel every bit of her skin against mine.

My mouth leaves hers and my tongue trails over her jaw to her neck. She lets out a moan and I release her wrist. All of her fingers tangle in my hair and around the back of my head. I can't help but move lower and run my hands across her perfect chest. The T-shirt is thin and her nipples can be seen straight through it. While I massage one, I suck the other one into my mouth, T-shirt and all. She moans and arches into me.

I shift my weight to the side, and while I still enjoy lavishing her with my mouth, I slide my other hand down her stomach and between her legs. What I find causes me to pause and I look up into her eyes. She smirks knowingly at me.

"Did you forget? I'm a dancer." Ahh, now I understand. She is completely bare and smooth. I drop my forehead onto her chest and moan. I've actually never seen a girl bare before, and although tonight is not going to be that night, I know it's coming soon.

I palm all of her and the heel of my hand presses lightly into her. She gasps and I smile while I begin moving my fingers. I know how to make her feel what she wants to feel, and as I slowly watch her come undone underneath me, I can't help but think that I have been given the most perfect gift of all . . . her.

She is so responsive, trusting, and open to me. I watch as she holds her breath, closes her eyes, and her flawless skin flushes pink. She's gorgeous and although I haven't told her . . . I'm so in love with her.

ALI

SOMETIME AFTER DARK Drew and I finally fall asleep. We did end up ordering room service, but we never made it out of the bed. By ten in the morning, we're packed and on the road home. Both of us are quiet this morning, but it's a comfortable quiet, and for that I'm thankful. All I want to do is sit here and relive every moment of last night over and over again.

When I walked into the room after my audition and saw Drew standing there, I felt at home. It was a feeling I haven't felt in so long that warmth washed over me from head to toe. It's interesting how easily that concept switches from being an emotional attachment to a person from a place. Maybe that's a part of maturity.

As children we're given a home, or a house to live in, and it provides a sense of constant comfort and safety. Throughout life, circumstances happen and the idea of home shifts to wherever a sense of belonging occurs. I feel like I belong with Drew and no matter where we are or what we're doing, I know that if I have him, I'm home.

My thoughts drift off to my dad. I suddenly feel very sad for him. I can only assume that what he and my mother had in each other is what I feel for Drew. To lose this kind of home would be devastating. A moment of insecurity washes over me as I think about what's going to happen over the next few months. Drew and I have never really talked about where he wants to go to college and this makes me nervous. I push this thought away. I can worry about all of this another day.

Looking over at Drew, he looks back at me. He gives me a small one-sided smile, squeezes my knee, and returns to concentrating on the road.

I can't help but admire how gorgeous he is. He's wearing a baseball hat. He says it's his lucky one and he brought it for me. His dark hair curls out a little underneath it, and he has on a pair of aviator sunglasses. I think it's cute that we wear the same sunglasses.

We keep the top up on the Jeep for the drive back, but we decide to still roll the windows down. I'm not going to lie,

February in Florida is beautiful. I do love the snow, but after living here, small doses of cold just might be better. "Cruise" by Florida Georgia Line comes onto the radio, and I smile at the irony.

Drew's thumb starts brushing back and forth across my knee and I blush at how it makes my stomach twist. The things he did to me last night and how he handled me—it was so much more than I ever imagined.

I can't even count how many times over the last couple of months he has slept with me at my house. Granted I've always been very aware of his physicality, but nothing prepared me for the onslaught of feelings I would have from just the little amount of skin-to-skin contact that we had. I thought that I had come to terms with him just sleeping next to me in a pair of boxer briefs, but intimacy lines were never crossed and I guess he became comfortable to me. The two of us wrapping ourselves around each other has become more like sleeping with my favorite pillow and blanket. Now, I don't know . . . things feel kind of different.

My eyes drift shut as I remember the feel of him when he laid us down on the bed. He's never laid directly on top of me before, and being underneath him and all his weight . . . I loved it. The feel of him settled between my legs—I wanted to keep them wrapped around him indefinitely.

"Why are you blushing?"

I look over at him and my blush deepens.

"Now you have to tell me." He smirks at me.

"Fine, I'm mentally replaying what your hands did to me last night." I can't see his eyes, but a smile breaks out across his face that shows he's completely pleased with himself.

"Hmmm. Well, I'm thinking that instead of mentally replaying it, sometime soon we can reenact it instead."

His hand slowly slides up my leg and stops at the top of my thigh. His fingers squeeze a little and I look over at him.

"You okay?" he asks.

"I'm more than okay, and I think that sounds like a great idea." I smile at him and wrap my hand over his, linking our fingers together. "Thanks again for coming with me. I know that you and I don't really talk about us, but it's important to me to that you know how much you mean to me, which is a lot. You'll never know what you being there for me this weekend meant. Thank you." Silence fills the cab of the Jeep.

"Ali . . ." His fingers gently squeeze my leg again. "There was nowhere else in this world that I would've rather been, than with you. Thank you for letting me come with you. I'm so proud of you."

Tears well up in my eyes. He'll never know either how much I needed to hear that.

ALI

IT'S BEEN A little over a month since my audition in Miami, and every day for the past two weeks I have been stalking my email account and the mailbox. I know from the massive amount of internet research that I've done on other people's audition process, that acceptance letters are usually received by the first of April. Every day I get more and more anxious.

School seems to be dragging by as well. The only bright side to being there every day is that I get to see Drew.

Leila and I are standing by my locker when he wanders over and stands in front of me. My senses are flooded, and as I breathe him in, my eyes wander and look him over from head to toe. He looks so good to me, and he wears T-shirts and jeans like no one else can. He's a foot taller than me, so by the time I make it up to his eyes, he smirks at me knowingly.

"So, a couple of us were thinking of going to Mainlanders Saturday night. Do you want to go with me?" Out of the corner of my eye, Leila rocks up onto the front of her toes and she smiles from ear to ear. I know she loves this place and any chance she gets, she goes.

"The dance club?" I ask him.

"Yeah. Beau and a few others are organizing a night out and I figured if you wanted to go, you could ride with me."

Of course I would want to ride with him. I want to go everywhere and do everything with him.

"So, you are definitely going?" I ask him.

"If you are." Drew has told me repeatedly that if at all possible, he would never give up one of our Saturday nights. This makes me smile because I know that he's saying he wants to be with me, no matter where.

Leila is watching us closely; her eyes are bouncing back and forth between the two of us.

"Okay, I'll go."

Drew smiles at me and it lights up my insides.

"Perfect. I'll text you later when I'm going to pick you up." He says this for Leila's sake, but I know that in approximately six hours after he finishes his swim practice he'll be all mine for the weekend.

"All right."

He winks at me and then strolls off for his next class.

"Girl, sooner or later, you are going to have to spill it," Leila says.

I keep my mouth shut and smile at her.

Saturday night we walk into the dance club, and as I take in the scene before me, I squeeze Drew's arm with excitement. I never allow myself to go out and do fun things. I've stayed so true to my routine for so long, and now that the audition is over, it's time to let loose.

This club is in what looks like an old warehouse. It has a

really great vibe. I can see why Leila likes it. The entire inside is wide open with second and third level balconies that wrap around the perimeter of the building. The ground floor is for eighteen and up, the second floor is twenty-one and overs, and I think that someone said the third floor is broken up into VIP sections. All of the balconies around each level overlook onto the main dance floor. I love it here already.

The bass is vibrating off of the walls, through the floor, and I can feel it move through me. A mash-up of "Shot Me Down" by David Guetta comes on and I immediately grab Leila. She'd made her way over to us as soon as we'd arrived. I grab her by the hand and lead her out onto the dance floor. I know I should've asked if anyone else wanted to dance, including Drew, but the music has taken over me. It's like an invisible force, pulling at me, and I just can't help myself.

The lights are low, the dance floor is kind of dark, and strobe lights are bouncing between us. Strategically, in each corner of the dance floor, there are large boxes of varying height. Karrie joins us, and in the corner closest to the guys, who have posted up at a few empty tables, we each stand on a box and dance for the next two hours. The music pulses through me and I am completely in my element. No one seems to mind that we're up here for so long, so we dance away and enjoy being in the spotlight. It feels so good to dance freely, and be unrehearsed.

Eventually, I need some water. I look over to Drew and see him talking to Beau and a few other guys that I don't know at one of the high top tables. He must feel my gaze because his eyes leave Beau and lock onto me. I was a little concerned that he might be bored, but the guys' tables have been pretty busy. They seem to know a lot of people here tonight. He smiles at me, while the people around him keep talking. I feel like I've just stolen one hundred percent of his attention, and I'm not ashamed to admit I like it.

Walking up to him, he hands me a water and wipes the sweat off of my face. I laugh because I'm certain I look like a complete hot mess.

"So, are you done with that box yet?" he asks me teasingly.

"Why? Are you jealous?"

He laughs and that sound is so much better than any music anywhere.

"Maybe . . . it's my turn." Drew takes the water, puts it on the table, and drags me out to the dance floor.

It never even occurred to me that Drew would want to dance with me, but being on this crowded dance floor, under the lights, and pushed up next to him—I am beside myself with happiness. I know other girls are looking at him. I mean, how could they not? He's tall and shockingly handsome, but he's here with me, and in this moment, I feel special. I feel like I belong to him and he belongs to me. I'm surprised to see how well Drew's moves are and with his hands all over me, if we weren't standing in a room full of people, I just might have stripped him down and had my way with him.

About an hour later, Leila grabs me by the hand and calls for a bathroom break. As we push through the door, she spins around and her eyes are blazing.

"Holy crap, Ali! What is going on?" She walks over to the paper towels and grabs a couple for us.

I begin wiping my face off when I ask her, "What do you mean?"

"You know exactly what I mean! You and Drew Hale! I mean, come on, I knew that the two of you had become friends. I even wondered after that kiss at New Years, but seriously, friends do not dance like that!" I can't tell if she's mad or excited.

"Dance like what? We were just dancing." I smile at her.

"Dancing! Honey, it looked like the two of you could have been doing a lot more than that. You know, I thought it was a little strange when he said he wanted you to ride with him, but the way he's been looking at you tonight." She lets out a long breath and fans herself with the paper towels.

"How has he been looking at me?"

She stops fanning and tilts her head to the side to examine me.

"You like him, don't you?" I see the corner of her mouth twitch; she wants to smile.

"It's not like that. How was he looking at me?" I have to know. It can't just be me that's the only one who's this affected.

"I think it is like that, and he was looking at you as if you were the only other person here. He's been watching you all night, and I'm not the only one to notice."

I don't know what to say to that. He spent most of the first part of the evening with Beau and their friends. I didn't feel like he was paying hardly any attention to me at all.

"And for the record, in all the years that I've known Drew, I've never seen him dance before . . . with anyone."

Knowing how important dance is to me, this warms my heart that he would step out of his comfort zone and do something he knows I love. I'm radiating on the inside.

"Leila, it's not what you think."

She walks over to the sink, washes her hands, and then throws the paper towels away. She looks up at me through the mirror and I can see her emotions shift. She's no longer excited by this conversation. She's starting to get irritated.

"Why don't you tell me what I should be thinking then? Are you with him?" She turns back around and her hands land on her hips.

"It's complicated." *And as much as I love you, it isn't any of your business.*

"What do you mean it's complicated? I thought we were friends, like really good friends. Why can't you tell me?" Her irritation now turns into anger.

"We are really good friends. It's just . . . I don't want to talk about him."

"I don't understand."

That makes two of us. How can I explain to her what Drew and I are when I don't even know myself?

"I'm sorry." This comes out more like a question than an actual apology.

"I don't even know what to say to you right now. You never really tell me anything and I honestly don't know very much about you at all. Some friendship we have here, Ali." Her lips press into a thin line and she pushes her hair back off away from her face.

"Leila, please. We are friends." My hands start to shake. Next to Drew, Leila is really my only other friend here and I hate that I'm upsetting her. I should just tell her something.

"Maybe, but you know, I thought we were better friends than this. I guess not. Whatever. Keep your secrets. Just re- member, I told you on the very first day that every guy wants to be them and every girl wants to be with them. You really are no different than all the others. Regardless of what you say or don't say, after this weekend and what everyone has seen, you have officially lumped yourself among all of the other Hale whores. Hope you're happy." She shakes her head at me and then turns around and storms out.

I don't know what to say, and I'm shocked by what she said. Am I just like all of the others? I don't think that I am, but then again, he's never told me differently, and it isn't like he's gone public with how he feels about me. Maybe I've been wrong.

I walk into the closest stall and close the door. I lower the lid and sit down. After everything that Leila just said, I need a moment before I head back out there.

I went from feeling the happiest that I have been in so long, to feeling the worst and most confused.

The bathroom door bangs open and a couple of girls come in laughing.

"Oh my gosh, did you see how good Drew looks tonight?"

It's Cassidy. I should have known. When did she get here, or has she been here all along? The hairs prick up on the back of my neck because I have a feeling I'm not going to like where her conversation is going.

"I did. I also saw that he seems pretty into that Ali girl," says Lisa.

Well, if Lisa saw this, maybe Leila wasn't too far off when she said that he's only looking at me tonight. A small smile crosses my lips.

"Whatever. You know as well as I do that he really isn't into her. He's using her like he's used all of the others."

What is Cassidy talking about? I've known him for six months and I've never seen or heard him talk about anyone else. She always seems so convinced that he's just using me, is he?

"I don't really ever remember there being others. If there were, he certainly didn't bring them out in public like he does her." I'm starting to like Lisa more and more.

"Oh, trust me. There are always others. He's Drew Hale. He can't help it. I'm pretty certain that this Little Miss Ali isn't his only side fling. It doesn't matter, though. Our time is finally coming and I can't wait to spend tomorrow with him. If everything works out this weekend, things will finally be as they should be."

Wait! She has plans to spend time with him?

"What time are you invited over?" Lisa asks.

Invited over? To his house?

"Ten. His mom thought it would be nice to have brunch together."

My stomach drops and I brace myself against the sides of the stall so I don't accidentally fall on the floor. I've never been invited to his house, and after all this time, I haven't met his mom either. He's never even asked me to.

"Well, that sounds amazing. I can't wait to hear all of the details." Leave it to Lisa to fuel her friend.

"Oh, you know I'll share. I'm hoping for a repeat of last summer."

Both girls break out into laughter and I feel like I'm going to throw up. I don't know why I ever thought that I could compete against someone like her. She's always going to be the type the guy brings home and I'm just going to be the one they spend the night with.

Tears fill my eyes. My heart is breaking. I just want to go home. Home . . . and here I thought that mine was him. Stupid me.

DREW

WATCHING ALI ON the dance floor tonight, it's official. Game over. Everyone needs to know that she is mine. She has always respected my need for discretion, but I can't do it anymore. I'm in love with this girl, and I'm not being fair to her.

When she walked out of her house tonight in that little black dress and those tall heels, I have never seen anything sexier. I think my jaw actually dropped open. Beau jabbed me with his elbow and smirked at me knowingly.

I hadn't really planned on doing any dancing tonight, but there was no way I was letting my beautiful girl come here and be hit on all night. Once she came down off of that box, I knew it would be game on. Random guys have been circling around the girls and watching them all night.

Most people have figured out or at least they suspect by now that she and I are together, but that doesn't mean I still don't get nervous about losing her. The only one who doesn't seem to have gotten the memo is Cassidy.

When I saw Cassidy walk in tonight with Lisa, I instantly scowled. I want Ali to have a good night out, and that girl is nothing but trouble for us when she's around. Shit, just the thought of her makes my blood boil.

I finally decide to make my way over toward the bathroom and I see Cassidy and Lisa leaving. I duck behind a group of people and am thankful that they don't spot me.

Ali walks out of the bathroom a few minutes later and the fire that was in her eyes is gone. Her head hangs down, her shoulders are slumped over, and her arms are wrapped around her stomach.

"Hey, you okay?" I walk up to her and wrap my arm around her, bringing her in close to me.

"Sure, I'm fine." Fine. Girl code for no.

"Did they say anything to you?"

She looks up at me and I can see so many emotions swimming in her eyes, mostly hurt, and I don't understand.

"No, but the question is, do you need to say something to me?" Huh?

"What do you mean?" She needs to tell me what happened because I need to fix this.

"Apparently nothing. Drew, I'm ready to go home."

Something is definitely going on with her, and I'm going to find out what it is. I was ready to go before we even walked in, so this sounds good to me. I take her by the hand, lace our fingers together, and we walk over to the table where Beau and Grant are standing to let them know we're leaving.

"Hey, we're out."

"Ah, but it's so early," Beau says. He then looks over to Ali and his eyes narrow. He sees it, too.

"Dude, we both got up a lot earlier than you today and probably will tomorrow also." Ali flinches. I don't understand.

"Whatever, man. I'll catch you later." He looks over at Ali and nods his head, "Tiny . . . and you two drive safe."

Beau and I bump forearms and I turn Ali to walk toward the door. I can't wait to get her out of here.

We pass Leila as we leave the table and she gives Ali a look of apology. Ali drops her eyes to the ground and pulls my hand to keep us walking. I shoot Leila a questioning look, and Leila's eyes fill with tears. What the hell is going on!

Out of nowhere Cassidy slides up next to me.

Ugh.

We stop walking, and I pull Ali behind me, never letting go of her hand. This girl seriously needs to stay away from us, and I don't want her anywhere near Ali.

"Are you leaving?" she asks with this sickeningly sweet fake tone.

I don't even acknowledge her question. It really isn't any of her business. I can see that she's getting flustered, but she continues on.

"Well, that's too bad. I was hoping to get to dance with you some tonight. No worries, I guess. We'll have plenty of time together tomorrow." A self-satisfied smile slowly stretches across her face. She and I both know what she is attempting to do, dropping that little piece of information.

My teeth clench and Ali pulls her hand out of mine.

My mom dropped this little bomb on Beau and I before we left tonight. I haven't had a chance to talk to her about this yet and she's not going to be happy. I feel her tense up behind me.

Shooting Cassidy a glare that says, *we're done,* I push past her, and pull Ali along.

Once we're outside, the cool air slams into me, calming me down.

"Ali."

She keeps right on walking into the parking lot and over to her car. She doesn't even look at me.

"Please stop." I'm not past begging if I have to.

She stops next to the car, but never turns around. "Drew, like I said inside, I just want to go home." She wraps her arms around her middle and looks at the ground.

I pull her keys out of my pocket and click open the doors. She pulls on the handle of the passenger door and I hold it open for her as she climbs in and buckles up.

"Will you let me explain?" She has to hear the pleading in my voice.

Her back straightens, she holds her head higher, and gives me a look that screams, *I have dignity and pride in myself.*

"You have nothing to explain. You don't owe me an explanation, a reason, or anything really. It's not like you and I were really ever together. We're just friends." She looks out the front window after she says this, and my chest starts to ache in that familiar spot.

"That's not true and you know it," I say quietly.

"Do I?" She looks me straight in the eyes and I swear I can see myself reflect back in them. They're glassy, and this is entirely my fault. "I just want to go home."

Letting out a deep sigh, I close her door and walk around to the driver's side.

The drive home is mostly silent. I can hear her breathing and she taps her foot on the ground.

"Ali, my father and Cassidy's are business associates. He invited them over for brunch." I need her to know that this is not my doing. I did not invite her over.

"That's nice. Tomorrow is supposed to be a beautiful day, so the weather will be perfect." She still won't look at me.

"Please don't be like this."

"Like what? How should I be?" Her voice picks up a little. Even though I'm looking at the road, I know the minute her eyes focus on me. "It's not like I'm your girlfriend. I mean, no one really knows about me. You keep me a secret. I've never been invited to your home, or to meet your parents, much less have brunch. Cassidy and Leila both say I have a new nickname. Apparently, I'm now a part of the elite club known as the Hale whores. Please, please, Drew, tell me how I'm supposed to be, because everything I thought was true about us now seems to be a lie."

"First off, Leila called you a whore?" I'm shocked at what she just said to me. I haven't heard that expression in years, and to have my Ali called this makes my blood race.

"Does it matter?" She sounds so defeated.

"Yes, it matters to me! And second, you and I are not a lie. I have never lied to you. In fact, I've told and shared more with you than I have anyone else. Ever!"

She doesn't say anything back to me. I know when she gets like this that I should let her be, so I do.

We pull into the driveway, I turn off the car, and the two of us just sit there. I hate that she's hurting. I should have told her about the brunch first thing when I saw her. Next to swimming, Ali, Beau, and Matt are all I have in my life. I can't lose her. I don't know what to say to her.

"I didn't invite her over. Think about this, please. I am with you. Only you. I asked you on our first date if you wanted to be mine, and you said yes. You became mine and I became yours. That's the way it has been for the last six months. You know this." I should tell her everything else, right here and right now. I should tell her all about my dad, about my life, and how I feel about her. Then there would be no questions and she wouldn't be hurting.

"Cassidy and Lisa keep telling me that you're using me like you used all of the others. She also says that I'm probably not the only girl in the picture right now. It makes sense when I think about it. Why else would you keep me a secret? I mean, it kind of bothered me a little before, but now that I think about it, it bothers me a lot. I'm worth more than this. You may have had your bevy of Hale whores in the past, clearly there have been enough to make this some kind of a thing, but I'm not now nor will I ever be one. You told me in the very beginning that you would never hurt me. Well, I guess you were wrong. Have fun at your brunch." With that, Ali gets out of the car and runs into her house.

I'm not sure how long I sit in the car. It's Saturday night, and I'm supposed to be with her. Those are our nights. If being in her car is the closest that I'm going to get, this is where I'm going to stay for a while. I lean my head back against the head-rest. I need to clear my thoughts and pull myself together. I've never used anyone or done anything with anyone that wasn't mutual. That name "Hale whores" is so blown out of propor-tion. She doesn't even realize that, and that name applies most-ly to Beau and not me. How can she think there's someone else? I know how—I've never told her differently.

It never fails. The minute I think that things are good, he shows up. My mind starts turning and the demon in my head starts speaking.

It's always going to be your fault. You're pathetic and worthless. Do you see the people that you say you love? They're hurting because of you. You hurt people. No one is ever going to want you. Why would they? No one is ever going to love you. You should feel ashamed of yourself.

Anxiety sets in. I lie my head down on the steering wheel and grip on to my hair. I try to control my breathing, but it won't slow down and my heart is racing. Sweat drips down my face, heat radiates off of my back, and my entire body shakes. She's hurting because of me and she's never going to love me.

The driver side door opens and Beau drops down so he's level with me.

"Hey, big bro. It's all right." He wraps his hand behind the back of my neck and pulls my forehead to his.

I can't stop shaking. I grip onto his shoulders and squeeze.

"Ali . . ." It's all I can get out.

"You need to calm down and relax," he says to me.

Together we breathe and the minutes tick by. Eventually, my fingers loosen on him and my heart starts to slow down.

"How did you know I was here?" I say hoarsely.

"I didn't. The parking lights on the car are on, and I was coming over to turn them off."

"Oh." I guess since I never opened the door, they never shut off.

"Have you been sitting here this entire time?"

I nod my head.

"It's been a while since I've seen you have one of these." He squeezes my neck.

"I know. It's just . . ."

"Yeah, I know. I heard Cassidy bragging. Listen, she'll calm down. Just give her a little space, and then in the next day or so just talk to her. It might be time to tell her."

"I never wanted to tell anyone. I don't know if I can."

"Why not?" Beau pulls back a little from me and looks me in the face.

"What if he's right? What if once she knows everything, she won't want me? I love her."

"I know you do, and you know he's wrong. You're everything, Drew. You always have been to me, Matt, and to mom too. You need to stop listening to him because we love you and I'm pretty sure there's a Tiny upstairs that loves you too."

"What if she doesn't?" I've just verbalized my biggest fear and a shudder rips through my body.

"Well, there's only one way to find out," he says quietly.

I know he's right, but the thought of life without her makes me feel lost.

"I hate him." Just thinking about him, my stomach hurts.

"Me too. Come on, let's go to bed. The sooner tomorrow gets here, the sooner you can talk to her." He's right again.

"All right."

Beau claps me on the shoulder and I climb out of the car.

"You've always got me. You know that right?" Beau asks.

At the moment, I can't say anything. I just pull him into a hug. We've never been very affectionate toward each other, but right now I can't hug him tight enough.

"You too." I breathe out.

Chapter Fifteen

ALI

I KNOW I shouldn't be watching his house, but I can't help it. Cassidy and her family arrived three hours ago and they still haven't left. Yes, I'm watching the clock, too.

Around 1:30 the door opens and Drew comes out holding her hand. My breath catches in my throat and I think my heart skips a beat.

Drew wears a pair of gray dress slacks and a white button-down shirt tucked in. He looks so handsome, and seeing him with her, I again realize that he's way out of my league.

Cassidy couldn't be ugly if she tried. I think that's one of the things about her that hurts so much. I'll never understand why he isn't with her. Every other guy at school seems to want her. She's breathtakingly beautiful.

In typical Cassidy form, she's wearing a white strapless dress that shows off not only her perfect form, but her perfect golden skin, too. She completes the outfit with a pair of gorgeous black patent leather heels and black and white jewelry to match. I couldn't look like her even if I tried.

Beau, Matt, and both sets of parents wander out to the porch while Drew takes Cassidy to their car. They're all giving them some space and I can't grasp what I'm seeing.

Drew leans over to whisper something in her ear and her hands reach up to hold onto his upper arms. Every part of me shakes.

I can't get any indication as to what he says to her, but when she tucks her face into him and he wraps his arms around her, I feel like my world is officially crashing in.

For months, I've been ignoring every little comment that Cassidy gives me. Even last night at the club when she again said that he was just using me, I blew it off. Yes, it hurt. But I've been trying to give Drew the benefit of the doubt. With the amount of time that we've spent together, there's just no way.

I know I shouldn't be watching them, but I can't turn away. Watching Cassidy's face as she snuggles into him, I see it switch from sad, to a smirk, and then to devastation. I'm confused by this, but eventually, she lifts her face to him and he leans down to kiss her. *He's kissing her!* It isn't a thorough kiss, but there is a pause in it that makes it seem intimate.

Drew looks up with a somber expression and glances over at my house. All the lights are off, so he won't know that I'm standing here, but at this point it doesn't matter anymore. I look over at the parents and three of them are smiling. Drew's mother, and both Beau and Matt are frowning at this little public display of affection.

Drew backs away from her and scowls at her, just before Cassidy slides into her parent's car as they step off the porch to leave. I have officially seen everything that I ever need to see.

I close my eyes and tears drip down my face.

Twice now in a year, I have had my heart broken. I'm so angry with myself and I feel so naïve for falling for him. After everything that had happened last summer, I never thought I would find someone else to love or to love me in return. Even though we've never declared love to each other, he had to of known. I feel so stupid.

Slowly, I close the plantation shutters and walk up the stairs to my bed.

Looking around my room, I find his T-shirt and pull it on. It still smells like him, and no matter how much he's hurt me, right now I need to feel close to him. I need to feel close to someone because really, I have no one.

The silence in the house echoes. This has become the theme song of my life.

At some point I fall asleep, which was good. The more I stay in dreamland the better. Around eight o'clock, I hear a knock at my balcony doors.

"Ali?" It's Drew.

I'm surprised he came over, but then again I guess he has to end it with me at some point. Knowing what he's going to say to me, I burrow further under the blankets. I'm not ready yet for him to tell me that I'm not good enough for him, so I don't answer the door.

"Come on, Ali, I need to talk to you."

My heart pounds in my chest. As if it isn't bad enough that he's breaking up with me, it dawns on me that I'm losing my best friend too.

"All right, Ali, I get it. I know that you're still upset, but at some point we do need to talk. I need to tell you about the brunch this morning, as well as so many other things."

I know what he needs to tell me and honestly, I just don't

want to hear it. About five minutes go by and I think that he's left, but he's still standing on the other side of the door.

"Ali, I have your car keys from last night. I'm going to leave them here on the doormat so you have them to get to school tomorrow. I missed talking to you today." And then he leaves. Each step he takes going down the balcony steps feels like a hammer pounding into my heart, and each step that he takes away from me feels like I'm breaking even more.

I roll onto my stomach and the tears return. I cry for hours. I cry for the memories that I have with him and I cry for the memories I'm pretty certain I'll never make with him. I can't understand why he would spend so much time with me, and then leave me to be with someone else.

What did I do wrong? I wasn't clingy. I wasn't needy. I never asked for more of him than I thought he was willing to give. I'm at a loss. If I ever do find someone someday who wants to love me, I need to know what it is so I don't do it again.

DREW

I DIDN'T GET any sleep. I hate knowing that I hurt her. I do understand why she feels this way too. If she had some guy that she had a history with over and their family too, I would be hurt. I get it. I've never even invited her over to meet my parents and here Cassidy and I are going to have to act like the happy couple.

I texted Ali good morning, but she never got back to me. The weather was supposed to be nice, but instead it's gray and I can tell a cold front is about to blow in. The water is choppy and there's no way I'm going to attempt to swim in it. Rip tides are always stronger and it wouldn't be safe. I'm sure she still went out for a run. If she wasn't so upset with me, I would have tried to have gone with her.

Dad is acting more crazy than usual this morning too. He's trying to come across as happy, but there's that edge to his tone that we all know so well.

Several times he mentions how happy he is that the Meyers family is coming over. How he had met Cassidy and thinks that she's a lovely girl. Beau and I both know what he's trying to say and at one point, a look of apology crosses Beau's face.

Dad doesn't know about Ali. Mom does, but she isn't going to say anything. We've all done a great job at keeping this little bit of information away from him. He's a very judgmental person, and although I'm certain that he would be pleased with who her father is, this connection wouldn't benefit him in any way and he would make his disapproval of her known rather quickly.

I look out the window and over to her house. It looks dark and quiet like always. I should be spending the day with her. She shouldn't have to be by herself. I see her front door open and she walks out to check the mail. Still after all these months, when I see her, she takes my breath away. Her hair is down and the wind whips it around. She glances up over to my house once, but that's it. A frown is on her beautiful face. She looks tired, and I feel my chest ache because I know that this is my fault.

She stops in front of the mailbox and stares at it. I'm not sure what she sees, but she doesn't move. Eventually, she opens the box, grabs the mail, and turns to head back inside. I can see her flipping through the pieces when she sees one that makes her stop. I watch her flip the envelope over and then back to the front. She slowly walks back into the house, and I know that's probably the last I'll see her today.

It doesn't take me longer than five minutes to realize once Cassidy and her parents walk through the door, what her crazy behavior has been about over the last couple of months. Both of our fathers are trying to push us together so they can use this relationship between us as leverage for business. My guess is that her father has been pushing her for months to get closer to me to get closer to my dad. Why didn't she try to explain all this? I would have understood. But then again, no one knows how controlling my father is, so maybe she thinks I won't understand.

My father wants her father as a business partner too. I know he thinks he'll get a better deal if we're dating, but there's no way.

When they're getting ready to leave, I see the silent plea in Cassidy's eyes and I feel sorry for her. I take a hold of her hand and walk her down to their car.

"Ah, look, Jim, aren't they so cute together?" My mother is even playing into this fake scene. I glance over to Beau. He's angry, but I also need to do this for him. Dad wants this, and I can't let Beau suffer because of it.

I look back at Cassidy and hate every moment of this. I lean forward so I can whisper in her ear.

"I get what's happening here. Don't worry. I'll play the part, but you need to understand that this means absolutely nothing, and I do mean nothing. I hate every moment of this, and you need to know that."

She flinches a little at the harshness of my words.

"But it could." Her eyes gaze up at me and I can see the longing in them.

Why this girl is so hopeful for me? I will never understand. I haven't been nice to her in months.

"No. You know that I'm dating Ali. She's my girlfriend and has been for almost six months."

Her hands land on my arms and shock registers across her face.

"What! But why? Just think about how much better our lives could be if we're together." Hurt is laced in her tone.

"Better for who? Better for our parents? Maybe, but certainly not for me, and I can guarantee you, certainly not better for you. And to be honest, why I'm dating Ali is none of your business."

She briefly closes her eyes and then they open and lock on to me. "You're wrong. My life would definitely be better if you were in it."

"Cassidy, I can be your friend, but I'll never be anything more. You seriously need to let this go. I'm sorry if this upsets you, but I've been clear on this matter for a very long time."

The sadness on her face is evident and she tucks her head into my neck on the opposite side of our parents. I know she doesn't want her father to see her. I really do understand her in so many ways. I put my hand on her lower back and pull her in closer to me.

"Look, I get it. I'm counting down the days until I'm out of here. So to make both of our lives a little easier, I'm going to kiss you goodbye. But . . . you need to remember everything that I said. It will mean nothing." She's trying to act relaxed, but I can feel the tension rolling off of her.

She looks up at me with defeat evident in her eyes.

"Okay, Drew."

I lean over and put my lips on hers. Honestly, after kissing Ali, I never thought that I would have to kiss another girl again. My stomach rolls and my heart aches. The kiss is brief and very innocent in the grand scheme of things, but it serves its purpose and I know that she and Beau will both be off the hook for a while.

I glance over to Ali's house. The lights are still off and I can only pray she didn't see any of this.

"Thank you." She says, while opening the door and sitting down in the back seat of the car.

Cassidy's facial expression is cool and triumphant. Her general disposition has done a one-eighty and an uneasiness settles over me. Why do I get the feeling that I was just played?

Chapter Sixteen

ALI

MY EYES ARE swollen and my head pounds when I wake up this morning. I turn off the alarm clock and roll back over. There's no way I'm able to go for a run today. The thought of him being out there too—I'm just not ready to see him yet.

Part of me wants to skip school today, but the fighter in me wins out and says, *Whatever. You're out of here soon anyway.* I need to keep my grades up, and skipping school over a broken heart really isn't a good reason.

I pull into the school as the first bell rings. Drew, Beau, and his friends are still standing in the parking lot talking. I feel Drew and Beau's eyes land on me and I take a deep breath. I really hope that he isn't waiting here to talk to me. Rubbing the dragonfly charm, I get out of the car and quickly walk away. I'm not ready yet to have any type of conversation with him.

"Ali!" I hear him behind me, but I don't stop. I just keep

moving forward.

Walking through the front doors, I can't help but notice the stares. Is it just me or does it seem like people are gawking at me more than normal this morning? Leila was right. Dancing with Drew Saturday night definitely encouraged them all to gossip about me.

Cassidy and her friends are standing at their lockers as I pass with Drew behind me.

"So Ali, we all know that you like to dance . . . imagine our surprise when we realized you could paint too." Cassidy's strange comment causes me to stop.

All four of them break out in laughter, and I look at her. Her eyes are dark and edgy.

"Hey, Drew," she says while looking at him with a sickly sweet smile. "Did you tell her about us yet?" She pins me with a celebratory look and I want to knock that smug grin right off of her face.

Drew stops next to me and he frowns. He places his hand on my lower back and I see all four of them drop their eyes.

Lisa gasps and confusion spreads across her face. Clearly, she's aware of yesterday's brunch details.

"Cassidy, what are you talking about painting?" I'm glad he asks the question, because I don't want to give her any more satisfaction than she seems to already have.

"Oh, Drew, haven't you heard or seen what she's done to The Cave? Coach Black was so stupid to give a key to someone like her. By the way, if you need me to, I'll be more than happy to explain what happened between us." Her tone is condescending and I can't take any more.

Anger fills every pore in my body. I walk right up to her and invade her space. She steps back and hits the lockers.

"Why are you such a bitch to me? What have I ever done

to you?" I'm shaking and my hands tighten into fists.

"You exist, and that's enough for me." Cassidy says in a low menacing voice. She rolls her eyes and brushes her hair off of her shoulders as if I'm doing nothing but wasting her time.

"Is that the best you can come up with?" This girl is no match for me. I'm better than her in every way. I would never purposely go out of my way to try and make someone else feel bad. She's the worst kind of bully.

I glance over at her friends, and all three of them are looking at the ground frowning. Not one of them will make eye contact with me.

"Why don't you go back to wherever it is that you came from? No one wants you here, and I do mean no one." She spits out at me.

She's right. She hits so close to the core of me with that statement that I'm certain she sees me flinch. No one wants me. I can't even make the argument that she's jealous, because in the end, she has him too.

"Cassidy, you don't speak for us, and you're wrong. I'd be really careful about what you say next." I didn't expect to hear Beau.

I look over and see that Drew is standing behind me on my left side and now Beau is on my right. To any outsider we would have looked like three united, but I know the truth.

Cassidy looks over to Beau and starts laughing. "Oh, Beau, when will you ever learn?"

Anger pours off of him as she continues to talk down to him like he's a child. It isn't lost on me that Drew never says anything, but then again, he never does.

I can't stand here and listen to any more. I turn and walk toward The Cave to see what she's talking about. I can hear the whispers all around me and I feel so alone. Maybe I should have stayed at home and in bed today after all.

There's a crowd outside the door to The Cave. They're all standing on their toes, pushing to try and see inside. As I approach, they part so I can walk straight up to the door.

I look through the window and my mouth falls open at the destruction of this room. Who could have done this? I open the door and slip inside to get a better look around. Drew followed me. I didn't know it, and he slips in with me. The door closes and silence surrounds us.

Tears fill my eyes and leak over. My already damaged heart, the one I thought couldn't possibly hurt any more than it already does, aches further.

The wrestling mat has been repeatedly stabbed, ripped to shreds, and discarded into a large pile in the middle of floor. My ballet barre is cracked in half and tossed onto the pile. The mirrored wall looks like it's been repeatedly hit with a baseball bat and is shattered from one end to the other. The surround sound speakers are hanging out of ceiling and the stereo has been smashed. Spray paint touches almost ever surface ruining the walls, floor, ceiling, and the back door . . . everything, and right in the middle of the back wall someone left a message that says, *I hate this school! It sucks and I wish I'd never been forced to come here!*

Whoever did this wants everyone to think it was me. I'm at a loss for why. Why?

Drew comes up behind me, and places a hand on my shoulder. I can't help but to turn around, fold myself up in his arms, and silently cry.

I feel as damaged as this room. I've spent so many hours in this one room over the last couple of months that in a way it's become a retreat for me and a safe place to express myself.

I'll never understand why someone did this to this room. It's then that I remember what Cassidy had said. I jerk back and look up at Drew.

"How did Cassidy know that I have a key to this room?" His hands slide to my arms, but he never lets go.

"I don't know. Someone must have known that you come in here and told her." His face looks as pained as I imagine mine does.

"Drew, I didn't do this!" Panic starts to wash over me and I begin to shake.

"I know, Ali."

The door opens and Coach Black walks in. He looks at the two of us, how we're standing, and then nods to Drew. Drew lets go of my shoulders and slides his hand down so he can lace his fingers with mine. He's taking a stand for me and I know it. Coach knows it too by the look on his face.

"Ali, I'm going to need you to come to the office with me." Coach's voice is calm and even.

"But why me?" I don't understand. Does he think that I did this too?

"We'll talk about it when we get there."

I look up at Drew and he squeezes my hand. I try to pull away from him, but he tugs me closer and kisses me on the forehead.

"It'll be all right. You'll see," he says and lets go of my hand. Together, Coach Black and I leave the room. I forgot about the audience outside. All of those people just saw me cry. They also saw me with Drew. Now that I think about it, his behavior to me isn't any different than any other day. He's standing here with me and not with Cassidy. But I can't be wrong about what I saw. I don't understand anything.

The walk to the office is one of the longest ever. I don't

know who did this or why, but I do know that I didn't and I'm going to have to prove that.

When we enter the office, I'm hit with the same tropical smell as when I arrived on the first day. I remember, that at the time, I thought it smelled so nice and now it makes my stomach turn. Leila is sitting up front and the look on her face is one of complete sadness. I avert my eyes. I don't want to look at her or talk to her. I didn't return her calls yesterday either.

We enter the principal's office and I'm surprised to see my dad sitting there.

"Dad? What are you doing here?"

His eyes narrow at me and he's fuming. "What do you mean what am I doing here, Ali? The question is, what have you been doing here?"

I gasp at his comment. He thinks that I did this. Everyone must think this.

"I haven't done anything except show up, get good grades, and dance!" I know that my voice is raised, but I feel like there's no one on my side. Again, I'm all alone and it's only me who's going to be able to stand up for me.

"Miss Rain, if you would please sit down," Principal Wright says authoritatively.

I look over toward the principal and he looks as displeased as my father. I sit down. My father is on one side of me, Coach Black is on the other, and one of the school's security officers is standing in the corner. I feel completely ganged up on and I didn't do anything wrong.

The heartache and pain that I felt a few minutes ago has numbed. Tears begin to drop. I can't stop them, but I can also barely feel them.

"Ali . . ." Coach starts talking to me and I turn to face him. Again with the calm, even voice he says, "Do you remember what I told you when you first asked if you could have access to the room?"

"Yes, but I didn't do this." He has to believe me.

"Maybe not, but again only you and I have a key that allows access to the room and we both know that I didn't do this." The expression on his face is sad.

I sit there quietly and look at the men in the room. Resignation fills me. It really doesn't matter what I say. To each of them, I am guilty. I fumble for the dragonfly charm. I need to feel it.

"You know what? I don't want the key anymore." I reach into my bag and pull out my keys, but the key to The Cave isn't there. I let out a gasp and look up at Coach Black.

"What?" His eyebrows furrow at me.

"The key, it's gone." Shock.

"What do you mean? Did you lose it?" Coach Black takes my keys from me.

"I don't know how. I just used it on Friday." My eyes bounce back and forth between Coach and Principal Wright.

"Well, did you leave them anywhere or lend them to anyone?" Coach asks me.

"No, but Drew drove us home Saturday night and I forgot to get them from him. I didn't go anywhere yesterday and he brought the keys back last night."

"Drew Hale?" Principal Wright asks.

I look over at him and see the confusion on his face. The Hale brothers are the golden boys of this school. They cross their t's, dot their i's, and fly under the radar as much as possible while proving what an asset they are to the athletic department.

"Yes, sir, but he wouldn't have done this. Besides, he was home until I got the keys back. They were having a family brunch." Not that I need to give an alibi for Drew, but I don't want him to get into trouble.

"I'm sorry to interrupt, but who is Drew?" All three of us turn to look at my dad. I want to roll my eyes because of course he doesn't know about Drew.

"He's my boyfriend." Not technically and apparently not anymore, but this is the easiest answer to give them.

"You have a boyfriend?" My dad is so clueless.

"Yes, Dad! For like the last six months. You would know that if you ever came home."

His eyebrows furrow down, his lips pinch into a thin line, and I see he isn't happy that I've just ousted him on his nonexistent parenting.

Coach Black clears his throat and my attention swings back to him.

"So here's the deal, Ali. As it stands right now you're being held responsible for this." I can see the apology in his face. He doesn't want to say this to me.

"What? But I didn't do it!" I can't help but to interrupt him.

"That's really irrelevant. I'm sorry to say that Principal Wright and I have decided that, until we can conclude this investigation, you're suspended."

Tears fill my eyes. "But you can't do that, and you know why!"

"We're not expelling you, but until we know exactly what happened we have to make sure that everyone knows that we won't tolerate vandalism of any kind."

"So you're just trying to make an example of me?" Disbelief.

"No, Ali, that room was your responsibility. Do you understand what I'm saying?"

"But I didn't do it," I whisper out. Tears now fall in steady streams and trail down my cheeks.

"Let me give you an example. Say your car is parked on the side of the road and someone comes along and crashes into it, side swipes it. They drive off and you never find out who, what, how, or why it happened. The car is still yours, and it's your responsibility to fix the damages. Does that make this clearer?" And now I know why my dad is here. Even though I got the feeling from everyone in the room that they know I didn't do this, I'm still going to have to pay for what the insurance company won't. I've heard enough.

"Fine." I wipe my face off, grab my bag and stand up to leave.

As my father and I exit the principal's office, I see Drew sitting in the chair directly outside of the door. I'm pretty sure he and Leila heard the entire conversation. I can't even look at either one of them.

"Allyson, I'll see you at home." My dad storms past me and walks out the front of the school. He used my full name. No one ever calls me that. It almost sounds strange coming from him.

"Ali?" Drew grabs my hand as I walk by, but I yank it from him and keep right on walking.

Beau is standing outside the office. I know he's waiting for me, so I stop in front of him.

"What!" I ask him.

His look is wary, almost like he's not sure of what to say. "Ali, I know you have so many things swirling around in your head right now, and I'm sorry, but you need to know that yesterday was about me. He did what he did for me." All of this crap with the school and my dad just went down, and he wants to talk about yesterday?

"Right. Do you think I'm an idiot? His message was received loud and clear." I'm so angry I could go toe to toe with him.

Beau pushes up off the wall and bends over so we're face to face. "No, I don't think you are an idiot, which is why you need to put out of your mind everything that you think you saw and listen to him. My brother loves you . . . and he doesn't love anyone." Beau's eyes narrow and he grits out his words as he speaks to me. He's mad at me now too, I give up.

"Well, I hate to break it to you, but he's never told me that he loves me, so I guess you bought into the act as well. I just feel so stupid. Beau, do you know happened to my keys yesterday?" I need to ask him because maybe he knows.

"Ali, it wasn't an act, and you know it. He's been with you one hundred percent of the way since the very first day of school back in August. Yes, I said August! You shouldn't feel stupid. You should feel amazing, because my brother is amazing. He's the best person I know, and if you can't give him the benefit of the doubt, even for just a little bit, then you don't deserve him like I thought you did."

I gasp at his words and the tension that is pouring off of him. He's left me speechless and I'm so confused.

Watching me, he stands up to his full height, glares at me one more time, and starts to walk away. "And, I don't even know what you are talking about . . . keys?" He shrugs his shoulders, turns around, and leaves.

I look back over into the office and see that Drew is no longer sitting there. He must have gone into the principal's office.

Whatever.

As I walk to my car, I try to think about what Beau said. He was very convincing in the way he talked to me. I know that he and Drew are super close, so maybe there's more to the story than I realize. Oh well, in the end it doesn't even matter. My thoughts turn back to Cassidy in the hallway when she said, "Hey, Drew. So did you tell her about us yet?" That one statement pretty much confirms everything I had thought. Beau is wrong. He doesn't love me.

Dad's car is sitting in the driveway when I pull in. Honestly, this is the last thing I need today. I walk up the steps to the front door and sitting right on top of the wooden pelican that Drew and I found at a yard sale is a blue dragonfly. I wonder if it's the same one I saw sitting on top of the mailbox yesterday. Like all of the others, its wings slowly beat up and down. I pause to look at it and wonder if it's somehow symbolic that it's sitting here waiting for me to enter into the firing squad. Every time something in my life happens, good or bad, there's a dragonfly. The coincidence of this isn't lost on me.

I take a deep breath and push through the door. I find Dad leaning against the island in the kitchen and he's still fuming.

"I can't believe that you were so irresponsible that you allowed this to happen!" he snaps at me.

What? Way to believe me. Way to support me! "I didn't do anything, Dad!"

"Were you or were you not the one who was given the key?" He pushes off the island and begins to pace.

"Yes, but I didn't give it to anyone else. I don't know how it disappeared!" This is the truth.

"Do you have any idea how much money this is going to cost me?"

"Whatever! Why are you paying for it? Isn't this what insurance is for? Oh, and by the way, I didn't do it!"

"You heard what he said, Ali! You are responsible! That's how it works, kiddo." He stops and stands directly in front of me.

"I'm not a kid." Does he really think he can come in here and talk to me as if I'm a child?

"Yes, you are, and speaking of which, you're grounded."
What!

"You can't ground me!" I'm now yelling at him.

"Watch me!" he yells back.

"Dad, I'm nineteen years old! In four months, I will be twenty! Let me put this in perspective for you . . . you got married at twenty and had a baby! I'm not a kid or a little girl anymore. I'm sorry if somehow over the last three years you forgot and missed the memo. Yes, Dad, just so we are clear here, you did forget my last birthday."

He stops what he's going to say and glares at me.

"Fine, give me your keys."

"For what?" There is no way I'm giving him my keys.

"I'm taking the car."

"Like hell you are! It's in my name. I will report that you stole it." I'm over being pushed around. I'm over him. I'm over Cassidy. I'm over it all.

"Do you realize how you are talking to me and in my house?"

"News flash, Dad, this isn't your house! It's mine. I'm the only one who lives here, and the only one who takes care of it. Did you forget that you moved me away from the only home that I've ever known and all my friends to a place that I have never been, and then you dumped me here and left? You left! I've been so alone and all by myself for months! I didn't lose one parent. I lost both. You know what, never mind keep your precious house. I'm out of here in less than three months anyway."

"Okay, and where do you plan on going, miss I-am-an-adult–now-and-can-do-whatever-I-want?"

His condescending tone rakes across my skin and he breaks my heart all over again. Why is it that he thinks so little of me that he assumes I would do nothing and go nowhere with my life? Not once has he asked me about my future. Not once has he been there for me since we moved. Again this just proves that the only one who's responsible for me, is me.

"College, Dad! I was accepted to Juilliard." Silence fills the room and we stare at each other.

"You got into Juilliard?" He sounds so surprised.

"Didn't I just say that?"

"Were you going to tell me? I didn't even know that you were still pursuing that."

"You wouldn't know that would you? I mean, when was I going to tell you, Dad? Oh wait I know, over one of our many family dinners, or over a cup of coffee before work and school in the mornings? You don't live here, you don't show any interest in me, and you don't care about anything going on in my life. So don't mock me about being an adult when I've been working so hard to make sure that I have a future. I'm the only one who's been looking out for me. Juilliard was always my dream. Why would you ever think that I would give that up? Besides, it's not like I have anything here for me." Silence stretches between us and I see regret etched onto his face.

"I'm sorry, Ali. I just didn't know how to do this anymore. I don't know how to be your dad without your mom. She was so good at all of this stuff, and I didn't even know where to begin. Every time I came over here and saw you, you seemed fine without me. I never felt like you needed me and you're technically an adult, so I thought you'd be better off without me. I'm sorry." A single tear rolls down my face. I hear what he's saying, but it doesn't make it okay. I did need him. More than he'll ever know.

"Just tell me one thing . . . why here? Why did you move us here?" He lets out a deep sigh and turns to look out the windows that face the beach. Silence stretches between us and I can see more sadness seep into his features and posture.

"I know that you'll think it's stupid," he says quietly, never turning to face me. "When your mother was told that the cancer had returned, we were sitting in the lobby of the oncology department, waiting to schedule her next appointment, and she had picked up a Southern Living magazine. There was an article in there about a bed and breakfast on Anna Maria Island, Florida. I guess that the owners had tragically died and that the daughter had moved back to take over. It talked about how the subtle differences that she had made were turning it again into a dream getaway location: the atmosphere, the ambiance, the culinary skills, and the peaceful beautiful backdrop of the Gulf of Mexico."

"Are you talking about Sea Oats up the road?" There are only a few bed and breakfasts on the island, and this one is by far the most beautiful.

"Yep, that's the one. Anyway, your mother looked longingly at the photos and said that if she could be anywhere in the world rather than where we were at that moment, she'd like to be here. I promised her that after all this was over and she got better, I would bring her here." He finally looks over at me and there are more tears in his eyes. "I guess I thought if we moved here, we would find that peace together, you and me, and just maybe somewhere I would be making her happy because I didn't break my promise."

I replayed every word in my head that he said. I now understand why he moved us here, but what I don't understand is why he didn't tell me this a long time ago? Things would have made more sense to me. I also don't understand how he thought we were going to find peace together when he didn't even give us a chance to do that. Wasn't I worth the chance? Whatever.

"Yeah well, it's too late now, isn't it? You know where the door is." I turn away from him and head for the stairs.

"Ali . . . please stop."

I can't talk to him anymore. I need him to leave. How many times am I going to get my heart broken?

I can't believe how much can change in just twenty-four hours. Yesterday morning, after opening the mail, and seeing that I was accepted, I was so excited. I couldn't wait to tell Drew. I wanted to tell him first, right away, and then after everything that happened yesterday afternoon, I just kind of forgot. I didn't really feel like telling anyone anyway.

I sit down on my bed and listen to the silence. I hear Dad moving around downstairs, and then the front door closes. His car starts up and I hear him drive away. More silence. The theme song has returned.

For the longest time after mom died, I felt like I had been abandoned, almost or maybe like what an orphan feels like, and even though I always had my dad, I still felt like part of me was missing. For months, I've been walking around with this emptiness inside that used to be filled with love from my mother. The emptiness is an ache, an ache so deep in my heart that there are days where I feel like I can't breathe. That's the thing about loss too. The emptiness that comes. It never goes away. And I wouldn't expect it to. That space in my heart belonged to her and only to her. She's gone . . . and so is her love.

When the front door closed, I felt the weight of that loss all over again. As if it isn't bad enough that every day I have to get up and live my life without her, I now know that every day I have to get up and live without him too. I was kind of already doing that, but I was still hanging on to the idea that he wanted me, at least a little. I guess I was wrong. No one wants me.

When I think about what it means to be an orphan or to be truly alone, there's one huge difference that separates me from so many others. I know what the perfect life is like. I don't have to imagine what it would be like to have two parents who love you. I had that and now it's gone. I know I should be thankful that I had it for a little while, but that just makes it hurt so much more. I feel like I'm drowning into myself.

Life is so unpredictable. Twenty-four hours ago I thought that things were looking up for me. I still had my dad, I finally felt like I belonged to my new school, I was accepted to my dream college, and I kind of had a boyfriend. But now, all that's left is the dream school.

I should just be thankful for being accepted to Juilliard and just say *screw the rest,* but what about love? Am I not deserving of that too? In less than a year, three people that I've loved have left me.

I look up and over as I hear the familiar tapping on the French doors to the balcony. I see a blue dragonfly through the window. Is this the same one from the front door? Is it following me? A surge of anger floods me.

Why did I ever think that a dragonfly was symbolic? There's no such thing as reincarnation. There is no such thing as gifts from angels. This dragonfly was not sent here to watch over me and it certainly isn't my mother. There is no such thing! It is just an insect.

I grab the closest magazine to me and throw open the doors. I see the dragonfly hovering midlevel and without even giving it a second thought, I roll the magazine up, and swing.

The magazine hits the dragonfly and the sound of the paper smashing down onto its beautiful body stalls me. A lightning fast piercing pain rips from my heart and through my chest. What have I done? I watch as everything moves in slow motion and the dragonfly spirals to the ground. It lands so quietly with one wing down, resting on the ground, the other up in the air. It doesn't move and neither can I.

My anger immediately recedes as panic sets in. My vision blurs as my tears return, and I whisper, "What have I done?"

The sky is gray, the water is rough as it hits the shore, and the temperature is dropping. I take a step toward the dragonfly just as a gust of wind picks it up, sweeping it across the balcony.

"No!" I dive into the corner to catch it with my hands before it slips between the wood slats and falls to the ground. The skin scrapes off of my knees, but I don't feel the pain. All I can feel is my heart breaking even further. I didn't think that it was possible to hurt more, but now I do.

"I'm so sorry. I didn't mean to." Sobs pour out of me, and I open my hands to look at the dragonfly. It lays there still, and I know I've killed it. I'm overwhelmed with remorse and loss.

I pick it up, pull it into my chest, and hunch over to protect it. Tears continue to pour out of my eyes and my chest aches so bad, I feel like I can't breathe. The wind has picked up and is swirling all around me, but I barely feel it. All that matters is that I hang onto this beautiful dragonfly.

I know that realistically it was just an insect, but it was beautiful and they've been coming to visit me here for months. I always felt like they were mine that they were sent to me, and I loved them.

A clap of thunder sounds from overhead and cold rain mixes in with the swirling wind. I can feel it falling all over me. Time passes. It could be seconds, minutes, hours—I don't know and I just don't care. All of the light that I thought I had found disappears and all I can see is darkness.

I give up. I am officially broken.

If the drops of rain could wash me away, I would let them.

DREW

I HEARD MOST of what was said in their meeting, and looking over at Leila, I know she did too. I'm certain that over the last couple of months she might have been suspicious of us, but for the most part, we just pretended to be friends.

"Six months, huh?" I can hear and feel the judgment coming off of her.

She assumes that I'm keeping Ali a secret because I don't want people to know about her, but that isn't it at all. I don't say anything back to her. I just give her a look of indifference. I mean, really it isn't any of her business anyway.

The office door opens and Ali walks out. Her eyes are rimmed red and because I know her so well, I can tell that she's about reached her breaking point. I grab her hand. "Ali?" She keeps right on walking, right passed me, and out the door.

Beau's standing in the hallway and she stops in front of him. I'm not sure what he's doing out there, but I want to physically remove him because she's choosing to talk to him over me. He's annoyed with her. I can tell by the look on his face and I can't watch anymore.

"Drew, can you come in here, please?" Perfect timing, I get up and walk into Principal Wright's office. The tension is stretched between Mr. Wright, Coach Black, and the security officer. I close the door and make my way over to sit down.

"Drew, I'm glad that you followed us down here. You're next on our list to question." Coach Black has always been so nice to me. Looking at him, I'm thankful for who he's been in my life.

"Now, I know you spend a lot of nights in The Cave with Ali, why is that?" He tilts his head to the side and looks at me.

"I don't feel comfortable with her being here by herself, so late at night."

"But why?"

What does he mean why?

"I don't know, Sir. You've seen her. She's got some fight in her, but she's so small. What if something was to happen to her?" The thought of that makes my skin crawl. I shiver not meaning to.

"Drew, we wanted to talk to you first before we get your father involved." I can't let this comment go.

"What do you mean involve my father? I haven't done anything!" The force of my statement isn't lost on them. I'm two seconds away from losing it.

"Lose the tone, Drew, and calm down. I get it. You know that I do." A moment of silence passes between Coach and me. I take a deep breath, trying to regain composure.

Relaxing my shoulders I ask them, "What do you want to know?"

"Tell us what you did over the weekend, starting with Friday night."

"Okay. Friday night, after swim, I met Ali in The Cave, and waited for her to finish rehearsing. We went back to her house, she made us a pizza, we watched a movie, and then went to bed. On Saturday, Ali and I met up with some other people at that club, Mainlanders, across the bridge. Sunday, Beau and I attended a brunch my parents planned, I did some homework, and then that was it."

"How long have you been dating Ali?" They know the answer to this. I'm not sure why they're asking again.

"Six months, but I wish it was longer." And isn't that the truth.

"Do you spend the night at her house often?"

Why is he asking me this?

"I'm not sure how that is any of your business?"

"Just answer the question. I find it relevant."

I don't want to answer him, but I also don't want to cause any problems either.

"Yes, I sleep at her house a lot." All three of them are staring at me.

"Her dad doesn't care?"

This is a sore subject for me. I'll never understand how he could just leave her all by herself.

"You're implying that he cares in the first place. Her dad hasn't been back to the house in at least a month. He lives in his condo, next to his office. Look, it isn't like what you're thinking, but keep in mind that both of us turn twenty in four months. We don't need permission or approval." I can't help the glare that I direct toward Coach Black. He doesn't react. He just continues with his questioning.

"So, did you hold the keys Saturday night, or did she?

"I did."

"And you drove home on Saturday night?"

"Yes."

"Why didn't you give her keys back?"

"Honestly, I didn't even think about it. My dad doesn't know that we're dating and he doesn't need too. She doesn't understand that and when I told her about the brunch with Cassidy, it hurt her feelings. Trust me when I say I don't ever want to hurt that girl's feelings, especially after what she went through last summer. I was still sitting in the car when she got out and ran into her house. I didn't have a chance to give them back to her."

"What happened to her last summer?" Principal Wrights asks me.

I look at all three of them. Shouldn't this type of stuff be in her transfer file?

"Her mom died."

All three of them stare silently at me.

"Look, it's not my place to talk about her business. I'd prefer it if you didn't ask me any more personal questions about her."

"Where did you put the keys in your house?" Coach Black is back to the questioning.

"On my desk in my room."

"Other than Beau or Matt, is it possible that anyone else was in your room?"

"I suppose that Cassidy could have wandered into my room. They were there for three hours and honestly watching her was not a top priority of mine." I better not find out that Cassidy did this.

"When did you give Ali back the keys?"

"Last night, I left them outside her balcony door around eight."

"Do you think that she left her house last night?"

"No. When she's upset she shuts down and goes to bed. Ali didn't do this. She's not mean or vindictive. She's just trying to get by the best she can by herself."

"Did she get accepted to Juilliard?"

Out of the corner of my eye I see Principal Wright's head pop up. He'd been taking notes on our meeting and judging by his reaction, I take it he wasn't aware of why Ali was using the room in the first place.

"I don't think she knows yet. The auditions were a couple of weeks ago, so she's still waiting."

He nods his head at me.

"Can you think of anyone who might have a problem with Ali and would try to pin this on her?"

"The only person at this school that seems to have a problem with Ali is Cassidy. I'm not saying that this is down to her, but I think her father has been giving her a hard time and really wants her and me to date. She's made her interest in me known since school started and I don't think she's been too happy with my response. Cassidy hasn't been subtle with her feelings toward Ali. It's bordered on bullying. Ali's always manages to handle it gracefully and let it go. She's a strong person."

I've gripped the armrests on the chair while talking about Cassidy. I didn't mean to, but now all three men in the room have noticed. It's clear this is starting to get to me and I've taken about as much as I can.

"All right, Drew, I think we're done here. Ali has been suspended until we can review some potential evidence we have. I have a feeling that the minute you walk out this door you're going to go and check on your girl, so knowing where you'll be, I will mark this as a sick day for you, but only today. Do you understand?"

"Yes, sir. Are we finished?" My leg starts bouncing in anticipation of leaving.

"You may go."

I pick up my bag and open the door to the office.

"Oh, one more thing you should know. This morning Cassidy made a comment to Ali that she couldn't believe you would ever give her a key. Ali and I both found this a little strange. No one but Beau and I know that she has a key." I glance one more time at each of the three men. I shrug my shoulders and walk out of the office.

Leila's still sitting there and I can tell she's been crying. Looking at her, I immediately know that Ali hasn't shared any of this with her.

"Don't, Leila." My tone to her makes it clear that her gossiping about Ali's life is not an option.

"I won't say anything, Drew, but please let her know that I'm here for her if she needs me."

I can't help but narrow my eyes at her. In the back of my mind, I can hear Ali say that Leila called her a whore.

She can read my reaction. "I didn't mean it. I was upset and I felt like she was lying to me. I'm sorry." Her eyes fill with tears.

I nod my head and leave the office.

Beau is waiting for me in the Jeep. He looks visibly upset over something and I go on alert.

"What's up with you?" I ask him.

"She knows?"

"Knows what?" I get a sinking feeling in the pit of my stomach.

"About you and Cassidy."

How would she know this?

"Did you say something to her?" He can see my irritation rising.

"No, I got the impression from her that she saw it all."

"Shit." No wonder she doesn't want to talk to me. I wouldn't want to talk to me either if I was her.

"I know. This is my fault, Drew. I know why you did it and I'm so sorry." I recognize this look on Beau. It's one I often have myself when it comes to him. Guilt.

"What did she say to you in the hallway?"

"That it was all just an act and she feels stupid."

Oh man. I run my hands through my hair and look up toward the clouds. Of course she thinks it's all an act. Again, I've never given her a reason to think differently. I've never really told her what she means to me, and that isn't fair to her. Oh, my sweet girl. I'm sorry.

"Listen to me. If Ali had talked to me last night, everything between her and I would be fine, but she didn't. However, I'm on my way to her and she will hear me now. Everything will be fine. You don't need to worry about us." I need him to relax and not feel responsible.

"But I do. I love you, big bro."

"Dude . . . you know I love you too. Ali and I will be fine. Didn't you just say this to me, like two nights ago?" I crack a small smile at him in effort to lighten his mood.

"She just looked so hurt and I love her, too. You've been so different with her around and you deserve her. She makes you happy."

"You're right, she does make me happy. But at this moment, she's hurting and I need to go to her. They are going to hold her responsible for The Cave and currently she's suspended from school."

Beau jumps up out of the seat. "What? But she didn't do it!"

"I know that and I think they do too, but Ali had the key and somehow she either lost it or it went missing. Ali's keys were in my room yesterday. I need you to keep your eyes on Cassidy, if you know what I mean." His mouth gapes open before slamming shut as he clenches his jaw. It's a mix of horror and anger that flashes across his face.

"You think Cassidy did this?"

"Yes."

"All right, I'm on it. You go take care of our girl." Beau climbs out of the Jeep as I turn it on. He looks back at me before he walks away and I can see how much all of this is affecting him. I know that he cares for her too.

It's kind of funny. I never wanted love, but that's all Beau's ever been chasing. It's why he's with so many different girls. He seeks connections with people because he's never gotten it at home. But the sad part is, he doesn't trust himself to love someone in return. I wish that I could help him with that.

I pull out onto Gulf Drive and head toward Ali's house. I pass a white Range Rover on the way and I know that Ali's dad has left her again. My heart breaks for her because even though I know what happened yesterday, she doesn't, and she thinks I've left her too.

The sky is dark, the temperature has drastically dropped, and the wind has picked up. I know the rain will hit any minute now.

I park the Jeep in my driveway and run across the road as the first drops hit. This storm is coming in fast and it doesn't look like it'll be going anywhere any time soon.

I knock on the front door and wait, but there's no answer. I crack the door open and call out her name. Silence. I can't help but feel a little panic. Her car is here, so where is she?

I walk into the house and peek into the kitchen to see that she isn't there. I take the stairs two at a time up to her room, but she isn't there either. I look in her bathroom, and it's empty. I sit down on her bed and rub the back of my head.

A howling wind blows outside. The French doors to the balcony fly open and slam against the house. I jump off of the bed to grab them when I hear her crying. I spot her instantly. She's in the corner of the balcony, curled up into a ball, and she's crying hysterically.

"Ali!"

She doesn't answer me as I rush over to her. She's soaking wet, shivering, and gasping for air in between sobs.

"Sweetheart, what happened? What are you doing out here?"

She shifts a little bit toward me and I lean over her to block the wind and rain. The crying doesn't let up any, so I lay my head on her back and sit with her, hoping she knows I'm here for her.

An indefinite amount of time passes and slowly I feel her muscles begin to loosen. She was so tense and so tight.

"Drew . . ." The sound of her voice, the agony that's so clearly evident, her saying my name—I just want to make all of this go away for her.

"Ali, please talk to me. What happened?"

"Drew, I killed it," she says between sobs.

"Killed what?" She's having a hard time breathing, so I rub soothing strokes up and down her back. "I need you to try and calm down."

"Oh, Drew . . ." More sobbing.

I'm not sure what I expected when I got here, but it certainly wasn't this. She and I are both soaked through and she's shivering. Enough of this, I pick her up and carry her into the house. I walk us into the bathroom and I sit her down on the counter. Her shivering is getting worse, so I go and turn on the hot water in the shower and close the door.

I really don't know what happened or what to do for her,

so I bend down in front of her and push on her chin to tip her head up. I need to see her. I need to see into her beautiful eyes.

"I killed it," she says, looking up at me. Her big brown eyes are so sad. She's killing me in this moment.

"You need to tell me what you're talking about because I don't understand."

She holds out her cupped hands and then slowly opens them to show me what's inside.

I recognize the dragonfly. It seems she too has noticed they've been flying around a lot lately. She was right. It's dead and one of its wings is broken in half.

"What happened?" I ask her quietly.

"I hit it." She lets out another sob and squeezes her eyes closed.

"Why?"

"I was so hurt and mad. I don't know. I didn't mean to kill it . . . I'm sorry." The tears continue to leak out and all I can think about is how much I love this beautifully broken girl.

"What made you so hurt and mad?"

"Everything! You, my mom, my dad, the people at the school, Cassidy, everyone. You don't understand. I was finally starting to feel more happy than I was sad. I felt like maybe my life was getting back to some version on normal, and I wanted it so bad."

I brush the wet hair off of her face and while she still cradles the dragonfly, she tells me everything about the last twenty-four hours. She tells me about getting the letter from Juilliard, seeing me with Cassidy, her conversation with the school, her dad, how quiet the house always is, how alone she feels, and how she hit the dragonfly. Sometimes I wonder how this girl is still functioning because life over the last year, and then some, hasn't been easy for her.

Slowly, I reach down, take the dragonfly from her, and place it on the counter. All of the fight in my sweet girl has left and she can't stop shivering. I carefully pick her up. She holds on tight while wrapping her legs around me, and lays her head on my shoulder. I know I should undress us first, but I don't. I kick off my flip flops and walk us straight into the shower, clothes and all.

The steam and the water are warm. I can feel her thawing out, and little by little her breathing returns to normal. She isn't crying anymore.

I think back to things she told me and it's not lost on me that she tells me she was accepted to Juilliard. I'm a little hurt she didn't tell me right away. I understand why she didn't, but there's a part of me that thinks she has to know how I feel about her. Of course I would want to know right away.

"Drew." She leans back a little so she can look me in the face. "I want you to know that more than anything in this world, I just want you to be happy."

"I am happy. You make me happy."

"I know things are going to change between us, but you have to know that over the last couple of months, you've become my best friend. Please, I don't want to lose that, to lose you. I can't lose one more person. I mean, I can see why you would want to be with her. She's beautiful . . .but . . ."

"Wait! What are you talking about?"

"I'm talking about you."

"What about me?"

"I saw you with her, Drew, and it's okay . . ."

This makes me angry.

"Stop! First off, you don't understand what you saw. There was a reason for what occurred in the driveway and if you would've talked to me instead of shutting me out then you would know. And second, it shouldn't be okay with you. I thought that you and I might have been starting something that was lasting. I thought I meant something more to you?" My heart pounds and insecurity seeps in.

"You do, and I thought that we were too, but everyone leaves me! What was I supposed to think? She's perfect and I'm barely here. I'm trying every day to hold it together and be somebody, but I don't know how to when I feel as if I'm not important to anybody. My mother died, my friends stop calling, my dad essentially leaves, my friend here calls me a whore, and the one and only guy I've ever fallen for doesn't see me. I feel as if I am vanishing." She lays her head back down on my shoulder and the tears return.

"I see you. And I'm sorry if I've made you feel that you aren't important to me, because you're the most important thing in my life. I know I should have told you every day, and I'm sorry. It's my fault you feel this way because I asked you to keep this quiet. Well, I don't want to do that anymore. I'm so sorry I hurt you."

She picks her head back up and looks me in the face.

"Then what were you doing with Cassidy, because being with me means you're most definitely not with anyone else."

She starts to slip a little, so I turn and push her against the wall with my hips. The wall absorbs some of her weight and I place my hands next to both sides of her head. I want to be as close as possible to her and I'm not allowing her let go of me.

Releasing a deep breath, I know it's time. "Ali, I always knew that one day I would have to talk about this part of my life with you. I just haven't been ready. You don't understand, my dad . . . he's . . . controlling. He's also very spiteful and mean. The things that he says to us and the things that he does . . . I didn't want you to know about it. No one knows about it.

Beau and I have never told a single person."

Confusion enters her eyes.

"But I don't understand. What are you talking about?" Her voice is etched with confusion and concern.

Of course you don't understand.

"My father, he's emotionally and physically abusive. I swim and I have to take my clothes off. So when he's unhappy with something I've done, he takes it out on Beau . . . do you understand now?"

She gasps. "He hits him?"

"Yes."

"Has he ever hit you?"

"Yes."

Silence falls between us and she places both of her hands on my face.

"My dad wants me to date Cassidy because he wants to be business partners with her dad. He thinks if we're together then he'll get a better deal. The thing is, he's being played because Cassidy's dad thinks the same thing. This is why she's been so crazy over the last couple of months. Her father is expecting the same thing from her. I told her when we were in the driveway that you're my girlfriend. Kissing her meant nothing, and that was it. It was a means to an end. Ali, he hurts Beau because of me. I can't allow that to happen. I promise that I wasn't being unfaithful to you, because I'm faithful to you! I have been since the day I first laid my eyes on you. I'm sorry you saw that, and I'm so sorry it hurt you." I lean my forehead against hers. Shame washes over me. I feel shame for my family, shame for what I did with Cassidy, and shame for how I made her feel. She deserves better.

"Why didn't you tell me this on Saturday night?"

"I didn't know how, and I tried to come over on Sunday

afterward to talk to you, but you wouldn't open the door for me. Why is it so hard for you to listen to me and believe me? What have I ever done to make you doubt me? You have to know that you hurt me too."

Her chin trembles and tears fill her eyes. "I'm sorry, Drew. I didn't know I was hurting you."

"I know you didn't, but please hear me when I say that I'm yours because I am and . . . you're mine." I don't wait another second before slamming my mouth to hers. Her legs tighten around my waist and I lean into her, trying to get as close as possible. Her fingers slide around my face and into my hair. She grips on, wanting me to be a little more aggressive. I know we have a few more things to talk through, but all of that can wait. I need her. I need to taste her, feel her, and show her that I love her, because I do. I'm so lost in her. I don't ever want to find my way without her.

"Drew," she mumbles against my lips. I pull back to look at her. "Why have you never tried to take things further with me? I know you've been with other girls, including Cassidy, but I just don't understand. I hear what you're saying to me, but yet I feel like you don't want me."

"Ali, I want you every second, of every minute, of every day. I think about it so much that I drive myself crazy. I know I haven't moved us forward, but I wanted to make sure I was what you wanted. And—"

"You are. You have to know that."

"I do and I was pretty sure that you did, but Ali, until you, I've only ever loved three people. And all three of them continually get hurt because of me. These feelings for you are new for me, and I feel raw and exposed sometimes with you. I never thought I would find someone that wanted to be with me. Most of the time, I don't even feel like I deserve you. You're perfect and beautiful and deserve someone so much better than me. I wanted to take this slower because you're different and I wanted to treat you different. It has never been about sex with you. It's just always been so much more."

"Wait . . . do you love me?" She looks me straight in the eyes and I can feel her question pulling all the way from my stomach.

"Yes . . . love you. Love you so much."

She stares at me.

The sound of the shower takes place of the silence in my ears, and this is the moment that I fear the most. Does she love me back? What if now that she knows the truth, she's changed her mind? I close my eyes because I can't bear to look at her anymore. I feel completely open.

"Drew, I love you. I've loved you for so long." Her voice is quiet and I open my eyes so I can see her lips move as they form around those words.

My heart pounds like it might explode.

My entire life, my father has told me that no one would ever love me. That I wasn't worthy of it and wasn't good enough for anyone.

I lay my forehead back against hers to catch my breath.

"Say it again." Tears burn in the back of my eyes. I don't cry and I need to pull it together. I'm thankful for the water of the shower because I don't really want my beautiful girl to see this. She's touched a place in me I never thought would be reached and the shattered parts of my heart are being put back together.

Her legs squeeze around me tighter, and my eyes move to lock onto hers. Her hands slide off my shoulders, and back up into my hair.

"I love you." Purposefully, she guides my mouth back to

hers. I could kiss her indefinitely and never tire of the way she tastes.

I pull back from her, breaking our connection, but my hips push into her a little more to keep her propped up on the wall. Very slowly I grab the hem of her shirt and pull it up and off of her. I drop it onto the floor and it makes a loud slap against the tile. She gives me a small smile and I can't help but reach out and run my fingers over her collarbone down to the swell of her breasts. She's so beautiful and she's mine. Forever with this girl will not be long enough.

Chapter Seventeen

ALI

HEARING DREW SAY that he loves me fills a part of my heart that's been empty for months. No one's told me that they love me in so long, and I didn't realize until he said it how much I needed it.

He lays his forehead against mine and I can feel him trying to get himself under control. I need to be closer to him, so I reach up and pull his head down to mine. Drew doesn't just kiss me. He consumes me. He explores every part of my mouth and then some.

When he leans back to pull my shirt off, inside I rejoice and think, *Yes! Finally!* Drew's fingers reach down and he skims them across my skin. Next to the hot water, his fingertips leave a trail of ice. My heart pounds in anticipation of what's to come. I love him so much.

Not giving him a second to change his mind, I reach down and grab the bottom of his shirt. His eyes leave my chest and come back to mine. He smiles at me. I pull his shirt up and off over his head. He reaches around and unclips my bra. Slowly he slides the straps down my arms and eventually pulls it away.

His eyes rake over me and I do the same to him.

All the time that he spends swimming has paid off immensely. His arms, shoulders, and chest are so well defined, muscular, and strong I can't even begin to describe how looking at him this way makes my stomach feel. I run my hands from his stomach up over his chest and he groans as he leans back in to claim my mouth.

Drew's control is gone, and this time he doesn't hold back. His lips and tongue have possessed mine and it's like he'll go crazy if he can't take what he wants from me right at this moment. I love how free he's being with me.

Although this is technically our first time getting naked together, I feel like we've loved each other this way forever. I'm completely comfortable with him, and being wrapped around him is sending my hormones into overdrive. This craving and these desires I have are only for him and I need to explore them. His hands are all over me and it feels so good. I can't get enough of him.

Slowly, I unwrap my legs from him and he puts my feet on the ground. Looking up through my eyelashes at him, I reach and grab onto his belt. His eyes darken with want and need.

Without breaking a beat, he helps me undo his belt and jeans. The tension in the air between the two of us is so thick, we could combust. Together we push down the heavy, wet fabric of his jeans and boxer briefs. Drew kicks them off to the side and stands before me completely, beautifully naked. I can't help but reach up and run my hands down over his ribcage and hip bones. Drew squeezes his eyes closed, drops his head backward under the water, and lets out a moan. This gives me the perfect excuse to see what it is I have been feeling for the past few months.

I think back to that first Sunday morning after New Year's. He was curled up behind me and I couldn't help but notice the effect that either I was having on him, or the fact that it was the morning, or maybe both.

I thought he was sleeping, but instead in a sleepy rough voice, he chuckled at me and said, "Just ignore it. I am. It's always going to happen, so no sense feeling awkward about it." After that, I never minded. Secretly, I kind of enjoyed it.

Drew reaches out and grabs my hand. He wraps it around him and then slowly moves my hand up and down. I'm amazed at how he feels. He groans and then drops his gaze back on me.

"Ali, please take the rest of your clothes off."

I don't even hesitate. My clothes are discarded.

One of his hands lands on my lower back, pulling me into him, and the other tangles into my hair. Drew tilts my head to the side and he tastes my jaw, neck, and collarbone.

When his mouth covers my breast, I can't help but arch my back, pushing my hips forward into his. Drew lets out a noise, letting me know he wants me as much as I want him.

I reach around him and turn off the water.

He opens the shower door and grabs us the two towels on the rack. The first one he wraps around me, and then the second he wraps around his waist.

"Mr. Hale, I hate to break it to you, but I'm not finished with you yet." He smirks at me.

"Is that so?"

Fire lights his eyes and my need for him pulses straight to

my core. Drew takes me by the hand and leads me out into the bedroom. He pulls his towel off and runs it over my head to dry my hair.

"Thank you," I say to him. He really is always so sweet and kind to me. Images of what his father has done, and possibly said to him, flash through my mind, and tears fill my eyes.

"You okay?" Concern registers on his face.

"I love you. I love you so much." I walk into him and wrap my arms around him. I want to tell him every day how wonderful, special, and loved he is. He deserves so much and my hearts breaks at the thought that he hasn't been given this. I can feel his heart rate increase, so I pick my head up to see what's going on with my handsome guy.

His eyes find mine and I can see the walls breaking down. "Love you. I really do and I'm sorry I hurt you." Pain is written on his face.

"I'm sorry I hurt you. I didn't stop to think and you deserve better than that. You've done nothing wrong."

"I should have told you everything sooner." His fingers brush the hair off my face and he tucks it behind my ears.

"It doesn't matter. I feel honored that you told me at all." I reach up and grab onto his biceps.

"Ali, I want to tell you everything. I don't ever want to keep anything from you. You're it for me and you're everything to me. You're all I'll ever want."

This declaration brings a wave of peace and security over me. I finally know how he feels and I don't have to wonder any more.

"I'm happy to hear you say that. After the audition, I had this revelation about what 'home' is, and home to me has become you. I thought I was losing you, and I can't tell you how horrible the last day and a half have been. I didn't answer the door last night because I was afraid you were going to tell me goodbye and I couldn't . . . I just can't bear the thought of not being with you."

"As long as you want me, you will never lose me."

I lean forward on my tiptoes, reach behind his neck, and pull him down to me. His tongue swipes across my bottom lip and then he gently pulls on it with his teeth. I arch into him because I want—need—more and am offering him everything. His taste is intoxicating, and I can't get enough of it.

Drew pulls my towel off and runs his hands straight up my backside. I moan at the sensation. His hands are large and strong. They make me feel possessed and cherished.

Drew walks us until the back of my knees hit the bed. Slowly, I lay down, scoot backward, and he follows. His fingers and his lips start at my ankle and work their way up my legs at a leisurely pace. He crawls between my legs and hovers directly over the juncture between my thighs.

"As much as I look forward to exploring this area in great detail, forgive me if right now I say that I just need to be with you, completely and wholly."

His fingers brush across me and the pulsing returns.

"Don't move." Drew slips off the bed and goes into the bathroom.

As he walks back toward me, he smiles and flips up the foil package for me to see. He climbs back onto the bed and straight over me, stopping to kiss my belly button.

"Why do you have that?" He looks up at me, our eyes connect, and he gives me a small smirk.

"Every guy keeps one of these in their wallet. That's just the way it is." He shrugs his shoulders.

"Oh, but we don't need that. I'm on the shot and I want to feel you . . . all of you. No condom." He pauses to look up at me.

"Why are you on the shot?" He crawls up the rest of the way, places his elbows beside my shoulders and both of his hands on my head. His thumbs brush back and forth across my cheek bones. The touch is light and it makes my heart flutter.

"Dancers don't do messy. The shot helps take care of that. I mean, have you seen what we have to wear?" He smiles at me and I can't help but blush.

"While I appreciate you being on birth control, what kind of guy would I be if I didn't make sure that I took care of things on my end as well?" He pauses gazing into my eyes. "Love you . . ." he whispers out.

He's right. I know he is. Maybe one day.

"Okay."

Looking up into Drew's handsome face, I feel like my heart could burst from happiness. Never in my wildest dreams did I actually think he would love me back. I knew he cared for me, but right now at this moment, I feel like the luckiest girl ever.

"I'm afraid I'm going to hurt you. You're so small," he whispers across my lips while ripping open the package.

"You won't hurt me . . . I promise."

Slowly and gently, Drew makes us one. It did hurt a little, but I was so caught up in the emotions of what was happening that the pain didn't really register. Drew's body, with mine, fills up every part of me, including my heart.

It's crazy to me that this could ever be done and not be filled with love. Being together and moving together, I can't help but feel flooded with passion and this profoundly tender affection for him. I adore him and he makes me feel beloved. This personal connection and attachment that we share—I never want it to end. The sensations he gives me run through me from head to toe. Every part of me tingles and this feeling is exquisite. I want to feel this way with him over and over again.

One of his hands slides down under me and pushes my hips to a different angle. His breathing changes and he tenses slightly. As he eventually stills, he lays his forehead on top of mine. My fingertips run through the light layer of sweat that's formed down his spinal cord and he shivers.

"Ali . . ." His eyes are still closed and his breathing returns to normal. "I don't know what to say to you right now, other than . . . love you." He nuzzles his head into my neck and cuddles me underneath him.

This feels like the safest home in the world.

Drew stays the rest of the day and the night with me. The world could have been ending and he wouldn't have left me. The only person to reach out to us was Beau. He wanted to check in, see how we were, and if we needed anything. Drew needed clothes, so Beau dropped some off at the balcony doors, along with food from Beachside.

Drew told me that he was really upset after I left and how he felt responsible for all of this mess between him, me, and Cassidy. We both told him not to worry about it, that we cleared the air between us and we were fine. Better than fine. Hopefully, soon enough his conscience will be free of this. It isn't his fault.

What I've learned about Beau is that he has a big heart, and he loves big too. He never wants to hurt or disappoint those that he loves. He and Drew are very alike with this quality.

Drew and I talked a lot. He explained how life was for him growing up, what his father expects of him, Beau, and Matt, and also how he treats his mother. I told him more about my life back in Colorado, and how I've really felt being here in this house, all alone. We talked about The Cave and what we both think happened. We talked a little about the future, and we also threw in a few rounds of "Stump Me."

It finally stopped raining sometime during the night, but temperatures dropped enough that Drew opted to skip his morning swim. Instead, we curled up around each other and pulled the blankets back over our heads. I hate that I'm not allowed to go to school today. After lunch I plan on calling Coach Black to find out if they've made any decisions.

After Drew left, I found a small, white jewelry box and I placed the dragonfly inside. I should probably bury it, but instead I wrap a piece of black satin ribbon around it, tie a bow, and place it in my jewelry box. In many ways, I'm just not ready to part with it yet.

DREW

I HATED LEAVING her this morning. This entire situation that she's been placed in really isn't fair. We all know she didn't destroy The Cave, and as much as they want to say they aren't using her as an example to what happens if you are caught vandalizing, that's exactly what they are doing.

Beau is waiting for me in the driveway as I walk out of Ali's house and lock the front door. A grin spreads across his face, and I more than happily give him one back. I'm pretty sure he can guess what we've been up to, but I'll never tell.

"So did you tell her?"

"Yep, I told her everything."

Beau looks off toward the beach. For so long this secret,

this terrible life, has been something that the two of us have just endured together. Now that someone else knows, it feels different. I feel different.

For him, I imagine that he feels vulnerable. Sharing secrets can make you feel weak, exposed, and in many ways it feels like it's a burden that you've unloaded on someone else. For me however, I feel free.

Ali completes me in a way I never thought was possible. She calms my heart and fills my soul with warmth and acceptance. Carrying around this hidden burden for so long has placed me into such a state of loneliness that I didn't even realize I was walking through life missing the best parts of it. I can blame it on the fear: the fear of discovery, the fear of ridicule, the fear of him. But in the end, maybe mostly, I feared myself. What does it say about me, that I allowed this to happen to my family and to me?

Ali has taken the heaviness that constantly weighs me down and lightened the load. I feel lighter, I feel stronger, and I feel hope.

In seventy-six days, with her by my side, I know that it'll be my last first day of my new life. A life that I plan on spending with her, no matter where that is, or where the wind blows us.

"You were right, you know."

Beau looks back at me. His eyes are slightly haunted and I wish that I could take this away from him like she's taken it away from me.

"How's that?" He shoves his hands into the pockets of his jeans.

"Well, turns out that there is a Tiny up those stairs who loves me."

Beau's grin returns. He reaches out and pulls me into a

hug. I worry a little that he might feel left out and left behind, but knowing Ali, she'll shower him with love just like she does to me.

"Yeah, I kind of have to rub it in and say I told you so." He pats me on the back and then let's go. "She's awesome, big bro, and she's perfect for you. You deserve her, and I'm so happy for you."

Hearing this come from him squeezes my heart.

"Thanks." A smile breaks out across my face. I can already tell it's going to be one of those days. I'm going to be smiling at everything.

We continue to look at each other, words not needing to be said. He's always understood me, and I've always understood him.

Beau needs to feel hope. He needs to continually hang on to the idea that once outside of this house, life will forever be different and better. He needs me and those around him to prove that our father is wrong, that he is worth something and capable of being loved. He needs to live knowing he's going to be accepted without fear of discovery. He's such an amazing person, and he's so strong. I wish he could see the inner strength that I do. His time is coming. I have faith in this.

I glance up toward our house and I see my mom standing in the window. She must have seen me coming from Ali's, but I don't care anymore. It's not like she's going to tell on me.

She has been watching Beau and me. Her hand is over her heart, and she's smiling down at us. I've never doubted that my mother loves us, but what I'll never understand is why she didn't love us enough to get us out. I've realized it's easy to say that about her now, but the reality is that I too had the ability to get us out years ago and I didn't do a thing. I can't really hold her responsible anymore. Each of us played a role in this, but every day our roles are changing, and soon this'll all be over.

"Burr, it's cold today." A shiver runs through me and I look down toward the water. The sky is blue, but the water is still a little choppy. I'm glad I opted to stay in and under the blankets with her. I'll just put in an extra half hour in the pool later.

"Yeah, let's go. I don't want to be late." Beau pulls his keys out of his pocket as Matt comes bolting out the front door and over to us.

"I've got to run by the post office first. I'll meet you there."

"Sounds good," he says while leaning forward to bump forearms with me. He wraps his arm over Matt's shoulders and turns them toward his car. "Hey," he says, glancing back to me. "Text her later and see if she'll make us some pizza to-night."

The unease that was floating in his eyes is gone, and I can't help but smile.

"Ha! You know she will, just for you."

He smiles at me. They climb into his Tahoe, and pull out of the driveway.

I look back up to the window, and place my hand over my heart just like my mom's is. Her smile grows even bigger and I can't help but think that so far this is the best day I've ever had. Everyone that I love this morning is smiling and happy, and so am I.

ALI

BEING HOME BY myself today was really boring. I did get a chance to catch up on some cleaning, laundry, and grocery shopping, but other than that I went for a run and didn't do much.

Coach Black said that I'm allowed to come back to school tomorrow. Hopefully they're getting closer to figuring out who did this.

Around 2:45 Leila comes walking up the balcony steps. Although it was cold this morning, right now the temperature is in the mid-seventies and it's gorgeous outside.

"I knocked on your front door, but no one answered." She sits down on the other chaise lounge next to me.

"It's kind of too pretty to be sitting inside," I say to her. I know she's here to apologize. She's called several times over the last couple of days, and I wasn't trying to blow her off, I just needed that time with Drew first. "I'm sorry I haven't called you back yet."

"Oh, Ali, I'm sorry for what I said to you. You know I didn't mean it. That was awful of me, and so not like me." Remorse fills her face, and I don't want her to feel bad anymore. There have been enough emotions going through all of us that really, I'm just trying to put what she said behind me.

"It's all right. It's over."

"So you forgive me?" Her eyes are pleading.

"Yes." I giggle at her.

"It's not funny. My feelings have been so hurt. And why didn't you tell me?"

"Tell you what?"

"Everything. Why didn't you tell me about your mom, your dad, the audition, Drew . . . I just don't understand. I thought we were, like, really good friends."

I'm not sure how she knows all of these things, and the look on my face must show this.

"Drew was questioned after you. A lot of these things came up, and I couldn't help but overhear." She looks at me sheepishly.

I smile at her to let her know it's okay.

"Well, I didn't tell you about my mom and dad because if I talked about it, that made it real. I so desperately haven't wanted any of it to be real."

She nods her head in understanding.

"The audition was something that meant a lot to me and my mom. I was trying to keep it that way. It was the last thing I had that was unfinished between the two of us. Now, there's nothing left. I did get accepted, by the way." I can't help but grin from ear to ear. I didn't realize how excited I would be to tell her.

"What! Oh my gosh! I was accepted to Parson's in New

York City. We'll be going there together!" She squeals and jumps off her chair to hug me. This is such great news.

"Congratulations! I knew that was your top choice, but you haven't said anything."

"I know. I was trying to secure financial aid before I mentioned it to anyone. We're going to have so much fun together." Her eyes sparkle and this is the Leila that I know and love. "So when are we going to talk about Drew?"

My face heats with a blush, and she giggles.

"I wasn't trying to keep him from you . . . it's just . . . he's a very, very private person."

"I know he is, and again, I'm so sorry for what I said. It was wrong of me. I knew that there was something more going on between the two of you. I started noticing the way he was looking at you at Grant's party back before Thanksgiving. When he kissed you on New Year's, there was nothing about that kiss that said, *hey this is our first time kissing*. I knew then, but you never said anything. I think that my feelings were just hurt because I thought you would tell me of all people . . . not that you had to. It's exciting to be dating someone, and I felt like you left me out. I've known both Drew and Beau for a very long time and, Ali, I've never seen him this happy. You should have heard him in the office after you left. He was pissed. And the look he gave me as he was leaving the office—if looks could kill, lasers would have been shooting out of his eyes."

I laugh, because I know this look.

"It's been a very slow-moving relationship. Let's just put it that way. I wouldn't change a thing, though. He's so sweet and very loving. There's so much more to him than anyone will ever know and I feel lucky to be the one he's sharing his life with."

She looks at me knowingly and my eyes fill with tears.

"You do realize that you're living every girl's dream come true right now."

I can't help but laugh again. However, based on the look on her face I get the feeling she isn't talking about every girl, and she isn't talking about Drew.

Leila ended up hanging out a little while longer. I invited her to stay for pizza and she was all in until I told her that Beau would be here too. Then she declined.

Drew, Beau, and Matt finally came over around 6:30, threw a comedy into the DVD player, and polished off all three of the pies that I made, including a pan of brownies.

The three of them laughed more at this movie and at each other than I've ever heard. It was music to my ears to hear them be so happy.

Beau decided to stay the night and their mom texted Matt when she wanted him to come home. Beau says he's officially claiming the guest bedroom.

As I'm turning off the lights, Drew throws me over his shoulder and runs up the stairs. I had left the balcony doors open while we were downstairs and now that the sun has dropped, my room is freezing. We close the door, jump under the blankets, and snuggle down together.

I'm half tempted to open them back up again if it means I get to snuggle longer with him.

"I have something I want to show you tomorrow when we get to school," Drew says to me.

"What is it?"

"Can't tell you. I want to show you." I can hear the smile in his voice.

"Well, that's not fair."

"Yes, it is. Besides, you're going to like it."

"Oh, really? Well, I happen to see something that I like right now."

He laughs.

"Come here, crazy girl." Drew pulls me on top of him and all thoughts about tomorrow are forgotten.

When we arrive at school the next morning Beau, Grant, and Ryan are standing in the parking lot waiting for us. Drew takes my hand as we walk over to them. All three of them notice this, and they smile. Besides Beau, they both knew. It's just no one has ever said anything.

Cassidy and her friends walk our way and the four of them slow down when they see Drew holding my hand.

"Drew! What are you doing?" Cassidy screeches.

Oh, she can't be serious.

Beau walks up to stand next to me, and Grant and Ryan fall in beside Drew and Beau. They are making a statement. I love when they do this, and I smile.

"Cassidy, how many times to do I have to tell you to stay away from me? What I do is none of your business, but since you're here, I'd like to introduce you to Ali, my girlfriend."

All three of Cassidy's friends gasp, but not her.

"But then again, you already knew this, didn't you?" Drew is mad.

"What about Sunday? Didn't that kiss mean anything to you?" She's trying to play the wounded role. If she thinks that she can manipulate either one of us, she's got another thing coming. *Stupid girl.*

She shoots me a smug look and I smile back at her. This confuses her. Leila, Chase, and a few other of our friends join our little circle. Each one of them letting Cassidy and her friends know that they're tired of this overplayed drama.

"Sunday? I've told you at least two dozen times that you

287

and I are nothing, and will never be. You know very well, the only reason I kissed you was to pacify your delusional father. That kiss wasn't even about you. It was a means to an end. Did you honestly think I wouldn't actually tell Ali about that? Better yet, after hearing the truth, did you think she would care?"

Even though the first bell has rung, a crowd of people have started to form around us. Drew never talks in public and people are coming from every direction to hear what he's saying.

"I don't believe you!" she screeches out again. Several people throughout the crowd chuckle and this throws her. She starts scanning the crowd, and we all see her looking for a possible adversary.

"Seriously, Cassidy?" Beau has had enough of being quiet. "Is there anyone here who thinks that Drew's lying?" He throws his hands in the air and spins around to look at the crowd.

No one says anything.

"How many times does he have to tell you before you'll get it in that very blonde head of yours? You do realize that you look crazy and kind of like a stalker."

"Beau! Shut up!" Cassidy stomps her foot.

"No! You shut up! Everyone is tired of this." Beau's cheeks flush with anger.

"This is all her fault!" She points to me.

Drew drops my hand, wraps his arm around my shoulders, and glares at Cassidy.

"Again! Is there anyone here who thinks this is Ali's fault?" Beau turns around, looking at the crowd. When his eyes land back on Cassidy, he smirks at her. "I didn't think so. Haven't you embarrassed yourself enough?"

Cassidy's face turns beet red and her eyes fill with tears.

She looks around at all of the people and then turns around to storm off.

"No more games, Cassidy. It's all over!" I know she can hear Beau as she pushes through the crowd. Everyone else hears him too.

Drew pulls me into him, and bends down so his mouth is next to my ear.

"You okay?"

"More than okay. I don't understand what is wrong with that girl. Geez, I hope for your sake, she leaves you alone now."

He chuckles in my ear. The warmth of his breath and the vibrations send goosebumps down my arm.

"I'm not worried about me. I'm worried about you."

"No, don't. She doesn't bother me. Really she doesn't. I mean, she's nothing to me, and in a few weeks when we leave, she'll be no one to us."

He pulls me in tighter.

"Seventy-five days," he whispers in my ear.

"What's that?"

"That's how many days away we are from leaving here."

"You're counting down?"

"I feel like I've been counting down for forever." He pulls back and looks into my eyes.

I understand why he says this and I reach up to place my hand on his cheek.

Drew bends down, and kisses me lightly on the lips. The second bell rings and people start moving around us. Why weren't they moving before? Were they watching us? Oh well, let them watch. He's mine, and I want the whole world to know.

"Meet me at my locker at lunch time. I still need to show

you something," he says as we walk through the front doors.

"Hmmm, secrets. I'm not so sure I like that, Mr. Hale." He throws his head back and laughs. I see people stop and look at us out of the corner of my eye. I totally understand. I would stop to hear him laugh too.

"Trust me, you'll like this one." He winks at me as he opens the door to our homeroom class.

DREW

LEAVE IT TO Cassidy to try and cause another scene. I seriously don't know what is wrong with that girl. I'm glad that Beau was here to finish that conversation. Confrontations with people are really not my thing. The only positive about it though is that everyone here now knows Ali is mine. Guys can stop looking at her and hopefully, at least while they're around me, they'll stop talking about her.

When Ali said in a few weeks we would be leaving here together, there was no question about this in her voice, and it was a statement of fact. She'll never know how happy she made me. I want to go with her, and hearing that she wants me too, that feeling of peace settles back over me.

Most of the morning moved pretty slowly. I'm not nervous to show her the letter. I'm more excited about seeing her reaction.

The bell to end fourth period finally rings. I jump out of my chair, and practically run to my locker. After what seems to take forever, Ali and Leila round the corner of the hallway. Her eyes land on mine and she smiles from ear to ear. She whispers something in Leila's ear. Leila looks up to find me, and smiles. She squeezes Ali's arm and skips off toward the cafeteria.

Everyone and everything fades into the background as she walks toward me. I can't help but to look her up and down. She doesn't even realize what those little shorts and those chucks do to me. She smirks, knowing my thoughts have just turned R-rated.

"I do believe you're once again up to no good." She stands right in front of me and seeing her smiling at me, melts my heart. I hope she looks at me like this forever.

"Why do you say that?" I smile back at her.

"Because I've seen this look before. It's like you've got a secret, but whatever it is, you know you're going to get your way, so you're feeling pretty confident in yourself."

I laugh at her assessment. She's pretty accurate.

I open my locker and hand her the letter.

"What's this?" She looks at me questioningly.

"Open it and read it." My heart races and my palms start to sweat.

Ali drops her bag on the ground, pulls out the letter, and unfolds it. I watch as she reads the lines and shock washes over her face.

"Is this for real?"

"Yes."

"When did you do this?"

"Last November, after you told me about your Juilliard audition. Coach helped me send in a late application, which is why I just got this yesterday."

"Why didn't you tell me yesterday?"

"Because I wanted to show you."

Tears fill her eyes and she throws her arms around me. "I can't believe you did this."

291

I wrap my arms around her too, and lay my head on top of hers.

"I told you . . . I've always been yours."

"I can't believe you got into Columbia!" she whisper squeals, and starts jumping up and down.

This causes me to laugh.

"I couldn't wait to tell you, but I had to make sure first. I didn't want to get your hopes up."

"This is the best thing anyone has ever told me, aside from you loving me. This is even better than my acceptance to Juilliard. I feel like this is Christmas and my birthday all wrapped up into one. I love you so much. Thank you, Drew."

I laugh again at the excitement radiating off her.

"Love you too. And don't thank me, just tell me that you want me."

She looks up at me and gives me another knowing look. Yes, I did mean that both ways.

"Come on, let's go out and get some lunch." I take the letter from her, put it back in the envelope, and return it to my locker.

"We're really going to do this?" She takes my hand, reaches down to grab her bag, and smiles up at me as we walk toward the door.

"Was there really any other option? What was the word that you used? Oh yeah . . . home. You're my home too."

Tears of happiness shine through her. I'm glad I decided to wait and show her. I'll never forget the look on her face. To me, that's priceless.

DREW

I DECIDE TO cut swim practice a little short today so I can run home and put on something a little nicer. Part of me wants to wait for Ali and maybe shower with her, but then again, it'll be a nice gesture to show up looking clean and ready to go.

After all of the things that have happened over the last couple of days, I think it'll be nice to take her out to dinner. We can get out of the house and celebrate.

I know I dropped a bomb on her today, but honestly I wasn't ready to go all in until I knew how she felt about me. I'm glad at the pace things have gone, but as we approach graduation, it's definitely time for us to begin making plans as to where we're going from here. If I have it my way, it'll be straight into an apartment in New York City. No dorms or other school living arrangements. I'm ready to start my life with her. I just want to be with her.

Beau's car is in the driveway when I pull in, and this surprises me a little bit. He's supposed to be at tennis practice with Grant, but today it's extremely hot outside, so I can't blame him for wanting to bail.

Walking into the kitchen, the first things that I notice are broken dishes and glass everywhere. It looks as if we've been robbed. Shock and fear course through me knowing that Beau is home. I scan the room and that's when I see them. My stomach drops and my emotions quickly change to pain and anger as I step toward them. I know he's done this. The question is, why?

My mother is curled up on the floor with her head in Beau's lap, and she looks unconscious. Her face is badly beaten and she has handprint bruises forming all over her. I tear my eyes from her and look at Beau. He too is sporting a black eye, a bruised cheek bone, bloody nose, and a busted lip. Blood drips off his face.

"What happened!" I yell at them.

"Oh, you should know." His voice is right behind me and it slithers up my spine. The hairs on the back on my neck stand up and rage rushes through my veins.

"Where's Matt?" I hiss out. I'm still looking at Beau. Panic slams into me, causing my hands to shake. I close them into fists, and every muscle through my back, neck, and arms begin to tighten. Beau shakes his head at me. Matt's not here. My heart instantly feels relief, but my body doesn't respond. Beau and I are locked onto each other. Fear is written all over him and I'm sure he can read the anger on me.

"You did this to them?" I look at him and he smirks at me. I'm now shaking all over.

"No, Drew, you did this to them. Did you really think I wouldn't find out about all of your sneaking around? I know about the P.O. box, the college acceptances, and even your first choice . . . Columbia."

"How did you find out about that? Who told you?" Disbelief and suspicion fill me. I haven't told anyone but Coach Black about the P.O. box until today, and I know for a fact that Ali wouldn't say anything.

"It doesn't matter. What does matter is that you're a fool if you think I'll allow you to do anything differently than what I have planned for you."

"Where I go to college and what I do with my life is not your choice! Not anymore! I'm nineteen years old, going on twenty, and I'm done with you!" Sweat begins to drip down the sides of my face. I never stand up against him, ever.

"You will watch your mouth, boy! Maybe I need to remind you again who's the boss here, and who is nothing but a worthless piece of shit!" He walks into the kitchen, grabs a pan off of the pot rack, and walks over to Beau and my mom. Looking at me, he sneers and swings. A dull ring of metal sounds as it makes contact with Beau's back shoulder blade.

He lets out a moan as he tightens his grip on our mom and continues to drape himself over her, she still hasn't moved.

The ringing echoes through my head, and I've lost all sense of sound.

My eyes blur, and all I see is red. I'm standing in the kitchen, looking at the two of them, and fighting the two battles occurring in my head. The first one is the thirteen-year-old boy who fears his father and believes him when he says he's worthless and unwanted, and the second is the nineteen-year-old young man who's bigger and stronger than this weak old man who's pathetic and still attempting to control all of us.

Something inside of me finally cracks. I can no longer take him hurting the people I love.

In slow motion, I see him grab Beau by the hair, whip his head back, and swing the pan with the full intention of bringing it down on him. Beau cringes, preparing for the pain, as I lunge forward and land squarely on my father, knocking him to the floor. His head bounces off of the hardwood, my fists instantly connect with his face, and I barely remember the rest.

Somehow in the midst of the massive beat down, Beau called 911. At some point, police officers enter our house, and it takes three of them to pull me off of him. I'm in a blind rage.

My father is immediately placed under arrest and hauled out of the house. He screams profanities at us, as if this makes a difference. We're all done with him.

An ambulance comes and EMT specialists load my mother onto a gurney and take her out the front door. She still hasn't regained consciousness. They try to persuade Beau to go as well, but he refuses.

I look down at my hands, and they're completely covered in blood. Walking over to the kitchen sink, I can feel several sets of eyes on me. I need to get his blood off of me. The water from the faucet stings as it rolls over my split knuckles. I can hear them talking to Beau, getting his statement, and I have no idea what's going to happen next.

I head to the kitchen table and sit down. I'm certain that I'll be arrested and for once, I just don't care. For years and years, I've laid in bed at night imagining what it would be like to finally be the one to break him. To put him in his place. To hurt him like he's hurt all of us. And right now, I want to live in this moment regardless of the consequences.

Two officers approach me, and both of them look solemn.

"Drew . . ." They glance at each other. One shakes his head, and then he looks back to me. "Son, we need to place you under arrest."

I don't say anything. I knew this was coming. I stand up.

"What!" Beau screams in the background. "What for?

Why?" He comes and stands next to me.

"Mr. Hale is pressing charges for assault."

"He can't do that! He did this to us. He's been doing it for years! Drew was protecting us!"

"Beau, is there anyone you can call?" The older of the two officers ask him.

Beau looks at me, tears fill his eyes, and I can see his heart breaking for me. He doesn't know how to help me.

"It'll be all right. Text Matt and tell him to go to Aunt Ella's. Let her know that he needs to spend the night and we'll explain later. Go down to the hospital and sit with mom. Everything will be fine. When she wakes up, the three of us can deal with all of this mess together, okay? Please, I don't want her there by herself."

He nods and leans into me for a hug. His tears are now unstoppable.

The younger of the two officers walks behind me, and the distinct sound of handcuffs echo through the kitchen as he clamps them down on me.

The adrenaline that's been coursing through my body over the last forty-five minutes has begun to dissolve, and I feel an overwhelming sense of tiredness. I'm drained, emotionally and physically. And if I am honest with myself, I'm scared. Of course Dad wants to press charges. He's that much of an asshole to not even care about my future. I'm an adult and should this stick, I'll permanently have a misdemeanor on my record, or even worse a felony since I hit him back with the pan. It was worth it though. I just have to keep telling myself no regrets.

The three of us walk down the front steps and the older officer begins reciting my Miranda Rights, informing me that I have the right to request an attorney. As we approach the back seat of the car, the younger officer pats me down just to confirm that I'm not carrying a concealed weapon. He opens the door and gently pushes me in.

A few of the neighbors have come outside to see what is going on, but in the end, I just lock eyes with Beau. He stands on the porch leaning over the railing.

As the police car pulls out of the driveway, the red and blue lights reflect off of the houses on our street. I'm thankful they don't turn on the siren, but I hate that I'm being subjected to this. An unwanted sense of anxiety and panic flood through me. The anxiety isn't for what I've done, it's more for the unknown. What's going to happen to me now? What's going to happen to Ali? How will she find out? Will she be disappointed in me?

My heart rate speeds up and it begins to get hard to breathe. This is the worst time ever to be having an anxiety attack. I'm trying to get this under control, but it's just not happening. It's so hot in the back of this car, sweat is soaking my clothes causing them to stick to me. My wrists, which are trapped behind me, start to hurt, and in general I'm overwhelmed by how uncomfortable I am.

The cops talk and their radio constantly goes off, but I don't have any idea what any of it means. By the time we pull into the station, I'm about ready to pass out.

The older cop opens my back door, takes one look at me, and unlocks the handcuffs.

"Son, I'm trusting that you won't be a problem if I remove these. We need you to take some deep breaths and calm down. It'll all work itself out." I immediately start rubbing my wrists and then the saber tattoo on my arm.

Beau's safe. Breathe. Mom's safe. Breathe. Matt's safe. Breathe. Ali's safe. Breathe.

Beau's safe. Breathe. Mom's safe. Breathe. Matt's safe. Breathe. Ali's safe. Breathe.

Slowly, my breathing returns to normal. The two officers didn't turn away from me, but they gave me as much privacy as they could.

Mustering up the strength and courage that I need to continue this, I take a deep breath, let it out, and remind myself that in seventy-five days, it's just her and me.

"All right, I'm ready," I say to them.

They step back away from the car so I can get out.

ALI

LOUD BANGING FROM the door leading to the outside thunders through the room and causes me to jump. No one ever comes to that door, but just in case, I always keep it locked. I put down the paint brush and rush over as the banging begins again. Instead of dancing, I'm a part of the cleanup process. Today, I'm painting over the graffiti on the walls.

I throw open the door and standing there gasping for air is Beau. He pushes passed me, comes into the room, slams the door, and spins me around so I'm back against it.

I'm shocked by his appearance, and I'm certain my jaw has dropped open. His shirt is ripped at the neck and covered in blood, one half of his face is red and swollen, his nose is bleeding, he has a black eye coming in already, and his bottom lip is split terribly and is still bleeding. He's shaking from head to toe.

Tears fill my eyes. "Oh my God. What happened to you?"

I say calmly and quietly. I take a step closer to him and he throws his hands up for me to not come any nearer.

Behind him, Coach Black enters the room, but Beau doesn't know this.

He takes one step toward me and slowly sinks to his knees. He's still struggling to breathe and then his control slips. Tears start to leak from his eyes and he drops his head.

Without even thinking, I walk to him and wrap my arms around him. His head presses into my stomach and he pulls me tighter to him. Silently, he sobs. I can't help the tears that fall over his obvious emotional state. He's having a complete breakdown, and my heart is dying for him.

I look up at Coach, and he slowly walks up behind Beau to put his hands on his shoulders.

At least five minutes goes by and Beau doesn't seem to be getting any calmer. Coach lowers himself to the ground next to Beau and pulls him off of me, folding him into his arms. Beau continues to cry as Coach wraps his arms around him and tries to console him.

I feel so overwhelmed when I think of all the places and people that Beau could have gone to, and he comes to me. He feels safe enough here with me, that he can be himself without fear or judgment and know that he's with someone who genuinely loves him.

I think about how happy I am to have Drew and Beau be a part of my life, and that's when it hits me. Where is Drew?

"Beau, where's Drew?"

His tears falter, and he stops breathing as he turns around to look at me. Panic is written all over his face and now I'm silently freaking out.

I ask him again, "Beau, where is Drew?"

Another tear drops and he lowers himself so he's sitting

on the ground. He pulls his knees up, leans his elbows onto them, and begins to run his hands through his hair.

"Beau?" I need answers from him before I flip out and go crazy.

"He's in jail." What?!

"What for?"

Beau looks over to Coach and then he looks back at me. He takes a deep breath.

"Dad found out about Drew getting into Columbia." He drops his eyes. Knowing how Drew feels about this area of their life, I can tell that Beau feels ashamed and embarrassed.

"How?"

"I don't think Drew knows. Either someone broke into his locker and found the letter, or maybe they overheard the two of you talking earlier today?" I can't imagine anyone breaking into his locker, so someone must have heard us.

"Did he tell you? Did you know?" I ask him.

"No. I think you were the only one and we all know that you didn't say anything." Of course I didn't. I never talk about Drew to anyone.

"So what happened?"

"Dad did what he always does. Except this time instead of him just going after me, he went after my mom too. She was half gone by the time Drew even got home." Beau's eyes fill with tears again, and in his mind, I know he's seeing his mom.

"Drew went ballistic and started beating the shit out of him. I called 911 from my cell phone, but when the police showed up, they arrested my dad and Drew. Dad is pressing charges for assault. Ali, I don't know what to do. I had to come here and tell you so you can go and help him. Please help him. My mom was taken to the hospital and I need to go to her." His voice is pleading to me and I'm at a loss for what he just

301

said.

"Beau." Coach Black has been listening to the conversation and I'm so glad he's here. I don't know what to do or how to help him. "This is what we are going to do. You're going to come with me. We need to take a little ride to the police station and you need to give a statement."

"I already did."

"You're going to need to give another one, and son, I'm sorry to say that you're going to have to be very in depth, specific, and thorough. Do you understand what I'm saying?"

Beau nods his head and lets out a sigh.

"Yes. I always knew this day would come and believe it or not, I'm ready." Coach and Beau both stand up.

"Okay, now Ali, you head on over to the emergency room and see what you can find out about Mrs. Hale. Shoot Beau a text, so he knows what's going on. Let them know that you'll be the only one who's available for her for a while. The boys will get there as soon as they can."

"Okay."

Coach Black leaves the room to go and grab his keys. I run over to the corner and pick up my bag. Even though the mirror on the wall is shattered, I can see Beau's blood all over the front of my shirt and I have to fight back the tears. I need to be strong for him. He doesn't need me to be an emotional head case right now.

Before I reach the back door, I stop in front of him.

He glances down at me, and he looks completely drained and defeated.

I drop my bag and jump onto him, wrapping my arms and legs around him. I probably shouldn't have in case he's hurt somewhere else, but I can't help myself. I know that I caught him completely off guard as he lets out a large "Oufff."

"Geez, Tiny, for someone so small, you sure are pretty solid," he chuckles.

I lean back a little and gently take his face in my hands, forcing him to lock his eyes with mine. "Listen to me. Everything is okay. It'll all sort itself out and everyone will be fine. Everyone is fine. From now on, all four of you won't have to worry about this or him anymore. It's all going to be okay." His eyes fill with tears, but this time they don't spill over. He gives me a small smile and I lean in to hug him again. He hugs me back. I kiss him on his cheek, and hop down.

He lets out another deep breath and smiles at me again. A little glimmer of hope in his eyes and I'm more comfortable leaving him knowing that he's in a better place than when he walked in.

Coach returns and the three of us walk out the back door together.

I don't ask any questions about where they're headed. I'm not really sure if either one of them would be able to give me any answers anyway. I watch as Coach wraps his arm around Beau's shoulders and I can't help but be thankful that the guys have someone like him on their side.

It only takes me about twenty minutes to drive over to the hospital. I really don't know if they'll tell me anything or if they'll even let me in.

Because it's a Wednesday evening, there are plenty of places for me to park, and in general, the emergency room department doesn't look to be all that busy.

The letters are large and red, and as the doors slide open, I feel a little nervous. I mean, this is going to be the first time I'm meeting Drew's mom. We've kind of been dating for months and I'm not even sure if I've passed her on our street.

I walk through the doors and up to the registration desk.

"Hi, I'm here to be with Mrs. Diane Hale."

"And you are?" She barely even glances at my face, but I see her take in my overall appearance.

"Allyson Rain."

"Are you next of kin?" she asks while opening up a large three ring binder that has *Visitors* written across the front.

"Yes."

"Okay then, I'll need to see some sort of identification, so I can check you in as an after-hours patient visitor." I look over to the clock and see that it's 5:30.

"Do you plan on staying a while?" She must be watching me.

"Yes, ma'am."

"Well, then you're going to need an after-hours tag. You may as well take care of that now."

I pull out my driver's license and hand it to her.

"Can you tell me how she is?"

"No, I'm sorry. I'm not allowed to give out patient information. If she isn't awake to talk to you, then one of her doctor's or a nurse will be by to answer your questions." She scans my ID, a tag prints out, and she hands it to me.

"Okay, thanks."

"Just walk through those doors and someone at the nurse's station will show you where to go."

"Thanks again." I walk through the doors and look around at the organized chaos that is the emergency room.

The nurse's station is immediately behind the doors and I see that the patient rooms are lined up one next to the other creating a U-shape around the station. The nurse closest to me seems to know who I'm here to see and she points to her room. I go and stand in front of the closed door.

I'm so nervous to go in to meet his mom. Will she like

me? Will she talk to me? Is she like my mother? Will she even want me here? Taking a deep breath, I only know one way to answer that question. I knock on the door and then slowly push it open.

Chapter Twenty

ALI

THE WOMAN LYING on the bed could have been the perfect poster model for domestic abuse. She has one black eye that's so bad it's swollen shut, her cheek is terribly bruised, and there are hand prints around her neck and on her arms. Her good eye is red and swollen. I can tell she's been crying. My heart aches for her. She watches me as I walk into the room and sit down in the chair next to her bed.

"Hi," I say quietly. I pull my legs up into the chair to make myself comfortable. She doesn't say anything back. I was hoping I might recognize her, but nope.

"I'm Ali."

Recognition flashes across her face, and I see her perk up just a little bit.

"Ali," she says this very quietly and very slowly. "You're so tiny, beautiful, and perfect." I watch as she looks me over. "It's very nice to meet you. I've wanted to meet you for so long."

"Really?" I don't know why this surprises me. For some reason I thought that she didn't know about me.

"Yes. I've seen such a change in Drew over the last couple of months. You've made him so happy, and I wanted to meet the girl that did this to him." She smiles at me. It's Drew's smile, and my heart squeezes.

"I didn't think that you wanted to meet me." Unwanted tears fill my eyes.

"Oh, sweetheart, that wasn't it. Drew's life has been so unhappy and complicated. I can imagine that he just wanted to keep his two worlds separate. It had nothing to do with me wanting to meet you or not. Can you blame him?"

"No, I guess not."

"I'm so happy you're here. I'm sorry it's under these circumstances, but I would like to know you." Tears now fill her eyes and together we stare at each other.

"Do you mind me being here?" I need to know if I'm making her uncomfortable.

"No, not at all. I'm embarrassed that you have to see me like this, but if you don't mind, then neither do I."

"Do you know anything about me?"

"No, except that Beau calls you Tiny. Now I see why."

I smile at his silly nickname. I need to remember to ask him why he calls me that. She flinches, squeezes her eyes shut, and lets out a slow hiss.

"Oh . . . Mrs. Hale . . . are you okay?" I stand up ready to jump into action.

She opens her eyes. I can see that the pain has passed, and I lower back down into the chair. "I suppose. He broke two ribs, but the medicine they gave me is helping. The rest is all surface damage. It'll go away. Can you please tell me what's happened to the boys?" She looks nervous as she asks this.

"Beau came and found me at school. He and Coach Black went down to the police station to try and get Drew released, and I don't know about Matt. I don't think he was there, but I'm sure that Beau has been in touch with him."

She gasps.

"Mr. Hale was arrested and he told the officers that he wanted to press charges against Drew for assault."

Tears fill her eyes and leak out.

"I know in this moment things feel really bad, but looking at the big picture, everything will be okay. It has to be. You, Beau, Matt, and Drew don't need to worry anymore. Does that make sense?"

"It does, but no matter what happens, as their mother I will always carry the guilt of letting this go on for as long as it has. I wish I had said or done something years ago." More of her tears come and she closes her eyes.

I reach out and take her hand. She looks back at me with guilt and sorrow all over her.

"I saw a quote once and it kind of stuck with me, it's by Ida Scott Taylor. "Do not look back and grieve over the past, for it is gone; and do not be troubled about the future, for it has yet to come. Live in the present, and make it so beautiful that it will be worth remembering." I want to make my life beautiful, and you should too. I mean, have you seen those gorgeous boys of yours lately?" She grins at me.

"You are so young to remember quotes like this. What happened to you?"

"My mom died 248 days ago. August 2nd." I drop my head and rub my free hand across my thigh. Even though it's been eight months, I still don't want to talk about it.

"Oh, sweetheart, I'm so sorry. Did you just move here?"

"Yes, the day before school started in August. I actually live in the house right across the street from you."

"Really? I didn't think that anyone was living there until yesterday when I saw Drew come out the front door."

"Yep, I live there. Just me."

She frowns. "What about your dad?"

"He's trying to start over with his life. I guess I just ended up not being a part of it." I look away from her. She doesn't need to know how much this hurts me.

"Drew stays with you?"

"Sometimes. Mostly, just Saturday nights. He doesn't like me being there alone."

"I can see that. He's very protective of those he loves." I don't know what to say to this. He just told me that he loves me, yet his mother who I have never met seems to already know. "Yes, he does love you. A mother can tell these kinds of things."

"Earlier today, when they were loading me up to come here, I heard Drew mention to Beau that only one person knew that he was accepted to Columbia. I'm assuming that's you?"

"Yes, I think so, but I just found out today. I don't know how Mr. Hale heard. I didn't even know that he wanted to go Columbia. He didn't tell me."

"Do you know why he does?"

"He said because he wants to be with me. After he found out about my audition last fall, he applied. Over the weekend my acceptance letter to Juilliard came in the mail. He was waiting until he knew for sure what my plans were before he told me."

"You were accepted to Juilliard? Ali, that's amazing."

"Thank you. I'm a dancer."

"You must be a wonderful dancer. I can't wait to watch

you sometime . . . if that's okay."

Tears come back to my eyes. I know I should be holding it together a little bit more, but I love Drew. He's my home and being here with his mom I kind of feel like she's mine too. I miss talking to my mom so much.

Drew's mom and I talk for hours. The nurses come in to check on her a few times but, we're so engrossed in our conversation that we barely even notice. At some point, I moved my chair closer to her and laid my head down on the bed. It's been such an emotional last couple of days that when she starts running her fingers through my hair, I just go to sleep.

Sometime around one in the morning, I feel a hand run down my back, and I sit up to see Drew standing there. I'm surprised they let him in this late, but I'm so happy to see him. I immediately stand up and walk into his arms. I want to hang onto him forever. He tucks his head down into my neck and I can feel him breathing me in and out. His skin still has a slight chlorinated smell to it. As familiar as this smell of him is to me, I can't help but frown because this means he hasn't even showered. Eventually, I pull back. I need to look him over from head to toe.

"Are you okay? I was so worried about you," I whisper to him. His face is etched with mixed emotions and exhaustion.

"I am now. How is she? What happened to her?" His eyes leave me and go over to his mother. She's still sleeping.

"She's okay, too. A little banged up, a few bruises, and he broke two ribs, but she seems strong. She'll pull through this."

He looks so sad.

"I'm sorry you had to come down here. Did the two of you get along okay?"

"Don't be, and yes. I loved every minute of talking to her. She's wonderful."

A little smile comes out of him as I say this.

"She is wonderful. It makes me happy that you finally got to meet her. I'm sorry it took so long."

"Don't be sorry." We both stop talking and just kind of stare at each other. "What happened to you?" I run my hands down his arms and chest. I pick up his hands and look at the damage done to his knuckles. They're swollen and they must hurt him.

"We can talk about it all in depth later, but it turns out Coach Black's brother-in-law is a local judge. Coach and Beau went to his house and had a little heart to heart. It seems that my father wasn't as secretive and discreet as he thought he was. Several people, including Coach Black, suspected that something has been going on at home.

"The judge filed a writ of habeas corpus, which says that I am to be brought before a judge, before booking—you know finger printing, photo and all that stuff. And it states that a prisoner can be released from unlawful detention, that is, detention lacking any sufficient cause or evidence. I've learned all kinds of things over the last few hours. A few statements had to be made and those combined with Beau's and my mom's set me free claiming it was self-defense. Whereas my dad is being charged with child abuse, assault, domestic abuse, and attempted murder."

"What? Murder?"

"Yep, apparently the hand print bruises around her neck showed them that he tried to strangle her. Whether or not murder was his intent is really irrelevant to them. Not a good move on his part. He's not allowed bail and is going to be tied up in the judicial system for a while."

"Drew, that's crazy."

"I know, but he's gonna get what he deserves. Now at

least we can all finally just live. Beau is having a bit of a hard time with all of this, but we'll help him through it."

"I saw him earlier. He came to me."

"I know. I'm glad he did. You're his family, too." My heart skips a beat and words don't need to be said. Drew wraps his hands around my face and lowers his lips to mine. "Love you," he whispers across my lips without breaking the connection. If I could have crawled inside of him and stayed there forever, I think I just might have.

Behind us, we hear a throat clear. We both jump back and turn to look at his mom.

Drew walks over to his mom and leans over to hug her. "Mom . . ." His voice breaks.

"It's all right, Drew. Everything is going to be okay. Just think about it, three good things happened to me today . . . wanna hear what they are?" He leans away from her and chuckles.

"Sure."

"First, I found out that you were accepted to Columbia in New York City. I'm so very proud of you. You have no idea. Second, I got to meet this beautiful, wonderful girl who has stolen your heart and made you so happy. You deserve to be loved unconditionally and I can't tell you what it means to me that you've found someone like her." She looks over and smiles at me. "And third, I finally get to live my life making beautiful memories that will be worth remembering."

I can't help but walk over to the other side of the bed and hug her. She listened to me and found it profound enough to remember and repeat.

"I'm kind of having a moment here watching the two women in my life interact like this. I'm not gonna lie. I'm definitely loving this, but it feels a little strange." All three of us

312

laugh and Drew's poor mom moans at the pain.

"Where's Beau?" she asks.

"He's in the lobby. They wouldn't let both of us come back."

"And Matt?"

"He's sleeping over at Aunt Ella's."

She lets out a sigh and relief sweeps across her body.

"Well, my favorite oldest son, how about you take this young lady home and get some rest. Send Beau back and I can see you both tomorrow."

"Okay, Mom. I love you." Drew bends down and gently gives her another hug.

"And I love you both."

My eyes fill again with tears and I smile at her. Our gazes lock, and she knows without me saying anything how much that meant to me.

Hand in hand, Drew and I walk out to the lobby. Beau has his elbows resting on his knees, and his head bent over in his hands. His legs bounce. Anxiety is written all over him. He jumps when he hears the sliding doors open and he flies out of his chair when he sees us. I let out a small gasp as I take in the damage to his face and clothes. Drew squeezes my hand tighter. That is his way of telling me not to make a big deal of it.

"Is she okay?" His eyes drift back and forth between the two of us, searching for answers.

"Yes. A little banged up, but honestly she seems lighter, maybe even happier, than I've seen her in a long time." Beau lets out a deep breath and runs his hands through his hair.

"Dude. I feel like I've been waiting for hours to hear that."

"What are you talking about? I text you when I got here," I say to him.

"I know, but part of me thought that you might have been leaving out some details because you didn't want me to worry and in the end, I ended up worrying more . . ."

"Beau, stop!" Drew says. "You're up anyways. Head on back there and go see her for yourself."

"Yeah, sounds good. I'll probably spend the rest of the night here."

"I'll be at Ali's."

"Okay, then I'll see you tomorrow."

The two reach for each other, bump arms, and embrace as only two brothers can. They're lucky to have each other.

Together, Drew and I walk out of the emergency room. He's still holding my hand, and I love that he doesn't want to let me go.

Being around Drew over the last couple of months, I've always felt that he has this edge to him, that he doesn't need anyone or really anything. I knew that he liked me and wanted to spend time with me, but for the most part I've felt that this relationship was very one-sided. I needed him much more than he needed me. But maybe that isn't the case. Maybe he does need me just as much. He's done a great job at hiding it.

DREW

NOT MUCH IS said on the ride home from the hospital. I'm not sure what to say to her, but I can't let go of her hand. Over the last eight hours, my emotions have gone from one extreme to the next. I was so angry at everything. I was angry at my mom for allowing this to go on for so long. I was angry at Beau because he didn't stop dad from hurting her. I was angry at myself for the life I've had to deal with. It just isn't fair. I was angry at everyone and everything.

Then once the anger dissipated, this crushing sense of sadness and guilt kicked in. It's the guilt that hurts and haunts me the most. It always does and I live with it every single day. What happened to them today was my fault. If I had just followed his plan, none of this would have ever happened. The thing is though, I'm not willing to give up Ali and they suffered because of it. If only I had walked away from her months ago like I should have. But that would have been like giving up air. You need air to breathe, and I need her.

Ali pulls into her driveway and parks the car. "Which house do you want to go to?"

"Yours. I need to grab some clothes first, though. Will you come with me?" I have no interest in ever going back into this house. It has so many horrible memories for me that I really just want to move in with Ali. She'd probably let me if I ask her.

When we walk through the kitchen door, I can't help but squeeze her hand tighter. The destruction of the kitchen, the mess and blood that's everywhere takes me right back to earlier in the day, and I freeze.

Somehow I've zoned out, and it takes Ali pulling on my arm and calling my name to bring me back. I don't realize I'm shaking until I look down at her and see she's holding onto both of my hands.

"Come on, Drew, let's get in and out, okay? Do you want me to go get clothes for you and I'll meet you outside?"

"No, I don't want you anywhere near anything in this house. Thanks for offering, though." I pull her with me up the stairs and into my room.

"Feels kind of strange. I've never been in your room before." She looks out the window and across the street at her house. This is my view to her.

"I know. I never wanted you to be a part of this life. I'm sorry."

"Don't be. I understand a little better now."

My room looks like a typical guy's room. I keep it very neat, and it's filled with swimming paraphernalia. I see her scan the walls. I have so many awards and framed articles that it would take her hours to read all of them. In the corner, I have a surfboard. She runs her fingers across it. On my desk, I have a large mason jar just like hers filled with shells and a piece of sea glass. She picks it up and smiles at me. She knows these are from our first date and she gives me a look that says this jar is definitely coming with us.

"Coach Black mentioned to Judge Thomas that somehow there was foul play involved. The acceptance letter was in my locker at school, so to try and fish out the true story of how dear old Dad came across this information he added another Federal charge onto his list of offenses. Federal statute says that any mail that has been opened, taken, or destroyed is considered obstruction of correspondence and is punishable. He immediately started backtracking and sang like a bird, throwing Cassidy under the bus. Apparently, she overheard us in the hallway. She must have been standing behind me, and after we walked off, she broke into my locker and took all the acceptance letters to my dad."

Disbelief and shock is written across Ali's face. Anger replaces them as her jaw tightens and she turns red.

"I guess I just don't understand why she would go to such extremes. She had to of known you would find out how he got the letters. I can't believe she broke into your locker! She has to be behind what happened to The Cave, too. I don't understand why she did it, but it really can only be her."

"I know. Coach Black said that we'll know more by Monday."

Ali sits down on my bed while I grab a bag to pack of few of my things. I know my mom is going to need some help once she gets home, but for right now, I only want to be with Ali.

When we get back to her house, I immediately drop my bag by her dresser and walk into the bathroom. I strip off all of my clothes and step into the shower. I need to wash off the visions, memories, emotions, blood, sweat, and dirt. I need this whole horrible night to disappear. I don't want any of it on me anymore. I place both of my hands on the wall and lean forward, allowing the hot water to wash down over me.

I look up at some point and see Ali sitting on the bathroom counter, watching me. Love and concern is evident on her beautiful face, but she leaves me alone and gives me some space. That's what I need at the moment.

Every time I close my eyes, I see Beau and my mom both bleeding and lying on the floor. I don't know how to erase this image and my heart rate starts to speed up again. I can feel the anxiety attack setting in and this is now my third one in four days. I can't control them, and they make me feel weak.

The water shuts off and Ali takes me by the hand, leading me out of the shower. I watch her every move. She runs a towel over my head, across my chest and back, wraps it around my waist, closes the lid to the toilet, sits me down, and straddles my lap. I lay my head on her shoulder. She holds me until the shaking stops, my breathing returns to normal, and I'm calm enough to get up.

"Let's go to bed, okay?" Her voice is so soft it's almost a whisper.

"Okay." I throw on a pair of boxers and climb into her

bed.

She changes her clothes and joins me under the blankets.

"I lied to you." It just kind of comes out.

"When?" She rolls onto her side so we're facing each other.

"The tattoo on my inner arm of 'Freedom' isn't about the feeling that I have when I'm swimming in the water. That's the answer I always give people. What it really means is that with each stroke I take, that swimming is my ticket out of here and away from him. When I see it through the goggles, it's a re-minder that I need to focus on swimming harder, faster, and longer because I know that no matter what, if I do these things, then one day I'll be set free. Free of him. That's why I got it tattooed there."

Tears well up in her eyes. "I don't know what to say to that," she says. "I know there are a ton of things you still don't know about me, but at the moment I can't think of any. I think that you officially won this round of 'stump me.'"

I give her a small smile, but I know she can see the ex-pression on my face change to grief. She's very familiar with this look.

"It's my fault this has all gone on so long." I feel like I'm confessing my biggest sins to her. They're all about to come pouring out of me and I don't know if I can stop them.

"How can you possibly believe that?"

"It's true. I'm the oldest and I'm also the biggest of the four of us. I should have put a stop to all of this years ago." My eyes fill with tears. I suck my bottom lip in and bite it. I don't want to cry in front of her. I don't cry, ever. "He hurt them over and over," I whisper to her. A tear leaks out against my will and runs down the side of my face.

The expression on her face lets me know that her heart is

breaking for the pain that I'm feeling.

I close my hands into fists. I know how to shut it off. I know how to shut out all emotions and not feel. It's something I've perfected over the years. Only now, it isn't working. Her hand comes up and brushes a piece of hair off of my forehead and she cups the side of my face. Just that little touch from her gives me a tiny sense of calm.

"Drew, why are you trying to take on the responsibility of what he did? He's a horrible, abusive, sick man. Those things that he did and said were his actions that you had no control over. This is all on him. You and Beau were children, his children, and he abused his privilege of being your father. You can't take the blame away from him and project it onto yourself. You didn't do these things. Those were his choices. You didn't do anything wrong." I hear what she's saying, but this is how I've thought about things for years and years. To accept that I might have it wrong or that I should have been looking at the situation with him differently is unfathomable to me. It's become so much of who I am and what I think of myself.

"Ali, I didn't protect them." I squeeze both of my eyes closed. They're burning. My chin trembles and I suck in air through my nose. A huge lump has formed in the back of my throat and now my tears start to drop. This emotion is so overwhelming that as hard as I try, I can't keep it in. I can't remember the last time I cried. Oh, yes I can.

"But you did. So many times that we probably couldn't even count them. And honestly, it probably wouldn't have mattered what you did the other times because he wasn't going to change and he would have found a way to be vicious anyway."

"I should have stopped him sooner."

"Sweetheart, you can't change what's already happened.

But you need to feel good about today. Take a deep breath, and remember you did stop him today. Today is all that matters and he won't touch any of you ever again." She's right.

"I did stop him today." I let out a deep breath and with it come more tears. Now he knows that no matter what, he can't control us anymore. I might be the cause of what happened to them today, but I have protected them and their future. From now on I'll always fight back and I will fight for them. Today, he lost his power and somewhere, where ever he is, he knows this.

Ali pulls the blankets up over our heads, and I know what she's doing. She's created a tiny bubble, which is a safe place, where only she and I exist. In this bubble, I fold her into my arms and cry. I cry until I can't cry anymore, and we fall asleep.

ALI

NOISE IN THE kitchen wakes me. I slip out of the bed and down the stairs to see what it is. Under no circumstances do I want Drew to wake up. He needs to rest.

I find Beau standing at the refrigerator and he looks up when he sees me.

"Hey, when did you get here?" I look at the clock and see it's 6:30.

"A few minutes ago."

I walk over to him and give him hug. I'm glad he's here.

"Why don't you sit down and I'll fix you something to eat."

He lets out a sigh and sits down at the kitchen table.

"Thanks." He looks so tired.

"Your face looks better."

"Yeah, the charge nurse responsible for my mom took one look at me and scowled. Next thing I knew, she was cleaning me up and stitching my lip. I probably should have gone in with mom. The nurse thinks I have a slight concussion, but whatever. It's all over now." I hand him three ibuprofen and a large glass of water.

"How does some scrambled eggs and a fruit smoothie sound?" Soft foods were probably best for him.

"Perfect. Thanks, Ali."

"Anytime, Beau."

Beau wanders into the living room and lies down on the couch. I hand him a bag of frozen blueberries for his swollen cheek bone and within five minutes, he's out cold. My heart aches for him and what he must be feeling. I cover him with a blanket and head back into the kitchen to make some breakfast. My guess is that Drew hasn't eaten either, so I pull out some potatoes for hash browns and a package of bacon.

Around 8:00, Drew wanders down into the kitchen and looks around. He's thrown on a pair of athletic shorts and although now's not the time to be looking, I can't help it. His size, his skin, his muscles—he's beautiful. He sees Beau and then all of the food I've made.

"Did you make this for us?"

"Yes. I thought you might wake up and be hungry."

He walks over to me and kisses me on the forehead. "Love you."

I lean into him a little. I can't help it. "Love you too."

Drew hands over his phone and I see a text from Aunt El-la. She's keeping Matt at home with her today. We agree that it's best he stays away from school. A huge part of me wants to go and get him. I feel like we should all be together, but it's probably for the best. He's still so young and he doesn't need to see Drew and Beau this morning. They too need a little time to reflect and heal without feeling like they need to put on an act for Matt.

Coach Black calls at 8:30 and lets us know that the three of us are excused from classes until Monday. As much as I hate getting behind on my school work this close to the end of the year, part of me doesn't care. I'll graduate no matter what, and I've already been accepted to Juilliard. I'm where I need to be, and that's with my guy and his sweet brother.

After Beau had called 911, a news crew showed up to the house, taking footage of their mom being loaded into the ambulance and Drew being arrested. Everyone knew by 9:00 the horror that the boys and their mom have been living with.

At 9:15, there's a knock on my door and I open it to find Leila standing there.

"Leila. Hey, how are you?" Worry lines are etched into her face and she's fidgeting with her fingers.

"I'm fine. I just wanted to come . . ." Her gaze leaves me and lands on Beau who's come up behind me. His body language is stiff and completely closed off, but the two of them look at each other as if I'm not even here.

"Beau," she breathes out. Tears fill her eyes.

"What do you want, Leila?" He's short with her and I see her flinch.

"I just . . . twenty-four hours," she says quietly and insecurely.

"Twenty-four hours of what?"

"A truce, a cease fire, whatever you want to call it. I just . . . please, Beau. Twenty-four hours." There's so much pleading in her voice and I can see the bricks of his walls start to fall one by one. The expression on his face shifts from one of speculation to adoration. I'm having an emotional whiplash just watching them.

"Okay," he quietly says to her. *What?*

"Okay?" She looks at him hopefully. He nods to her and she expels the biggest breath while passing by me in a blur and landing straight in his arms.

To say I'm shocked at the embrace these two are giving each other would be an understatement. My jaw must have dropped open because I hear Drew come up beside me to close the door.

Looking over at him, he chuckles, takes his finger, and pushes my jaw up.

"Come on, let's leave them alone for a while," he says to me.

"Did I miss something? I don't understand." As we pass by the two of them, Beau tucks his face further into her neck and shoulder, and Leila's fingers weave into his hair. *What?* This is not a casual hug. This is a very intimate one that has clearly been shared before.

"When we were kids, they used to be best friends." I didn't know this little fact about them.

"What happened to them then? I always thought she didn't really like him." Drew takes my hand as we walk up the stairs together.

"I'm not sure. He would never tell me, but I do know that after whatever went down between the two of them, he hasn't been the same."

"That's really kind of sad."

"Maybe, but it's their story to work out."

"Huh."

Back in my room, Drew gets a text from his mom. She's going to be released late afternoon, so we decide to take a nap before he leaves to go pick her up. Beau was planning on staying and hanging out with me, but it looks like his plans might have changed.

I crack the balcony doors to let the sounds of the beach float into the room. I've become so accustomed to it that sometimes I wonder how I'll ever sleep again without it. Drew and I climb into bed, bury down under the blankets, and I snuggle up next to him so I can be wrapped in his arms.

DREW

MONDAY MORNING, WE all drive to school together, dropping Matt off first. We know today is going to be a tough day, so we decide to stick together. None of us have any intentions of staying after school, so the minute the bell rings we're out of there.

I park the Jeep in my usual spot, and Grant and Ryan pull up next to us. The five of us get out of our cars. I take Ali's hand, and all of us just kind of look at each other. Beau drops his gaze to the ground and I want to beat my father's ass all over again. I hate that Beau feels like this. Beau's face still has the stitches and some significant bruising and swelling. Only a little of it has faded to yellow and the pain that was inflicted upon him is still evident.

Grant walks up first, and throws his arms around Beau, giving him an awkward but heartfelt hug. Beau laughs and returns the hug. Ryan follows next and Beau visibly relaxes. I toss my arm around Ali. I don't need any affection from them, I get all I want from her.

The bell rings.

Ali and I turn to walk away first. Beau is behind us with our friends flanked on both sides of him. We walk into the school like it's no different than any other day.

I drop my arm and take a hold of Ali's hand. She looks up at me and gives me the biggest smile. I'm making her happy.

I continue to focus on her as we make our way to the lockers. I can feel eyes on us and whispers behind us. At this point, who knows what they are gossiping about? It could be about my family or about Ali and me. I'm hoping that it's about us because I want the whole world to know that there is an *us*.

"Hey, Drew, can I talk to you for a minute?" The sound of Cassidy's voice has me freeze mid-step.

I cannot believe that she has the audacity to approach me. Of course she would try to do it here. It's not like she's going to come to my house or anything. Ali and I both turn around to see her standing behind us. She's by herself and her friends aren't anywhere around. Her eyes are filled with tears and I can see the shame, regret, and disgrace all over her. The funny thing is . . . I don't care.

I look her over from head to toe. I can feel my face getting red, and Ali squeezes my hand because she can see and feel that I'm angry. I narrow my eyes at her. "No, Cassidy. I will never talk to you again, and you are to never speak to me ever again. Do you understand? Don't even look at me, Beau, or Ali. I told you over and over again, and you just couldn't let it go. Do you even realize what you've done or how bad things could have ended for Beau, my mother, or me? You're a horrible and selfish person. Stay as far away from us as possible, and I'm going to forget that you ever existed." She physically flinches and the tears now stream down her face.

Leila walks up next to Ali and crosses her arms across her chest while glaring at Cassidy. Beau, Grant, and Ryan have come up behind me. She looks around at all of us and stops when she sees Beau's face. She lets out a small gasp, but it was enough for all of us to hear.

"Cassidy!" She turns back to look at me. "Leave, now!" My voice has risen and she jumps at the tone.

I didn't realize this, but the entire hall has filled with people who are watching the scene before them and not one person says anything. It's stone quiet. Cassidy looks around one more time at everyone staring at her and then she runs between Grant and Ryan for the front doors.

Letting out a sigh, I loosen my hand against Ali's and look at Beau. A moment of silence passes between us, and Beau nods. He knows I want annihilate her, but he also understands that we need to move forward. It's time to be done with bullies.

Without taking my eyes off of Beau, I say, "Show's over . . . go to class." Immediately, there's movement and commotion around us. Beau smirks at me because between the two of us, I'm never the one to exert the force of our popularity. I can't help but grin back.

By lunch time, I realize that the majority of the school gossip is about Ali and me. After all, who really cares about someone else's parents? Most kids have their own drama to deal with at home and don't want to be bothered by any more.

We've just walked back into the school from lunch when Coach Black approaches the three of us. "Drew, Beau, Ali, will you please follow me to the office?" His voice is somber and his eyes dart to the ground. At first I think that it might be to scold us because Beau left campus, but as Coach pushes open the office door, we all see Cassidy sitting in a chair next to Principal Wright's office. She's no longer crying, now she just looks pissed. I can't help but shake my head at her. Were any of the tears real, or were they always just a part of her scheme?

One by one we pass her as we enter. She doesn't acknowledge any of us—she knows better.

"All right, kids, please take a seat." Beau and I put Ali in the middle. I smile to myself as I realize that this is how it's always going to be for her. She never again has to stand alone. She'll always have us on both sides of her.

None of us say anything as we watch Coach go and stand next to Principal Wright.

"So here's how this is going to go. Instead of bringing each of you in here separately, we decided that it was best to just get this all over with one time. In the end, it all comes back to events that affected the three of you, so if you don't mind us speaking openly and candidly in front of each of you, we'll get started." I look over at Ali and Beau, and they in return look at me. I'm sure that confusion is evident on all three of our faces. Being the oldest, I decide to speak for us.

I look back at Principal Wright and shrug my shoulders. "Sounds good to us." Neither Beau nor Ali disagrees with me.

"We understand that this last week has been extremely difficult and emotional for all three of you. Please believe us when we say that by prolonging disciplinary action, the time allowed us to have a better grasp of what actually occurred in said events."

"Today, we're going to address two different situations that happened here on campus. It shouldn't come as a surprise, but we do have a state of the art security system here. We have cameras hidden all over the campus that the student body isn't aware of, and after this meeting, we would like to keep it that way. Ideally, it's for safety measures for the students, but you never know when it may come in handy." Principal Wright pauses his little speech. I think that he's giving us time to digest what he just told us. Coach Black puts his hand on the back of Principal Wright's chair, and he zeroes in on Ali.

"Last Sunday night, thanks to the security cameras that cover the parking lot, we were able to identify the license plate of a black Mercedes that pulled into the parking lot at approximately 9:45 in the evening. A young lady with brown hair under a baseball cap, wearing dance gear and carrying a bag gets out of the car and enters the cave through the outside door . . ."

"But it wasn't me!" Ali has started to panic and I reach over and grab her hand.

"Calm down, I'm getting to that."

She takes a deep breath and reaches up to grab the dragonfly charm.

"The license plate shows that the car is registered to a Ms. Darla Meyers." I squeeze her hand a little tighter because we all know where this is going. "As you can tell from the name, Ms. Meyers is Cassidy's cousin who lives down in Sarasota. The police approached her last Friday for a statement, but due to the nature of the other events, we haven't been able to discuss any of this with you yet."

From my neck to my ears, I am burning. I knew that Cassidy was involved in this. We all did.

"Turns out that Ms. Meyers was over at Cassidy's parents' house for dinner Sunday night and Cassidy said that she needed to run out and get something that was needed for school. She used the excuse that Ms. Meyers car was blocking hers and that she would be right back. When the police officers investigated the trunk, they found a bag full of old spray paint cans, a hammer, a pair of large trimming sheers, dance clothes, a ball cap, and a brown wig. Ms. Meyers agreed to remain quiet about her interaction with the police. Otherwise, she would have been found guilty of disrupting a police investigation, as well as it would further make her look like an accomplice to the crime. She stands by her statement that she had no idea what Cassidy was up to."

"So what happens now?" I can't wait any longer to hear. We all know that Cassidy is guilty. What I want to know is what the will the punishment be.

"Well, I wasn't finished Drew, so hang on," says Coach Black. "After talking to Beau and you on Wednesday night down at the police station, I had the security company pull video footage of the hallway as well. You said that Ali was the only person who knew about the Columbia acceptance and that you kept the letters in your locker. We wanted to see if there was anything suspicious that occurred there as well. And, what do you know, about ten minutes before school is let out, we see Cassidy with a paperclip breaking into your locker and removing a stack of envelopes. Your father's story pans out. She did tell him and give him the envelopes."

I can't take it anymore. I let go of Ali's hand, jerk to my feet, and begin pacing the room. "Why? I don't understand!"

"Well, we just finished asking her the same thing and her exact words were that she 'needed to get rid of Ali.'"

"So you're telling me that all of this is because she's jealous of my girlfriend?"

"No. I don't think that she's jealous of her. There's more to her story than that, and most of it is around her father. According to her, he told her to do whatever was needed to get close to you. So, she tried to have Ali expelled and then she thought if your parents knew about her, they would end the relationship and she could take her place. She said that none of it was personal against Ali. It was all business for her father. Who knows, though? It's out of our hands now."

I know how manipulative fathers can be, and I kind of

know how Cassidy's is. Although I can sympathize with how he made her feel, I'll never forgive her for what almost happened to me. She tried to break up Ali and me, and destroy the one thing that I've ever found that was just for me. She broke into my locker and stole my personal things. She went to my father behind my back and in return, he almost killed my mother. I'm having a hard time even comprehending all of this. How does she even sleep at night?

"Wait, how did she know that I got into Columbia?"

"She was standing behind you and heard your entire conversation with Ali." Coach Black watches me as he tells me this. He can see how angry I am. I place my hands on Principal Wright's desk and lean forward. I grip the edge so tightly that my knuckles are strained and white.

Ali's hand rubs across my lower back and it instantly slows down my blood, which thunders through me. I look over at her and she's crying. Tears are silently pouring down her face and in that instant, I forget about me. I drop down in front of her.

"Hey, shh . . . don't cry. It's over, okay." Her hands have moved to her lap and I cover them both with one of mine, while wiping her tears away with the other. I can feel Beau, Coach Black, and Principal Wright all watching me and I don't even care. All I care about is this girl and how she feels at this moment.

"I know. It's just . . . so much has happened and all of this is because of me. I'm so sorry." She bends over at the waist, covering our hands, and starts shaking as she cries into her lap.

Beau reaches over and puts his hand on her back. He looks at me and in that one look I can see him screaming at me to fix this, fix her. He doesn't want her to feel this way. I don't want her to feel this way, and she needs to understand this.

"Ali, please look at me," I say quietly. She turns her head to the side and her eyes lock onto mine. Sadness, guilt, and tears pour out of them and all I can think is, *no, my sweet girl.*

"I'm going to repeat to you what a very wise and beautiful person said to me last week and I really want you to listen, okay?"

She nods her head as her tears continue to drip off of her face.

"Why are you trying to take on the responsibility of what she did? Those are things that she did and they're her actions that you had no control over. This is all on her. You can't take the blame away from her and project it onto yourself. You didn't do those things. Those were her choices and now she has to live with them. You didn't do anything wrong. Beau, Matt, my mom, and I—we all love you. Nothing changes that. This isn't your fault. Do you hear me when I say you haven't done anything wrong?"

"I do hear you." *Sniff.* "I'm just so sad for what you all have been through and if I wasn't . . ."

"If you weren't what? In the picture? With me? My girlfriend? Nothing changes. You know me well enough to know that no matter what, Cassidy and I were never going happen. Even if you had never moved here . . . it was never going to happen." She nods her head at me, sits up, and looks over at Beau.

"Don't look at me." He cracks a smile. "It wasn't going to happen with me, either."

She lets out a small grin and runs her hands across her face to wipe it off.

Beau grins at her and she smiles back.

"So what happens now?" I ask Coach Black.

"Well, we really aren't at liberty to say, nor do we know

much, but here's what we can tell you. She stole The Cave key from you. You're the only one who was given permission to use that key or that room after hours. A school break-in refers to an unauthorized entry into a school building when it is closed, such as; after hours, on weekends, et cetera. Vandalism of school property refers to willful or malicious damage to school grounds and buildings or furnishings and equipment, such as: glass or mirror breakage, graffiti, and general property destruction. Both of these things combined may mean criminal charges for her. As for breaking into your locker, criminal charges for this aren't usually likely, but then again, we don't know what's going to happen considering how she did this after the fact of The Cave. The school hasn't decided whether or not it's going to press charges. As all three of you know, a parent's influence can cause one to do unexpected things. Do we think she should go unpunished? No, she knows right from wrong. But do we want to permanently mark her record? She's eighteen. Do you understand what we're saying?"

All three of us nod our heads. We do understand. She won't go unpunished, but if her father has been anything like ours, she's been punished enough. She too just needs to move on from here.

"I don't think you should press charges." Beau and Ali both turn to look at me. Ali gives me a small smile. I swear this girl is the most forgiving person in the world.

"I think you're right," Ali says. "Maybe she just needs the opportunity to move on and start over." I love this girl. Had it been anyone else sitting here next to me, they most likely would have fought to have her persecuted. But not my girl, she believes in second chances and do-overs.

ALI

TWO HUNDRED AND ninety-one days.

I'm still counting the days. I've often wondered when I might stop, but I'm just not ready to yet.

It's been six weeks, and the dust has finally settled from most of the drama. I'd like to say that once Drew's dad was arrested and the school discovered what Cassidy did to The Cave, that things got easier, but they didn't. Things just became different.

Drew stopped talking about that night, and slowly all three of them began to heal. Drew refuses to move back home. Secretly, I was super excited, and surprisingly, his mom is okay with this. She has Beau and Matt, and in a way I can tell that she needs them more.

Prom was a few weeks ago and Drew sweetly asked me to be his date. Mrs. Hale took me shopping for my dress, and she only had to hug me once after I broke down and cried because

I missed my mom. My dress ended up being champagne colored, strapless, sparkly, and short. Drew loves my legs, so when I paired the dress with a pair of tall, gold strappy heels, his jaw dropped at the sight of them. I still smile when I think about him standing at my door in a tuxedo, holding a huge bouquet of flowers. He takes my breath away, as he said I did to him.

His mom took a ton of pictures of us and I've added a new photo next to the one of my mother on my book shelf. Now each morning, I have two that I must look at.

Beau and Leila called another twenty-four hour truce, and the four of us went to dinner and prom together. I still can't figure the two of them out, but whatever. I just want them to be happy . . . especially Beau.

Graduation is in a few weeks. Drew reminds me daily how many days we have left here, but I think now his countdown is more out of excitement than it is relief.

A seagull flies over me and squawks. I turn my head to watch it soar down the beach. I decided to skip my run this morning and instead I came out to enjoy the calmness that the morning can bring a new day.

On my shoulder lands a cold drop of rain. The second drop hits just above my knee and I look up directly over me as the third drop hits my wrist. There's a single white plume perfectly silhouetted against the morning sky. A few more light drops hit my face and I realize how good and hypnotic this feels. The contrast of the cold clear rain and the warm humid air humbles me. I close my eyes and tilt my head backward to welcome it. I don't flee, dodge or hide, but instead I sit up and let Mother Nature cleanse my outsides, just as strength and love have helped heal my insides. And as suddenly as the rain has come, it moves past me. As it does, I felt both lighter and a sense of freedom.

I once wished that the rain drops would wash me away, but now I feel like they're here to help my soul grow. Storms will come and storms will go, but it's the rain drops that provide life to the world. They sparkle like glitter and shine in the sun. They magnify the light and make the colors brighter.

I look down the beach and see that Drew has hit his turn around. He's headed back toward me and for no reason at all, my heart flutters. Every single thing about him does it for me. It isn't just the fact that he's so handsome. It's the little things, the details that constantly draw me in.

It's his clothes and the way they hang on him, the texture of his hair, the feel of his cheek against mine and the light stubble that brushes across it. It's his eyes and how I feel when they land on me, his own unique smell, the sound of his voice, the way he chuckles more than he laughs, and his hands.

Drew's hands make me feel safe and wanted. They aren't too big or too small, and his fingers aren't too thin or to thick . . . they're perfect for me. I love when he brushes my hair off of my face, or applies pressure on my lower back, letting me know he's there. I love when he holds my hand and when he wraps them around my head to draw me in for a kiss. I also love when he slides his fingertips across my skin, causing not only trails of fire, but chill bumps at the same time. His hands alone cause me to become lost in thought.

But besides the things that everyone can see, it's the things that can't be seen at all that I love the most about him. Over the last year, I've heard people call him arrogant, proud, and self-entitled, but he isn't any of those things. Drew is quiet, private, and a little shy. He's sweet, thoughtful, and kind. He's overprotective and he always knows the things that I need, even before I do. He's easygoing and he doesn't sweat the small stuff. He finishes the things he says he's going to and he always stands by his word.

Drew has provided me with a sense of home. He's made me realize that I have more strength and determination in me than I thought possible. Everyone needs support and everyone needs love, but it's these things that just enhance what people can already do on their own. I'll never be able to thank him enough for the love and confidence he's given me. He's seen me at my worst and still somehow loves me anyway.

A new dragonfly has made its home on the balcony. I love to sit in the chaise lounge and watch it as it moves from place to place. I think about the blue dragonfly often. In so many ways, it did provide me a sense of comfort for months and months, but now when I see one instead of clinging to the idea of hope . . . I feel happiness. Inside, I can feel my heart beat unbroken for what seems like the first time in a long time. Whoever said that the dragonfly is connected to the symbolism for change was right. I have changed and grown so much in this last year.

I look up and see Drew heading out of the water. He spots me and his face lights up with the biggest grin. In this moment, I hear my mom whisper joy and light.

DREW

IT'S MEMORIAL DAY weekend, and for no reason at all, my sweet girl decides she wants to have a picnic. She packs the lunch, I go gas up the boat, and by 9:30, Matt, Beau, Ali, and I are on the water.

Beau and Matt spend a lot of time with us. I know Ali

doesn't mind, and I appreciate it since we'll be leaving them soon. I never thought that it was going to be this difficult, but really it is. I love them.

As I sit behind the wheel, I can't help but watch as the three of them laugh together and think, I'm the lucky one. Ali has one arm wrapped around Matt. He leans into her, and both of her feet are propped on Beau's lap. For some reason, one that I will never understand, good fortune fell at my feet and I'll cherish her every day. It's moments like these where I know one thing . . . I know what happy is because she shares it with me.

Someone once said, we all learn everything we need in kindergarten. Nope. I learned it from a brown eyed, gorgeous girl who grew up in the snow and never asks for anything of anyone because she's always too busy giving. She's taught me that it's the simple things in life that are best. Life is only hard if you want it to be that way. And every day, you get to choose what you want to do, how you're going to react, and how you're going to treat people.

Ali is kind, forgiving, and incredibly optimistic. I'm trying to be more like her.

The traffic on the water is heavy today, but like any other day, no one stops to appreciate our little slice of heaven, our little island. Several boats are parked off shore, but mostly people are having fun on their boat and swimming around.

I lay down a large sheet and Ali pulls out some of her homemade pizza. I think poor Beau just about died and went to heaven. He lives for the days when she'll make him pizza. The two of them with their crazy pizza addiction. They're perfect dining companions for each other.

"So, Ali, I got you a present," I say to her.

"What?!" She jerks to a sitting position. A huge smile

takes over her face and if Matt wasn't here, I might have kissed it off her.

"Now, now . . . patience." She rolls her eyes at me. "Just kidding." I open up my backpack and pull out a gift wrapped box.

"Drew! What did you do?" A few pieces of her hair have fallen out of the messy knot on top of her head and that spot in my chest aches. Oh, what this girl does to me.

"Don't get too excited. It's not that fancy."

She snatches the box from me and rips it open. Inside she pulls out a large, perfect, conch shell. She knows what to do with it, and immediately holds it up to her ear. She looks over at me and listens to the sounds of the water.

"I love it." She smiles at me and I can see genuine gratitude for the gift shine off of her. All I did was give her a simple shell. I love that she appreciates everything, even the little things.

"It's to take to New York. I know how much you love the sound of the waves and this way when you miss it, you'll have a way to hear it."

She lowers the shell and looks at me. She doesn't need to say anything. Her big, beautiful brown eyes say it all. She gets up off the sheet, comes over to me, and sits down on my lap.

"Thank you." She leans in and kisses me. I kiss her back. I've wanted to kiss her for at least the last hour. She tastes so good.

"All right, all right! Drew, Tiny, I just can't take any more of y'all's romantic crap." We both start laughing and Ali throws a piece of pizza crust at Beau.

"Seriously, Beau, why do you call me Tiny?" I'm so glad that she's finally asks him. I'm curious to know too.

"Because you are a Tiny Dancer." He grins at me as he

says this, like I'm supposed to know what that means.

"Like the song?" she asks.

"Yep. First, you're super tiny—that's the given—but second, there's a line about a ballerina dancing in the sand." He says this as he throws his arms out, and sings the line as if he's Elton John himself. "The ballerina was one of Elton's best friend's wives. She was always around them and supporting them, kind of like you. Drew is my best friend and well, you're kind of like his wife. The sand part was just a perfect coincidence. "

He couldn't have given her a more perfect answer and her eyes fill with tears. Both of us look at him speechless.

Ali gets up off my lap, walks over to him, flops down onto his lap, and all four of us start laughing. She gives him a big hug.

"For that, Beau Hale, I'll share my brownies with you." She hops up and heads over to the cooler.

"You made brownies?!" Beau's excitement level just shot off the charts. It really doesn't take much to make him happy.

"Uh huh!" She opens up a Tupperware box and gives them to Matt to hand out.

"Oh, you are the best! Hey, did you know that both of your last names are kind of similar? Get it, Rain and Hale?"

"Beau, you might want to recheck your spelling there." Ali laughs at him.

"I know, I know . . . but Rain and Hale is kind of cool." Now that he mentions it, it is kind of cool.

"After all these months, is that all you've got?" she's taunts him.

"Oh no, I'm full of good info. For example, did you know that the state of Florida is bigger than England?" He wiggles his eyebrows at her.

340

"Well, the name Jeep came from an abbreviation used in the army. G.P. for General Purpose vehicle." She gives him a *take that* look.

"Ali, I didn't know that. That's a good one," I say, smiling at her. I lean over to give her a high five and Beau huffs at us.

"Yeah, well, Drew, did you know that conception occurs most in the month of December?" I could have spit out the brownie.

"What! Why are you telling me this?" Ali laughs, whereas I am looking at Beau like he's crazy.

"You know why . . ." Beau smirks at me and I give him the look that Ali calls the, *I'm up to no good* look.

"All right, sounds good, don't you think, Ali? When the time is right, we can remember that. Just think how awesome that will be, Uncle Beau."

"Ugh . . . you just gave me the creepy shivers! Not cool, man. Not cool. I'm too young to be an uncle."

"You think you're too young? I'm only eleven!" Matt says. All four of us bust out laughing.

"Come on, let's go for a swim." I say. Everyone jumps up off of the blanket and Matt takes off for the water.

"Last one in is a rotten fish." I love this kid. I look over to Beau, and see that he's watching Matt. I know that he has reservations about taking his shirt off.

"Who cares, Beau? There's only family here." He looks over to me and I smile at him. I can see that our conversation is confusing Ali.

"You're right." He cracks a crooked smile. We both pull off our shirts, and turn for the water.

It's then that she sees what makes Beau so uncomfortable. Two thirds of his back is covered in scars. Not just any kind of scar, but a burn scar. She lets out a gasp and he stiffens, slows, and starts speaking to her without turning around.

"Please don't ask." How could she after hearing the insecurity and pleading in his voice?

"I won't . . . I promise." I look over at her, and see tears well in her eyes. Her gaze locks onto mine and I can see that she knows. The scars are somewhat new. They cover too much of him to be old.

"Thanks, Tiny." He runs ahead, catches up with Matt, and launches him into the air. Matt squeals with laughter and makes a huge splash. As I run down into the water, I smile back at her because I want her to know that I appreciate her silence.

Ali walks to stand on the water's edge, and watches the three of us laugh and play together. She's smiling and I can see that she's happy. She pulls out her phone and takes a few photos of us. I'm glad because I want to remember this day. I hope she heard me say that there's only family here, because it's the truth. She's our family and we are hers.

Epilogue

DREW

Fourteen Months Later...

RIGHT AFTER GRADUATION, I packed mine and Ali's belongings and on June fifteenth, we drove away from the place where we found each other, to move forward where we can find ourselves. We've officially been living in New York City now for over a year, and both of us survived our first year of college.

We each agreed that we wanted to forego the standard college life of living in a dorm, and given that we're both financially stable for the time being, an apartment was the way to go.

We were lucky enough to stumble across one that was available on the Upper West Side, right in the middle, between our two schools. Ali had called her admissions office and made an inquiry about anything that might be open and sure enough, we were in luck. This condo we're in belongs to a former student, turned well-known singer, and due to her crazy schedule, she decided to sublet it. The distance from Juilliard to Columbia is four miles. The apartment is small, but it has two bedrooms and the building has a doorman which makes me feel more comfortable for Ali when I'm gone overnight for swim meets.

Beau decided to join us too in New York after he graduated. He also thought that Columbia would be a great place for him. Over the last couple of years, Columbia has repeatedly won the Ivy League Tennis Title, and that was all Beau needed to see.

For our twenty-first birthdays, Ali and I, Beau, Matt, my mom, and Leila head to the beach. The girl who owns our apartment has a friend who owns a house out on Dune Road in the West Hamptons. He agreed to rent it to me for a weekend based on her referral. Instead of having a party, Ali wanted low key with the people that we love. Leila and Ali have become closer since moving to New York and knowing what I had planned, there was no way Leila was going to miss out.

In front of our loved ones, on the beach, I got down on one knee and proposed. It had to be on the beach—after all, that's really where we started.

Some might say that we're too young, but Ali wants to wait a year and that'll make us twenty-two. I couldn't care less. If she'd let me, I would marry her tomorrow.

The thing is . . . she and I have never been young. We both were forced to grow up quickly based on the circumstances of our lives and in return, we both know the direction we're headed and what we want out of life. Although we came together slowly, she was mine and I was hers the minute we laid eyes on each other. It's been almost two years. And most importantly, she's the love of my life.

As long as I have my way, there'll never be anyone else. The pull that I have toward her is like the need to breathe and without either one of those things, I would die.

I completely surprised her, which is exactly what I wanted. She never saw it coming and I love that after two years I can still "stump" her.

Ali and her father have slowly been trying to rebuild their relationship, and somehow over the last year or so, he's become friends with my mother. Although he couldn't be here with us this weekend, the minute the excitement died down, my mother was on the phone giving him all of the details.

Ali and I both cried. I seem to do that a little more frequently lately. Ali jokes with me that it's years and years of emotions that my body is trying to get rid of and clean out, and maybe she's right. Alex Tan says, "Perhaps our eyes need to be washed by our tears once in a while, so that we can see life with a clearer view again." I think he was right. Maybe if I had cried a little more over the years, I would have not only seen things differently, but felt them differently too. As it is now, I finally feel worthy, wanted, and loved.

ALI

TWO WORDS.

That's all that was said. That's all that I needed.

Two words . . . seven letters that have forever changed my life.

Sitting in an Adirondack chair, with my knees pulled up under me, I stare out across the sand toward the water and I enjoy the silence. I once called the silence that surrounds me the theme song to my life, but what I've learned over the last two years is that I was listening to it all wrong.

It's the silence that allows you to enjoy each moment and hear your heart when it speaks.

A warm breeze blows in off of the Atlantic, and the smell of wet sand and salt is in the air. My hands run up and down the armrests of the chair and my fingers glide over the dents, bumps, and lines of the wood underneath them. The wood isn't perfect and that's what makes it unique. At this moment, I love this feeling and there's no other chair in the world I would rather be sitting in.

Very slowly, the horizon begins to have an orange glow. Watching the colors change and blend from a yellow to orange to pink to blue—it's amazing to me how much the world lights up before the sun even peaks over the horizon.

I hear the sliding glass door open and close behind me. Drew comes up next to me and hands me a cup of coffee.

"Whatcha doin?" he asks quietly.

I look up at him and even after all this time, he still takes my breath away. Drew has that just climbed out of bed look. His hair is messy, there's a hint of stubble across his face, he's wearing a gray T-shirt, and a pair of pajama pants that are slung low on his hips.

"Watching the sunrise. I've never see one before." He looks from me out to the horizon.

"Now that you mention it, I don't think that I have, either." A moment of silence passes between us and a feeling of contentment washes over me.

"Isn't it beautiful?" I whisper to him.

"I think that you're beautiful."

I look back up at him. He's still standing and smiling down at me.

"Will you do something with me?" he asks.

"What's that?"

"Dance with me." He holds out his hand.

"But there's no music."

"Does there need to be?"

I shake my head at him, set down the coffee cup, take his offered hand, and climb out of the chair.

"However, future Mrs. Hale, you happen to be in luck. I found the perfect song for us." Drew picks up a remote and hits a button. Music quietly fills the deck. The song is "Feels like Rain" by John Hiatt. It's perfect.

Drew places his hand on my hip and pulls me into him. I wrap my arms around him and lay my head on his chest. He smells as good as he looks.

I know the moment the sun peaks over the horizon because the warmth from the sun's rays hit my back. A golden haze has taken over, and as we turn to watch the sun rise higher into the sky, I snuggle in a little closer to him to feel the beats of his tender heart.

Drew's fingers slip under the hem of my shirt and he lays his head down on top of mine.

"Hey, Ali . . ." His voice vibrates through him and into me.

"Yeah." His arms pull me in a little tighter.

Two little words that when spoken, calm my soul. Two little words that remind me I'm home. Two little words that between us say it all.

"Love you."

BEAU

I KNOW WHAT people think of me, especially now that the drama of my family has gone public. They all think that I'm some damaged guy who's searching for love and seeking connections with other people since I didn't get it at home.

But they couldn't be more wrong.

The truth is . . . I know what love is. I found it a long time ago and now I spend my days trying to forget about it. I wish that loving someone was a choice, but unfortunately it's not.

Every day I wake up thinking about her, and thinking about a love that's unwanted and not returned. And the thing that kills me the most, I have no idea why.

I would have done anything for her and I would have given her everything . . . in fact, I almost did. I almost gave my life for hers.

The worst of it wasn't the physical pain, but the emotional pain that came from what she left behind.

I should be over this by now. It's been years. Everyone around me is moving on, and I suppose it's time that I do too.

I just wish that forgetting someone like her was as easy, but it's not. It would be like trying to wipe the sky free of all the stars, only to have them return the next night.

One day, I'll figure out how to make every night starless . . .

From the Author

Thank you for reading *Drops of Rain*, book one in the Hale Brothers Series. If you enjoyed this book, please consider leaving a spoiler free review.

Listen to *Drops of Rain's* Playlist
http://bit.ly/1omtzsS

Acknowledgments

THE BIGGEST ACKNOWLEDGEMENT that I need to make is to my beautiful husband. This book would not be written if it wasn't for him. For years, he's watched me write bits and pieces of stories that would flood my mind and my heart. Stories that just couldn't stay confined and needed to be told. Thank you my love for believing in me, supporting me, and encouraging me to write everyday even if it was just one sentence. You've always known that I could do it and I am thankful that you have carved this path for us in our life together to allow me to pursue my dreams. If you're a bird, I'm a bird and I'll follow you always.

To my boys, you bring me so much happiness, joy, and light. I would not be who I am without the two of you. Davy, thank you for always being so excited about my story. I loved coming around a corner and finding you reading bits and pieces of it on my laptop, and you will never know how much it meant to me that you wrote a poem about rain. It is a beautiful Cinquin poem. Matty, thank you for supplying me with endless smiles and snuggles. I will forever hear you in my mind asking, "Mama, are you working on your book?" I love you both very much.

Mom, thank you for all that you have given to me. It's

because of you that I know I don't have to be perfect at something, but I can still be great at it. You've always encouraged me to chase the things that I love and follow my heart. I also need to thank you for my love of romance novels. I pulled my first Danielle Steel book off of your bookshelf and was forever changed. I know that I am a hopeless romantic, but hey . . . I still believe in fairytales. I love you.

Kelly, my beautiful non-fiction reading bestie. Oh, how I have tortured you with hours and hours, days and months of talk and text about dragonflies and teenagers. No one has been on this journey with me like you have. Thank you for listening to me, brainstorming with me, and for being enthusiastic about every step in this endeavor. Toes in the sand, buckets in hand! You and me…

Brandie, almost twenty years ago we were sitting on the pullout couch of my college townhouse. You were flipping through a random Composition book that I had lying around and you said, "You should be a writer!" Well guess what?!! I am! You've always known where the heart of me lies, I'm thinking it's that sisterly bond that we have. Thank you for always listening to me ramble on about fictitious characters, and thank you for always being my biggest cheerleader. I love you.

Zoe, my friend and writing partner. The last six months would not have been the same without you. Together, line by line, we have worked our way through two beautiful manuscripts. You were such a huge part of the plotting, changing, and rewriting that I will forever feel blessed to have you a part of my life. I think it's fair to say that we have talked all hours of the day and night . . . and look what we've accomplished! Thank you for being a part of this adventure with me. I can't wait to do it all over again.

Michelle H., my beautiful friend, you have been there for me every step of the way. Thank you for continually pushing away my insecurities, sharing with me parts you loved, and for challenging me on the parts you didn't understand. Ali's backstory is remarkably better because of you. Let's see . . . how can I thank you? I know! I just might owe you a lifetime of Pho! Love you . . .

To my friends: Heather Y., Sejal, Nichole, and Shawna thank you so much for your enthusiasm and support. Handing over *Drops of Rain*, I was very nervous. You'll never know how much I appreciated all of wonderful comments and positive feedback. Thank you. Oh! And this is where I apologize to each of you for having to read the unedited version (can't you just hear me laughing). Next time will be better, I promise!

Michelle F., I really do think the dragonfly that John gave you from the museum was the perfect gift given at the perfect time. Dragonflies are known to life their life to the fullest. They are considered the ballerina of the insect world, meaning they dance their way through life. Remember, the dragonfly, in almost every part of the world symbolizes transformation, change, happiness, joy and light. Whenever you see a dragonfly be happy and think, "joy and light"; because, "We are of this light."

This special thank you is for Malinda. I joined a private group on Facebook and dropped a post looking for a beta reader for my revised manuscript. Malinda offered to read my story while vacationing on a cruise and once she returned she would give me super honest feedback. Needless to say, after one very long nail biting week her email came in. Yes, my beautiful friends who read the book told me that they loved it, but this was my first review from someone completely unrelated to me. Reading her email, I was speechless. It's scary putting something you've poured yourself into out there, but her words to me were beautiful. I cried tears of joy and I will never forget her. Thank you, Malinda.

Elle Brooks, this journey with you into the world of self-publishing has been amazing. I think you are a brilliant writer and I can't wait to see what you come up with next! Cheers to us with our pink Moet Champagne!
http://ellebrooksauthor.wix.com/blog

E.k. Blair, I will never be able to thank you enough for the infinite amount of industry wisdom you have taught me. Over many cups of coffee, you've answered all of my questions and shared so many of your friends and contacts. Forever, I will treasure your friendship! Thank you.
http://www.ekblair.com/

Chelle Bliss, thank you so much for your willingness to help me. Being a new author, I am super appreciative to all of those who have taken the time to explain things, guide me, and point me in the right direction . . . that is to the U.S. Copyright Office Online! Congratulations on all of your much earned success! http://chellebliss.com/

Ari, from Cover it Designs, I love my cover. Thank you for bringing my first novel to life with its *beautiful* cover. I look forward to working with you more in the future . . .

Jade, from Black Firefly, thank you for your services. I appreciate you always being there to answer my questions, continually explain the process, and to help me put out the best novel that *Drops of Rain* can be. Chrystal from editing, you hold a special place in my heart. After having to tackle my manuscript . . . you know why. Thank you Chrystal!

Vanessa, from PREMA, how can I thank you enough for stepping in when I needed you most. Thank you for calming my nerves, making sure that all of my questions were answered, and delivering to me a very shiny and clean manuscript. I look forward to picking your brain and sending you many more manuscripts.

To Donna from *The Romance Cover* and to Kaylee from *K&S Book Blog*, thank you so much for answering any random question that I might have had. I did have quite a few. My favorite to date goes to Kaylee, "What is a blog tour?" Thanks again ladies, I hope to one day meet you both!

To the 100+ bloggers . . . WOW! I never in my wildest dreams imagined that I would have been received with such open arms. The interest in *Drops of Rain* and in me has left me feeling humbled and so very grateful. Writing this book has been a dream come true. Thank you for helping me and sharing *Drops of Rain* with the world. I look forward to further building relationships with you for years to come.

And finally . . . to the readers: Thank you, Thank you, Thank you! I hope that you loved reading *Drops of Rain* as much as I loved writing it. My wish for you is that you always have happiness, joy, and light in your life. Take care . . . Kathryn xoxo.

About the Author

OVER TEN YEARS ago my husband and I were driving from Chicago to Tampa and somewhere in Kentucky I remember seeing a billboard that was all black with five white words, "I do, therefore I am!" I'm certain that it was a Nike ad, but for me I found this to be completely profound.

Take running for example. Most will say that a runner is someone who runs five days a week and runs under a ten minute mile pace. Well, I can tell you that I never run five days a week and on my best days my pace is an eleven minute mile. I have run quite a few half marathons and one full marathon. No matter what anyone says . . . I run, therefore I am a runner.

I've taken this same thought and applied it to so many areas of my life: cooking, gardening, quilting, and yes . . . writing.

I may not be culinary trained, but I love to cook and my family and friends loves to eat my food. I cook, therefore I am a chef!

My thumb is not black. I love to grow herbs, tomatoes, roses, and lavender. I garden, therefore I am a gardener!

I love beautiful fabrics and I can follow a pattern. My triangles may not line up perfectly . . . but who cares, my quilts are still beautiful when they are finished. I quilt, therefore I am a quilter.

I have been writing my entire life. It is my husband who finally said, "Who cares if people like your books or not? If you enjoy writing them and you love your stories…then write them." He has always been my biggest fan and he was right. Being a writer has always been my dream and what I said I wanted to be when I grew up.

So, I've told you who I am and what I love to do . . . now I'm going to tell you the why.

I have two boys that are three years a part. My husband and I want to instill in them adventure, courage, and passion. We don't expect them to be perfect at things, we just want them to try and do. It's not about winning the race; it's about showing up in the first place. We don't want them to be discouraged by society stereotypes, we want them to embrace who they are and what they love. After all, we only get one life.

In the end, they won't care how many books I actually sell . . . all that matters to them is that I said I was going to do it, I did it, and I have loved every minute of it.

Find something that you love and tell yourself, "I do, therefore I am..

Ways to Connect

www.kandrewsauthor.com

https://www.facebook.com/kathryn.andrews.1428

https://twitter.com/kandrewsauthor

COMING SOON
In The Hale Brothers Series

Starless Nights
(Book 2)

https://www.goodreads.com/book/show/22076624-starless-nights

Unforgettable Sun
(Book 3)

https://www.goodreads.com/book/show/22607887-unforgettable-sun